Praise

'Tense and compelling, a genuinely thrilling read'
Elizabeth Haynes

'Brimming with tension, riddled with doubt and suspicion, insidious and compelling with a terrifying ending that had me catching my breath' Sue Fortin

'A tense, gripping domestic noir that shows just how fast the dream of a new life can turn into your worst nightmare'
T.M. Logan

'A scorchingly good thriller' Lisa Hall

'This is a must read for anyone who lives to delve into psychological thrillers!' Linda Strong

'With brilliant main characters and a wonderful plot, this book is a real page-turner. I would highly recommend this book'
Stephanie Collins

'I absolutely adored this book' Lu Dex

'Great book … keeps you guessing!! If you love twists and turns then this book is for you!' Diane Merrit

'With twists and turns that will wrong-foot you all the way, a dash of dark humour and a strong emotional punch, this is an excellent debut that more than earns its place within the genre'
S.J.I. Holliday

DIANE JEFFREY is a *USA Today* bestselling author. She grew up in North Devon, in the United Kingdom. She now lives in Lyon, France, with her husband and their three children, Labrador and cat.

Diane's debut psychological thriller, *Those Who Lie*, was a Kindle bestseller in the UK, the USA, Canada and Australia. *He Will Find You*, set in the Lake District and Somerset, is her second novel. *The Guilty Mother*, Diane's third book, was a *USA Today* bestseller and spent several weeks in the top 100 Kindle chart in the UK. *The Silent Friend* is her fourth book.

Diane is an English teacher. When she's not working or writing, she likes swimming, running and reading. She loves chocolate, beer and holidays. Above all, she enjoys spending time with her family and friends.

Readers can follow Diane on Twitter, Facebook, or on Instagram, and find out more about her books on her website:

🐦 www.twitter.com/dianefjeffrey
📘 www.facebook.com/dianejeffreyauthor
📷 www.instagram.com/dianefjeffrey
www.dianejeffrey.com

Also By Diane Jeffrey

The Guilty Mother
He Will Find You
Those Who Lie

The Silent Friend

DIANE JEFFREY

ONE PLACE. MANY STORIES

HQ
An imprint of HarperCollins*Publishers* Ltd
1 London Bridge Street
London SE1 9GF

www.harpercollins.co.uk

HarperCollins*Publishers*
1st Floor, Watermarque Building, Ringsend Road
Dublin 4, Ireland

1
This edition published in Great Britain by
HQ, an imprint of HarperCollins*Publishers* Ltd 2021

MIX
Paper from
responsible sources
FSC™ C007454

This book is produced from independently certified FSC™ paper
to ensure responsible forest management.

For more information visit: www.harpercollins.co.uk/green

Printed and Bound in the UK using 100% Renewable
Electricity at CPI Group (UK) Ltd

"The band that seems to tie their friendship together will be the very strangler of their amity."

WILLIAM SHAKESPEARE, *Antony and Cleopatra*, Act II, Scene 6

Prologue

I wonder how you knew. I keep replaying our whole conversation in my head, but I can't pinpoint what gave it away. I'm glad you found out. Relieved. I should have told you the truth months ago, but I've grown fond of you and I was scared of losing you.

When you carry a shameful secret inside you, it becomes a heavy burden that weighs you down. The longer you put off telling the truth, the harder it gets. You try to paint as accurate a picture as possible, but in the end you add another coat of lies. And then another. Until you almost believe in the alternative reality you've depicted.

You know what it's like. You were also hiding something. You tried to tell me your secret, but I was the last person you should have told. I reacted badly. I was unsympathetic. What I should have said was that none of what happened was your fault. I am culpable, but not you.

If I could go back, would I do things differently? I don't think so. What choice did I have? If I'd been honest with you from the start, you would never have befriended me. Our friendship was important to me. I'm truly sorry that things turned out this way. I hope you can find it in your heart to forgive me.

Chapter 1

Laura

As Laura entered the flat, her phone pinged with a text. She groaned. It was time to make up her mind. But after mulling things over for the last fortnight, she was still indecisive. Kicking the front door closed behind her, she dumped her handbag and shopping on the floor.

It was always dark and gloomy in her flat, even on sunny days like that Saturday. Although poky, it was her refuge, and at the end of a working day, she liked to shut herself off from the outside world and relax with a book or a film. She kept the place obsessively clean and tidy, although no amount of bleach and polish masked the smell of damp.

'I'm home,' she called out, shrugging out of her coat and slipping off her shoes. Harry barely acknowledged her from his usual place on the sofa.

'Lazy cat,' she muttered affectionately, picking up her bags and making her way into the kitchen.

She put away the shopping before fishing her mobile out of

3

her handbag to read the message. Just as she'd thought. It was from Claire.

> You have to come.
> Please.
> xoxo

Laura couldn't go. How could she get out of it this time? Last year, Claire had found cheap flights from Belfast International to Alicante. She'd tried to talk Laura into going with her and the others. A whole week in August. It would be great craic, according to Claire, all that sea, sun and sangria.

Her mother had said something catty. She usually did. How her father had put up with her for so long was beyond Laura. She'd been like that even before he died, although she became worse afterwards, when he was no longer around to keep her in check. Laura remembered her mother's words as if it were yesterday. 'Better ditch the bikini,' she'd said. 'They'll mistake you for a beached whale.'

Laura wasn't nearly as fat as her mother liked to make out. A little overweight, yes, but she was surely of average build for a citizen of Northern Ireland. And she didn't even own a bikini. Cursed with a ghoulishly white Celtic complexion, Laura tended to stay out of the sun. Which was one of the reasons she didn't go to Spain.

Even so, she'd been flattered that her colleagues had asked her to go to Alicante with them and grateful that Claire included her all the time. They were poles apart, she and Claire. Laura had freckles, eyes the colour of seaweed and scraggly ginger hair whereas Claire was skinny with cobalt blue eyes and long shiny jet-black hair. She was beautiful. Popular, too. Everyone at the library adored her.

In the end, Laura had lied. She said she'd been invited to the wedding of one of her cousins. She had twelve cousins on her mother's side, and they were all married except for one: Declan. Same-sex marriage would have to be legalized in Northern Ireland before Declan and his partner could get married. But Laura's colleagues knew nothing about her family and so, as implausible as that excuse was, it got her out of the trip.

Afterwards, she'd listened to the suntanned girls reminiscing about their holiday in Spain. They talked about nothing else for a week. *The weather was lovely! We were bladdered! The paella was cracker! Spanish men have such firm arses!* It had all made Laura rather envious.

In turn, Laura told them a bit about the fictitious wedding. She'd spent hours during the holidays devouring novels. As the main characters tied the knot at the end of a few of her summer reads, she used that for inspiration.

She made herself a cup of tea now. Sitting next to Harry on the sofa and cradling the mug in her hands, Laura thought of all the reasons she couldn't go this year. A week in France.

'Who would look after you for a start?' she said to Harry, stroking his soft fur.

Plus, she didn't have a passport. Deep down she knew these were excuses rather than reasons not to go. She could easily apply for a passport and her neighbour, Mrs Doherty, would happily take in the cat.

She'd have to make up a story. Perhaps she could buy her flights – Claire said they were cheap – and then drop out at the last minute. One of her uncles could die or her mum could break her leg. Then it wouldn't look like she hadn't wanted to go in the first place.

Lyon. That was this year's destination. There were direct flights from Dublin. Laura had never been to France. She'd never been abroad unless you counted their family holidays on the mainland. They'd taken the ferry to Scotland – from Larne to Stranraer – four or five times when she was little, when her dad was still alive. But she'd never taken the plane.

And this was the main reason Laura didn't want to go. She had an irrational fear of flying. Her stomach pitched at the thought of boarding an aircraft. She couldn't stand the idea of putting her life into the hands of a pilot she couldn't see. She knew it was safer to travel by plane than by any other means of transport, but that didn't help. She didn't mind taking the boat. She could swim if the worst came to the worst, or at least stay afloat until help came. But if something went wrong in the plane, she couldn't fly. Or hover. This was why she'd bottled out of going to Spain the previous year. Silly, but there it was.

But France tempted her more than Spain. A lot more. Laura was a Francophile. She'd taken French A-level and gone on to read French at Queen's. She read novels in French, her favourite writers being Guy de Maupassant and Marcel Pagnol; she watched old French films, especially by New Wave cineastes; and listened to *France Info* every day on the radio. She'd always wanted to go to France. It was just that she'd imagined travelling there by boat as far as Scotland or England, then by train and on the Eurostar.

Lyon. What did she know about Lyon? Not a lot. Nothing whatsoever, come to think of it. It was quite far south, wasn't it? She googled it on her smartphone and scrolled through the Wikipedia page. South-East France, foot of the Alps. The basilica of *Notre-Dame de Fourvière* ... Silk weaving ... *Fête des Lumières* festival ... *Frères Lumière* cinema ... Roman theatre ... Interpol ... gastronomy.

Claire wanted to go to Lyon simply because *The Naturals* were playing there in August. The local rock band was playing on their doorstep in March – in the SSE Arena in Belfast, which would have been a lot handier, but tickets had sold out in less than ten minutes when they'd gone on sale six months previously. *The Naturals* were performing at two venues in France – Paris and Lyon. Claire said hotel prices in Paris for August were astronomical. So Lyon it was.

Lyon wasn't by the sea. There would be no risk of turning red like a cooked lobster at the end of a day on the beach. Plus Laura loved *The Naturals*. They'd long been her favourite band. Her cousin Declan was friends with the bass guitarist – they'd been at school together. Connor, that was his name. She met him once before he was famous after a gig he and his group had done in *The Dirty Onion*. He was a ride, Connor. Not very tall, but muscular. She'd loved his smile and the mischievous twinkle in his clear blue eyes.

She looked up, catching her image reflected in the black TV screen. She gave herself a stern look while she thought things over. An opportunity. That's what this trip was. Declan was always saying she should do something out of her comfort zone.

Picking up her mobile, she texted Claire.

OK! Count me in!

Claire's reply came straight back.

Yay! You won't regret it!
xoxo

Laura hoped Claire was right. But as she climbed into bed that night, she already regretted her decision. She couldn't put her finger on why exactly, but going on holiday with her friends to France seemed like a very bad idea. She wrestled with a strange gut feeling she was heading towards some inevitable disaster. Pulling her covers up to her chin, Laura closed her eyes and told herself she was being ridiculous.

Chapter 2

Sandrine

Sandrine shook Antoine as he lay in his bed, the covers kicked off onto the floor. He didn't respond, his body warm and yet seemingly lifeless. Was he ill? She spent her life worrying about one child or the other, even though her elder son was now officially an adult and her younger son wasn't far behind.

'Antoine,' she said, shaking him again, 'you're going to be late for work.'

He opened one eye, looked at her, then closed it again. 'I've set the alarm on my phone,' he said.

'You won't have time for breakfast if you don't get up now.'

'I work in a supermarket, *Maman*. The bakery there has *croissants* and *pains au chocolat*. And they have freshly squeezed orange juice.'

'You won't work there for much longer if you arrive late,' she said playfully, picking up the quilt from the floor and throwing it over him. Pulling it over his head, Antoine groaned.

'If you hadn't stopped my pocket money, I wouldn't have to work there at all,' came his muffled voice. 'I could have a lie-in on Saturdays like Maxime.'

Sandrine didn't know if he was joking or not. She glanced around his room. As usual, it was tidy and orderly, unlike his younger brother's bedroom. Even the posters on Antoine's wall were neatly aligned. His clothes were folded in a neat pile on a chair by his bed whereas Maxime always left his clothes discarded in a heap on the floor.

She smiled to herself, marvelling, not for the first time, at how alike her boys were, and yet at the same time how different. They couldn't have looked more similar if they'd been cloned. They had the same features, the same expressions and gestures. Sandrine and her husband Sam sometimes mistook one for the other in their photo albums. They had to examine the pictures closely to work out who was who. Max didn't have the green flecks in his eyes that Antoine did and Antoine's eyebrows were darker and more sharply defined.

Not only did they look alike, they also liked many of the same things – video games, jigsaw puzzles, fishing, the beach and the sea, dogs and cats. They had the same tastes in music: R&B, rap and rock. But Antoine was bookish while Max preferred the outdoors. Max had been cuddly as a child and was still affectionate whereas from a young age, Antoine had been fiercely independent and detached.

Antoine's alarm went off, cutting off Sandrine's thoughts. She left the room and went to join Sam for breakfast.

'Do you think he's depressed?' she asked Sam.

'No! You worry too much,' he said fondly as she sat down opposite him at the kitchen table.

She couldn't help worrying about her boys. That was her job as their mother. Indeed, she felt that bringing up her children was her only job, as she'd given up teaching years ago when

Antoine was born. She'd intended to go back to work, but it hadn't been necessary financially and she'd enjoyed her role as a stay-at-home parent. She had friends and didn't feel isolated. Perhaps she'd get back into teaching – at least give some private lessons – once the boys left home. That might distract her from feeling grief over an empty nest when the time came.

'I'm sure you're right,' she said. 'I'm just concerned about him, you know, since … well, what happened with Océane.'

Sam reached across the table and put a hand on her arm. 'That was months ago,' he said. 'I doubt he even gives her a thought these days.'

Sandrine wasn't so sure. Antoine had told her he wanted to marry Océane. He'd been smitten. It had been a few months since Océane had broken up with him, but she didn't think Antoine was over it yet. It was as if a light had gone out behind his eyes and hadn't yet come back on. He didn't smile as much. He didn't laugh at all.

Antoine sauntered into the kitchen a few minutes later, dressed with his hair combed. Standing at the worktop, he tore off a hunk of *baguette*, and took a bite.

'Catch you later,' he said, his mouth full, waving the bread as he made for the front door.

'Have a nice day,' Sam called after Antoine, but he got no reply other than the sound of the front door slamming shut. 'See?' Sam said, turning back to Sandrine. 'He's a typical teen.'

When Maxime emerged, sporting a bedhead and pyjamas, Sandrine and Sam had almost finished their breakfast. He kissed first Sandrine then Sam on both cheeks.

His back turned to them as he made himself toast, he said, '*Mamie* and *Papy* have invited Antoine and me round this Sunday. I said yes. Is that all right?'

'Of course,' Sandrine said noticing Sam blanch at the mention of his parents. 'You know it is.'

Sandrine had only met Sam's parents once, briefly, on the day

Sam had introduced her to them and announced their engagement. It had come as a complete shock to his parents. They'd had other ideas for him and they took an instant disliking to her. They made it clear they didn't even want to get to know her and would sever all ties with Sam if he insisted on marrying her. There was a huge row and Sam and Sandrine were unceremoniously thrown out of the house before they'd even sat down to eat lunch.

'Is your uncle picking you up?' Sandrine asked, pushing the argument to the back of her mind.

'Yes.'

Sam's parents lived about forty kilometres away, in a suburb to the south of Lyon. His older brother took Antoine and Maxime along with his own children to see their grandparents, and she was grateful to him for that. It was important to Sandrine. It was bad enough that she'd come between Sam and his parents. She didn't want to come between her sons and their grandparents, too.

In the first year or so after their marriage, Sam had spoken little about his parents, but over time he'd told her anecdotes about his brother and him when they were children and it was obvious he'd been close to his parents despite a somewhat strict upbringing.

But Sam rarely discussed the family rift with her. Sandrine hoped Sam's parents would come round eventually. She knew Sam would jump at the chance to be reunited with them. But the more time passed, the less likely it seemed there would ever be any reconciliation. Not as long as Sam remained married to Sandrine.

Maybe that was partly why Sandrine had abandoned the idea of returning to work. She was close to her parents, although not as close geographically as she would have liked, and she desperately wanted her own family to be a loving one, too. The fact that Sam was no longer in touch with his parents because of her

11

made Sandrine all the more determined to make her home a happy one. Sandrine was an only child, and she was glad Antoine and Maxime had each other.

To Sandrine, family was everything. And she would do anything for her sons. To make them happy, to protect them. Cook and clean for them, lie or even die for them. Anything at all.

Chapter 3

5 MONTHS AFTER

Laura

'How did your appointment go?' Declan asked, handing Laura a beer. She was sitting on the sofa, next to Declan's partner Patrick, who had his feet up on the coffee table, a bowl of crisps on his lap and a bottle of beer in his hand.

It had been several months since that night and Laura still couldn't tell her therapist everything. She couldn't tell her cousin the whole truth either. 'Put it this way. I enjoyed it more than lunch with my mum afterwards.'

'I'll bet. How is the old battle-axe?'

To say Declan wasn't especially fond of Laura's mum would be a massive understatement. Noreen was his father's sister, the youngest of five children, and the only girl. She'd grown up used to getting her own way. Noreen had never warmed to Patrick, and so Declan had accused her of being homophobic. Laura didn't think she was. It wasn't personal. Her mother was objectionable and offensive towards pretty much everyone. But Declan had had a heated argument with his aunt, saying that having married a Protestant, Noreen of all people should show compassion towards couples that society ostracized. They'd never really patched things up, which made for an awkward atmosphere at family reunions.

'Fine. Herself. You know.'

She was lucky to have Dec and Pat in her life. Declan was nine years older than her. He'd always been more like an older brother than a cousin, perhaps because like her, he was an only child. He had the same ginger hair and green eyes as she did and was the only person she knew who had more freckles than her. Pat was tall, dark and lanky, very different to Declan, but they had the same tastes in everything and nearly always agreed with each other. Laura had never heard a cross word between them.

'So, your appointment?'

It had taken Laura a while before she felt able to talk to a complete stranger about what she was going through. To begin with, her GP had put her on small doses of beta-blockers to help reduce the symptoms linked to her anxiety – her frequent sweats and racing heartbeat. He'd suggested a prescription for light sleeping tablets or anti-depressants, although she could tell he wasn't in favour of either. Laura had refused anyway. And finally he'd convinced her to go and see a therapist and referred her to Dr McBride, a psychologist who specialized in patient adjustment to anxiety and depression, post-traumatic stress disorder and major trauma.

'It went well, I suppose. He said it's perfectly normal – you know, after an experience like I had – to have difficulty falling asleep and flashbacks for several months. We did some breathing exercises. I think they might help calm me down if I get any more … panic attacks.'

Declan nodded. 'Go on.'

'According to Dr McBride – Robert – I shouldn't repress my feelings …' Laura had lost count of how many times she'd had to describe her feelings and at this point that's what she'd had to

14

do yet again – guilty, unmotivated, helpless, sick and, most of all, unworthy. 'But I'm to continue to work on replacing the negative emotions and thoughts with positive ones.'

'Sounds like it was beneficial,' Pat said before taking another swig of his beer.

'Uh-huh,' Laura said, noncommittally.

She was still mortified that she was seeing a shrink in the first place. Her mother had always branded people with mental health problems as "weak" and "self-absorbed" and although Laura didn't see eye to eye with her mother on this subject as on so many others, she didn't want those labels applied to her.

'So, when are you seeing your man again?'

'I have another appointment. Same time next week.'

'Baby steps,' Declan said, putting his arm around her shoulders and giving her a squeeze. 'You'll get there.'

'Hmm,' Laura said.

Robert was gentle and had an easy-going, avuncular manner. Even though she felt more and more comfortable talking to him, she knew she wouldn't make any headway until she could voice what had really happened that night. Each time she had to recount the events in detail, she omitted the worst part. She remembered it clearly, although she wished she didn't. She'd replayed it in her mind hundreds of times, ashamed of how she'd reacted and wondering what she should have done. It was all too horrific to put into words, so she'd cut those few seconds out of the description she'd given her therapist and even Declan.

Pat brought Laura back to the present. 'Chinese or Indian?' he asked, sliding forward on the sofa to pull his mobile out of his back pocket.

'I fancy a curry,' Laura said.

'Indian it is.'

'Do you want another beer?' Declan asked.

'Better not. I'm driving.'

'You'll let us know if there's anything we can do, won't you? Pat and I are here for you.'

'Thanks, Declan.'

They watched a romcom on Netflix while they ate dinner, plates balanced on their laps. Laura surprised herself by laughing at one point. The sound was foreign to her and she stopped abruptly, riven with guilt that she could laugh at all.

'Are you going to eat that?' Pat asked after a while.

'What?' She followed Pat's gaze and realized she'd barely touched her meal. 'Oh. No. I'm full.'

Pat took the plate from Laura's lap and proceeded to load large forkfuls of tikka masala into his mouth.

'He has that much appetite he needs two gobs, so he does,' Declan whispered to Laura.

'Hey! I heard that.'

Laura was tired and couldn't concentrate on the film, even though the plot didn't seem particularly complicated. She was glad of the company, though, and enjoyed Dec and Pat's banter.

When the end credits started to roll, Declan walked her out to her car. 'Safe home,' he said.

Laura yawned all the way home. Perhaps she would nod off no problem for once. She felt more relaxed than she had for a while. Today had been one of her better days.

Harry weaved a figure of eight around her legs as she cleaned her teeth, then he followed her into the bedroom, taking up his usual night-time position on her pillow as she got ready for bed. As she pulled up her pyjama trousers and they promptly slipped down to her hips, she realized how loose they'd become.

Her mother was right. Well, partly. Laura remembered their conversation over lunch.

'Are you sure you don't want more than a salad, dear?' her mother had asked. 'My treat.'

'No, I'm not hungry,' she'd replied, thinking that eating lunch with Noreen in *The Ivory* was not her idea of a treat. Or anywhere

16

else for that matter. It inevitably meant being subjected to jibes about being overweight, or "obese", if Noreen was to be believed.

'At least there's a silver lining in all this,' her mother had commented, smiling at her beatifically.

'In all what?' Laura had asked, staring at her blankly, her eyebrows pinching into a frown.

'You know, your near-death experience,' she'd continued. 'You've lost tonnes of weight.' Laura had choked on a cherry tomato.

Looking down and appraising her tummy now, Laura realized she had indeed lost several pounds. She didn't feel good for it, though.

Her eyelids felt heavy and her body cried out with exhaustion. But as always when she tried to get to sleep, images flashed in front of her eyes – even as she squeezed them shut – a series of film-like stills of people frozen in the strobe lights as they ran for their lives in every direction while she stood rooted to the spot, compelled to watch the slideshow. She could hear the rapid gunfire, smell the stench of fear. Above all, she could clearly see the face of the Frenchman who had saved her life.

And then lost his.

Chapter 4

Sandrine

Sandrine slid the snapshot out from under the book in the drawer of the coffee table and stared into her dead son's round face. He was looking directly at the camera, his eyes the same colour as Sam's, hazel with green tinges that flashed wildly whenever he was angry or sad. She stroked Antoine's cheek with her forefinger as she sat on the sofa, a solitary tear plopping onto the photo in her lap as her son grinned up at her. He still had braces on his teeth then. He must have been about fifteen. Only four short years of his life left, although no one could have predicted that at the time.

Sandrine had photos of Antoine hidden everywhere, although Sam – in one of the rare moments when they'd talked about what it meant to have lost Antoine that way – had asked her to take them all down. It was easier for him, he'd said, not to have a constant reminder.

Sandrine saw her son everywhere, even without the photos. She imagined him lounging in front of the television or sitting

18

on the empty chair next to Maxime at the kitchen table. When she closed her eyes, she could visualize him so clearly it was as if his image was printed on the insides of her eyelids.

She was sure the same thoughts and images went through Sam's head as hers. Identical memories of their son. The first time Antoine managed to swim a whole length of the pool, when he broke his arm falling from a swing, his first medal at judo, the afternoon the boys had all fished together in their grandfather's pond in Brittany and Antoine was the only one to catch any trout, the day they realized he was taller than Sam … Memories that would forever more be bittersweet.

Sometimes, when she and Sam were sitting across the kitchen table from each other or next to each other on the sofa, they were so close she could reach out and touch him. And yet, the distance between them seemed too far to travel. They blamed themselves and each other, wondering what they would do differently if they could go back in time. They couldn't talk about it. They couldn't find the words. And so they barely spoke to each other, even though they both knew that saying the wrong thing was better than saying nothing at all. What was left unsaid loomed large in the small space between them, making the air rancid with resentment and reproach. They were each alone in their grief.

Since it had happened five months ago, Sandrine struggled to keep afloat as every day more waves of sorrow broke over her. She had so many regrets. She wished she'd been a better mother. If only she'd paid more attention to her son. She hadn't known anything about his plans for that evening, although that wouldn't have changed anything. Even if she'd asked him where he was going and he'd told her, she wouldn't have stopped him. She couldn't have foreseen the danger. Could she?

She hadn't seen Antoine that day. For once, he'd left the house before she got up. She knew he'd had breakfast – he'd unloaded the dishwasher and cleared his plate and mug into it. But she didn't know what he was wearing that day and she didn't remember their last conversation. That still tortured her. Were her last words to him kind? Banal? Good morning or goodnight? Or did she nag him for something inconsequential like talking with his mouth full or playing his music too loudly? When was the last time she'd told her son she loved him or that she was proud of him? When was the last time he'd made her proud? Or smile?

She looked at the photo of Antoine one more time, drinking him in, then put it back under the book and closed the drawer. She rose to her feet, knowing she had to get out of the house and get some air.

She put on her coat and shoes, slung her handbag over her shoulder and stumbled through the door. Her legs felt unsteady as she walked to the bus stop. She could feel people's eyes on her, boring into her. They must have thought she was drunk or drugged.

She saw her neighbour, Angélique, cross the road, throwing disapproving glances over her shoulder and pulling her toddler by the hand to the safety of the pavement on the other side. Angélique had once been a good friend, but all Sandrine's friends avoided her now. It was as though her bereavement and affliction were contagious; as though she would jinx them or their children.

The background noise on the bus had a calming effect on Sandrine and chased the thoughts of her dead son to a recess of her mind. She looked out of the window as the bus hugged the River *Saône*, the road following its meanders. Sandrine lived in a suburb to the north-east of Lyon and hadn't been into the city centre for many months, but she soon found herself walking across *La Place des Terreaux* and into the wind.

She glanced at the Bartholdi Fountain to her left. Once, when her parents had come to stay, she'd shown them around Lyon and was amazed to discover almost as much about the city as they had. How was it that when you lived in a place, you were always the last to visit its sights? The fountain's four sculpted horses pulling the chariot represented rivers racing out to sea, Sandrine recalled, although she couldn't remember which rivers. She stopped for a moment and studied the monument, wishing she could gallop away or flow out to sea. She'd grown up by the sea and she missed it.

Pulling up the collar of her coat against the cold as she passed the city hall, Sandrine headed for *La Rue de la République*. There were people everywhere, walking up, down and across the shopping street in undisciplined hordes. She felt as if she were swimming upstream, struggling against the current, but at the same time she appreciated the impression of blending into the crowd. There was little chance she'd see anyone she knew; no one here knew her or anything about her. She could pretend to be normal.

It wasn't until Sandrine saw the red and white signs for *SOLDES* in the window of a perfumery that it dawned on her why there were so many shoppers in town. This was the first Saturday of the January sales.

She'd forgotten her gloves and her hands were freezing, so she stopped at Starbucks to warm herself up. When the barista called her name and handed her the vanilla latte she'd ordered, she turned round to see there were no free tables. She spotted a seat in the corner, opposite a woman with a baby, and made her way over.

'Do you mind if I sit here?' Sandrine asked.

'Not at all.'

Sandrine sat down. The baby was pulling on a tuft of his mother's long brown hair, which spilled out from under her glittery bobble hat. He was giggling and gurgling at noises and grimaces that his mother made. The game amused him for a few minutes before he began to whimper. Holding her baby in one arm, his mother opened a cavernous baby changing bag with difficulty and brought out some mineral water, a baby bottle and a transparent plastic container with milk powder in it. Then she tried to unscrew the cap of the bottle of water with one hand.

'Can I help you?' Sandrine asked, expecting the woman to talk her through making up the formula. To Sandrine's surprise, the woman stood up and thrust her son at Sandrine while she got everything ready for the feed.

Sandrine cooed at the baby, soothing him. It had been several years since she'd held a baby. He wasn't tiny, but she was careful to support his head anyway. He looked at Sandrine with wide eyes and she thought he was about to cry, but instead his mouth opened, forming a large "O". Then his mother reached out to take him back. Sandrine watched as she sat back down and the baby latched on to the teat of the bottle, guzzling hungrily.

'Thank you,' the woman said, shooting a grateful smile at Sandrine. 'That was very kind of you.'

'You're welcome.'

'A lot of people think bottle-feeding makes you a bad mother. They say mothers who breastfeed bond better with their babies.'

Sandrine nodded, hoping she wasn't trying to strike up a conversation. Sandrine had breastfed both Antoine and Maxime, but there was a lot more to motherhood than choosing between formula or maternal milk. She used to think she wasn't doing a bad job as a mum, but she was no longer so sure. She wanted to be a good mother to Maxime but her younger son seemed estranged from her now.

As she watched the mother with her baby boy, a memory from twenty years ago erupted into Sandrine's mind: holding Antoine, her miracle baby, for the first time, seconds after he was born.

She and Sam had tried for a baby for so long. And just when they thought it might never happen, Sandrine finally got pregnant. At the seven-month scan, they asked if their baby was a boy or a girl. But the gynaecologist shook her head and wouldn't answer the question. That was when they realized something was wrong. Their baby girl, Léa, had no heartbeat.

Sandrine had been inconsolable and Sam had been so

supportive, even as he grieved himself. One night, six or seven weeks after they'd lost Léa, he held Sandrine in his arms and they made love. Sam was gentle, as if afraid she would break. She cried when it was over.

Her period hadn't returned since the pregnancy and so she was nearly four months gone by the time she realized.

'Women are quite fertile immediately after giving birth,' her gynaecologist said.

It took her another fortnight to pluck up the courage to tell Sam. She was surprised he hadn't noticed – her bump was getting prominent by then.

They were terrified. They didn't dare to dream or hope. They didn't make plans, but the baby's room had already been decorated – for Léa. And so Antoine came along. Two days after his due date. Their miracle baby. A heavy, healthy baby boy.

Sandrine didn't want to tempt fate again, but after a while she became anxious. What if something happened to Antoine? What if he got sick? What if she lost him? Her irrational fear that one day she might no longer be a mother grew stronger than her fear of having another miscarriage or stillbirth so she stopped taking the pill to see if anything would come of it. Something did. Maxime. She thought of her boys as her two princes, but never as the heir and the spare. She loved them both equally. But the fear she'd had of losing Antoine, which diminished gradually as the years went by, turned out to be founded in the end.

The media rarely mentioned it now. It was yesterday's news. But that didn't make it go away. Like everyone else in France, and the rest of the world, Sandrine had seen those images broadcast over and over again on the television. They continued, even now, to play on a loop in her head like a film she couldn't turn off.

She'd added a sequence over time, the product of her imagination, based on survivors' accounts. It showed what had happened inside the arena. There was no real footage of that. There had been no cameras. People filming the concert with their mobile phones had stopped when the first rounds rang out. The film in Sandrine's head paused on the same frame every time, at the exact point where, in Sandrine's mind, her son had lost his life. One second alive. The next dead. In a heartbeat. In the blink of an eye. In the squeeze of a trigger.

An invisible hand clutched Sandrine's throat and she couldn't breathe.

The woman stared from across the table. 'Are you all right?' she asked, startling Sandrine out of her reverie.

Standing up on shaky legs, Sandrine grabbed her coat and handbag. 'Goodbye. Have a nice day,' she said automatically, her voice sounding unfamiliar, even to her ears.

The cold air hit her like a slap to the face as she stepped outside. She walked up the avenue, back the way she'd come. In the window of an estate agency, she caught sight of a slim woman, stooping at the neck like a question mark so that her shoulder-length lank brown hair fell over her face. It took Sandrine a moment to realize that this elderly woman, who was still clinging to her forties, was her own reflection. Forcing herself to stand tall, she peered into the window.

Unsurprisingly, there were no signs in the window of the estate agency for the winter sales. Almost two weeks into January, and the *Meilleurs Voeux!* stickers, wishing everyone a happy new year, hadn't been taken down yet. Underneath it, glossy photos showed expensive flats for sale or for rent in the city centre. Sandrine gazed at them. She couldn't afford to buy a flat in the city centre, and wouldn't want to live here anyway. She liked the anonymity here, but she didn't care much for the bustle and noise. She longed to go back to Brittany, to be near her parents, by the sea.

Then a thought burst into her mind. Why didn't they move? What was stopping them? They could easily sell up here and buy a house near her mum and dad. Get away from it all. Sam could set up his business there easily enough. He'd come with her, wouldn't he? Would she go if he didn't?

But even if Sam did get on board, there was Maxime to consider, not that they saw much of him these days. He slept over at friends' places most nights now, during the week, coming home once in a while to dump his dirty washing and pick up clean clothes. She'd failed one son; she couldn't abandon the other.

Chances were, though, Maxime wouldn't be living with them much longer. He planned to move to Marseille after his *baccalauréat* exams this summer. She would talk to Sam about this idea, sound him out. The more she thought about it, the more convinced she became that this was what they needed. A new home. A fresh start.

Sam was still at work when she got home. She made her way into Antoine's bedroom. She'd cleaned it after his death, as though he were coming back any day and she wanted to welcome him home. She hadn't washed the bedclothes, though. She climbed into his bed, pulling the quilt over her mouth and nose, and breathing him in. She often did this when she found herself alone in the house, but as the months went by his scent had faded and the covers smelt only of her perfume now.

Tears streamed down Sandrine's face, rolling into her ears and onto Antoine's pillow, as she lay on her back in his bed. Did he know how much he was loved? Or had they been afraid to love him after losing Léa? Had they spoiled him? Perhaps they hadn't spoiled him enough.

She wasn't aware she was tired. Not any more than usual, anyway. Sleep was something Sandrine had given up on. It had become irregular and elusive. She slept through the night only occasionally now, and when she did she felt less energized than if she'd lain awake for most of it. It wouldn't have occurred to her she might fall asleep during the day.

She woke up groggy and disoriented. It took her several seconds to work out where she was and a few more to realize she wasn't alone. Daylight had faded now and she could make out only a silhouette. Someone was sitting on the bed. Sandrine sat bolt upright and screamed.

'Shhh. It's me.' Sam put one hand on her shoulder. In his other hand, he was holding a steaming mug, which he passed to her. She saw worry etched around his mouth and in the green flecks of his hazel eyes.

'Thank you.' She was touched by his thoughtfulness.

For a while, neither of them spoke. Sam didn't ask her what she was doing in here, or if she came in here often. He must have worked that out for himself. Maybe he sneaked in here, too, when she was out somewhere.

Sandrine blew across the mug and sipped the drink, crinkling her nose. It was too sugary. Sam said proper mint tea was sweet and that's the way he always made it.

They'd bought the house from a couple of elderly Moroccans, whose garden had a bed of mint running riot behind the clothesline. Sam had wanted to dig it all up. It took up too much space, he'd said, but Sandrine felt it was part of the legacy of the house and liked the smell when she hung out the washing, so instead they found recipes to cook with it and froze it so they could make herbal teas during the winter. The smell of mint and the memory it carried slowed down Sandrine's breathing and heartbeat.

'Sam, I've been thinking,' she said. 'When Maxime has finished his exams later this year, we could move away. I'd love to move back to Brittany. You like it there, don't you?' He didn't answer. She tried to read his expression, but his face was inscrutable. 'We could get a house near the sea,' she persisted. She could hear the quaver in her voice.

'My family's here,' Sam said.

'Your family! Your brother is the only one who talks to you! And even he's …'

'He's what?'

'Nothing. Forget it.'

Sam's face clouded over and Sandrine regretted her outburst. After all, it was because of her that Sam had fallen out with his parents. It had been cruel of her to use that as an argument. She put her hand on Sam's to placate him, but he pulled away.

'We need to stay here. For Maxime.' The green blaze in Sam's eyes belied his calm tone. In that moment she saw Antoine in Sam and had to look away.

'Max plans to go to Marseille,' she muttered.

'We've already lost one of our sons,' Sam continued, as if he hadn't heard her. 'We can't risk losing the other one.' He got up and left the room, closing the door behind him and leaving her in the dark.

She set the mug on the bedside table and curled up again in Antoine's bed. Oblivion. That was what Sandrine needed. She scrunched her eyes tight shut in an attempt to go back to sleep. But it was futile. Antoine's face swam into focus as her imagination conjured up the photo she'd stared at earlier. She tried to hold on to that image, to zoom in closer. But it was as if, from behind her closed eyelids, her vision blurred and the colours faded to sepia. Her mind was playing a cruel trick on her, reminding her she would never see her son again.

27

Chapter 5

1 MONTH BEFORE

Laura

It wasn't until she stepped out of the flat to go to work that she was reminded what day it was.

'Happy birthday!' It was her neighbour.

'Thank you, Mrs Doherty,' Laura said, locking the door to her flat. 'It's so good of you to remember.'

'Ah, it's an easy one to remember, so it is,' the elderly lady replied. 'It's the anniversary of my husband's death.'

Laura was thrown for a second. 'Oh. I'm sorry, Mrs Doherty. I didn't know that.' Laura hadn't even known there had been a Mr Doherty.

Her neighbour made a dismissive gesture with her hand. 'Sure, when you start to forget dates, you start to lose your head, so you do.'

Mrs Doherty's brain was still razor-sharp, but her arthritis meant she was losing some of her mobility, so Laura ran errands for her whenever her hips were playing up. 'Do you need me to get you anything, Mrs Doherty? I can pick up some shopping after work if you like?'

'Och, no pet, thank you. Right as rain today.'

Mrs Doherty nodded towards her tartan shopping cart and wheeled it over to the lift, which they rode down to the ground floor together. Then Laura headed for the bus stop.

The library opened at 9:30 but Laura and her colleagues usually arrived half an hour early so they could have a chat and a cup of tea together before work. As usual, Claire was already in the staffroom when Laura arrived that morning. She was wearing a flowery sundress with sandals. She had her back to Laura and was pouring milk into four mugs.

'Good morning. What a pretty dress!' Laura said.

Claire turned round, her large hoop earrings rocking energetically from side to side with the movement.

'Hiya. Happy birthday!' She put the carton of milk on the counter and picked up a small, beautifully gift-wrapped box, which she held out to Laura.

'You shouldn't have. That's so sweet of you.'

'Are you excited?' Claire asked.

Laura frowned. Did she mean about the present? About turning thirty?

'Four weeks tomorrow!'

'Ah. Oh. Yes. I still have a few things to get before then, but I can't wait,' Laura said, as a small knot of trepidation tied itself in her stomach.

Laura picked off the Sellotape and opened the present. It was a necklace, a colourful glass pendant on a red ribbon. Laura remembered admiring a similar necklace around Claire's neck a few months ago.

'It's beautiful,' she said, moved. 'Thank you.'

As Claire was tying the necklace around Laura's neck, Ava and Sarah arrived. Both in their mid-twenties, they were the same height and build, when Ava wasn't wearing heels. But the similarities stopped there. Sarah had fine blond hair, scooped back into a ponytail, and wore a serious expression as her default setting. Ava, on the other hand, had an unruly mane of thick, dark hair and flawless skin with permanently rosy cheeks. She had prominent front teeth, which were all the more noticeable as they were naturally very white and she smiled a lot.

'Happy birthday,' they chorused. They came bearing gifts, too. Laura hadn't expected any of them to remember, let alone buy her presents, and for a moment she was choked up. They looked at her expectantly, Ava flashing her signature wide smile.

Claire finished making the tea and handed round the mugs while Laura opened Ava's and Sarah's presents. Ava had bought her an orange and yellow chiffon scarf.

'It's beautiful, thank you.' Laura tended to wear black in the hope it flattered her body, so she could wear the scarf or the necklace with pretty much anything in her wardrobe. It might make her outfits more summery.

Sarah had bought her a set of mini Yankee candles.

'That'll help brighten up my flat,' Laura said, realizing she'd complained to Sarah the other day about how grubby her flat was. 'That was thoughtful of you.'

Looking at her colleagues now, Laura felt a little spark of excitement at the idea of going to France with them. They were kind, thoughtful people. They would have fun together. Once they got off the damn plane. She drained her tea and went to get ready.

She was running Rhythm and Rhyme that morning and by eleven o'clock, she and a group of under-fives with their accompanying adults were stomping like elephants, prowling like tigers and jumping like kangaroos around the room. After that day's story, *The Tiger Who Came To Tea*, which was always a firm favourite with kids and carers alike, Laura did some finger-counting rhymes to end the session. When the half hour was up, she was exhausted and sweating like an animal herself.

The rest of the morning raced by and it was only when her stomach rumbled that Laura realized it was past midday. She ate lunch with her mother on Fridays. It had become a thing. Seeing as it was her birthday, maybe Noreen would take her to *The Titanic Pub and Kitchen*. It was just round the corner and Laura liked it there, as much for the atmosphere as for the food, although her mother considered it to be a tacky tourist trap.

Her mum was talking to Ava when Laura found her in the entrance hall. As they left, Noreen hissed, 'She has a face only a mother could love, that one.' Laura nudged her, afraid Ava might have overheard. 'It's true. She could eat an apple through a tennis racket with those teeth.'

Laura could feel her face burning. As they stepped outside, she turned to her mother. 'Ava's nice and that's not—'

'Oh, come on. I was joking. I'm sure she's a lovely girl. Many happy returns of the day,' she said, deftly changing the subject before Laura could protest any further. 'I didn't get you a present,' she continued. 'I thought we could choose something together in your lunch break.'

'What? Now? We won't have time to eat if we go shopping.'

'Well, it'll not do you any harm to skip a meal now, will it? Let's go to CastleCourt. I'll buy you some clothes for your holidays.'

It was a strange experience. Laura hated clothes shopping and tended to buy stuff online. She tried on garments her mother chose – things she wouldn't normally buy herself – and then blushed as Noreen made her walk up and down and do twirls in front of the changing cubicle in Debenhams. Laura felt as if she was being made to parade naked along a catwalk in front of a large audience, certain the other shoppers were staring at her. With each outfit, Laura tried to gauge her mother's reaction, hoping for approval, but expecting to read disappointment in her expression. But Noreen remained impassive.

Laura had to admit, though, her mum had an eye for this.

The colours Noreen picked – greens and blues, with white rather than black, suited Laura's pale complexion and went well with her ginger hair. Plus the clothes were comfortable. Her mother splashed out and bought her three dresses, five T-shirts, a pair of jeans and two pairs of shoes. She'd always been generous with her money, her mum. Laura decided to go on a diet. She'd look better in her new clothes if she were a bit slimmer.

She returned to the library ravenous. Her stomach growled all afternoon and by the end of the day she had a headache. She was glad the library closed early on Fridays. She could stop off at the supermarket on the way home and get what she needed to make herself a healthy dinner. Veggie lasagne, maybe. And some soda bread. That wouldn't hurt. Especially as she hadn't had any lunch. And she'd buy a bottle of wine for Mrs Doherty to thank her for agreeing to look after Harry while she was away next month. Then she could curl up on the sofa and read for a bit before getting an early night.

But her colleagues had other ideas.

'It's your birthday. Let's go for a drink!' Claire suggested as they finished work.

'What about a drink and a meal?' said Sarah. 'I'm starving and it's not good to drink on an empty stomach.'

'Ooh, it's Friday. Let's make it a girlie night out,' Ava said.

Laura left the bags of new clothes in the staffroom and allowed herself to be persuaded to go out. She'd been for a drink with Claire a few times and she'd had lunch with Sarah and Sarah's mum on at least two occasions. But she'd never socialized with Ava. She didn't know her as well as the others.

'What did you have in mind?' Sarah asked Ava.

'Might as well get something to eat in Muriel's, seeing as it's not far, then we could move on to The Spaniard?'

Laura wondered if Ava was planning a pub crawl. She'd been to The Spaniard once with Declan and Patrick, but she'd never heard of Muriel's.

Ava filled her in. 'Muriel's Café Bar. Gins to die for. Food's great, too.'

Laura found Muriel's to be a classy bar, despite the knickers suspended on clotheslines around the ceiling, a wink at the establishment's past as a brothel, according to Claire. They were lucky enough to get a window seat upstairs. Ava was right. The food and the gin cocktails were delicious. And Ava turned out to be a hoot.

Over Cajun chicken burgers, pepper fries, nachos, guacamole and mixed berry mojitos, the conversation turned to their respective love lives. Sarah had a steady boyfriend, Claire had a string of exes, Laura was embarrassed to admit she hadn't been out with anyone for more than two years. Ava, who wasn't at all ashamed of her single status, regaled them with stories of her latest disastrous dates.

'I've been on two so far this month,' she said, 'and I'm starting to think I'll never find Mr Right.'

'What was wrong with these two?' asked Sarah.

'Well, first there was Aiden. Other than the chunky chain around his neck, he was fine.'

'You didn't see him again because he wore a necklace?' Sarah asked, incredulous.

'No. I'm not that shallow! I'm not finished.' Ava took a gulp of her gin. 'At the end of the evening, he offered to drop me home and asked would I mind if we called in to see his granda on the way. He said it was "a difficult anniversary."' She made air quotes with her fingers. 'So, I said, yes, of course. I figured his grandmother must have died on that date or something and it was hard on the old man.'

'So, what did he mean?' Laura asked, absent-mindedly twirling the paper umbrella from her cocktail between her fingers.

'He took me to Milltown Bloody Cemetery,' Ava continued. 'It was the anniversary of his granda's death.'

'No!' Laura suppressed a giggle as Claire's mouth dropped open.

'It was eleven o'clock at night and I was in a graveyard for feck's sake. I was bricking it. I even texted me ma so she'd know where I was in case anything happened to me.'

Ava paused, for breath or to drink more gin, Laura wasn't sure which. She had no idea if Ava was exaggerating or even making all this up, but as Declan often said, you shouldn't let the truth get in the way of a good story.

When she'd finished laughing, Claire spoke the words Laura was thinking. 'I can't understand how no one has snapped you up, Ava. You're lovely, smart and funny. Any bloke would be lucky to have you.'

'So what happened on the second date?' Sarah prompted before Ava could respond.

'That one didn't get off to a great start,' Ava said. 'As soon as Liam walked into the restaurant, he said, "From your photo I was afraid you'd be out of my league, but now I've seen you in the flesh, I feel more confident." I almost walked out, but I thought I'd give him a chance.'

'Not the best chat-up line,' Laura agreed, giggling.

'No, indeed. Anyway, when I went to the ladies', the waitress was in there. She told me I was his third date that week. It was only Wednesday! I climbed out the toilet window and called a cab.'

It was one o'clock in the morning when Laura's cab dropped her home. She'd had a wonderful evening and knew she would have a hangover.

'I'll do some exercise tomorrow,' she said to Harry. She could go for a walk, a swim or even a bike ride. Tonight had been a temporary blip, but she'd get back on her diet tomorrow. She didn't need to lose that much weight and she still had a whole month before the trip to France.

Yeah, right. Who are you kidding?

The little voice in her head – the one that sounded like her mother, the one that had made her feel worthless all her life – was clearly a lot less optimistic about her chances of success. She ignored it.

'And I'll carry on brushing up on my French,' she added. Laura had studied French at Queen's University but she hadn't finished her degree. She'd had glandular fever and a sizeable student loan that needed to be repaid, so in the end she'd got a job at Belfast Central Library and dropped out of her course before the obligatory year abroad. She'd kept up her French over the years, though, and had been studying every spare minute since she'd bought her plane ticket to Lyon.

She found she was looking forward to this trip now. She'd never been adventurous or gregarious. A week's holiday with some friends was exactly what she needed.

Chapter 6

1 MONTH BEFORE

Sandrine

Sandrine was convinced this would be their last holiday as a family. She intended to make the most of their week here at her parents' house in Brittany and spend some quality time with her sons. She was surprised the boys had agreed to come this year. For a few summers now, they'd been asking if they could go somewhere else for a change. They'd certainly prefer to go on holiday with their mates from now on rather than with her and Sam anyway. As it was, Maxime had plans to go camping somewhere in Provence for a few days with his friend Benoît when they got back.

It was good to see Antoine smiling again. He seemed to finally be over his break-up with Océane and to have found a sense of purpose in life again. Sandrine had seen him typing on his mobile a couple of times. He'd hastily put his phone away each time she'd caught him, which made her wonder if he had a new girl-friend. But when she asked who he was writing to, he told her it was one of his mates. He hadn't shown much interest in social-izing for a while, so she took that as a good sign.

On their fourth day there, Sandrine and her mother went to Douarnenez, the nearest town to her parents' house, which Sandrine considered to be her hometown. Their only mission was to buy vegetables at the street market to make a ratatouille for dinner, so they took their time and wandered around the cobbled streets, then sat on the *terrasse* of a street café and drank *citrons pressés* – squash made from freshly squeezed lemons. When they got back to the house, it was calm – almost too quiet – without the others.

Sandrine's father, Sam and the boys had gone fishing for the day. Her father used to spend long afternoons fishing trout from a large pond in his own garden, but it had been replaced by a little fishing boat and a permit years ago. He'd bought his boat when Sandrine's mother had made him drain the pond to avoid any accidents after an incident involving Maxime.

Sandrine winced as she thought about that day. She'd had the fright of her life. She remembered it clearly despite the sedative she'd been given by her mother's GP. Sam and her father had been in the front garden, mending the fence. When she'd called everyone for lunch, Maxime hadn't come. According to Antoine, Max had wanted to feed the ducks. Maxime was only five at the time and he couldn't swim. Sandrine had raced out the back door and down the grassy slope to the pond.

Sandrine's father kept repeating that the pond was neither big nor deep. It was both, and Sandrine was aware that a child could drown in just a few centimetres of water, but her father was trying to convince himself and everyone else there was no way Maxime could have drowned.

Sam had always been Sandrine's rock and she'd clung to him like a limpet. He remained calm even though she could see panic in his eyes. He held her up when her legs threatened to give way. If it had been the other way round, if one of the boys had gone missing on his watch, she wouldn't have been so forgiving.

Sam had called the emergency services, and Sandrine's

mother had called the doctor for Sandrine. There had been one awful moment when one of the divers from the fire brigade had held up what looked to be a small item of clothing he'd found in the middle of the pond. But it turned out to be an old towel.

It wasn't until two police officers and the doctor took Sandrine back inside the house that they'd heard it. A thudding. A fist on wood. At first, Sandrine thought there was someone at the front door and immediately assumed it was bad news. But the knocking was coming from along the hallway. Then there were shouts and people came running in from the garden. One of the firefighters used a crowbar to prise open the door to the cupboard in which Sandrine's mother kept her cleaning stuff. It appeared to have been locked from the inside.

Sandrine couldn't understand what Maxime had been doing in the cupboard all that time. He'd been missing for over three hours. But he hadn't seemed at all disturbed by the experience. Much to everyone else's amusement he said he'd fallen asleep while playing hide-and-seek.

'That was a great hiding place,' Sandrine said through tears of relief as she scooped Maxime into her arms. 'It took a lot of people a long time to find you.'

That caused a ripple of laughter to sweep through the hallway.

But even now, all these years later, Sandrine couldn't raise a smile as she replayed the incident in her head. Standing in the kitchen next to her mother, prepping the vegetables for the evening meal, she didn't know if it was the onions or the memory that brought tears to her eyes. It was definitely the memory that put the same sour taste of fear in her mouth, a taste of what it would feel like to lose one of her sons. Distressing. Disturbing. Devastating. It was any mother's worst nightmare. She fervently hoped she'd never feel sheer terror like that again.

Sandrine didn't realize she was shaking until she cut the tip of her finger with the knife. It wasn't a deep cut, and although it stung only slightly, it was enough to dissolve the past and carry Sandrine firmly back to the present.

'Are you all right?' her mother asked, reaching for a first aid box in the cupboard above Sandrine's head.

'Yes,' Sandrine said. 'I wasn't concentrating.'

She washed away the blood with cold water from the tap. As she was putting on a plaster, her father, Sam, Antoine and Maxime burst noisily into the kitchen with their day's haul – mainly turbot and sardines. There was a lot of it. Some of it would go in the freezer for now.

Without having to be asked, Antoine washed his hands, put one of the turbots onto a chopping board, wiped it with kitchen towel and expertly filleted the fish with a knife, opening it along the side and then slicing it along the backbone.

Maxime watched his brother work.

'You could pitch in, you know,' Antoine said.

'You're doing a great job by the look of it. You don't need me,' Maxime replied.

'Well, can you fetch me a beer, then?'

'Well, just this once,' Maxime said. '*You're* the barman.'

Sandrine caught the look Antoine threw his younger brother. 'What's this about being a barman?' she asked.

'Change of career plan,' Antoine said.

'You're not serious.'

'No, I'm joking. Relax, *Maman*.'

'Are you still working at the supermarket?' Sandrine knew Béatrice, Antoine's boss. They'd gone to the same Friday evening Pilates class for a couple of years.

'Er, no. Not anymore.'

'Why not?'

When Antoine didn't answer, Sandrine looked pointedly at Maxime.

'He got the sack,' Maxime supplied, sheepishly. He pulled a

face at Antoine and mouthed an apology as he handed him a can of lager.

'You got sacked?' Sandrine turned to Sam. 'Did you know about this?'

Sam shook his head and carefully took the knife from her hand. She hadn't realized she'd been waving it around.

'Why? What happened?' Sam asked, his voice much calmer than Sandrine's. 'What did you do?'

'Nothing.' Antoine lowered his head. 'It was a mutual decision. I found another job. The supermarket job was just Saturdays. With the bartending, I can do a few evening shifts as well and earn more money.'

'In a pub? A nightclub? I hope it's not cash in hand,' Sam said.

'No. It's all above board. In *La Voie Lactée* – the concert hall in the seventh *arrondissement*.'

Sandrine didn't feel reassured and it must have shown on her face because Antoine said, 'Don't worry, *Maman*.'

Was it Sandrine's imagination or was Antoine being cagey? She sighed. He'd probably turned up late for work a few times too many, in which case she couldn't blame his boss. She hoped this wouldn't make things awkward between Béatrice and her. She didn't want to have to shop elsewhere. She also hoped the new job wouldn't get in the way of Antoine's studies after the summer holidays. Bar work would mean late nights. Unless it was just a summer job. But before she could ask, her mother had ushered everyone out of the kitchen and into the sitting room for an aperitif. Sandrine pushed the conversation with Antoine out of her mind.

Later, as they ate their dinner of fish, mashed potatoes and ratatouille, Sandrine looked around the table at everyone's contented faces and knew they mirrored her own. She wished they could stay longer. The sea air and climate in Brittany would be far kinder than the stifling atmosphere in and around Lyon.

An intense heatwave had been predicted for the rest of July and all of August.

The rest of the week went by quickly – too quickly. Sandrine was still reluctant to leave as they loaded their suitcases into the boot of Sam's car the following day. It would be considerably hotter in Lyon – thirty-eight degrees, according to the forecast – and she was dreading it. Instead of heading home, she felt as though they were driving away from it.

Chapter 7

2 DAYS BEFORE

Laura

'Where the hell is Claire?' Sarah asked for the fourth time in five minutes.

They were sitting in the waiting area at Europa Bus Centre, looking out through the dirty windows for their coach. Sarah jabbed at her mobile, then, holding it to her ear, she grimaced at Ava and Laura, muttering, 'It's gone to voicemail again. I'll leave a message this time.' Into her phone she said, 'Claire, our bus leaves from stand fourteen in …' she held her mobile out in front of her, examining the screen '… three minutes. You're not going to make it.'

As Sarah ended the call, their coach pulled into the bay. They stood up and headed for the automatic doors.

'Damn it! Where is she?' Sarah said, as she stepped outside, wheeling her suitcase.

Laura followed, suddenly feeling nauseous at the idea of going ahead with the trip without Claire. At the door she faltered, causing Ava to bump into her. Turning to apologize, she saw Ava shiver.

'It's like brass monkeys out here,' Ava said. 'It's supposed to be August, for feck's sake.'

Laura took in the pink T-shirt, short denim skirt and high wedge sandals. She could make out the goose bumps on Ava's arms and wondered why she didn't put on the light cardigan tied around her waist.

'Baltic,' Sarah agreed. 'The forecast is for thirty-eight degrees in Lyon today.'

How could they talk about the weather when Claire was about to miss the bus?

'Sounds lovely,' Ava said.

'I think that's pretty hot,' Sarah said. 'As in heatwave-hot. A heatwave here is like nineteen, twenty degrees,' she continued. 'I think we're in for a climate shock.'

Laura had checked the weather in Lyon every day for the last week. She'd never known temperatures anywhere near that high and had been hoping it would get cooler the week they were there. But that wasn't what the forecast said.

Ava seemed unfazed, though. 'Bring it on!' she said.

'Hiya, girls, what's the craic?' came a voice from behind Ava. It was Claire. Laura's face broke into a relieved smile.

'Better late than never,' Sarah muttered under her breath. Laura remembered Claire once remarking that Sarah had a saying for every situation.

'What are yous talking about?'

'The weather,' Ava and Sarah said in unison.

'As you do,' Claire said.

The bus driver, a small young man in his thirties, loaded their suitcases into the hold of the coach. Laura caught him admiring Claire's bare legs when he straightened up again.

She found herself sitting next to Ava on the coach with Claire and Sarah in the seats behind them. As the bus careered round the corners, Laura felt glad she'd got the window seat. She sometimes got travel-sick.

As if reading her mind, Ava said, 'We'll be out of Belfast soon. It'll be a smoother ride once we get onto the motorway.'

'I hope so. The driver clearly fancies himself as the next Eddie Irvine,' Laura said.

'Who?'

'Oh. He was a Formula One driver. From Newtownards? My father was a fan.' *Apparently*. At the thought of her father, Laura's heart clenched.

'Was he killed?' Ava asked.

Laura's eyes and mouth opened wide. *How did she know?* 'M … my father?'

'No. I meant Eddie Whatshisname. You said *was*.'

'Ah. No. Eddie Irvine. He wasn't killed.' *My daddy was.* 'He retired from racing, that's all.'

Laura fell quiet after that and Ava soon gave up trying to make small talk, becoming engrossed in her book and leaving Laura to her thoughts.

Over twenty years after his death and she still missed her father with a raw, visceral pain. And yet, the few memories she had of him were vague. Perhaps they weren't recollections at all and merely images pieced together from what she'd been told about her father over the years. She was only six when he was murdered.

She'd spent her childhood trying to patch up her mother, who had understandably gone to pieces. Laura had tried to make Noreen proud, but no matter what she did, it was never good enough, never enough.

'You remind me too much of your father,' Noreen would say to Laura.

Laura didn't look a lot like him – she got her red hair, freckles and pale skin from her mother's side of the family. So she supposed that meant she must have a similar personality. Laura liked the idea of being like her da. But she wondered if Noreen secretly wished she'd lost her daughter instead of her husband. Laura sometimes felt as if she'd lost both her parents that day.

Tears sprang to her eyes, so she followed Ava's example, pulling her novel out of her handbag to take her mind off her father. But after a few minutes, Laura realized she'd read the same paragraph four or five times and hadn't taken in a word of it. She closed her book with a sigh. She still felt nauseous, so she looked out of the window. The bus was hurtling along at an alarming speed. At least they should arrive at the airport in good time.

But just outside Dublin, they hit traffic and came to a standstill. At first Laura's nausea was replaced by relief.

Until Ava looked at the time on her mobile and said, 'It's going to be tight now.'

Sarah spotted it first. There had been a car accident, a collision between a white car – a Ford Fiesta, maybe, which was on its roof, and a badly damaged grey Audi a few feet away from it. There were also emergency vehicles with flashing blue lights – Garda cars, ambulances and fire engines – and a lot of broken glass. There was no sign of the drivers or any passengers. Laura hoped they were all right. They had a good view of it all from the bus, although Laura tried not to look. Once the traffic had trickled by in the one lane left open, the bus picked up speed again.

'We're going to be late,' Ava said.

Oh no. They couldn't miss the flight. Not now. Laura had psyched herself up for it. Plus she'd received her passport and gone on a diet – although she'd not lost much weight in the end – and spent months brushing up her French. And she did want to see *The Naturals*.

'No, we'll be all right,' Claire said. 'We'll have to get a move on, though.'

'At least we're in the bus and not in one of the cars back there,' Sarah said.

Despite her impractical footwear, Ava sprinted into the airport first, making a beeline for the Aer Lingus check-in area. The others followed, zigzagging around travellers pulling suitcases or pushing luggage trolleys. Laura jogged as fast as she could, struggling to keep up. Her heart was hammering, partly due to the physical effort and partly because she was terrified of losing the group. Thank goodness her new suitcase had wheels.

'Take a carry-on,' Claire had advised Laura when they'd bought the tickets. 'If we all travel light, we won't have to pay extra in Dublin or faff around when we get to Lyon.'

Laura only had the one suitcase. It had once belonged to Noreen. It was massive and heavy even when empty, so she'd rushed out and bought a smaller one.

'We don't need to go to the Aer Lingus desk,' Sarah called after Ava. 'We've already checked in online.'

This was true. Claire had talked Laura through it on the phone and she'd printed out her boarding pass. She also had it on the app on her phone.

'Sensible Sarah,' Claire said jocularly. Laura was grateful to Claire for keeping calm. It was saving her from losing it.

Ava stopped by the departures board. 'The gate's up,' she announced.

'That way,' Sarah said, pointing towards a sign for Security.

The two of them started to run again, but Claire called them back. 'The gate's up, but the flight's not boarding yet. We don't need to rush.'

Laura followed the others through security, watching what they did and copying them. She hadn't known to put liquids into small containers and transparent plastic bags, so most of her toiletries were confiscated.

'Not to worry,' Claire said cheerfully. 'I've got shampoo and conditioner and we can always buy some more when we get there.'

In the end they got to the gate with five minutes to spare before boarding. Laura needed to rest but the seats were all taken, so she slumped to the floor with her back against the wall. Sarah sat down next to her.

'You should check your suitcase in that metal stand over there,

Ava,' Sarah said. 'It looks like it's about to burst open. If it doesn't fit in there, you'll have to pay for it to go in the hold.'

Ava wheeled her suitcase over to the baggage sizer and as Sarah had predicted, it didn't fit. Claire offered to take some of Ava's clothes in her luggage.

'You have to pack your own things,' Sarah said. 'It's a safety thing. You're not supposed to carry anyone else's stuff.' Everyone looked at her. 'What? You're not. Just saying.'

Claire and Ava ignored her, knelt on the floor and transferred some clothes from Ava's suitcase into Claire's. Sarah messed about on her phone. Laura resisted the temptation to take out hers and send a text to Mrs Doherty to ask after Harry. It had only been a few hours since she'd dropped off the cat at her neighbour's.

And then it was time to board the plane. Laura's stomach clamped in panic. By the time they'd got onto the plane and found their seats, she felt as if she were about to faint. Claire had to put her case in the overhead bin for her. Laura sat down, sandwiched between Claire and Ava. She fumbled with the safety belt – it seemed complicated and her hands were shaking.

'Is something the matter?' Ava asked as she deftly attached and adjusted hers.

Helping Laura with the seatbelt, Claire replied for her, 'She's never flown before.'

'Away on!' Ava exclaimed, then added, 'Sure, the pilot can't be worse than that buck eejit bus driver.'

Laura tried to grunt her agreement, but it came out as a sort of squeal.

'The plane's the safest means of travelling, so it is,' Claire said, patting Laura's hand.

'There's a first time for everything,' Sarah said from across the aisle. There was no one next to her, but some passengers were still standing, stowing luggage or waiting for someone to sit down so they could get to their seats.

'Do you want the window seat?' Ava asked.

Laura managed to shake her head and force a smile.

'You should never swap seats on a plane,' Sarah piped up again.

'Why not?' Ava asked, leaning forwards to look at Sarah.

'Well, in case the plane crashes and they have to identify the bodies.'

Laura blanched.

'Not helpful, Sarah,' Claire said.

'What? It's true.'

A large man put an end to their conversation as he lifted his suitcase to put it in the locker above Sarah's seat. Claire nudged Laura and nodded in his direction. They observed him as he shrugged off his jacket. Laura could see huge wet patches under his armpits as he raised his arms again to cram his jacket on top of his case.

'Um, I'm in the middle,' he said, turning round to Sarah, who got up and squeezed past him into the aisle to let him get to his seat. As the man wedged himself into the seat next to her, Sarah turned towards the others, wrinkling her nose and waving her hand in front of it.

As Sarah sat down again, Ava said to Laura, 'I bet she wishes she could swap seats now.'

That made Laura laugh in spite of the kittens tumbling around in her tummy.

Shortly after everyone had boarded, Laura heard the thrumming of the aeroplane's engine and felt it vibrate through her. She was suddenly cold and regretted putting her cardigan in the overhead locker. She rubbed the goose pimples along her arms. With her eyes glued to the flight attendant, she hung on his every word during the safety demonstration, wondering why no one else was paying attention.

They were several rows away from the nearest emergency exit, which did nothing to reassure Laura. By the time the flight attendant got to the words *brace! brace!*, Laura had freaked out. Her mind conjured up images of masked hijackers, crashing aeroplanes, inflatable yellow slides, and black boxes sinking to the bottom of the Irish Sea. As the plane accelerated along the runway, Laura gripped the armrests so tightly her knuckles turned white. Claire placed her hand on Laura's arm.

Once they were airborne, it got worse. The plane turned abruptly, tipping to such an angle that Laura could see the ground out of Ava's window. She closed her eyes, convinced they were going to flip upside down. The plane continued its ascent, but the higher it climbed, the bumpier it got. Laura wanted to ask Claire what was happening, but the words got stuck in her throat.

But Claire seemed to sense her unease. 'It's OK, Laura. It's just a wee bit of turbulence,' she said.

Laura wasn't convinced, but the plane gradually righted itself and once it was cruising horizontally and had stopped bouncing up and down, she began to relax.

Until there was a strange ding. 'What was that?' It came out as a whisper and Laura was surprised she'd been heard over the noise of the plane.

'It's to let you know you can take your seatbelt off,' Ava said, pointing at the sign above their heads.

'Why would I want to do that? I'll never get it back on again.'

Ava laughed. 'You can go for a wander.'

'Wander where?'

'Well, the toilet, for example.' In a more serious tone, Ava added, 'You know what your problem is?'

An unbidden image of her mother's face flashed before Laura's eyes. That was a question Noreen asked Laura often, and there were various possible answers to it. *You've no self-confidence / dress sense / common sense* or *you're always gurning / talking / thinking about yourself.*

Declan had recently asked Laura the same thing. 'Do you know what your problem is?' She'd shaken her head and waited for him to enlighten her. 'Your mother,' he'd said.

'You need to get out more,' Ava finished, folding her cardigan to use as a makeshift pillow.

Laura forced herself to chuckle. 'Yeah, I know. I'm not very good with people, though.'

'What on earth makes you think that?' asked Claire, who had been listening in on the conversation. Laura shrugged. 'That's so not true,' Claire said. 'You're brilliant with those kids when you do Rhythm and Rhyme at the library. You were really patient with that old man the other day, even though he was very rude, and a lot of our regular readers specifically want you to recommend books for them.'

Laura didn't know what to say to that and the three of them were silent for a while. She glanced at Sarah, who was asleep. After a few minutes, Laura could hear Ava snoring. She suddenly felt tired herself. She'd got up early this morning and now her anxiety was dispersing, it was taking her energy with it. As the plane began its descent, Laura nodded off, only to wake up a few minutes later with a jump as it landed.

As soon as the four of them stepped off the plane, the heat hit them. They walked towards the terminal building, wheeling their suitcases. The pilot had told them there was a slight breeze in Lyon, and Laura had assumed this would feel refreshing, but she felt as if she were surrounded by people, all aiming hairdryers on full blast at her.

'Oh my God. My clothes are sticking to me already,' said Sarah, flapping her T-shirt away from her with her free hand.

Once inside, they followed the signs for the *Douanes* – passport control – and soon stepped outside into the intense heat again.

'Shall we get a taxi?' Sarah suggested. They'd been planning to take the tram into Lyon. 'It won't cost much if we split it four ways and there'll be air conditioning in the car.'

'Good idea,' Claire said.

Laura heaved a sigh of relief. The journey had been a total nightmare so far. There had been no end of obstacles along the way – Claire had almost missed the bus; they'd all nearly missed the plane. The bus ride and the flight had both been horribly stressful. But here they were. They'd arrived safely in Lyon, all four of them.

As she got into the cab, she felt anticipation and excitement flow through her body, even though it was sweating profusely. The worst bit was over. Or at least, Laura hoped it was.

Chapter 8

THE DAY BEFORE THEY DIED

Laura

Laura lay wide awake, her earplugs not quite blocking out the snores coming from the other twin bed. She'd always been a light sleeper and she couldn't remember the last time she hadn't spent the night in her own bed. She'd not slept well and she didn't feel particularly energized. She did, however, feel hungry.

A tempting smell of coffee was drifting its way towards her from the kitchen of the aparthotel. Or perhaps it was her imagination. Laura threw off the sheet and tiptoed out of the room so as not to wake Ava.

Claire and Sarah were both up already. Claire was sitting on a bar stool, dressed in denim shorts and a grey tank top. Sarah, who was still in her nightie, was fiddling with a coffee machine.

'Morning. Come and have some brekkie,' Claire said. 'I've been to the bakery and bought some *croissants* and *pains au chocolat*. And some of these bright pink praline *brioches*. Some sort of local speciality, apparently. Hopefully they taste better than they look. The lady in the bakery spoke a bit of English, luckily, although she didn't seem to understand a word I was saying.'

'Oh? Did you try out your GCSE French on her?'

'No.' Claire chuckled. 'I just repeated everything more loudly in English. I think it was the Norn Iron accent that threw her.'

Laura laughed.

'I'm making coffee,' Sarah announced unnecessarily, without turning round. 'Milk's that UHT stuff. Bloody disgusting. So we're having black coffee instead of tea. When in Lyon and all that.'

By the time Ava emerged, Claire and Laura were poring over a map of the city of Lyon and the guidebook, planning their day's sightseeing. Sarah was checking bus, tram and tube routes on the Internet on her phone.

'The basilica of *Notre-Dame de Fourvière* is a must-see,' Claire said.

'We could take the funicular,' Sarah suggested.

'Why don't we walk?' Claire said. 'You can go through the Rosary Gardens, it says here. It would be nice to go for a wee dander after all that travelling yesterday.'

Laura thought if it was going to be as hot as yesterday, they'd be better off taking the funicular, but she kept that to herself.

'Sounds good,' Ava said, her mouth full of *croissant*.

Sarah googled *La Voie Lactée*, the arena in the seventh *arrondissement* where *The Naturals* were performing their gig the following evening. '*La Voie Lactée* means the Milky Way,' she said, reading from her phone. 'It has a capacity of fifteen thousand – that's massive! It opened as a concert hall in 1985, but it was previously used as a hospital during the Second World War and an armoury in the 1920s. The original building opened in 1910 as a cattle and pig market and a slaughter-house.'

'Yuk!' Ava exclaimed.

Laura's imagination created a graphic scene of row upon row of pig carcasses hanging upside down on huge metal hooks and dead cows lying on a bloodstained concrete floor. She shuddered, dispersing the image.

The walk up to the basilica turned out to be less of a "wee dander" and more of an uphill hike. Thankfully, it was in the shade, but it was hot even so, and they were all sweating liberally by the time they were halfway up. Laura's right knee was throbbing, although she put on a brave face and said nothing of her discomfort to her friends.

The panoramic view from the top made the climb well worth it. They could see for miles – as far as Mont Blanc. And inside the basilica, it was cool. Laura was struck by how sumptuous and ornate everything was. The walls with their mosaics and gold leaf, the colourful stained-glass windows. You could probably enter this building every day for the rest of your life and still notice a detail you'd never picked out before.

Ava dipped her fingers in the font and crossed herself with the holy water. No one said anything. Laura had known Ava was Catholic. Her name was Irish for a start and she wore a gold necklace with a crucifix pendant. Sarah was a Protestant. Laura didn't know what Claire was – she didn't know which part of Belfast she lived in or which school she'd gone to. Her surname – Quinn – didn't give anything away. Laura didn't care either way. Here she was, on holiday with her friends, and religion had never been an issue between them. In fact, they'd never discussed it. But it had mattered a lot more when Laura's parents were her age.

When Laura's father had announced to his parents that he was going to marry Noreen, they'd disowned him, and so Laura had never met her paternal grandparents. She wasn't even sure if they knew she existed. They'd never forgiven her father for marrying a "Taig" – a Catholic.

Laura's mummy had taken her to mass when she was younger; her daddy had taken her to Orangemen marches. Northern Ireland was a very different place when Laura was a small child.

The two religions could coexist now, but they'd caused a lot of damage to many Northern Irish families during the Troubles, including Laura's. A lot of damage and a lot of death.

Laura couldn't go there. She dismissed her thoughts before they got too dark, before she upset herself thinking about her father's untimely death. Instead, she forced herself to listen to Sarah who was reading aloud from an online guidebook she'd brought up on her phone as the four of them walked around the basilica.

Afterwards, they visited the Roman amphitheatre, then walked down the hill to *Le Vieux Lyon*, the old quarter, to get a beer before going back to their aparthotel. They'd had a lovely day. The only thing that marred their enjoyment was the heat. They drank litres of water and walked in the shade, but the heat was oppressive. It was like being in a sauna, except you couldn't come out and jump into a cool pool or dive under a cold shower. They didn't walk all that far, but Laura felt drained.

It was as they were sitting at a table in the shade in a charming cobbled square that Laura heard it. A Northern Irish accent. And then another. She turned round and looked behind her. And then she saw them. The four men were sitting at the table behind her. She gestured over her shoulder.

'Oh my God. It's *The Naturals*,' Ava exclaimed, loud enough for the members of the band to hear. Sarah spluttered on her beer.

'I'm Ava,' she said, getting up and reaching across the table to shake their hands.

Claire coughed.

'Oh, and these are my friends Claire, Sarah and Laura.'

'I'm Niall, the lead singer.'

Ava rolled her eyes, which made Laura giggle. It might be obvious to Ava, but Laura didn't know the names of the members of the band. Apart from Connor.

'This is Rich, our guitarist and my backing vocalist,' Niall continued. Laura looked at Rich, who had tight blond curls and tanned arms. 'This is Tom. He's our drummer.' Tom was tall with a receding hairline and a nice smile. 'And last but not least our bass guitarist and my best mate, Connor.'

Having dispensed with the introductions, they pushed their tables together. Laura ended up next to Connor. As he sat down again, she got a whiff of his aftershave – a pleasant citrusy, musky scent. Thinking she was probably giving off a rank smell by now, Laura tried not to sit too close to him.

Niall did most of the talking, and he was the main topic of conversation. Ava acted like an overexcited groupie, taking photos of them with her phone, asking them for their autographs and trying to wangle backstage passes, all of which amused Laura and seemed to please Niall no end.

'So, yous have come all the way over to Lyon to see our gig, then?' Connor asked Laura.

'Yes,' she said. 'We got here yesterday. We're staying for a week. I've seen you play before, actually. A long time ago. In *The Dirty Onion*. I was with my cousin, Declan.'

'Declan. Of course. I remember now. I knew I'd seen you before! I didn't dare say it in case it sounded like a cheesy chat-up line!'

They laughed at that. Connor was easy to talk to and as they chatted together, Laura tuned out the others and almost forgot they were there. She no longer felt the heat, either.

Niall paid for another round of beers.

'So, are you nervous about tomorrow?' Laura asked.

Connor, who had been upbeat until then, didn't answer for a few seconds. A cloud passed over his face. 'I'm terrified,' he said.

'Well, I suppose it's normal to get nervous before you go on stage,' Laura said. 'And it's a big arena.'

'Aye, I do get stage fright – we all do,' he said. 'There's always a lot of adrenaline and it's not such a bad feeling. But this time,

I feel like … I don't know … it's daft … It's more than that this time.'

'How so?'

'Och, it's pathetic. I think I've got myself worked up or perhaps the heat has gone to my head. I just don't feel good about this concert.' He shrugged. 'I can't explain it.'

'I think I know what you mean,' Laura said. 'I felt like that on the plane. It was the first time I'd flown, and I imagined all sorts of things going wrong – the plane crashing, hijackers on board, you name it, it went through my mind. But all my worries turned out to be unfounded. We landed safely. It will be fine, you'll see. I'm sure you'll be grand.'

'Thank you,' Connor said, sounding sincere. 'You're right. I'm panicking over nothing.' He smiled at Laura, but it didn't reach his lovely blue eyes.

Chapter 9

THE NIGHT THEY DIED

Laura

They all agreed that the musicians playing for the opening act were pretty "meh", as Claire put it. Whenever the lead singer of the French band sang into the mic, high-pitched feedback filled the auditorium. To his credit, he carried on regardless.

'I hope they get the sound system sorted out before *The Naturals* come on,' Sarah shouted over the music.

Laura was more concerned about going for a pee before *The Naturals* came on. Sarah had wanted to be as near to the stage as possible and had insisted on them all arriving at the arena an hour and a half before the doors opened. They'd waited at the front of the queue in the still-blazing evening sun, taking it in turns to sit in pairs in the shade of the plane trees along the boulevard. Laura must have drunk nearly a litre of water and they'd bought a plastic beaker of beer each when they'd got in.

'I'll come with you,' Ava said during the interval.

'You'll lose your place,' Sarah warned.

'We can push through the crowd,' Ava replied. Then, turning to Laura, 'How's your leg?'

Laura's knee was sore, and a little swollen, from all the walking they'd done. She hadn't wanted to say anything to her friends because she didn't want to slow them down or complain, but she was hobbling noticeably by the end of their first day here.

'Holding up,' she lied. She was in agony. She'd take a painkiller when they went to the loos.

There were loads of people waiting for the toilet and Laura and Ava were at the back of the queue this time.

'There's no one waiting in line for the men's bogs,' Ava said. 'Let's go in there.'

'*Hé! Qu-est-ce que vous faites?*' a man yelled as they passed the urinals. Ava darted into the only free toilet cubicle and the man continued to shout at Laura.

Laura muttered an apology: '*Je suis désolée.*' Then she ran out of the men's and took her place at the back of the queue for the ladies', which had grown a little longer.

'You head on back,' she said when Ava returned. 'You'll miss the start of the concert.'

'You sure? I'm happy to wait for you.'

'No, you're all right,' Laura said. 'I'll find you no bother.'

'If you're sure,' Ava said.

Laura wasn't, but Ava had already gone.

When Laura eventually came out of her toilet cubicle, she heard squeals of delight and applause. *The Naturals* must have come on stage. She took a packet of paracetamol out of her handbag and stuck her head under the tap so she could swallow down a couple of tablets.

As she was washing her hands, a man entered the toilets. Laura was about to point out that the men's was opposite, but before she could come up with the words in French, she caught his eye in the mirror. There was something about the way he stared at her through his insistent dark eyes, something unsettling, and Laura's half-formed sentence died on her lips.

She felt nervous suddenly. She was on her own now, alone with this stranger. She gave him a taut smile, but his expression didn't change. He wiped his forehead with his bare arm and Laura realized he was sweating profusely. Laura, too, had sweated outside while they'd waited to get in, but in the toilets the air conditioning was on full blast and it was almost too cool.

His gaze did not waver and Laura wanted to run, but she was frozen to the spot for some reason, as this man's reflection held her eyes. She noticed his arms were tanned, but his face was deathly white. He had a short, scraggly beard, but his hair was neat as if he'd recently had it cut. He was younger than her, of average height and build, wearing dark clothes. She watched, trembling now, as he walked purposefully to the cubicle at the end. She saw him struggle with the door, which was apparently locked. But he got it open somehow and entered, banging the door behind him. Laura heard him lock it from the inside.

Stuck to the toilet door with tape was a sign, a piece of white paper. Two words had been written on it by hand with a black marker pen, but in the mirror, the letters were back to front. Laura turned around, taking in the words. *HORS SERVICE*. Out of order. Without drying her hands, she hurried out of the toilets as fast as she could on her dodgy knee.

The band had kicked off with one of their most popular songs, "Always & Anyway", and the audience was jumping up and down. Laura had difficulty weaving her way through the crowd towards the stage. She certainly wouldn't be jumping up and down; her knee was killing her. The closer she got to the stage, the hotter it seemed to get. The lights had dimmed and she couldn't see her friends. Where were they?

The Naturals finished playing "Always & Anyway" and suddenly Laura was swamped by a fog of dry ice. She stood still, waiting for it to disperse, hearing the opening chords strike up to her favourite song, "Don't let this be the end". She sang along and relaxed a little, even though she was still separated from her friends. They couldn't be far away. There were only two or three rows of people between her and the stage now.

Then, as a strobe light flashed, she caught sight of Ava, her head above those around her thanks to her vertiginous heels, and next to her, a good few inches lower, Sarah's blond ponytail swinging from side to side as she swayed in time to the music. She heaved a sigh of relief and trod on some toes as she elbowed her way towards them.

A hand tapped her shoulder. Whirling round, she found herself face to face with Claire.

'I was coming to find you,' Claire shouted in her ear. 'Are you all right?'

'Yes,' Laura said. 'Thank you.'

'I was … worried. I thought maybe … lost or something.' Laura couldn't hear Claire properly over the music.

'What? No. Long queue, that's all.'

Just then there was a loud bang. Laura froze.

'What was that?' she shouted near Claire's ear.

Claire shouted back. Laura caught two words. "Firecracker" and "percussion".

Claire didn't seem worried, so Laura tried not to be. But it had seemed a bit loud to be a firecracker. And it didn't sound like the drums. It had sounded more like a pneumatic drill starting up and stopping abruptly. Or a detonation. But that was ridiculous.

There was another loud bang with a white flash somewhere to their right, followed by a screeching sound through the loudspeakers as Niall fell to the floor of the stage, clutching his mic in his hand. On one of the giant screens, Laura saw him fall. The whole crowd had witnessed it, too. People started running in all directions, pushing and shouting.

Laura wanted to run as well, but she was paralysed by fear, like a deer caught in headlights. She looked at Claire, whose hand was clapped to her mouth, wide eyes glued to the stage. The music had stopped abruptly, replaced by loud dissonant screams from the crowd. Glancing at the big screen again, she saw Connor kneeling beside Niall, his hands on the frontman's chest. The other musicians – Tom and Rich – had fled. Was that blood? Was Niall bleeding?

Another bang – a gunshot. Then a salvo of shots. Four or five people fell to the ground, a few feet away from them.

'Oh God! Oh fuck! Laura! Ava's been hit!'

As hordes of people stampeded away from the danger, Claire pushed her way towards Ava and Sarah. Without thinking, Laura followed, oblivious now to the pain in her knee. Her head was ringing with the sound of gunfire even as the next burst broke out, momentarily drowning out the screams, Laura's among them. Suddenly the lights went out. They came on again a few seconds later, but Laura could no longer see Claire.

But she saw them. Three of them. All wearing dark clothes. All armed. They were making sweeping movements from left to right, then from right to left, with their automatic weapons – Kalashnikovs? – shooting aimlessly. She watched, helplessly, as rows of human dominoes collapsed in front of her.

They want to kill as many people as possible, Laura thought, terror ripping through her like wildfire. She barely registered the deafening volley of bullets flying close to her before she went down. She would never know what made her drop to the ground. Shock? Survival instinct? She did know she wouldn't have made it far if she'd tried to run. She wasn't much of a runner, even without her bad knee.

Where was Claire? Where were Ava and Sarah? Claire's voice came back to her: *Ava's been hit!* Was she injured or dead?

Making herself as small as possible on the floor, Laura tried desperately to think of something nice. It could be her last thought. But her mind was blank with terror.

This time the firing was relentless. She had no idea how long it lasted, but it seemed interminable. Fifteen seconds? Twenty seconds? Bullets raining, hailing, all around.

Laura couldn't be sure because she could still hear the shots resounding in her head, but she thought it had stopped. There were far fewer people now. Had some of them escaped? Had they all been shot?

'*Maintenant! Cours!*' She heard shouts and was conscious of people in the pit getting to their feet and running. She didn't dare to move. Was it over?

No sooner had that thought entered her head than it started up again. They must have been reloading. That's why it had stopped. Suddenly someone fell on top of her, someone who had been gunned down while trying to escape. She half-pushed, half-kicked the deadweight off her, her screams blotted out by the noise of the automatic weapons. But she'd reacted without thinking and she instantly regretted it. The dead body would have shielded her, acted as a camouflage as she herself played dead underneath it, and now she was exposed. She didn't even know if the victim was a man or a woman.

When they finally stopped firing again, there was an eerie silence. No screaming, no crying. Or maybe Laura's ears were no longer working. She was overwhelmed by a strong stench – sweat mixed with a pungent odour of powder from the weapons and something metallic, which Laura recognized as blood. The smell of fear; the smell of death.

Opening her eyes, through streaming tears she saw one of the armed men kick a body lying in a pool of blood on the floor near her. There was no movement, no sound. He moved on to the next person. Another kick with his black boot. This time a groan. More shots rang out and the body jerked suddenly. The man had shot him dead.

Oh God. He's killing the ones who aren't dead. He's finishing them off, she thought. A whimper escaped as she willed herself not to scream. The shots continued to echo in her ears.

'*Bien joué, Zak,*' one of the other two called out, laughing.

These men – these *gun*men – were having fun. Laura felt bile rise into her throat and it was all she could do not to retch.

Pretend to be dead. Don't move if he kicks you. The thoughts in Laura's head were loud and frantic. Even as she willed herself to stay still, she could feel herself shaking uncontrollably, as if she were cold in this stuffy place. She was sure her body trembling would give her away. She closed her mouth to stop her teeth chattering, but she kept her eyes open. One of the gunmen was pointing his weapon at a man and a woman. He shouted something Laura didn't catch and the couple dropped to their knees. The man was pleading; the woman was crying hysterically.

'*Am. Stram. Gram* …' With each word, he moved the weapon, aiming it first at one, then at the other. He was playing Eeny Meeny Miny Moe! He would shoot one of them! Laura was horrified.

'*… Ce sera toi!*' And with that, he took aim at the woman and shot her. She fell with a thud, face down onto the ground. The man threw himself on top of her, crying as hysterically as the woman had just seconds earlier. The gunman shot him, too, in the back.

A sharp kick to her side. Laura was unprepared for it and cried out. The game was up. She curled into a tight ball, her arms over her head in a futile attempt to protect herself. But instead of shooting her, the gunman hauled her to her feet. Her legs were too weak to hold her up and she fell back to the floor, but he picked her up again.

That's when she recognized him. The one they'd called Zak. It was the man who had gone into the ladies' toilets as she was coming out. He had an amused expression on his face. He recognized her, too. A thought dawned on her then. Had he hidden his weapon in the ladies' loos? Is that what he was doing? Getting his gun?

64

'Laura!' It was Claire's voice. Laura turned her head to the left, then to the right, but she couldn't see her friend.

'*Ah! Vous vous connaissez.*'

Now she saw her. She was walking towards them, followed by one of the gunmen, who was pressing his weapon into the middle of her back.

'*Tu choisis,*' Zak said into her ear.

Laura sobbed. No translation came to her. The sentence was easy, but its meaning was way too difficult to grasp. She couldn't even find the words in French to say she didn't understand. What did he want her to do? 'Oi ... Irish,' she stammered. 'English.'

'*A toi de choisir,*' Zak said, loud enough for only Laura to hear. 'You choose.'

Laura's heart stopped as she grasped his meaning now.

'Who should live? Who must die? You or your friend?' Zak said. He pointed his gun at her, then at Claire, who was whimpering. '*Toi ou elle, bordel! Choisis!*'

Chapter 10

THE NIGHT THEY DIED

Laura

Laura shook her head frantically then covered her face with her hands.

It happened so fast. Zak swung the Kalashnikov to his right and fired two rounds. Peeping through her fingers, Laura saw Claire fall to the ground and lie, crumpled in a heap. Laura sank to her knees. The only noise now was her wailing.

Claire, oh God. He's shot Claire. Claire's dead. What has he done? What have I done?

Zak jerked his weapon upwards to indicate Laura should get to her feet. Laura noticed the two other gunmen had rounded up six or seven other people and were making them walk towards the stage. Zak pushed his machine gun into Laura's shoulder, forcing her to turn round, away from him.

'Move!' he growled, pushing his weapon into her back now. 'Walk!'

She had to step over – even step *on* – dead bodies as she did what Zak ordered. She told herself not to look around her, but she couldn't help it. Death was everywhere. This was a massacre. Carnage. Mounds of dead bodies. She could only have looked for a second or two, but she knew these images would be etched on her brain for the rest of her life.

If she could get out of here alive.

She allowed herself a faint glimmer of hope when, backstage, she spotted an illuminated sign for an emergency exit. But the gunmen – the terrorists – made them go up a winding staircase, then through a door that led to the balconies.

They heard subdued crying as they came through the door. There were more spectators – more *survivors* here. Three of them. They'd been hiding behind the chairs, probably too terrified to take the stairs to the ground floor in case they found themselves face to face with one of the assailants. They, too, were forced to join the group.

Hostages. That's what they were. They were hostages being held by terrorists.

'*Tu as le sac?*' Zak asked one of the other gunmen.

'*Quel sac?*'

'*Le sac avec la munition, idiot!*'

'*Ah, non. Merde! Je l'ai oublié en bas.*'

'*Vas-le chercher, tête de con!*'

Another tiny flicker of optimism as Laura understood they'd left the ammunition in a bag on the lower level.

They all waited while one of the gunmen went back down. They saw him, from the balcony, as he emerged onto the stage, then leapt off it into the pit where he jumped over bodies like he was playing hopscotch in a playground. He looked up at them all and laughed. Laura felt sick and looked away.

Suddenly more shots rang out and then a bigger bang. The commotion had come from below. Laura hadn't seen what happened, but she did see the look of shock on Zak's face. He recovered quickly.

'*Avancez! Pas un bruit!*' he hissed, and to Laura, 'Move! Keep quiet!'

'*Putain! Ils l'ont eu!*' This from the other terrorist.

'Oh, God. What's going on?'

Laura didn't realize she had spoken her thoughts aloud until the hostage standing next to her, a woman about her age, whispered to her in English, 'It's the police. They've killed the other one. The one who went to fetch the ammunition.'

They went through a door behind the balcony area and found themselves in a corridor, dimly lit by emergency lighting and the faint glimmer of a streetlamp through a small, dirty window. There was a staircase to the end of the corridor. Laura supposed it led to the wings. She was in shock, but her mind was surprisingly lucid. She was desperately trying to come up with a plan to escape. Could they make a run for it? If all of them ran, would some of them make it? The terrorists had no more ammunition. Except what was already in the magazines of their rifles. What could that be? Thirty bullets each, maybe? Two terrorists. About ten hostages. Laura's chances were slim to non-existent.

'*Assis! Dos contre la porte!*' Zak shouted, indicating with his rifle that he was giving this order to Laura, the woman who had whispered to her and an older man. Laura didn't move. She'd understood perfectly, but her body refused to obey. 'Sit down, your back against the door,' Zak translated when Laura didn't move. 'Do what I tell you,' Zak said, locking his eyes onto hers, as he'd done in the toilets earlier that evening. He had a dangerous gleam in his dark gaze. 'Do what I say and I won't kill you.'

Laura grabbed on to that promise as if she was drowning and he was throwing her a lifeline. He had just slaughtered dozens of people, including Claire, but she had no choice but to trust that he would let her live. She sat down, her back against the door, as Zak had instructed.

But then the hostage next to her shattered any brief illusion she'd created in her head. 'When the police begin their assault, they will come through this door.' She had whispered, but Laura could still make out the panic in her voice. She took the woman's hand and squeezed it.

One of the men issued another order. She didn't understand, but the other hostages, who were sitting against the walls of the corridor were taking out their mobiles and sliding them across the floor towards the gunman. The women were handing over their handbags, too. Laura followed suit.

She tried hard despite her alarm to concentrate on what they were saying. Her life might depend on it. She understood they were looking among the hostages for a married couple. Two hands went up. They made the man stand up, asked him his name.

'Henri,' he said, his voice quavering.

Then he had to retrieve his phone from the pile. Zak asked Henri's wife her name. The first time it came out as a sob and she had to repeat it.

'Elodie,' she said. '*Je m'appelle Elodie.*'

Laura listened as Zak told Henri what to do. She got the gist of what he was saying. She looked at Elodie, whose tear-streaked face was ashen. Laura knew her own face must look like that, too.

Unless Laura was mistaken, Zak had told Henri to take his mobile phone to the police inside the building. It occurred to Laura that the police probably didn't know exactly where they were for the moment, and that their hiding place in the corridor would no longer be a secret. But that didn't concern the terrorists. They wanted to negotiate. They told Henri if he didn't come back, they would kill Elodie and throw her body out of the window.

'*Et Henri,*' the other terrorist added, '*N'oublie pas de leur dire que nous avons onze otages ici!*'

So there were eleven of them. Eleven hostages at the mercy

of two terrorists. The terrorists were using them as a human shield.

Laura, the man sitting next to her and the woman whose hand Laura was still holding had to move away from the door to let Henri out. Elodie didn't make a sound, but her wide eyes and open mouth reflected sheer terror.

While Henri was gone, two or three of the mobile phones on the heap in the middle of the floor started ringing at more or less the same time. The two terrorists looked at each other, then at each of the hostages in turn.

'*Ça y est! On doit passer aux infos!*'

'He thinks they must be on the news,' her neighbour whispered, confirming what Laura had understood.

There were relatives and friends at home who must have seen or heard the news about the terrorist attack and now they wanted news of their loved ones. Tears sprang to Laura's eyes. Another mobile began to ring as Henri knocked on the door and gave the terrorists some kind of prearranged password.

Laura looked at Henri's wife as he came back into the corridor. Her face showed no relief. Did she and Henri have children? Maybe Elodie had thought if one of them could get away, that would be better than neither of them.

Zak ordered Elodie to find her mobile. She crawled over to her handbag, unzipped her bag and pulled out her mobile. She handed it to Zak and returned to her place, sitting against the wall. Henri wrapped his arms around her. Then Zak told the other gunman – Laura caught his name: Ali – to turn off the other phones. At least four were still ringing. One of the ringtones was the same as Declan's. The tears spilled down Laura's cheeks.

Ali stomped over the bags and mobiles and then bounced up and down on them like he was on a trampoline. He continued to jump, giggling all the while, even after the phones were all silent.

'*Arrête, Ali!*'

Ali did what he was told and stopped jumping. He unzipped his cardigan, clearly hot after exerting himself. Underneath he was wearing a black T-shirt and, to Laura's horror, a suicide vest.

Oh God. No one is going to get out of here alive, Laura thought. *We're all going to die. Them. Us. Everyone.*

Chapter 11

THE NIGHT THEY DIED

Laura

It became obvious to Laura that neither of the terrorists had a clear plan of action. They appeared to be making up a game plan as they went along. If Ali was wearing a suicide vest, the chances were Zak had one as well. Why had they taken hostages if they were going to kill themselves? Or would detonating the explosives be a last resort? Laura thought their main aims had been to sow terror and attract publicity. She suspected they'd already achieved that. The rest hadn't been mapped out in detail. Perhaps the part after their killing spree didn't feature in the original plot at all.

Even more disturbing to Laura than their apparent lack of strategy was their unpredictability. They oscillated from acting defeated to having fun. Ali had been sitting, slumped against the wall, staring vacantly at the ceiling. Laura got the impression he was waiting for the end, waiting for the police to make their assault, but perhaps he was psyching himself up, deciding when he would blow himself up – and everyone else with him.

But then he sprang to his feet. He aimed his weapon at a large man, ordering him to take off his trousers while he mocked him for his chubbiness. He made another man bark on all fours and Henri's wife, Elodie, had to stand up and sing what sounded to Laura like a nursery rhyme.

Zak waved the woman's phone around, as he asked his colleague what they should demand from the police.

'*Un hélico?*' Ali suggested, shrugging.

'*Ouais. Bonne idée. Un hélicoptère.*'

Laura started to shake as it dawned on her that she and the other hostages were only useful as bargaining tools. And the terrorists had no idea what to use them to bargain for.

Ali opened the tiny window and peered out, half of his face glowing in the light from the streetlamp outside. It made Laura think of the character of Dr Jekyll and Mr Hyde. Except that Ali was pure evil. Laura was convinced he had no good side to him. As if to confirm this, he turned and fired a few shots randomly out of the window into the boulevard below and then squealed in joy. '*Je l'ai eu! Je l'ai tué!*'

A chill lined her stomach despite the heat. He'd just killed someone. A passer-by, perhaps, who happened to be in the wrong place at the wrong time, or a police officer who had been doing his job. And he'd enjoyed it. He'd have no scruples about shooting all eleven hostages dead before he blew himself up.

They must know they'll die one way or the other, she thought. *That's the only possible ending for them. And they want to take out as many people as they can before they go. Isn't that the general idea of a terrorist attack? As much destruction and death as possible.* She tightened her grip on her neighbour's hand.

Zak shouted at Ali to get away from the window and instructed a hostage to stand there instead. He was told to report on any movement he saw outside and let them know if the police approached or if he spotted snipers taking up their positions.

The phone in Zak's hand rang. He showed it to Henri and asked him something Laura didn't catch. Henri nodded and Zak took the call. After a while, he said into the mobile in French, 'I'll think about it and call you back.'

Laura listened as Zak explained the situation to Ali. The Brigade of Research and Intervention wanted to swap a member of their team with one of the hostages. Laura assumed they were dealing with a special unit, perhaps police who were specialized in terrorism or negotiation.

'*Il veut qu'on libère une femme,*' Zak added.

A woman. The police wanted them to free one of the *female* hostages.

Laura looked round, her heart pounding so hard it hurt her chest. The other female hostages were studying each other, too. The woman sitting next to Laura pulled her hand away. Besides Laura and her neighbour, there was Henri's wife and two women who were obviously related – mother and daughter, Laura guessed.

Five female hostages. Laura had a one in five chance of getting out of here alive. Her survival instinct kicked in and she tried to catch Zak's eye as he rang the policeman back. She shut out everything except the sound of his voice as she focused on what he was saying.

Laura understood the gist of the conversation from listening to Zak's side. Zak had agreed to allow a female hostage to leave in exchange for a female member of the task force – the BRI, as he called it. 'Tit for tat,' he said.

Laura didn't think Zak could care less if the police officer was male or female. He was playing. But apparently there were no women on the team. Laura's heart sank. In the end, Zak agreed to let go a female hostage in exchange for a male member of the police unit.

She tried again to catch Zak's eye, and when he looked at her, her heart clenched painfully. Her life was in this man's hands. And his hands had blood on them. She didn't consider herself to be superstitious, but she crossed her fingers behind her back.

But her hope was short-lived as Zak ordered Henri's wife to

stand up again. After peeling off his T-shirt, revealing that he, too, was indeed wearing a vest packed with explosives, Zak held Elodie to him with one arm, his free hand on the detonator of his suicide vest. His Kalashnikov was slung over his shoulder.

Laura and the two other hostages sitting against the door were ordered to stay sitting but move away from the door. Laura shuffled forward on her bottom.

There was shouting through the door – the police officer who was to swap places with Elodie was there.

Zak shouted instructions back at him. Laura didn't understand, and felt even more terrified than she was already, if that was possible. Did the policeman know there were hostages behind the door? Did they know not to shoot?

Then the man next to Laura was ordered to open the door – just a crack – and the police officer squeezed his way into the corridor. Laura was struck by how young he was. He looked younger than she was. And yet, he appeared confident. If he was scared, and he must have been, he was hiding it well. He was dressed all in black, like the terrorists, except for the white lettering across his back: BRI.

Ali checked him for weapons and then told him to sit next to Laura. He did so, and out of the corner of her eye, she noticed him slip a mobile phone behind his back. She almost turned her head to look, but she stopped herself before she gave the game away, realizing just in time that this was the reason the police officer had wanted to come in. Everything that was said from now on in this corridor – every order the terrorists gave and every discussion the pair of them had – would be transmitted to the police task force outside.

She looked into Zak's eyes again. They were flashing wildly. He was still holding Elodie against him, holding her up.

'Get up!' he said to Laura in English. He spoke so quietly she thought she'd misheard. '*Debout!* Get up,' he repeated, more loudly this time. 'Stand up!'

Laura got to her feet. Her legs were so weak she wasn't sure she could stay standing for long, but she held her head up high and looked Zak in the eye. She was sure he could see how frightened she was even though she was trying to appear defiant.

'You can go,' he said, speaking softly again.

Her first thought was that it was some kind of trick. Would he shoot her in the back as she turned away?

'What are you waiting for?' he suddenly shouted, making her jump and galvanizing her into action.

She turned and pulled at the door. It wouldn't open. She pulled the handle down harder and then she was out. The heavy door to the corridor slammed shut behind her.

Several pairs of gloved hands seized her, mauled her, rubbed her roughly the length of her body. She was being searched. The police were checking she was unarmed, as if she were one of the terrorists. Or perhaps they were checking that the terrorists hadn't planted explosives on her, making her into a human booby trap.

Four or five people, dressed in black and wearing helmets, bombarded her with questions as they propelled her towards a fire exit. She managed to give her name, her age and her nationality and tell them where she was staying. They asked her to describe the terrorists.

'There are two of them. There were three. I think one was shot dead. In their twenties. Beards.' She gave their names. Zak and Ali. She could barely get the words out and it was an incoherent jumble of French and English. 'Eleven hostages. Ten now. Plus the police officer who took my place.'

'*C'est bien, Laura.* That's very good.'

She understood someone warning her in French not to look below, trying to shield her from the sight of the carnage. Claire's dead body was lying down there. Were Ava and Sarah there, too? Ava had been shot, but she might be alive. She might be among the dead bodies, waiting for help. She hoped Sarah had somehow got out of the building unscathed.

'*Ne regardez pas.* Don't look,' one of the police officers repeated from behind his helmet. She had no intention of looking, not even to try and spot her friends. But she could clearly see the images of the bloodbath every time she closed her eyes.

As the double doors at the far end of the balcony were held open for her, the sounds she heard were somehow even worse than the sights she'd seen. A cacophony of different ringtones coming mainly from the pit and lower level. It transported her for a split second back to the corridor, to the moment when some of the hostages' phones had started to ring at the same time.

As she stumbled down the steps, the noise in her head was so loud it threw her off balance – the ringing of the mobile phones competing with the ringing in her ears from the shooting. Then she was outside. Someone wrapped an emergency blanket around her. Suddenly it all became too much. The colours, the sounds, the faces, the urban smell of the street, everything became distorted and rushed at her at once, and her legs gave way beneath her.

She was lifted onto a stretcher. Lying on her back, she felt as if there were a weight on her chest, pinning her down. At the same time, she felt a strange lightness, as if she were floating above herself. She gulped the fresh air, but it winded her. She lifted her arms to protect her eyes from the yellow onslaught of the streetlamps. Faceless firefighters stared down at her, and spoke to her in reassuring tones, but it looked and sounded like they were underwater.

She closed her eyes, even as she dreaded the brutal picture that would come to her. But this time, a different image swam into focus and instead of the carnage, she saw the face of the young policeman who had taken her place as a hostage. His features were so sharply defined it was as if she were staring at his photo. But in her mind, he no longer appeared confident and brave, as he had when he'd come through the door into the corridor. He looked terrified.

Chapter 12

THE NIGHT THEY DIED

Sandrine

The end credits for the film Sam had been watching began to roll. He flicked over to the 24-hour news channel, as he always did last thing in the evening, to catch up on current events.

'Sandrine, look,' he said, waving the remote control in the direction of the television.

She'd been lying on the sofa reading, her legs across Sam's lap. She turned her head to see the breaking news banner with the words "*LYON: ATTENTAT TERRORISTE*" – terrorist attack – and sat bolt upright. She snatched the remote control from Sam's hand and turned up the volume.

'Isn't that—?'

'That's *La Voie Lactée*.'

'Sam, was—?'

'Shh. Listen.'

Sam took Sandrine's hand. She knew what he was thinking, but it seemed that he couldn't find the words to say it and didn't want her to.

The journalist reporting live from the location of the event was several metres away from the concert hall, talking animatedly at the camera from his position in front of a red and white cordoned-off area. But in the background, behind the fire engines with their flashing blue lights, they could make out the building.

'Here's a reminder of what we know so far,' the reporter was saying in an appropriately serious tone. 'About an hour ago, a few minutes into a rock concert by Irish band *The Naturals*, three gunmen entered the concert hall *La Voie Lactée* here in the centre of Lyon, and opened fire on the crowd.'

'Sam, was Antoine due to work tonight?' Sandrine breathed.

'I don't know. I think so. I'm not sure. Oh fuck.'

Sandrine couldn't remember the last time she'd heard Sam swear. Her heart raced.

The reporter went on to say that several concertgoers had managed to escape through fire exits and windows, but many more people were still inside the arena. That night's concert, he added, had been a sell-out event and the venue had a capacity of up to fifteen thousand spectators. The implication was obvious: the death toll would be high.

'A hostage situation is ongoing inside the arena,' the journalist said, pointing behind him. 'The number of hostages has not yet been confirmed, nor do we know the number of gunmen or their motives. We don't have any information yet on the band members themselves.

'Police officers from the Brigade of Research and Intervention are on site. It is not clear if they are planning an imminent assault or if they have made contact with the terrorists.'

For a minute or so, they sat in silence, glued to the news report.

Then Sam snapped into action. 'You call Antoine on his mobile and I'll get my laptop,' he said, springing to his feet. 'There's usually a Facebook group or something in situations like this.'

'What do mean?' she called after him.

'You know, so you can mark yourself as safe, so your loved

ones don't worry. It'll be easier to look it up on a computer screen than on a smartphone.'

Sandrine grabbed her mobile from the coffee table. She noticed she had a missed call and realized her phone was switched to silent mode. She didn't recognize the caller's number and they didn't appear to have left a message. A wrong number, probably. She flicked the sound button on and turned the volume up as high as it would go. Her hands were shaking so much she almost dropped the phone.

When she called Antoine, his phone went straight to voicemail. She left him a message, asking him to call her urgently, then sent him a text saying the same thing.

Sam came back, his laptop under his arm. Sandrine was struck by the deathlike pallor of his face. She felt the blood drain from her own face.

'Where's Maxime tonight?' she asked, her voice at least an octave too high. 'Is he coming home?'

'No idea,' Sam said.

So she tried calling Maxime. This time there were several rings before she got voicemail. She left him a message. She tried to speak clearly and calmly, but the words sounded jumbled, even to her.

She remembered the missed call. Could it have been Antoine ringing from a friend's phone to say he was all right? Another thought pushed that one aside. Perhaps it was a friend of Antoine's, calling to say he'd been injured. Or worse.

She brought up the recent calls on her mobile and rang back the caller. It, too, went to voicemail. It was a female voice. A name Sandrine didn't recognize. Sandrine didn't leave a message. She should have done. The caller could have been one of Antoine's friends.

'Do you know the names of Antoine's friends?' she asked. What sort of a mother was she to be asking her husband that? But Antoine no longer saw his schoolmates – Matthieu and Gabriel.

80

Although they'd grown up together, they had drifted apart after they'd left school. Sandrine had no idea who he hung out with now. Guys from his course, he'd said when she'd asked.

'No,' Sam replied. He sounded sheepish, and she realized he was thinking along the same lines.

Sandrine had met one of his friends recently. Antoine had shepherded him out of the house as soon as she'd arrived home, but he'd seemed nice enough. He'd introduced himself or Antoine had introduced him, but she couldn't remember his name and wouldn't know how to contact him even if it did come back to her.

She'd lost her train of thought. She was struggling to focus. She looked down and saw the mobile in her hand. She needed to do something, ring someone.

'I got a call from a number I don't recognize,' she told Sam. 'Should I ring back?'

'One of Antoine's friends?'

'I don't know. She didn't leave a message.'

'She?'

'I called back and got her voicemail greeting. I didn't leave a message, either.'

'Then, no. Don't bother her again. It's late. If it was urgent, she'd have left a message. It's probably a wrong number.'

Sandrine nodded. She thought about calling Océane, but Antoine hadn't spoken about his ex-girlfriend for months, so the chances he ever spoke *to* her were remote. It hadn't ended well. They'd had mutual friends, but as far as she knew, Antoine didn't see them anymore.

'Should we ring the hospitals?'

'No,' Sam said firmly. 'They'll be rushed off their feet if people have been injured. Stay off the phone altogether,' Sam said. 'That way, when Antoine calls, he can get through.' He seemed more lucid than she was. He brought up the Facebook crisis page on his laptop. Sandrine watched over his shoulder. None of Sam's

Facebook friends were marked safe. 'It's early days,' Sam said. 'I don't think he uses Facebook much nowadays. He probably didn't think to mark himself as safe.'

Sandrine's mobile rang in her hand, making them both jump. 'It's Maxime,' she said to Sam, then into the phone, 'Max, are you OK? Have you heard from your brother?'

Maxime hadn't even heard the news, so Sandrine filled him in with garbled explanations. Maxime promised to come home immediately.

Sam got up and paced the living area. Sandrine stared at her phone, willing it to ring with an incoming call from Antoine. Then she watched the news again for a few minutes, but the journalist had nothing new to report. It occurred to Sandrine that she might see Antoine on the television – she could see some survivors in the background wrapped in shiny space blankets that looked like tinfoil. From time to time the camera zoomed in on them and although none of the faces were clear, she desperately scanned the screen for her son.

The next half an hour seemed to last a lifetime. Sandrine could feel the fear weighing her down, pushing her into the sofa. Her mouth was dry and her stomach was coiled in a painful knot.

When Sandrine could no longer hold in her tears, Sam stopped pacing the room and sat down, taking her into his arms.

Just then Sandrine heard the front door and leapt to her feet. Sam followed her as she rushed into the hall. A surge of disappointment rose inside her when Max came in and was instantly knocked back down by a feeling of guilt. She'd been expecting Max, but she had hoped Antoine might saunter in, unharmed and unaware of what had been going on in Lyon this evening.

Maxime walked Sandrine back to the sofa with his arm around her shoulders. The gesture made her cry, but he didn't pull away.

'I'm going to drive there, see what I can find out,' Sam announced.

'Drive where?' Sandrine asked.

'To *La Voie Lactée*.'

'You won't get anywhere near it,' Max said.

'It doesn't matter. There are journalists around. They may know something.'

'They won't know any more than what they're already reporting,' Sandrine said.

'I'll come with you, Dad.'

'No!' Sandrine and Sam exclaimed together.

'Stay here and look after your mum,' Sam added.

Max stayed up with Sandrine for another hour or so, his physical presence giving her a little strength, if not comfort. Max fidgeted while Sandrine stared blankly at the television. For a while the report played on a loop, punctuated by an interview here and there with an expert on hostage negotiation or counter-terrorism, but then news broke that the terrorist attack was over.

Sandrine sat forwards on the sofa, her body tense. But the journalist's report was vague. He was unable to state how many of the hostages – if any – were alive. Nor could he say how many terrorists there were or whether they'd been apprehended or killed.

'It's late,' Max said. 'There's nothing more we can do for tonight. Chances are, we're worrying about nothing and Antoine's fast asleep on someone's couch.'

Sandrine forced a weak smile and nodded, although something in her gut told her this wasn't how it would pan out. Once Maxime had left the room, the panic she'd been trying to contain swirled through her entire body. She was now convinced Antoine had been working tonight. He was dead; she knew it. She tried to block out the thought that he'd died because he was doing his job. She felt sick to her stomach, knowing she'd encouraged him to work – forced him to – by stopping his allowance after he'd turned eighteen.

'You're old enough to stand on your own two feet now,' she'd argued.

The slamming of a car door intruded on her thoughts. She remained sitting on the sofa with bated breath, hoping that Sam would come in and dreading that the police would knock on the door. But when she heard nothing further, she figured it must have been the neighbours. They tended to party late at weekends.

In the end, the police did come, but they didn't knock on the door, they burst through it. Sandrine had been dozing on the sofa, her thoughts incoherent with the onset of sleep. It took her a moment to realize she wasn't dreaming.

There were officers everywhere. All wearing black clothes and bulky bulletproof vests with the word POLICE written on them in white. Some were wearing black balaclavas; others helmets. Sandrine didn't think she'd ever seen so many people in her house, not even all those years ago when they'd first moved in and invited all their friends to a house-warming party.

She was dragged from the sofa, her heart pummelling in her chest, and pushed against a wall while an armed police officer patted her down and secured handcuffs to her wrists.

Seconds later, Maxime, also handcuffed, was half-pushed, half-dragged into the room. Sandrine noticed that his eyes were darting all over the place. His hair, which was standing on end, served to heighten the terror and bewilderment painted on his face. Behind him, more black-clothed police officers emerged, carrying things she recognized as Antoine's. One of them was carrying his laptop inside a transparent case. They marched towards the front door and out into the night.

There was an urgent discussion among the police officers in the living room. She caught a name. One she knew well. *Samir Hamadi*. More people, rushing in and out of the room, their boots thundering along the tiles and wooden floorboards elsewhere in their one-storey house.

Then one of them shouted at her, 'Where is he? Where's your husband?'

'At *La Voie Lactée*,' she managed. She caught the look he threw one of his colleagues, even though she could only see his eyes through his balaclava. 'He went there when he saw the news,' she added.

'Does anyone else live here? Is anyone else staying here?' another officer asked her.

'Yes. My elder son lives here.'

'Not anymore,' the officer commented wryly. Before Sandrine could process his words, he jerked his masked head in the direction of the television and added, 'How ironic. You were watching TV, were you? At this hour?'

'I was worried.'

'I'll bet you were.' He gave the order for Sandrine and Maxime to be led outside and then addressed Sandrine again. 'So, your husband has gone to the concert hall. Clearly, you both knew your son was involved.' His disdain was palpable.

'He works there. My son. He's a barman,' Sandrine protested. 'He serves beer,' she added unnecessarily. Then his words sunk in. 'What do you mean … involved? You're not saying … surely you don't mean …? Antoine can't be involved in this. There has been a misunderstanding.' She turned her head to look at the TV screen. There was no way the massacre and destruction being described on the news had Antoine's name stamped on it.

'Antoine?' the officer barked. He sounded confused, and she pinned every last hope she had for Antoine's safety to this. Could there be a mistake?

Everyone stopped walking and looked from him to Sandrine.

'Madame Hamadi.'

It didn't sound like a question, but Sandrine breathed a reply. 'Yes.'

'How many sons did you have?'

The question troubled Sandrine. She picked up the past tense. She bent over as the realization hit her like a blow to the stomach. She was almost certain she only had one son now. It was every mother's worst nightmare to lose a child and up until this moment, Sandrine had believed that losing one of her boys was the worst possible thing that could happen to her. Now she realized she'd been wrong. She was hauled upright again.

'Two,' she said. 'Antoine … and …' Unable to point with her hands cuffed behind her back, she nodded in front of her at Max, who was also flanked by police officers. 'And Maxime.'

'Are those their real names, Madame Hamadi? Is Antoine your older son's real name?'

Sandrine was surprised at her lucidity. She knew what was coming next. She knew even before she answered that her life had already changed forever. 'Yes,' she said defiantly. It was as if by affirming his identity – or denying part of it – she could erase what he had done. She paused. 'Their middle names,' she relented in a whisper, lowering her head. 'We call them by their middle names. No one uses their first names. We gave them Arabic first names. Zakaria and Hamza. My husband is of Algerian descent.'

'No shit,' she heard someone comment behind her.

'Is your husband, Samir Hamadi, involved in this, too?' someone else asked. 'Is that why he's at the arena?'

'No! No!' Sandrine cried.

The officer again gave the order for Max and Sandrine to be taken away. Then, he leaned towards Sandrine and said, 'Your older son, Madame Hamadi, you called him *Antoine* …' he spat the name out '… but he called himself Zak.'

Chapter 13

THE NIGHT THEY DIED

Sandrine

Sandrine and Maxime were taken in separate police vehicles to the *Hôtel de Police* in the eighth *arrondissement*. Sandrine was led into a small room where she was told to sit down on a plastic chair. The windows in the room were so high up she couldn't see out of them. She could only make out from the black panes that it was still dark outside. It resembled the sort of interrogation room she saw in all the crime series she liked to watch on television. For a few seconds, it seemed as if she'd walked onto a film set instead of into her worst nightmare.

Sitting next to her was a lawyer who had been appointed when she said she didn't have one. He'd introduced himself as Maître Guillet. He was around Sandrine's age and height, and he had a firm handshake.

Two men and a woman were sitting opposite her, also on plastic chairs, a wide table stretching like an abyss between her and them. They hadn't introduced themselves. They'd merely said they were members of the SDAT – and explained that this was an anti-terrorist unit of the judicial police.

Anti-terrorist. Terrorist. Sandrine couldn't get her head round that word. She looked down, overcome with a feeling of intense shame, and noticed her knuckles were white from gripping the sides of the chair.

The questions began. They were easy at first. She was asked to confirm her full name, those of her children and her husband, where they lived and worked. One of the men was quite brusque, not rude, but not friendly. The other man said relatively little. The woman spoke softly and sympathetically. Sandrine focused on her. All in all, their treatment of Sandrine was more civil and cordial than she'd expected, but that did little to allay her fears.

Then the questions came like punches, one after the other, in quick succession. She found she couldn't recover from one blow before she was dealt the next. They kept asking her the same things. Had she known about this attack? Had she even suspected her son was implicated in terrorist activities? Was he brought up as a Muslim? Was she aware that Antoine – or Zakaria, as they called him – regularly attended a mosque? Did she know how he'd been radicalized? Was there anyone in his circle of friends who might have influenced him? What about a member of the family? Could she describe his friends? Had anything happened to him that might have made him vulnerable? Did he have any activities or interests? What did he do in his free time?

Following the solicitor's advice, Sandrine didn't give any overly detailed responses. On the contrary, she kept her replies as succinct as possible – answering 'no' or 'I don't know' to everything, muted by an overwhelming desire to protect her dead son. She didn't know the person who was forming in her mind with each new question. It was as though they weren't talking about the son she knew – Antoine – and as if the man they were describing – Zakaria – was a complete stranger to her.

It dawned on her that Antoine had had another side to him,

a side he'd kept hidden or that she'd refused to recognize. She'd only seen his good side, blinded by unconditional love. She hadn't known the person Antoine had become at all.

They took a break after a while – Sandrine had no idea how long, but they had been interviewing her for hours. She was led to a cell and allowed to rest, but she didn't sleep. The bed was as hard as the floor, with no sheets or pillow. It wasn't designed to encourage sleep. She lay down and thought long and hard about what they were asking.

With hindsight, bright red flags were flying high. She should have known. She'd known her son. She'd brought him up. How could she not have realized?

But on some level, she understood she was still not being entirely truthful with herself. She'd suspected something was wrong for a while. On numerous occasions she and Sam had discussed things that Antoine had said or done that they'd found strange, but they'd always come up with rational explanations.

There was the fact he no longer saw his friends from school, for a start. They'd put that down to them going their separate ways after school, but Gabriel and Matthieu still hung out together. She'd seen them. Then there was the company he'd been keeping instead, his new friends. They hadn't met any of them except for the one she'd encountered briefly that day when she'd come home before Antoine and his mate had left.

But something struck her now. Like Antoine, his friend had been growing a beard. At the time, Sandrine had thought nothing of it. Lots of young men had beards and goatees. It seemed to be fashionable, although Sandrine had hoped it was a phase. She thought her son looked far more handsome without the facial hair. Sam had been on at Antoine for weeks to shave off his beard. Looking back on it now, she wondered if it was one of many signs she'd overlooked. She got the feeling that all along she'd failed to see what was hidden in plain sight.

Another recent memory wormed its way into Sandrine's mind.

She'd seen Béatrice, Antoine's former boss at the supermarket, a few days ago when she'd gone for some groceries. She replayed their conversation in her head.

'I'm so sorry about dismissing your son,' Béatrice said. 'I had no choice. Some of the female employees were complaining about him.' Sandrine looked at her, wide-eyed. What was Béatrice implying? 'He won't talk to them apparently. He doesn't even say hello. He'll only talk to the male employees.'

'Oh.' Sandrine feared Béatrice was about to say that the girls were accusing him of something far worse and the motive for his dismissal came as a relief. 'I'm so sorry,' Sandrine said. 'I think he may be shy around girls. His girlfriend, Océane, split up with him a few months ago and he has taken it badly.'

Béatrice had nodded and accepted Sandrine's explanation. But had Sandrine been making excuses? Had she realized there was something wrong about the fact that her son wouldn't even exchange pleasantries with his female colleagues?

And what about Antoine's break-up? He'd been depressed. He'd spent days in his room and had barely eaten. Sandrine's worries were assuaged when he met new people, got a new job and started going out again.

Oh, God. Was that what had made him vulnerable? His break-up? Had that opened him up to radicalization? He'd always been impressionable, even as a young boy. Sandrine had put it down to him trying to make friends, a normal boy trying to impress an in-crowd. *Oh, Antoine.* Tears flowed down her cheeks.

Her cell door was opened and she wiped her face with the backs of her hands, fighting to regain control of her emotions as she was brought back into the interrogation room.

'You had a phone call, Madame Hamadi,' said the gruff police officer, the one who had conducted most of the interrogation so far. 'Yesterday evening. Someone rang your mobile, but you didn't answer the call. Was that some kind of code? Who rang you, Madame Hamadi?'

'No one rang me,' Sandrine protested. 'I called my sons. First Antoine, then Maxime.' She paused, suddenly remembering. 'No. No, you're right. I had a missed call. I noticed when I picked up my mobile to call my sons. But I didn't recognize the number.'

'It wasn't a code? Your son wasn't calling to tell you something?'

'No. It wasn't his number.'

'Do you know Henri Charbonnier or Elodie Charbonnier?'

'No. Those names mean nothing to me.' But something was niggling at the back of Sandrine's mind. *Elodie.* She did remember that name.

'The phone call came from Elodie Charbonnier's mobile. Our records show you rang her back, Madame Hamadi. Less than twenty minutes later.'

It came to her then. The voicemail. Her name was Elodie.

'I thought my son might have called me from a friend's phone, you know, to say he was safe, or maybe a friend of my son's was ringing to say ... Antoine wasn't safe. So I rang the number. It went to voicemail. But I don't know anyone called Elodie, so I assumed it was a wrong number.'

'Elodie Charbonnier was one of the hostages. Your son, Zakaria, was using her phone to talk to one of our colleagues from the Brigade of Research and Intervention. Had he arranged to call you as some sort of code?'

Her son had called her. Why had Antoine called her? Had he been scared of dying? Was he having second thoughts?

'No. No. I honestly don't know why he would have called me. What time did he call?'

'Madame Hamadi, we ask the questions here not you,' the officer said at the same time as his female colleague said, 'About an hour before it was all over.'

Sandrine burst into tears. If she'd taken the call, would she have been able to talk him out of what he'd done? Was it already too late by then? In that moment she hated herself for having left her phone on silent mode. She'd failed her son minutes before his death. More importantly, if she'd heard the phone ring and taken the call, perhaps she could have saved some of his … victims.

As if reading her thoughts, the female officer added, 'It might have been to say goodbye. I doubt there was anything you could have done at that stage.'

Through her tears, Sandrine threw the woman a grateful look. She had grey eyes and thin lips, a long, narrow nose. Mid to late thirties. A nice voice. Sandrine knew nothing about her other than that. But she felt certain this woman was a mother.

After an hour or so, Sandrine was taken back to her holding cell and advised to get some sleep. She lay on her back on the bed, if it could be called that. It was so uncomfortable it made Sandrine think of an examination table at the doctor's or a stretcher. Without any sheets, she felt cold despite the hot night. Through the small, rectangular window above the door, faint strip lighting glowed from the corridor, emphasizing the gloom of the cell. Sandrine stared at the ceiling, her body still, apart from the shaking that wouldn't stop.

Chapter 14

THE NIGHT THEY DIED

Laura

The ride on the stretcher was bumpy as they rushed through the street. Her eyes squeezed shut, Laura felt for an instant as if she were back on the flight from Dublin to Lyon, terrified as they flew through turbulence. She hadn't known what fear was until tonight.

There was a strange quietness, or maybe she was just deafened to the noise, for when she opened her eyes again, she could see people everywhere: injured victims swathed in reflective space blankets like her own – some sitting on the pavement; some walking slowly, heads down – the streetlamps throwing an eerie spotlight on them against the backdrop of the dark night. People in uniforms ran in all directions – police, firefighters, other officials in high-visibility vests.

They passed three men in civilian clothes – concertgoers, maybe – two of them carrying a metallic barrier, the kind used to block off roads or keep pedestrians on the pavement during a parade, now a makeshift stretcher for an injured middle-aged man. Turning her head to look at him, Laura caught his eye. He looked as distressed as she felt. But while she was unscathed, physically at least, he was bleeding profusely from his shoulder despite the compress that the third man was holding to the wound. Laura thought it must be a bullet wound.

'Laura, can you hear me?' It was one of the police officers running alongside her, speaking to her in English. He didn't wait for a reply. 'We are taking you to our command centre for a debriefing. It won't take long, but we have to act quickly. We need you to assist us by answering some questions. Can you do that? Laura?'

They turned into the main road. Flashing blue lights bounced off the walls. The noise suddenly hit Laura as if someone had turned on the television with the volume up too high. She had the impression she was playing a small part in an action film. This wasn't happening to her. She was just an extra. It wasn't real. But it wasn't fiction, either. It was surreal.

A safe distance from the concert hall, they suddenly stopped in front of a restaurant. The stretcher was lowered and Laura was helped off it and ushered inside.

'My friends ... I think they're still ...' She tried to point over her shoulder.

'We're doing everything we can.'

There were at least twenty police officers in the restaurant, most of them armed and wearing black uniforms and bulletproof vests. There were floor plans on the walls, helmets on the tables. This must be where the tactical unit had set up their command centre to plan their assault. They sat her down on a chair. Everyone else was standing except for two men sitting at her table. One of them fired questions at her in English. The other scribbled notes on a pad. There were no introductions. They already knew her name.

Could she describe the terrorists? What were their names? How old were they? What sort of weapons did they have? Were they heavily armed? How many hostages? Male? Female? Were they sitting? Standing? Where exactly? Could she show them on this floor plan? Could she give a detailed description of the corridor? Was there anything or anyone blocking the entrances and exits?

She heard someone translate what she was saying. Laura had grasped how vital this was. The lives of the other hostages depended on the assault the tactical unit was preparing. They would aim to rescue all the hostages; they would aim to kill both the terrorists.

She tried to answer quickly and clearly, but her mind felt numb and she wasn't sure how intelligible her replies were, even in English. She did her best to remember things that might be significant. The bag of ammunition left on the lower level, the suicide vests Zak and Ali were wearing, the window in the corridor and the stairs at the end of it, the hostages and the police officer sitting against the door.

After ten minutes at most, the questions stopped. Laura heard orders being given in French, but she tuned out. Then most of the officers ran out of the restaurant. They were ready to make their assault.

'The paramedics will take you to hospital now, Laura. We'll need you to come to the police station so we can take a written statement within the next forty-eight hours. *Le Capitaine* Fournier from the RAID unit will accompany you to the hospital and arrange all that. Is that OK?'

She nodded and it sent a bolt of pain through her head. She felt as if she were in free fall, her mind and body shutting down at the same time.

She was helped to her feet and led towards the door. As she stepped outside, she caught a glimpse of a bus passing beyond the police cordon tape, its passengers all wrapped in glittering survival blankets. One or two passengers had their heads against the windows, their expressions vacant. No one appeared to be talking. It was a strange sight and a disturbing one: a city bus, white with a horizontal blood-red stripe, carrying out its scheduled service as usual, with locals on board going home from a situation that was anything but normal.

Then the colours swirled into one another, the shiny gold, the red and white. Laura heard herself groan. She felt the hands on her arms tighten, catching her as her legs refused to hold her up. She was lifted onto another stretcher, which was hoisted onto a red emergency vehicle – a fire engine, perhaps – and an oxygen mask was fixed to her mouth. Comforting voices spoke to her and two kind faces peered at her with concern. The doors slammed shut, the siren wailed and the vehicle began to move. A wave of nausea engulfed her and for a moment she thought she would throw up.

'*Ne vous inquiétez pas, Madame. On vous emmène à l'hôpital,*' one of the paramedics said over the siren as they carried out various checks on Laura.

Remembering the man she'd seen earlier on the improvised stretcher, Laura protested. 'No! No! I'm not hurt,' she said. 'There are lots of injured people. Take them. I don't need to go to hospital.' It came out in English. Either no one understood the foreign language garbled into the oxygen mask or they chose to ignore her.

When the vehicle came to a halt and Laura's stretcher was lifted out of the ambulance, she noticed the name of the hospital carved into the stone facade. HOPITAL EDOUARD HERRIOT. Under it was a long line of people, stretching up the road. She assumed she would be taken to an overcrowded waiting room, but she was wheeled along a corridor and into a small cubicle where she was seen to immediately.

The doctor pulled a curtain for privacy, shutting out *le Capitaine* Fournier. The RAID officer said something to Laura, but she didn't catch it. She couldn't even tell if he'd spoken in French or English.

The doctor introduced himself, but Laura didn't get his name. It was written on a rectangular badge on the lapel of his white coat, but she couldn't make it out. She didn't seem to be seeing or hearing properly. She found it difficult to take anything in. She still felt sick and dizzy. She wished she could vomit; perhaps the nausea would go away then. She thought if she could cry, that would evacuate some of the stress, but the tears didn't come. The doctor's English sounded less fluent than Laura's French, but she was grateful for his efforts.

'I'm not injured,' Laura said. 'I told them that in the ambulance. You must have other patients who need more urgent treatment than me.'

'You were one of the *otages* …'ostages, yes?'

'Yes.'

'Then you need urgent treatment.'

'But there were lots of people queuing outside at the entrance to the hospital.'

'Ah. We 'ave a lot of patients from the attack, yes. Many, many patients. Some of them are gravely injured. But the people in the queue, they are waiting to donate blood. They are not injured or patients.'

Laura's eyes welled up. She didn't know what the time was, but she did know it was the wee hours and she was moved by the thought that several people who had seen the news had come to the hospital late at night to do their bit to help the victims of this atrocity.

Then it occurred to Laura that this would be international news. She had to get a message to her mother and her cousin to let them know she was safe. But she didn't have her phone. She didn't know a single phone number by heart, not even her mum's landline. She only knew the number to her childhood home, but Noreen no longer lived there.

But surely no one would know yet. News travelled fast, but everyone back home would be in bed. It would be better if her mum heard about this first thing in the morning. She didn't want to wake her up in the middle of the night.

As he was examining her, the doctor asked Laura where she was staying. Laura's heart and head started to pound at the same time at the thought of going back to the aparthotel alone. Unless ... was there any chance Sarah was there? Claire was dead. Ava had been shot and Laura still had no idea if she was alive or dead. But Sarah?

'Who are you in Lyon with?' the doctor asked as if reading her mind.

'My friends ...' A scene burst into her mind. Zak shooting Claire dead with two rounds of his Kalashnikov. Claire collapsing to the ground. It was such a vivid memory and so fresh that Laura could see the blood flying from the back of Claire's head along with ... she couldn't think about it. It was indescribable.

Finally the tears came. Laura's body became racked with uncontrollable sobs. She was vaguely aware of the doctor's hand on her shoulder, but it brought her no comfort.

The doctor took the names of Laura's friends and made a call from the phone on his desk. He replaced the receiver, shaking his head, and Laura assumed it was bad news, but then he said, 'It seems that they 'aven't been admitted to this 'ospital.' His French accent was very pronounced. 'Not yet, anyway. But it's possible they are 'ere and we don't 'ave their names. We can check again in the morning.'

Laura nodded.

'We 'ave already in place a ... how you say? ... emergency psychological support unit, yes, in a *pavillon* of this 'ospital,' he said. 'We'll keep you in overnight for observation. You're in shock. And you may 'ave concussion. Tomorrow you will be taken in charge by the emergency unit.'

Laura wasn't sure what the doctor meant, but she was relieved she didn't have to go back to the aparthotel alone tonight and after a while her sobs subsided.

The doctor called for a nurse who helped Laura off the examination table and into a wheelchair. As she was pushed towards the lifts, Laura saw a clock on the wall. It was gone three a.m. There was no sign of the police officer.

When they reached Laura's ward, the nurse insisted on fetching her a hot chocolate from a vending machine. Then she helped Laura into a thin hospital gown and gave her a tablet and a plastic cup of water.

'*Pour vous aider à dormir,*' she said, enunciating slowly. Pressing her hands together against her cheek and tilting her head, she closed her eyes to mime someone sleeping in case Laura hadn't understood.

Laura lay staring at the ceiling, but even with her eyes open she could see his face. The police officer who had taken her place. What had happened to him? What was his name? She blinked to dispel the image, but instead the police officer's face morphed into someone else's – the face of a younger man, with a beard and light brown eyes flecked with a dangerous green glint. She knew *his* name. She would never forget it. He was called Zak.

Laura didn't think she'd be able to sleep, but within minutes she sensed herself slipping and welcomed the feeling of oblivion the drug was circulating through her body.

Chapter 15

THE DAY AFTER THEY DIED

Laura

When she was woken up for breakfast a few hours later, she felt sluggish and hung-over. It took her a split second to remember where she was and why but then the events of the previous night came crashing down on her. She looked at the tray – some French bread with a mini jar of *Bonne Maman* jam and a pot of natural yoghurt. She managed to eat a little. She was sipping her tea – black, there was no milk – when the doctor on duty came to examine her. He took her pulse and her blood pressure and asked if she was in any pain. She asked about Ava and Sarah.

'I'm sorry,' he said in French. 'I don't know anything about them, but a nurse will come to take you to the emergency psychological unit. They will find out about your friends there.'

Laura asked the doctor if she could take a shower first. She felt dirty. She'd sweated abundantly the previous evening with both the heat and the night's stress. But it was more than that. She felt as if she'd been tarnished by the whole experience. She shuddered, remembering the terrorist called Zak talking in her ear. She'd felt his beard scratch her cheek as he'd held her against him. She might still have a bit of his DNA on her body somewhere, flakes of his skin in her hair or droplets of his dried saliva on the back of her neck.

'Of course,' he replied, in English now, looking pleased with himself for it.

Laura stayed for a long time in the shower. There was some hair and shower gel in the metal shower caddy and she used it to scrub herself all over. She turned the temperature up as high as it would go so that the water almost scalded her.

When she felt cleansed, she got out of the shower and dried off, but she had only her dirty clothes to put back on or the hospital gown. She pulled on the underwear, short cotton trousers and T-shirt she'd been wearing the previous day, instantly feeling soiled again.

As she came back into the ward from the bathroom, Laura spotted a woman standing next to her bed, looking out of the window. She was wearing a white sleeveless vest with "SAMU 69 CUMP" in black capital letters across the back. As Laura approached, the woman turned and her face broke into a soft smile.

'My name is Karima. I'm a nurse,' she said. She had dark hair, dark eyes and olive skin. Her melodious voice inspired confidence in Laura. 'We have set up an emergency medico-psychological unit. It is made up of psychiatrists, psychologists, GPs and nurses like me. We aim to assist you in any way we can. We're based in another part of this hospital for now. When you're ready, I'll take you to one of our consulting rooms.'

'I need to ring home first,' Laura said. 'I haven't spoken to my mother.'

'We'll sort all that out. Don't worry.'

'Your English is excellent,' Laura heard herself saying, an observation rather than a compliment.

'It was my favourite subject at school and my parents

encouraged us to travel a lot. Also, I'm addicted to TV series on Netflix. I don't feel guilty about being a couch potato if I watch them in English.'

Laura nodded. She wasn't up to making small talk.

'If you've got all your stuff, we can go,' Karima said.

'I have nothing,' Laura replied.

'OK. I can get a wheelchair to take you if you like. It's a bit of a trek.'

'I can walk.' Her knee wasn't as sore this morning. There was irony in there somewhere. The only pain she'd been in when she was admitted to hospital had now subsided and it wasn't from an injury sustained in the terrorist attack anyway.

Laura followed Karima to the lift, which they rode to the basement, then through a labyrinth of underground galleries until they got to the consulting room.

'Take a seat,' Karima said, pointing to a plastic chair and sitting down on the swivel chair on the opposite side of the desk. She gave Laura a weak smile. 'Now, you said you haven't spoken to your mother. Does that mean your family doesn't know you're safe?'

Laura shook her head. 'My mobile … the terrorist … he confiscated all the mobiles.'

'This has made headlines the world over. We need to do that straight away.' Karima handed her the desk phone.

'I don't know my mum's number by heart.'

'OK. Do you know how we can contact any member of your family or a friend or even a colleague? We could find a number on the Internet, maybe?'

Laura thought about that. 'What day is it?' she wondered aloud.

'It's Friday.'

Everyone would be at work. Except for her mother, who was retired. They would have her mother's landline and mobile numbers at the library. Laura had listed her as next of kin on the forms. But she didn't want to ring the library. They would ask after Claire, Ava and Sarah. She needed to get a message to her mother, though. Urgently. Noreen would be going to pieces. How could she handle this? A terrorist attack? Another one. She would relive the shock of losing Laura's father.

She could try and get hold of Declan. It might be better if he dealt with Noreen. Declan was an estate agent. They could get hold of him at the office if he wasn't out doing a viewing. Karima found the number online and punched in the digits and moments later, they heard the UK ring tone through the speakerphone. Declan himself answered and Laura burst into tears at the sound of his voice. Somehow she managed to tell him she was in hospital, but not injured.

'Oh, Jaysus. We've been so worried. Thank goodness.'

'I haven't got my mobile,' she said. 'Can you let Mum know I'm all right?' She wasn't all right, far from it, but she was safe. And that was more than could be said for some.

'Of course. I'll call her straight away.' She thought she could hear Declan's voice cracking. 'What about your mates, Laura? Are they safe, too?'

'Claire is … no. Claire isn't … Ava was shot, too. I don't know if … I don't know.'

'Listen. I'll fly out. I can travel back with you. Can you give me the name of your hospital and your hotel?' Laura told him. 'And have you got something to note my mobile number with?'

Karima, who was listening in, jotted down Declan's number.

When Laura had finished talking to her cousin and stopped crying, Karima said, 'I heard you tell your cousin about your friends. Can you write their full names for me?' She slid a piece of paper and a pen across the desk towards Laura.

Laura wrote down Ava's and Sarah's full names. Ava Duffy. Sarah Lynch. She wrote Claire's name as well – Claire Quinn – even though she'd seen Zak shoot her dead. She wanted Karima to find out about Connor and Niall, too, but she didn't know their surnames even though they were sort of famous. A vivid memory came back to her: Niall bleeding on the stage as Connor attempted to stop the haemorrhage. It had looked pretty hopeless. Laura tried to suppress the sob that rose in her throat and it erupted as a subdued squeal.

She handed the piece of paper back to Karima.

'That's good.' Karima spoke to her as if addressing a child.

'One of my friends … Claire … she's dead. I don't know about Ava and Sarah.'

'I'm so sorry about Claire. We'll do our best to locate Ava and Sarah. Now let's see if we can get your phone back for you so you can ring your mum later. What make and model is it?'

Laura gave her the make. She didn't know the model. 'It has a protection case with a photo of my cat, Harry, on it,' she said. She wished she were at home watching TV on the sofa with Harry curled up beside her. That thought almost set her off again. She should never have come to France.

'They took my handbag, too, but that's not so important.'

'What's in it? Your passport?'

'No. A purse with some cash. A few notes. Not much. Some headache tablets. That's about it. My friend Sarah made us leave our passports and bank cards at the hotel and carry our key cards on us, in our pockets, just in case.'

'OK. Describe the bag anyway.'

'Small, rectangular. Red and blue flowers on a white background.'

'Make?'

Laura shook her head. It was a cheap bag she'd picked up from a crafts stall at Folktown Market in Belfast.

'OK. A police officer from the RAID accompanied you here last night – Captain Fournier. He will be back this morning. I will ask him to chase up your phone and your handbag.'

'Thank you.'

'In a few minutes, you'll meet Dr Rivoire. She's a psychologist.

She's very nice. Before that, I need to ask you a few questions and fill out some forms.'

Laura's heart clenched at those words. 'I can't … I don't want to talk …' She couldn't answer any questions about what had happened last night. Karima's English was excellent, but she wouldn't understand. There were no words in any language to describe the barbaric brutality Laura had witnessed.

'Basic questions,' Karima said hastily. 'Your name, address, telephone number. We already have most of the details, but I'll check them. I won't ask any questions about your experience. If you want to talk, I can listen. If not, that's fine.'

Laura breathed in deeply and exhaled slowly. She nodded.

It didn't take long. When she'd finished, Karima said, 'I'll just let Dr Rivoire know we're ready for her.' Karima picked up the desk phone and placed a brief call to her colleague. 'She's on her way,' she said to Laura.

As they waited, Karima checked through the forms. The silence became too much for Laura. 'I like your necklace,' she said, for want of something better to say. On a gold chain around Karima's neck hung a gold pendant of an ornate, open hand.

'Thank you,' Karima said. 'It's a *hamsa*. My parents are from Tunisia. Muslims believe it protects us against the evil eye. I believe they have something similar in the Jewish faith.'

Laura remembered the gold crucifix Ava wore on a chain around her neck. Her throat constricted as she thought of Ava. Witty, lovely Ava. Where was she?

The door opened and a small woman with frizzy brown hair entered the room. She was wearing a white lab coat over a blue T-shirt.

'I'll leave you in Dr Rivoire's capable hands,' Karima said, vacating the swivel chair, for the psychologist to sit on.

Karima was right. Dr Rivoire was nice. Her English was also excellent. She explained that her role was to attempt to attenuate the effects of the traumatic event Laura had just experienced. She told Laura what to expect in the days, weeks and months to come. It didn't sound good. Anxiety, difficulty sleeping, depression … the list went on.

'I strongly advise you to seek help from a healthcare professional when you get home,' she said to Laura.

It was late afternoon before Karima returned with some news for Laura. 'Your friend, Sarah, was injured in the attack,' she said.

'Is she here? Can I see her?'

'She is here, but I'm afraid you can't see her. She is in the operating theatre. Her injuries are serious. She was shot in the back.'

'Oh, God. Oh, no. Will she be … How serious?'

'I'm sorry, Laura,' Karima said, pulling her pendant from side to side. 'That's all I know for now.'

'Are you sure it's her? How can you be sure?'

'She had a library card with her name on it in her wallet.'

Karima didn't have any news of Ava. Laura didn't know if that was a good sign or a bad one. The nurse looked as helpless as Laura felt.

'Could she have been taken to a different hospital?' Laura asked, grabbing on to that idea as it came to her.

Karima shook her head. 'Unlikely,' she said. 'This is the nearest hospital. The injured were brought here. Even if she had been admitted to a different hospital, her name would come up on our computer system.'

'Oh.'

'Sarah's parents haven't been contacted. No one knows how to get in touch with them.'

'What about Claire's and Ava's parents?'

Karima shook her head.

'They would have contact numbers for them at our place of work,' Laura said. 'Belfast Central Library.'

Laura looked at the clock on the wall. It was nearly half past six here, which would make it shortly before closing time with the time difference – 5:30 on Fridays.

'It'll still be open,' she said. 'Just about.'

Karima looked up the number online for the library.

Laura hadn't wanted to speak to anyone at the library, but they might not give out the information to Karima for security reasons even if they'd heard about the attack.

'I'll do it if you like,' Laura said, reaching out for the phone. 'They know me.'

'If you're sure.'

She spoke to Orla, a young colleague who had started working there not long ago. Orla didn't know where Laura was or what had happened, so Laura managed to keep the phone call mercifully short. She noted the contact details for Sarah's, Ava's and Claire's parents and then pushed the sheet of paper across the table to Karima.

'I'll just pass these on to someone to contact your friends' parents,' Karima said, standing up and striding towards the door.

'I'll call them,' Laura heard herself say.

'We have people trained for this,' Karima said. 'It's too much for you and it's against protocol.'

'But I was there,' Laura said, surprising both Karima and herself with her forceful tone.

Karima paused, one hand on the door handle. 'I can't allow you to contact Claire's parents,' she said.

'I know Mrs Lynch, Sarah's mother. It would be better if she heard it from me.' Laura could hear a quaver in her voice and was suddenly a lot less sure of herself.

Karima looked reluctant, but she sat down again and punched in the number for Mrs Lynch, Sarah's mother. She put the speakerphone on again.

As Laura relayed to Mrs Lynch what Karima had told her, she realized that the poor woman was making a huge effort to keep it together. Laura could feel the tears coming again. She tried

107

hard not to break down. She'd insisted on making the call and Mrs Lynch was being so brave. She couldn't give in to her own tears.

'How about yourself?' Mrs Lynch asked.

'I'm at the hospital but I'm ... I wasn't injured.'

'I'm sure you're in shock, pet. You're in the right place. What about Claire and Ava?'

Laura glanced at Karima to gauge her reaction. The nurse made some sort of gesture, but Laura couldn't tell if she was nodding or shaking her head.

'Claire was ... shot ... she's dead. And we don't know if Ava survi ... where Ava is. She's not been admitted to the hospital.' As she said those words, Laura realized this meant that Ava was probably dead. She'd been shot, so she couldn't possibly have gone back to their accommodation without being treated.

'Have you spoken to the families of the other two girls?' Mrs Lynch asked.

'No. They have people here to inform the families.'

'I'll give them a ring anyway, pet,' she said. 'I know Ava's and Claire's parents. I'm sure they'd rather hear the news from a friend than a stranger.' Laura had only met Mrs Lynch a few times and didn't know Sarah's father. She thought Sarah probably got her practical, sensible side from her mother. 'When Sarah comes round, will you tell her we're on our way over?'

'Yes, I'll do that, Mrs Lynch.' Laura gave Sarah's mother the name of the hospital. Then she said goodbye and hung up.

Karima said there might be a bed available in the hospital for Laura. She also offered to find clothes for her. But Laura wanted to change into her own clean clothes and so it was decided that she would go back to the hotel and come in again the next day for a follow-up visit. Karima cut out a tablet from a blister pack strip and handed it to Laura with instructions to take it before she went to bed to help her sleep.

At Karima's suggestion, Laura rang Declan on his mobile before she left. He'd booked flights from Dublin to Lyon. He would be with her the following evening.

'Pat has pulled a sickie. He's coming with me,' Declan said.

The heat took her breath away as she stepped outside. Karima had organized medical transport to take Laura back to the aparthotel and a taxi was waiting to the side of the main hospital building. The engine was running and the inside of the car was cool from the air conditioning.

'Have you got the key for your hotel room?' Karima asked, opening the car door for Laura to get in. The key card was still in Laura's pocket. 'Don't worry,' Karima said. 'We're here for you. We may have some more information tomorrow. We'll see you first thing in the morning. And your cousin will soon be on his way to pick you up.'

But as the taxi pulled away, Laura had never felt so alone. She hadn't wanted to spend another night at the hospital, but at the thought of going back to the aparthotel, her stomach lurched in dread. There would be no one there. Sarah was in hospital, badly injured. Ava was at best injured, but it seemed far more likely she was dead. And Claire. Oh God, Claire. She'd been shot before Laura's very eyes. Laura kept seeing the moment flash before her, kept hearing herself screaming and the shots from the automatic weapon.

She became aware of her nails digging painfully into the palms of her hands. She looked out of the car window, trying hard to focus on something – anything – to replace the images in her head. She couldn't process what had happened to Claire yet. She couldn't take in what she herself had done.

Chapter 16

2 DAYS AFTER THEY DIED

Sandrine

Sandrine must have dozed off in the end for she woke up with a start. They had come for her. More questioning. This time she was interrogated by a different team. Three men. One small, one tall, one bald. No woman on this team. They took it in turns to ask her questions. The focus was now on Sam's family. Sandrine gave fuller answers in the hope that she would soon be released.

'How would you describe your relationship with your parents-in-law, Madame Hamadi?' the bald one asked.

'I don't have any sort of a relationship with any member of my husband's family,' Sandrine said. 'Except for my brother-in-law who we see occasionally.'

'Why is that, Madame Hamadi?'

'His parents were against our union, our marriage,' she said. 'They're devout Muslims.' She stopped, as the realization of what those words would imply for her interrogators sank in.

'And you're …?'

'Nothing. I'm nothing. An atheist, I suppose. They might have accepted me into the family if I'd been willing to convert to Islam.'

'But you weren't?'

'No.'

'Did your son have anything to do with that side of the family, Madame Hamadi?'

Your son. Sandrine sobbed as the thought she'd had when she was arrested came back to her now. She had only one son now. But they didn't mean Maxime. They were talking about Antoine. Zakaria. They already referred to him in the past tense.

'Antoine got on well with his uncle, my husband's brother. Abdel comes to the house sometimes. He gets on well with both Antoine and Maxime.' She paused. 'He got on well with Antoine and …'

'That's all right, Madame Hamadi.' It wasn't. Nothing was all right now. Her whole world was upside down. 'Go on.'

'My sons go – went – with him to see their grandparents sometimes. Their cousins, too. I was glad Abdel took them. It was important to me.'

'Where do Samir's parents live, Madame Hamadi?'

It took Sandrine a second to realize he meant her husband.

'About forty kilometres away. In Vénissieux. Near the park.'

'*Le parc de Parilly?*'

'Yes.'

'And does Samir see his parents at all?'

'No. They disowned him when we got engaged. His name's Sam. No one calls him Samir.'

'Why is that, Madame Hamadi?'

Good question. Sandrine searched for an answer, but couldn't find one immediately.

'Did you know him as Samir before his parents disowned him?'

'No. Only his parents called him Samir. He has always been Sam to me. I think he'd rejected his religion before his parents rejected him. He grew up feeling like he was living in two worlds, but he felt more French than Algerian.'

'And yet he gave both French and Arabic names to his sons.'

The intonation suggested it wasn't a question, but Sandrine answered anyway. 'Yes. It's part of who he is and it's the same for our children.'

'Even though he wasn't on good terms with his parents?'

'Yes.'

'And even though he wasn't a practising Muslim.'

Sandrine stared at him then. She held his gaze before answering slowly. 'That has nothing to do with it.'

As the bald officer cleared his throat and looked away, his tall colleague took over. 'Was your son religious, Madame Hamadi?'

'I didn't think so. But you seem to know more than me on that score.'

'Did he ever express a wish to go to a mosque?'

'No, but then he would be unlikely to tell me that, I suppose.'

'Do you remember him ever showing an interest in religion?'

Sandrine suppressed a yawn. She felt exhausted. And over-whelmingly sad. She wanted to be on her own. She closed her eyes. A scene came to her. All four of them sitting at the table for an evening meal. It must have been one weekend six months or a year ago, when Abdel had brought the boys back from their grandparents'. They'd been talking about the fact they never ate pork. Antoine had brought up the subject. Sandrine didn't know why exactly, but Sam had an aversion to pork. It probably stemmed from his upbringing. So, they never bought any and never cooked pork dishes.

The conversation turned into an argument. Antoine stormed out of the room, yelling at Sam over his shoulder, 'You've always been a lapsed, lukewarm Muslim. You're a hypocrite, too. Look at you. You won't eat pig, but you'll drink wine no problem!'

Sandrine opened her eyes. The officer was looking at her, waiting for an answer. 'No, I don't,' she said.

Sandrine was held for over thirty exhausting hours. When she was finally released, on the Saturday afternoon, her lawyer, Maître Guillet, told her that Sam was still being held in custody. At the thought of going home without him, Sandrine felt weak and would have collapsed to the ground if her lawyer hadn't caught her.

'Maxime, too?'

'No. He was released a few hours ago. He's still waiting for you. Come with me.'

'But Sam … When will my husband—?'

'He can be held for a maximum of ninety-six hours unless …' The lawyer broke off, biting his lip. He looked tired, too.

'Unless what?'

'Well, unless the police want to charge him,' he finished.

'They won't do that, will they?'

'I don't know, Madame Hamadi. If the police have evidence that indicates your husband was in some way tangled up in this or knew about Antoine's … subversive activities, he could be charged with conspiracy in relation to a terrorist enterprise. I think that's the most likely worst-case scenario.'

The most likely worst-case scenario. What on earth did that mean?

Before she could ask him, he said, 'It might be a good idea to call someone to pick you up. I'll make a statement to the press on your behalf.'

'Thank you.'

Maxime was sitting on a bench in the vast entrance hall. He stood up as soon as he saw Sandrine and she clung to him as if she were drowning and he were her rescuer.

They were allowed to wait in a large room – much larger than the one Sandrine had been interviewed in – while Sandrine called Angélique, her friend and neighbour, to ask her if she would come and pick them up. But Angélique didn't answer her mobile. That was strange. Her kids would have finished their naps by now. Sandrine often went round to her friend's house at this time of day. Angélique would be making her children a snack right now, texting on her phone while she did so.

She tried again, and this time Angélique answered. Sandrine explained where she and Maxime were and asked if Angélique would mind coming to fetch them.

'I can't right now,' her friend replied in a voice Sandrine didn't recognize.

'Oh. We could wait for a while if—'

'I said no, Sandrine. Please don't call again.'

Angélique ended the call and Sandrine looked at the phone in her hand, her mouth open.

'Don't worry, Mum,' Maxime said. 'I'll text Benoît. His sister got her driving licence last week.' He tapped away at his phone with his thumbs at incredible speed and seconds later, it pinged with a message. 'They're on their way, Mum,' he said. 'Come and sit down.'

'I'll wait with you,' Maître Guillet said. Sandrine had forgotten he was there. She told him there was no need, but it sounded hollow, even to her ears. She found his presence comforting and was glad when he sat down with them.

When Maxime's friend arrived with his older sister, Maître Guillet left the building with them. As they stepped outside, a swarm of reporters clamoured for Sandrine's attention. The lawyer leaned in and said in Sandrine's ear, 'You go with Maxime. I'll distract them. Don't say anything. Don't react to anything they say.'

Maxime took his mother's arm and guided her towards where the car was waiting. *The getaway car*, Sandrine thought. She felt like a criminal.

As they walked away, their heads down, Sandrine heard her lawyer's loud voice as he made a statement for the press. 'My client has been released from police custody and no accusation or charge has been retained against her at this stage of the procedure.'

His tone of voice indicated that was the end of the matter, but the journalists had no doubt been congregating outside the police station for a while and continued to bombard him with questions.

As Benoît's sister drove them home, Sandrine leant back against the headrest in the back seat of the car and closed her eyes as silent tears streamed down her face. She could see Antoine's face as if it was etched on the insides of her eyelids. Her son. Her firstborn. Her miracle baby. Antoine was dead. She'd brought him into this world nearly twenty years ago. She'd given him life. And he had taken lives. People had lost their sons, their daughters, brothers, sisters, mothers, fathers, loved ones, friends. The death toll hadn't yet been confirmed. They would find out soon enough exactly how many people had died. But the number of people whose lives Antoine had destroyed would never be known. It was inestimable.

Sandrine had been in the police station for hours. She had a splitting headache and she was physically and mentally drained. But, although she'd been given a brief summary of what had happened at *La Voie Lactée* before her interrogation began, her own questions remained mostly unanswered.

One question demanded attention more than the others inside her sore head. She knew she would ask herself the same thing every day for the rest of her life: What could she have done to prevent this?

Chapter 17

2 DAYS AFTER THEY DIED

Laura

The first time she heard it, Laura was sitting on the bar stool in the kitchenette of the aparthotel, staring at her untouched mug of tea. Her heart raced and sweat broke out in beads on her forehead. *What was that?* Then she heard it again. A loud bang. She dived to the floor.

Slowly her brain kicked in. The noises had come from outside. It was quiet now. Perhaps it was car doors slamming or a vehicle backfiring. As her pulse slowed, she wondered if this was the way it was going to be from now on. Would she dive to the ground or run for cover every time someone knocked on the door or accidentally dropped something on the floor? Would banging noises always trigger such emotions and reactions? *Trigger.* Now there was a word that was laden with meaning, *loaded* with meaning.

She got to her feet. She needed to do something. She couldn't just wait around for the taxi to come and take her back to the hospital. She'd been up and dressed for a while and she'd packed her suitcase. She decided to pack her friends' bags, too. She would leave them in reception later. She walked to the sink and tipped away her tea.

She got through the task she'd set herself on automatic pilot. She left Claire's things till last. The smell of Claire's perfume on her clothes caused tears to trickle down Laura's face. Claire would never wear these clothes again. Luckily, Claire hadn't unpacked much of her stuff. Laura felt a bit calmer once she'd closed Claire's suitcase.

The packing didn't take her long. When she'd finished, she looked at her watch. She still had a few minutes to wait. She paced the apartment for a while, from her bedroom, where she tried not to look at Ava's empty bed, to the dining area with the kitchenette in the corner and into the living area. She felt a little calmer but the silence was becoming unbearable. She was alone in an apartment where only the day before yesterday there had been four of them.

Sinking on the sofa, she looked at the blank TV screen. The day before, Dr Rivoire and Karima had advised her against watching the news. Karima had told her that all three terrorists had been shot dead and all eleven hostages had been saved.

'Eleven?' Laura had said.

'Yes,' Karima said. 'There were eleven hostages altogether.'

'Including me?'

'I suppose so.'

'Not counting the police officer who swapped places with me, then.'

'I don't know about that.' Karima's reply had come a beat late, and Laura didn't believe her.

She picked up the remote control and turned on the television. It was a French news channel. On the screen, three pictures appeared with the names of each of the terrorists underneath. The photos looked uncannily – or perhaps deliberately – like

117

mugshots. Laura shuddered, transfixed by the photo in the middle. She read the name. Zakaria Hamadi. Zak.

Her hands shaking, she flicked through the channels until she came to Sky News. There would undoubtedly be the same images, but at least she could listen to the latest developments in her own language.

She watched the report, her body rigid except for the rapid rise and fall of her chest as her breathing became laboured. Turning on the TV was a mistake. She should have listened to Dr Rivoire. But now she was paralysed, compelled to listen, eyes riveted to the screen.

Five minutes later the adverts came on and she somehow managed to point the remote control at the television and switch it off. Leaning forwards on the sofa in a daze, her head in her hands, she rocked back and forth, moaning as she did so.

He was dead. His name was Pierre Moreau. He'd been a member of the Brigade of Intervention and Research. He had swapped places with her and he had died.

'It should have been me. It should have been me.' The words went round on a loop in her head as the moaning grew louder and louder.

She had no idea how long she stayed like that, rocking to and fro on the sofa with her hands over her ears, but after a while the wailing stopped. Her breaths were now coming in erratic gasps and she felt an overwhelming need to get out of the flat. As if on automatic pilot, she stood up, albeit on wobbly legs, slipped on her shoes, put her key card into her pocket and left the aparthotel.

She waited outside in the shade, leaning against the wall until the same taxi driver as the previous evening came to take her to the hospital. He spoke no English and didn't say much in French, either, which suited Laura. When she arrived at the hospital, she was greeted by Karima who led her to the same consulting room as the day before.

'I've got some good news for you,' the nurse said brightly. 'About Sarah?'

Karima's face fell. 'Oh, no. I'm afraid not. I'll ask for an update on her in a moment, OK? I ... well, you should be able to get your mobile phone back later today.'

'Oh. Thank you.' Laura could hear the disappointment in her own voice and forced a smile so as not to appear ungrateful. 'Any word on Ava?'

'No, I'm afraid not. I passed on all the phone numbers you gave us to the police officer.'

Laura grasped the subtext. It would take a while to identify all the bodies in the concert hall and when they did, if Ava's body was among them, her parents would have to be notified before anyone else. Following Sarah's advice, they'd all left their passports at the aparthotel. Laura hadn't brought her driving licence to France; Ava had probably left hers at home, too. She might not have had any ID on her at all. There was a chance, though, that Ava had been brought to hospital unconscious and that no one knew who she was. Laura clung to that.

'Speaking of which,' Karima continued, snapping Laura out of her thoughts, 'the police would like to talk to you. They're keen to take a statement before you go home because as one of the hostages, you're a key witness.'

Laura nodded. The prospect of having to go through any of that night's events was more than she could bear, but at the same time she was painfully aware that she was alive and others hadn't been so fortunate. She didn't feel lucky right now, but compared with her friends she was.

Privately she thought her story wouldn't be any different to those of the ten other hostages, all of whom could explain much better what had happened than she could, if only because they spoke the right language.

'You have to go to the *Hôtel de Police* – the police station. Captain Fournier will arrange for a car to pick you up and he will go with you. Your mobile phone is at the police station, too.'

Laura nodded again. 'I'm ready.'

True to her word, Karima rang through to Intensive Care to find out how Sarah was doing. Judging from Karima's face, the news wasn't good.

'She's critical but stable,' Karima informed Laura, hanging up the phone.

'Can I see her?'

'I'm afraid not. No visitors yet. Except her family when they get here.'

Critical but stable. What does that mean exactly? Laura wondered as she left the hospital later in the afternoon. She got the feeling Karima wasn't telling her everything, just as she'd withheld information about the police officer, Pierre Moreau. It was probably better that way. Laura didn't think she could take any more bad news for now.

Dr Rivoire came to see her before she left. She urged Laura again to seek help from a professional once she got home. Events like this could trigger depression or post-traumatic stress disorder, according to the psychologist. She'd written a letter in English for Laura to take to her GP for an urgent referral.

When the police car pulled up in front of the *Hôtel de Police*, Laura looked up at the imposing building. It didn't look like either a hotel or a police station, but more like some big corporate company headquarters. Captain Fournier got out of the car with Laura to take her inside.

Laura was surprised to see several reporters in front of the building. They were all shouting questions at a slim woman with shoulder-length brown hair and an adolescent boy, her son maybe, who was holding her arm as they emerged from the police station. They were followed by a small, suited man. The woman kept her head down and Laura caught no more than a glimpse of her as the pack of journalists closed in like bloodthirsty hounds. She felt sorry for the woman.

Taking hold of Laura's arm, Captain Fournier steered her to the right, giving the crowd a wide berth.

As they were about to enter the police station, Laura heard someone shout, 'Madame Hamadi! Madame Hamadi!'

Laura's legs threatened to give way and she stumbled. She whirled round. She remembered that name. She'd heard it on the news that morning. Zakaria Hamadi. The terrorist they'd called Zak. Madame Hamadi. Was that woman his mother? Laura's initial pity was replaced by a rush of rage. She wanted to shake the woman and scream at her.

She made to run after her, but Captain Fournier was still holding her arm and pulled her back. She stared after the woman and teenager, but she couldn't get a good look at them through the ring of journalists around them. They got into a car. As it roared off, Laura allowed herself to be led inside.

Captain Fournier introduced Laura to *Le Commandant* Roche, a member of the judicial police investigation team. The commander explained that he would take Laura's statement. Captain Fournier typed up her account while Commander Roche talked to Laura. He spoke to her in perfect English albeit slowly, as if dealing with a child. Unlike Captain Fournier, who was wearing a uniform, Commander Roche was in plain clothes. He had thick salt and pepper hair and striking green-grey eyes. Laura guessed he was in his early fifties.

The whole thing was easier and quicker than Laura had feared. She was able to tell them what had happened without breaking down and without getting the feeling she was reliving that night. She felt strangely detached throughout, as though she were giving an account of an incident someone else had experienced a long time ago. She assumed they'd already heard similar accounts from the ten other hostages anyway.

The hardest part was recounting how Claire had died. There was no way Laura could describe this in any detail, but to her relief, her succinct account seemed to satisfy Commander Roche.

He was far more interested in her encounter with Zak in the ladies' toilets and nodded enthusiastically when she surmised that this was where the terrorist had hidden his automatic weapon.

She went over it again, this time in more detail as the whole incident came flooding back to her. For a moment she could see Zak's face in the mirror, holding her gaze. The reflected image was so clear that she could see the out of order sign on the door of the toilet cubicle behind him with its letters appearing backwards. She felt the hairs prickle on her arms.

When she'd finished her account, Captain Fournier printed out her statement. He'd typed it up in French. The commander asked her to read it through and say if there was anything she didn't understand, wanted to amend or realized she'd forgotten to mention.

As Laura signed her statement, she glanced at her watch, thinking of Declan. He and Patrick would have landed by now. This would all be over soon. She could go home.

As if reading Laura's thoughts, Commander Roche asked her if she had made travel arrangements to go home.

'My return flight is in a few days' time, but I'll try to change it. I'd like to go home as soon as possible,' she said. Then she remembered her phone. 'My cousin is on his way. I need to contact him. The nurse at the hospital said I could have my mobile back.'

'I'll see to that,' the captain said in French to his superior. 'I've spoken to someone about Mademoiselle Davison's handbag and mobile phone.'

A few minutes later, Captain Fournier came back, carrying a mobile phone in one hand and her bag in the other. Commander Roche took the items from him and brought them over to Laura as his colleague said goodbye to her and strode away along the carpeted hallway.

'Are these your things?' the commander asked.

'Yes, thank you.' Laura turned over the mobile and looked at the picture of Harry printed on her phone case.

'Thank you for coming in today,' Commander Roche said. 'You've been very helpful.'

She was about to stand up, taking this as her cue to leave, but a woman appeared at the door that the captain had left open. She was pretty and petite with long dark hair. She looked about Laura's age. The commander spotted the woman and rushed into the hallway.

Laura looked at her phone. She'd turned it off for the concert. Maybe there was still some battery left. If not, her charger was at the aparthotel. She would go back there now. She'd wait until she was outside the police station to turn on her mobile. She probably had a few missed calls and text messages from people who knew she'd come to Lyon to see *The Naturals*. But the first thing she would do was ring Declan.

Laura stood up. Through the open door, she could see the commander, his back to Laura and his hands on the woman's shoulders. They were talking fast, in French and in hushed tones, and Laura had to concentrate to make out the words.

'You shouldn't be at work, Romane,' he said. 'You should be at home.'

'Is that her?' Romane asked. 'Is that the hostage he swapped with?' With a jolt, Laura realized the woman was staring at her as she said this. Curious, Laura walked towards her.

'Yes. Look, I'm sorry about Pierre. We're all utterly devastated by what happened. It's a terrible tragedy. We have lost a selfless hero and a remarkable human being. But you must go home, Romane. If you wait for me downstairs for a few minutes, I'll drive you home.'

Pierre. Laura wondered if she'd heard correctly. Pierre Moreau? The police officer who had lost his life to save the hostages? Laura's eyes widened and she saw the commander wrap the woman in his arms as she began to cry. Was this woman – Romane

123

– one of Pierre's colleagues? Or something more than that? Laura took a few more steps towards the door, closer to them. She was standing in the doorway now, but they didn't notice her.

'They wanted a female member of the task force,' Romane sobbed into the commander's shoulder. 'I was there. I was the only woman on duty. Pierre said there were no female officers. He went in because he didn't want me to. I told him that morning … If I hadn't told him … If only I hadn't—'

'Romane, I don't know what you said to Pierre. But it wouldn't have made any difference. He was incredibly brave. You know he was.' The commander turned his head and spotted Laura only a few metres away from them. 'Please, Romane,' he whispered, 'wait downstairs for me. I'll be there in a second.'

His voice still low, the commander turned to Laura and said in English, 'I'm so sorry about that. We lost a colleague in the terrorist attack, as you probably know. He was that lady's boyfriend. She's understandably distraught.'

So Romane was Pierre Moreau's girlfriend. It bothered Laura that Commander Roche had felt the need to apologize on the poor woman's behalf.

Romane shuffled down the hallway, hugging herself around the waist. She threw Laura one last look over her shoulder. As their eyes locked briefly, Laura wondered if they were both tormented by the same question: why had Laura survived while a courageous, commendable police officer from the Brigade of Research and Intervention had died? Or maybe Romane felt the same way Laura did because Pierre Moreau had saved her, too. *It should have been me.* Those exact words might be going through Romane's head.

Laura had encountered violent death before. She hadn't witnessed it and she hadn't been told all the details, but she'd imagined it several times over the years. Her father's murder. It was always there, lurking in a corner of her mind, ready to pounce every now and then and overwhelm her all over again.

It struck Laura that her story was now intrinsically bound to her father's with brutal, bloody ties. Similarly, the terrorist attack linked her to Romane even though she didn't know her and would probably never see her again. But they'd both had a brush with death and lost people they cared about. As the policewoman turned away, Laura realized nothing would ever be the same again for either of them. Their memories, feelings and lives would be divided into a before and after the night the others had died.

Chapter 18

2 DAYS AFTER THEY DIED

Sandrine

As the hours dragged by, Sandrine became more and more unsettled. She'd barely slept last night, hadn't eaten much today and couldn't hold it together even for Max's sake. He'd gone out half an hour ago, leaving her to her thoughts. She needed Sam. Where was he? Why were they still holding him in custody?

Her mind began to play tricks on her, sowing seeds of doubt and nibbling away at the implicit trust she had in her husband. Could Sam be involved in this? She rejected the thought as soon as it entered her head, but it was replaced by a taunt: *You didn't think your son was capable of this and look what he did.*

She did believe it, though, somewhere deep inside her. She hadn't known she'd created a monster, but she could admit to herself that she and Sam had been ignoring signs that Antoine was up to no good for months. If anyone had been able to see this coming, it should have been her. How could she not have known? What kind of a mother was she? The same questions, over and over.

She combed through her memories, looking for answers. But only recollections of happy times came to her – Antoine smiling triumphantly after cooking dinner for the whole family for the first time, Antoine cracking a joke and he and Maxime roaring with laughter at it, Antoine proudly and earnestly confiding in her that he was in love and wanted to marry Océane. Portraits of good times, reminding her of everything she'd lost, bittersweet, as if her mind was deliberately deriding her with the memories it was whipping up. Memories of Antoine before he became Zak.

When her mobile phone rang, she started, the loud ringtone slicing through her thoughts. It was Sam.

'Sam! What's happening? Why—'

'They're letting me go, Sandrine. I'll be home in an hour or so.'

Relief flooded through her, washing away some of her fear.

'Do you want me to come and get you?' she asked.

'No, don't worry about that.'

'But there will be reporters everywhere. You can't take the tube or the bus. And it's a long way. I'll come and get you.'

'I've ordered a taxi,' he said.

She looked at the time on the clock on the wall. It was late, way past dinnertime. Sam would be hungry, but there was nothing to eat in the house. Sandrine hadn't set foot outside since she'd come home the day before. She was terrified of bumping into people she knew and of their reactions. She hadn't dared turn on the television. She knew Antoine's name would be all over the news and everyone who knew them would know by now what he'd done. Angélique, who was her friend, wanted nothing more to do with her. What would her other neighbours say, if they spoke to her at all?

Sandrine paced the floor while she waited for Sam – and Max – to come home.

She'd already cleaned the house. It had been a mess after the police had searched it. The only room she hadn't been able to bring herself to clean for now was Antoine's bedroom. She would do it, but not yet. She hadn't even looked inside it. She'd just quietly closed the door, as though she didn't want to disturb her son while he was sleeping. But she didn't know what to do with herself while she waited, so she went to the kitchen and put on her rubber gloves, looking for something else to scrub or polish. Anything to keep herself occupied. Then she took them off again, throwing them into the sink. She went back into the living room and, against her better judgement, turned on the television.

Antoine's name and photo, along with the names and photos of two other young men, were on the screen. Sandrine's heart missed a beat as she recognized the man on the left. She read his name aloud: Ali Belkacem. He was the friend of Antoine's she'd met in this house that day.

'The Islamic State has claimed responsibility for the attacks that were carried out in response to a recent French airstrike that resulted in ten Jihadists killed at the border between Algeria and Mali,' the news reporter was saying. 'This was part of the anti-insurgent *Opération Barkhane* led by the French military against Islamist groups in Africa's Sahel region.'

Sandrine stared uncomprehendingly at the screen. Algeria? Mali? The terrorist attack on the *La Voie Lactée* had happened in Lyon.

'The number of victims is now estimated at around eighty dead and around three hundred injured,' the journalist continued. 'The victims include the band's frontman, Niall O'Donnell, who was shot dead on stage.'

'Oh God, oh God,' Sandrine murmured over and over.

'We know that the three terrorists were French citizens,' the newscaster continued, 'and they have all now been confirmed dead – one of them was shot dead by police in the pit of the concert hall. He was subsequently identified by his driving licence as Ibrahim Traoré, a twenty-year-old man of Malian origin. The other two terrorists, Zakaria Hamadi and Ali Belkacem, both

French citizens, who had taken eleven hostages into a corridor on the upper level of the arena, detonated their suicide vests when the police launched their assault.'

Tears blinded Sandrine. She cradled her head in her hands, peeping through her fingers like a child watching a horror film. She didn't want to see any more, but at the same time she was unable to tear her eyes away from her son's face.

'The eleven hostages were all rescued without injury,' the newscaster continued. 'However, Pierre Moreau, a member of the Brigade of Research and Intervention, lost his life saving them. Moreau, who had just turned thirty, had swapped places with one of the female hostages. He managed to introduce a mobile phone with an open line into the corridor where the hostages were being held, enabling the tactical police team to monitor the situation. Moreau died when one of the terrorists, Zakaria Hamadi, detonated his vest during the police assault.'

As the shot cut to the Interior Minister issuing a statement, Sandrine ran out of the room, but didn't make it to the toilet in time. Instead, she was violently sick all over the clean tiled floor in the hall.

Sandrine turned off the television before cleaning up the mess. Her earlier reluctance to show her face outside her home was suddenly replaced by an urgent need to get outdoors. She looked through the window. There didn't seem to be any journalists. They would be here soon enough – she was sure of it.

She put on a cardigan and as an afterthought, went to her bedroom to find a straw hat. She pulled the sunhat low over her forehead and tucked her hair inside at the back. Then she put on her sunglasses. She glimpsed her reflection in the hall mirror. The sun had gone down and she looked conspicuous. Not for the first time, she felt like a criminal herself. *Not a criminal; the mother of a criminal*, she thought, stepping outside. Then, *How could you do this to me, Antoine?*

She walked quickly, her head down, to the supermarket, which

129

was half a kilometre away. It stayed open late and she should make it before closing. She fervently hoped that Béatrice wouldn't be working this evening or that she would at least be inside an office somewhere on the premises so Sandrine wouldn't see her. She didn't think Antoine's former boss would be sympathetic towards her.

She kept her hat on as she raced round the aisles, grabbing a roasted chicken, warm inside the thick paper bag, a ready-washed salad and a stick of bread. She didn't think to pay at the self-service checkout and realized her mistake as soon as she saw the look on the cashier's face. A woman of around Antoine's age, the cashier bored her eyes into Sandrine's, not looking down once as she picked up Sandrine's items and scanned them one by one with painful slowness.

Sandrine's hands shook as she opened her purse and fished out a fifty-euro note. She handed it to the cashier who snatched it and opened the till. She tidied the note into the till then slammed the drawer shut. Sandrine, who was already hot from her brisk walk in the heat to the supermarket, could feel herself burning even more under the younger woman's penetrating gaze.

No words had been exchanged between the two women, but the message was clear. Sandrine was not welcome and there was no point in asking for her change. Sandrine wondered if this was one of the female members of staff Antoine had refused to speak to. She found she couldn't blame the cashier for her attitude and lowered her head in shame.

Turning to go, she almost walked into Béatrice, who was standing in her way, her arms folded across her chest.

'You've got a nerve, coming in here,' Béatrice snarled. Sandrine said nothing. She was sweating and desperately needed to get outside, but she was ensnared like an animal in a trap. She would have to physically push Béatrice to get past her. 'Find somewhere else to shop,' Béatrice continued. 'You're no longer one of our valued customers.'

Later, as she told Sam about what had happened in the supermarket, she realized she had no recollection of walking home. She didn't remember getting the dinner ready either. The time between leaving the supermarket and Sam arriving in the taxi was a total blank.

Max had come home a few minutes after Sam. He'd eaten hungrily and retired to his room. Sandrine and Sam sat at the table, their food almost untouched on their plates.

'Do you think it's my fault?' Sandrine whispered, voicing the question that was still writhing around in her head, torturing her. 'Should I have seen this coming?'

She put her elbows on the table, covering her ears with her hands, as if afraid to hear Sam's reply.

Sam got up and stood behind her, holding her tightly to his chest. 'You mustn't blame yourself, my love,' he said.

But in that moment, she did, and she also blamed Sam, perhaps even more, although she couldn't have explained why and she wasn't going to share that with her husband.

'Why not?' she said. 'Everyone else will.'

Chapter 19

Sandrine

Sandrine often thought of him as two different people: her son Antoine, as she'd known him, and the terrorist Zak, whom she'd never met. She couldn't reconcile the two in her mind. Her son had been obedient and helpful; loving and intelligent. He was gentle and sensitive. Zak had been downright evil and savagely violent. She was unable to get her head round the fact that Antoine and Zak had coexisted, that they were, in fact, the same person. She hoped that Antoine had had enough influence over Zak at the end to make him demonstrate some compassion.

She knew Antoine had become Zak long before the night he died and this thought plagued her. Had he always had this in him? Had he shown any remorse? Should she have seen this coming? In her mind, she went over incidents, seeing things he'd said and done in a new light. She remembered things he'd done to Max when they were younger, like sticking chewing gum in his hair or putting a plastic snake in his bed or even on one occasion throwing a tantrum followed by a fork, which had left angry red prong marks on Max's forehead for a couple of days afterwards.

She remembered the day at her parents' house when they'd thought Maxime had drowned in the pond, only to find him locked in the cleaning cupboard. Antoine had admitted the next day that he'd played a role in his younger brother's disappearance.

None of this behaviour had been nice, but she'd considered it normal at the time. Now she wasn't so sure. Had these been warning signs they'd overlooked, or worse, ignored? Sam refused to talk about Antoine, but he listened. Last time she'd shared her doubts with him, he'd dismissed them.

'You're reading too much into it,' he'd said. 'That was standard sibling behaviour. My big brother did that sort of thing to me, too.'

She wished Sam would remind her of the good times and the good things Antoine had done, or failing that, tell her stories about the naughty things their friends' children had got up to as kids when they'd turned out all right. Then she wouldn't feel as if she should have foreseen this.

These thoughts occupied her mind all the time, and one day it came to her. She might find what she was looking for in the garage. But before she could do anything about it, Sam arrived home. It was nearly dark, but it was still fairly early and Sandrine hadn't been expecting him yet. His face was drawn. Perhaps he was tired or maybe he wasn't feeling well and had finished up at work earlier than usual.

'How was your day?' She asked him the same thing every evening. They talked less and less, but they kept up common courtesy, said their pleases and thank yous, their good mornings and goodnights. But Sandrine knew it was a meaningless question.

He gave her an equally meaningless reply. 'Fine.'

She imagined Sam's day must have been anything but fine. It was Sam's company, which was a relief, as she was convinced he would have been sacked had he worked for anyone else. But it was a small web design business, and she knew that one of his employees – the web developer, whatever that was – had handed in his notice immediately after the attack. She wondered about the attitude of those who remained. Were they unpleasant behind Sam's back? To his face? Or were they understanding?

'Are you hungry?'

'Not yet. I'm going to take a shower before dinner, warm myself up a bit.'

She waited until she could hear the water running in the bathroom. Then she slipped into the garage. She wrapped her long, woollen cardigan tightly around her. The garage was insulated, but it wasn't heated. They had storage space in the roof in here. There were boxes containing clothes the boys had grown out of, board games they'd stopped playing with and books they'd finished with. They used to do car boot sales every now and then so the boys could make some pocket money from the stuff they no longer needed.

Antoine's room had been ransacked during the police raid and they'd taken away anything personal. Even here, in the garage, all of the boxes had been opened. She had to hand it to them, they'd been thorough. But whatever they were looking for – ammunition or bomb-making equipment, Sandrine supposed – there was none of that in here and nothing inside the boxes had been disturbed.

Sandrine climbed up the ladder and with difficulty she brought down two of the boxes. Inside were school reports dating right back to when Antoine and Max had started nursery school at the age of three. Sandrine had also kept most of their exercise books and drawings.

She sat on the concrete floor and started on the first box. She knew what she was looking for. Signs. Paintings with lots of black and grey, that sort of thing. Or perhaps something in an essay Antoine had written.

After twenty minutes, though, all she'd found was a sheet of A4 paper inside a homework book on which Antoine had written lines for one of his teachers as a punishment. *I must not bully.* The same sentence over and over. And hidden in the middle, *not today, anyway.* Sandrine didn't know if the teacher had spotted this small act of rebellion or what the initial act of bullying had been.

She took out another exercise book. English. Antoine had liked foreign languages. He'd always had excellent marks in English and Spanish. As a former English teacher herself, Sandrine had read to the boys from English picture books when they were little.

And that's when she found it. It dropped out from between the pages of the exercise book and fell onto her lap. A cream envelope. With the word "*Maman*" written on it in what was unmistakably Antoine's spidery handwriting.

For several minutes, Sandrine simply stared at it. It was clearly a letter, but she had no memory of it. Then she picked it up and turned it over. The envelope was still sealed. Why hadn't Antoine given this to her? When had he written it? And how did it end up in here?

Sandrine knew that the answers to the questions racing around in her head were probably inside the envelope, but she couldn't bring herself to open it. Instead she turned the envelope over and over in her hands as tears rolled down her cheeks.

She heard Sam calling her from within the house, but she didn't answer. She didn't trust her voice to call back to him past the lump in her throat, and anyway, she needed to be alone for a few more minutes. Even as tears blurred her vision, she couldn't tear her eyes away from that one word – "*Maman*" – on the envelope. She could hear Antoine's voice in her head saying it. A teardrop plopped onto the ink. She blotted it with her thumb, but it smudged. This upset her more, although she didn't know why.

The fact that she'd found the letter in a box from the storage

135

space in the garage suggested it had been written years ago and then forgotten among the pages of Antoine's old schoolbooks.

But Sandrine didn't believe that. She still clung to the unwavering certainty she'd had since Antoine had died that he would have said goodbye, and she didn't believe the phone call he'd made moments before his death from the hostage's mobile was supposed to be that goodbye. She didn't like to consider what he'd wanted to say in that missed call. Sometimes she hoped he wanted to express his regret; sometimes she was secretly glad her phone had been in silent mode. But *this*, this was his last letter, or his *adieu*, or whatever you wanted to call it. She was sure of that.

The police had asked Sandrine several times if Antoine had written a letter or a notebook. They'd turned his bedroom upside down – the whole house, in fact – without discovering anything like that. At the time, she hadn't known if they thought he'd recorded details of the planned attack, possibly incriminating someone else, or if they believed he might have left behind some sort of pre-confession.

Antoine must have realized the police would raid their home. He probably anticipated that if he left a letter lying around it would be confiscated. And so he'd hidden his last letter for his mother here, in a cardboard box in the roof space of the garage, between the pages of one of his school exercise books. He knew she would find it one day. He may even have imagined that his mother would go rifling through his school exercise books, looking for signs and answers, just as she'd been doing. He'd known her so well. Better than she'd known him in the end.

Taking a deep breath, Sandrine gently opened the envelope, careful not to rip it. Her heart was pounding, beating out of control, out of time with her slow movements. She wasn't sure she wanted to read what her son had written. Did he try to explain? Did he expect her to understand? Forgive him?

Her thoughts were interrupted by Sam calling her again from

inside the house. Again she ignored him, but seconds later he burst into the garage. His eyes widened when he saw her sitting, cross-legged on the ground.

'Sandrine! Come into the house.' He walked towards her, grabbed her hand and pulled her to her feet. 'It's freezing in here. You're crying,' he continued. 'What are you doing in here?'

By way of an answer, she held out the envelope. He was still clutching her hand in one of his. He took the letter with his free hand and examined it.

'From …? Is this from …?'

She looked him in the eyes, willing him to say their son's name. When he didn't, she said, 'From Antoine, yes. It's his writing.'

'Where did you find it?'

'In a box with his schoolbooks.' She pointed behind her and saw him look over her shoulder at the open boxes. 'I think this might be his last letter. His confession or his goodbye or whatever you want to call it.'

'What makes you think that?'

'I've always thought he would leave a message to say goodbye. Or sorry. And we have cream envelopes like that in the house.'

'How did you know to look through the boxes?'

'I didn't. I was looking for …' Sandrine hung her head, shamefaced. 'I wanted to see if there were signs, you know, in his essays or drawings.'

Sam nodded, as if he'd had that thought, too. 'What does the letter say?' he asked tentatively.

'I don't know. I haven't read it yet.'

Without another word, he led her into the house. They went into the living area. Sandrine noticed Sam had lit the log burner. They sat down on the sofa.

'Shall I read it?' he asked.

'Yes.' She leaned into him, breathing in his familiar clean smell, but it did little to calm her.

If Sam was troubled that the letter was addressed only to

Sandrine, he didn't say so. He took three pieces of paper out of the envelope and unfolded them. He started to read aloud. But he only managed the first sentence: 'By the time you find this letter and read it, I'll be dead.'

They read the first two pages in silence, Sam looking up at the end of each page and Sandrine nodding when she'd caught up so he could turn the page or hold up the next one. *I don't want to think about how much I'm going to hurt you*, Antoine had written. There followed several paragraphs from which such self-loathing flowed that it brought a lump to Sandrine's throat and tears to Sam's eyes.

Antoine anticipated all the questions that Sandrine would ask herself. They seemed to stand out, as if highlighted, on the pages and Sandrine knew they would be etched on her brain from now on. *You'll wonder, as I do, when I began to turn bad. You'll ask yourself if this is your fault and what you did wrong.* But Antoine hadn't given any answers. He'd asked himself the same things.

Then the tone changed. From what he'd written, Antoine believed his actions were a necessary evil. *I mustn't bottle out*, he'd written. *The world will be a slightly better place afterwards. That's what I have to tell myself.*

'He was brainwashed,' Sam muttered as he turned the paper over.

Sandrine was blinded by tears as she read the last page. She knew there were whole sentences and even paragraphs that her mind was refusing to absorb. It was too hard to assimilate everything her son had written.

She wiped her eyes on her cardigan sleeve, sighed and read out the last sentences aloud. Her words – or rather Antoine's words – came out as a whisper: 'I know you and *Papa* will blame yourselves. Don't beat yourself up too much, *Maman*. Hold on to the happy memories. You've always loved me unconditionally. Please don't stop. Your son, by any name, Antoine.'

For several minutes neither of them spoke. Sam put down the

pages of the letter and the envelope on the coffee table and took Sandrine's hand.

Sandrine couldn't get the ending of the letter out of her head. Her son had asked her not to stop loving him. That was a given. She couldn't stop loving him even if she tried. Maybe it would be easier if she could. But the question rattling around in her head was had her son loved her? And if so, how could he have done this to her?

It was Sam who broke the silence. 'It's like a suicide note,' he said. 'His mind ... he wasn't right in the ... such destructive thoughts. He knew he was going to die.'

Sandrine made a sound in her throat, something between a whimper and a scoff. She found herself wishing her son had committed suicide, which was a deeply disturbing thought, but it would have been easier than this.

'It wasn't suicide,' she said softly. There was a world of difference between wanting to take one's own life and wanting to take the lives of others. 'It was mass murder.'

Chapter 20

3 MONTHS AFTER

Laura

'Tell me about your nightmare,' Dr McBride said, leaning forwards. He picked up his clipboard from the low table and looked at her intently, pen poised, ready to take notes. This was her cue to talk.

Laura didn't want to go through it all again. She'd already told Declan about it in detail and it had been like reliving the whole incident, albeit with a drastically different outcome. But she supposed if she'd been able to wipe out the night of the terrorist attack and its aftermath from her memory, there would be no point in her seeing a psychologist. Now she was here, she thought she should make an effort.

She sighed. 'There were loud noises. It took me a few seconds to realize what they were. I thought that it was maybe a firecracker or the drums, from on stage, you know?'

Robert nodded.

'The terrorist called Zak was holding his automatic weapon to Claire's head and I wanted to save her. I had to run around people's dead bodies to get to her. At one point, I even trod on someone's foot. It wasn't ...' The foot, in a man's black trainer, had no longer been attached to its body. 'That bit's not relevant.'

She paused. As she was recounting her dream, it seemed very real. She could still picture the scene in detail. It had been so vivid in her mind. She could even smell the powdery odour from the weapons and the metallic stench of the blood.

She could still hear their voices, too, as clearly as if they were standing next to her: Zak's voice, saying to Claire, *Choose! You or her!*, followed by Claire screaming, *Shoot Laura!* She shut the voices out, refusing to listen to them.

The choice Zak had forced Laura to make between herself and Claire always ran like a leitmotif through her nightmares. But there was usually a variation on the original theme, a deviation from what had actually happened. In this particular dream, the tables had been turned. Zak had forced Claire to choose instead. Laura wondered what Claire would have said, had she been in Laura's shoes.

'Go on.'

'Well, Zak was still aiming the weapon at Claire, but before he could shoot either of us, I grabbed the Kalashnikov and gunned down the terrorists. And that was it.'

Laura was picking at the skin around her thumb. It had become a habit. She sat on her hands to stop herself.

For a second or two, Robert said nothing. Laura studied him. His stocky frame was stuffed into a suit that was too small for him, his appearance at odds with that of his office, where everything – the armchairs and cushions, the low table, the large print of a beach cairn – had obviously been designed to create a relaxed, comfortable atmosphere.

'How did you feel?'

'Scared during the dream, but the fear sort of transformed into anger when I woke up.'

'Do you think that might carry a positive message?' Robert

asked. 'Perhaps it shows you're refusing to be a victim. Or maybe it shows you want revenge?'

Laura shrugged. That wasn't how she'd interpreted it. For her, the heroic deeds she'd been capable of in her dream highlighted what a coward she'd actually been. In a fight-or-flight situation, she'd done neither. She hadn't retaliated and she'd remained rooted to the spot. She put this to Dr McBride.

'What do you think would have happened if you had made a run for it, Laura?' he asked gently. They'd been through this before.

'I expect Zak would have shot me in the back,' she said.

'And what would he have done if you'd fought back?'

A half smile briefly played on her lips. She knew where he was going with this. 'He'd probably have shot me down.'

'Do you think it would be fair to say, then, that your survival instincts kicked in? You couldn't put up a fight – the terrorists were armed. And for that very reason, if you'd attempted to make a run for it, you would certainly have been killed. You said so yourself. Don't you think the fact that you neither fought not fled could be what saved you?'

Yeah, that and the fact my friend was killed instead of me, Laura thought to herself. But she hadn't told Robert about that part yet. She hadn't told anyone. It had become a shameful secret she couldn't share, a heavy burden that weighed her down but that she insisted on carrying alone.

Of everything that had happened that night, one incident preyed on her mind more than anything else. The moment when Zak had ordered her to choose between Claire's life and her own. Laura had caused Claire's death and that haunted her night and day. This was what lay behind her recurrent nightmares.

You choose! You or your friend? Who should live? Who must die?

What should she have said? What could she have done? Was there a right answer? One that would have saved both of them? Laura tortured herself with this. She rewrote the scene in her dreams, believing in alternative outcomes, until she woke up and realized all over again that she'd been clinging to a lifeline that had never been thrown.

Zak had made a choice of his own, which also tormented her. He chose to release her. Why did he talk to her? Why did he treat her differently? Was it simply because he recognized her from earlier in the ladies' toilets? Laura thought there must be more to it than that. She suspected Zak had seen something in her that he recognized, some shared characteristic. Much as she hated the idea she had something in common with Zak, she couldn't come up with any other explanation.

'All right,' Robert said, nudging Laura back to the present. 'So you're still having difficulty sleeping and you wake up often when you do sleep due to nightmares. What about the panic attacks?'

'Just as frequent,' Laura said. Then, seeing him frown, she added, 'The breathing techniques you showed me help, though.'

'And did you go to the group therapy session I recommended last Thursday?'

Laura had gone, but she wasn't going back, that was for sure. The hour-long session had taken place at Belfast City Business Centre, a brown-brick building that Laura had found austere and unwelcoming. Most of the people there had been friendly enough, though, but none of them had problems she could relate to. Among them were a bloke in his thirties who was recovering from losing a testicle to cancer but struggling to get over losing his girlfriend, a fifty-year-old woman who had dominated this week's discussion with an elaborate account of her various suicide attempts and an old woman who had either led an unbelievably hard life or else was a compulsive liar. She shook her head at the memory.

'You didn't go?' he asked.

'Yes, I did,' Laura said. 'But it wasn't for me.' While she sort of liked the idea of talking to someone who'd had a similar experience to her, she didn't want to talk about her trauma with a group of complete strangers who were unlikely to understand something she found hard to put into words herself.

'That's a shame. Group sessions can be therapeutic,' Robert said. 'But they're not for everyone. I think you're doing well, Laura. I hope you'll keep coming here regularly. You're talking about the experience itself and your nightmares much more openly and you're getting much better at dealing with your anxiety. In a future session, I'd like to focus more on your social relationships, if that's OK.'

'Social relationships?'

'Yes, you know, your relationships with friends, family, colleagues, that sort of thing. Your social life, too, and whether that has changed as a result of your experience.'

Social life. That would be a short conversation. She'd never been particularly outgoing.

'How did it go?' Declan asked when she emerged from Dr McBride's office into the waiting room. Whenever he was free, he drove her to the consultations. It was just as well since she might have bottled out and cancelled a few otherwise.

'All right,' Laura said. 'I'm getting there. Slowly.'

'Baby steps,' he said. It was his mantra. 'Shall we get a cup of tea or something before I go back to work?'

Work. She was sure Robert would broach that subject sooner or later if they were going to be talking about her social relationships – or lack of them. He was all for her facing her fears and overcoming avoidance.

She couldn't afford to stay off work forever. She'd have to go back at some point. But she couldn't bear the thought of returning to the library knowing that Claire, Ava and Sarah wouldn't be there. She wasn't even interested in books anymore. She'd tried to distract herself with a few good novels, but she couldn't follow the plot in any of them and each time she'd given up after a chapter or two.

'So, what do you say?'

'Sorry, Declan, what?'

'Do you want to grab something to drink?'

'No, I should let you head on. I'll catch you later when you get home.'

Once Declan had dropped her off, Laura began pacing the living area of her flat, looking at the phone in her hand. She'd been thinking about Sarah since Robert had brought up her friends and colleagues. She thought about her a lot. She'd texted her a couple of times. But she hadn't once been to see her. She felt awful about that, but she couldn't bring herself to do it.

It was strange because although she felt the need to discuss what she'd been through with someone who would understand, she'd been avoiding Sarah. Maybe it was because Sarah had come out of it so much worse than she had. A few weeks after coming home from France, she'd bumped into Mrs Lynch in Belfast. Mrs Lynch told her that Sarah was in a wheelchair. How could Laura discuss her nightmares, flashbacks and fears with Sarah when she might never walk again?

Did it not occur to you that she might feel the need to talk to you? She has lost her friends and colleagues, too, and she couldn't go back to work right now even if she wanted to. Perhaps she needs your support. For once, the voice in her head berating her didn't sound anything like her mother's. It was unmistakably her own.

The call went to voicemail. Laura left a message, asking Sarah if she'd be up for a visit one of these days. She decided that if Sarah didn't get back to her, she'd ring again. She'd neglected her friend for far too long.

Chapter 21

Sandrine

In the months following the terrorist attack, Sandrine had hardly left the house. The incident in the supermarket had unsettled her. She understood Béatrice's reaction. Everyone she knew would react the same way as her son's former boss. But she was even more terrified of bumping into strangers who knew who she was, like the cashier who had kept her change. Above all, she was troubled by the idea that she might meet someone who had known one of her son's victims – a family member, a friend or a loved one.

Her home had become both a self-imposed prison and a safe house. But she couldn't stay confined there forever. She needed to get out for some fresh air. Her town was in the foothills of the *Monts d'Or* and Sandrine thought it unlikely she would run into many people walking along the woodland paths on a cold weekday. So she put on a coat, gloves, woolly hat and some walking boots and set off.

It was snowing lightly, but it wasn't yet sticking on the ground.

Sandrine felt calmer than she had for many weeks. It was good to be out in the elements. She should make it a habit to get out and walk a few kilometres every day.

As she walked, the snow got heavier. And suddenly a memory hurtled unbidden into her mind, hitting her hard, like an icy snowball in the face. She and Sam had taken the boys up here one winter, to the top of *Mont Thou*. Antoine was about ten or eleven at the time and Max seven or eight. They'd built a snowman, had a snowball fight and sledged down the slope on the plastic toboggans Sam had bought from the supermarket.

Winded by the memory, Sandrine stopped walking and bent over, trying to catch her breath. She remembered Antoine pulling his younger brother's sledge as well as his own as the two boys trudged back up the hill. A rush of love enveloped her.

She thought of the cliché about the Inuit people having fifty or so words for snow and wondered why there was only one word for love. In French, *aimer* meant both 'like' and 'love', which seemed inadequate to describe all the different emotions love could encompass. There should be more words. Love was not enough. That scary, heady feeling of falling uncontrollably in love when she'd first met Sam had nothing to do with the secure, trusting relationship they'd grown into after twenty years of marriage. Similarly, she loved both her sons. But now, after what Antoine had done, she no longer felt the same way about him as she did about Maxime.

She still loved Antoine. How could she not? Loving him was both the easiest and the hardest thing she'd ever done. For where once her love had been unconditional and unquestioning, it was now tinged with shame and tainted with guilt. She'd lost her son. But what Sandrine had lost couldn't be equated with the loss of the families of her son's victims. How could she grieve for her son when others were grieving because of him? She told herself she had no right to pain when her son had inflicted such unspeakable pain on others.

In the beginning Sam would say, 'It's not your fault. It's not our fault.' He repeated it so often that it almost became a mantra. Privately Sandrine thought that he was trying to convince himself as much as her. But no matter how often he said those words to her, or how often she said them to herself, she continued to carry her guilt with her everywhere, wrapped around her like a shroud.

Sandrine turned around and walked back the way she'd come. Despite her gloves, her hands were aching from the cold. When she reached her road, she let out a loud sigh of relief. She realized theirs was the only house in the street with no traditional candles on the windowsills for Lyon's annual festival of lights.

Sandrine didn't notice the broken glass at first. The writing had grabbed her attention instead. She stood by the car in the driveway and stared at the huge red letters daubed across the front door. The paint had run, making it appear as if the three-word obscenity had been written in blood.

She took two slow steps forwards. The glass crunched under-foot. She looked down at the tiny fragments, glittering like diamonds in the late afternoon sun. Then she turned her head and saw that the car window had been smashed. Peering through the broken window, she could see a brick on the passenger's seat. She leant in closer and worked out what was sitting on the driver's seat as much from the stench as from the sight of it. Faeces. Human excrement, by the looks – and smell – of it. Someone had put shit in her car, or more likely, had got into the car and defecated.

Turning away, she bent over and retched. Nothing came up. She hadn't eaten since breakfast. Straightening up, she read the words on the front door again. *Fils de pute.* Son of a bitch. In three monosyllabic words, the graffitist had managed to insult both Antoine and her.

It had been a while since their property had been defaced. It had happened five or six times altogether. The last time was back in October. She and Sam had come home from a week at her parents' house in Brittany to discover dog mess smeared across their porch and the racial slur "*Sale Arabe*" – Filthy Arab – scored into the paintwork on the driver's side of Sandrine's car. The vandals didn't display much imagination. Different forms of the same idea every time.

Sandrine sighed and forced back the tears that threatened to spill down her face. They hadn't been badgered by journalists, as she'd feared at first. There had been a few, but they'd remained civil. They had mostly called on the phone rather than at the door. They'd been pushy, but polite, feigning sympathy and trying to cajole them into telling their side of the story.

But this sort of intrusion into their lives was much harder to deal with. It made no difference to Sandrine if the messages were racist or not. It didn't matter who specifically was targeted – Sandrine herself, Sam and her, or Antoine. There was disrespect and disgust in the insults, but for Sandrine it was the act itself that exuded sheer hatred.

And yet, saddened as she was, she felt relatively little animosity towards the vandals, whoever they were. Each time she cleared up the mess, had the car repaired, changed the slashed tyre with Sam, or scrubbed off the graffiti, she felt as if it was all no more than she deserved.

She walked stoically towards the front door. Careful not to stain her clothes with the still-wet paint as she opened it, she went inside, returning a minute later with a bucket of hot soapy water, some rags, a sponge and a bottle of solvent.

Sandrine rolled up her sleeves and got to work. Some of the paint came off easily enough as it hadn't had time to dry. She'd taken off her woollen gloves, but she'd forgotten to bring out her rubber gloves. She looked at her hands, startled. They looked as if they were covered in blood rather than red paint. Startled, Sandrine fetched her rubber gloves and went back to scrubbing the door, then she swept up the broken glass and finally cleaned out the mess in her car and shampooed the car seat.

When she'd finished, she washed her hands, scrubbing at some stubborn traces of paint under her nails and on her palms. Then she took a long, hot shower.

As she was coming out of the bathroom, she heard Sam's car pull into the drive. She knew he would notice the broken car window and the faint red smears on the front door. He'd be furious.

'Sandrine!' he shouted, bursting into the house. 'We have to go to the police.'

'Sam, they won't do anything about it. You know they won't.'

'We can't accept deliberate damage to our private property, Sandrine,' he said. 'It's been going on for far too long and we never report it.'

They never reported it because Sandrine always refused to. She was grateful to him for not blaming her. He could easily have said '*you* never report it' instead of 'we'.

'You're right,' she conceded. 'I'll go to the police station tomorrow.'

Later that evening, as Sam watched the television and Sandrine sat silently next to him on the sofa, she realized that until now she'd accepted other people's treatment of her unquestioningly: she'd been upset, but not surprised, when her friend Angélique no longer wanted anything to do with her; she'd understood when Béatrice had barred her from the supermarket and she'd felt sorry for the cashier; she repaired the damage to her home every time without complaining. She'd taken it all as her due, as if it were part and parcel of her son's legacy.

But perhaps she should shift her focus from penance to repentance. She didn't believe in God. Religion had caused more than enough problems in this world in Sandrine's view. But she did feel a strong need to atone for her son's wrongs.

The terrorist attack had impacted countless people, not just those who had been in the epicentre of the event – the victims and their families, the witnesses, survivors and first responders, but it had also indirectly touched many others all over the world. The ripple effect, wasn't that what it was called? The term didn't seem appropriate to Sandrine. Instead of small circles spreading across the surface of a pond, she visualized a tsunami building up in the ocean.

A plan was forming in her head. There was something she could do, but she couldn't do it without Sam. He switched off the television and listened without interrupting as she told him what she had in mind. For a few seconds, he didn't react and Sandrine thought he would refuse to help her. But then he nodded slowly.

'All right,' he said. 'Let's do this.'

Sandrine leapt up from the sofa and almost ran to the kitchen, where she grabbed the pad and pen they used to make their shopping lists. Sam followed her at a more sedate pace. Then, sitting side by side at the kitchen table, they batted around ideas and Sandrine jotted them down. This was how she could reach out to the people who had suffered at the hands of her son and make amends.

Chapter 22

4 MONTHS AFTER

Laura

No sooner had the Hallowe'en decorations come down than the Christmas decorations were up. All over Belfast – in the shops, in the squares, in people's homes. The big Christmas Lights Switch-on had taken place the previous evening at City Hall. It seemed to get earlier every year.

Laura usually got out some tinsel, baubles and fairy lights, which brightened up her dull flat for one month a year, although she never could manage a Christmas tree, artificial or real. She hated the sight of them. Even the smell of them reminded her of her father, arousing a memory Laura did her best to suppress.

This year, though, she wouldn't be putting up any decorations at all. She wouldn't be sending any Christmas cards, either. She would have a turkey dinner with Noreen and no doubt work her way through most of the chocolates in the Quality Street tin. She would watch a lot of TV, as she did every year. But it didn't seem right to be celebrating.

Like Claire, Ava had been killed outright in the terrorist attack, as Laura had found out a week or so after coming home from Lyon. Claire's and Ava's families would be spending their first Christmas without them. Laura knew what it was like to be without a loved one at this time of year. Especially when that loved one had been mercilessly murdered.

Laura knew Sarah wouldn't be in a festive mood either. She would have Claire and Ava on her mind, too. Laura had rung Sarah several times over the previous weeks but each time the call went to voicemail. Why didn't Sarah answer or ring her back? Maybe she didn't actually get her mobile back that night. Or perhaps she didn't want to meet anyone who would drag up memories of the horrific ordeal she'd had to face. She might resent the fact Laura hadn't got in touch earlier. Laura could hardly blame her.

A few days ago, she'd walked to Sarah's flat in Belfast, but the name on the buzzer had changed. She must have moved away, which stood to reason. She couldn't live there alone, on the second floor with no lift, if she was in a wheelchair. Laura knew Sarah's parents lived twelve miles away, in Bangor. She should look up their number or get it from her colleagues at the library again. At least that way she could ask after Sarah.

Christmas, Sarah, the anniversary of her father's death. It all made Laura feel low and lonely. She was having dinner at Declan and Patrick's that evening, which she was looking forward to. But in the meantime, she needed to be around someone or find something to keep herself occupied. She rang Noreen and asked if she could pop round, but her mother had other plans.

'You can't expect me to drop everything for you, dear,' Noreen said.

She didn't fancy staying in, watching Netflix with only the cat for company. So she went to the pool. She was a hopeless swimmer, but it did her good and she got out of the water afterwards feeling tired but pleased with herself. On her way through the foyer towards the exit, she noticed a flyer on the noticeboard for Zumba lessons. That sounded like fun. A good way to meet people and make new friends. She took her phone out of her bag and snapped a photo of the flyer.

Once she got home, she made herself a sandwich and, sitting next to Harry on the sofa with her feet resting on the coffee table, she booted up her laptop. While doing her lengths in the pool, she'd reflected on her last session with Robert. He'd suggested it would help her to learn from other people's experiences, but she didn't want to try group therapy again. There was bound to be help on the Internet, though.

She typed keywords in English into the search engine and trawled through several online articles, reading eyewitness accounts of terrorist attacks such as the Madrid train bombings in 2004 or the London Underground bombings in July 2005. She scrolled through similar stories in French by survivors of the 2015 terrorist attack on the Bataclan theatre in Paris and the 2016 truck attack in Nice.

Then she spotted the image of someone she recognized. She clicked on the link below the picture and watched the video. It was an interview for a French news channel with Henri Charbonnier, one of her fellow hostages. He recounted how he'd been forced to take his mobile phone to the police so that the terrorists could negotiate with them. Laura remembered it well. Zak had threatened to kill Henri's wife, Elodie, if he didn't come back.

These were people who had been in the corridor with her. If anyone could understand what she was going through, they could. But this wasn't what she was looking for. She didn't want to read in-depth descriptions of something she remembered clearly herself. She wanted to find inspiration from survivors and learn from them. How had they coped? What steps did they take to carry on living their lives afterwards? Above all, she wanted to know how they'd got rid of that crushing feeling of guilt at surviving when their loved ones hadn't.

And that's when she stumbled on it. A support portal for survivors and families of the victims of the terrorist attack at *La Voie Lactée*. The website looked to be still partially under construction and when she clicked on the various tabs, not all the pages opened. But there were already resources such as helpline numbers, where to get treatment, advice on how to support a victim of terrorism and on how to handle media attention as well as links to charities for people who wanted to make a donation.

What grabbed Laura's attention, though, was the forum. On it, people had started threads by sharing their experience or asking questions, and for most of these posts, there was an overwhelming number of supportive answers.

You could read the posts on the forum without registering, but you had to be a member to publish a message. Laura started to fill in the online form with her email address and her country of residence. She chose a username and a password. Easy enough so far. Then came the reason why she wanted to join. This was optional, but Laura didn't want to leave that box blank. She typed in French, *To connect with people who have had a similar experience to me.* The profile picture was also optional. Laura skipped that bit. Finally, she just had to click on all the photos showing traffic lights to prove she wasn't a robot and that was it. A message appeared to inform her that her application was now pending approval by a moderator.

She didn't expect to get confirmation straight away – according to the message, it could take up to twenty-four hours – and the support portal didn't even enter her thoughts that evening at Declan and Patrick's.

Her cousin and his partner were in great spirits and it was good to catch up with them. They'd made a half-hearted effort at putting up Christmas decorations, which consisted of some worn-looking tinsel around the picture frames on the walls and a small tree by the radiator that had shed more needles onto the floor than it had kept on its branches.

Two or three times a week since it had happened, Laura had come here for dinner. Declan and Patrick took it in turns to make the meal and Laura brought the beer or the wine and the dessert. Patrick was no cook and whenever it was his turn, he either had the food delivered or else picked something up on his way home, although he varied the takeaway restaurants – Chinese, Indian, Sushi, fish and chips …

That evening it was Patrick's turn and pizza. They usually watched a film or a series, but this evening they played a card game. Declan won, which was just as well since he was a notoriously bad loser.

'What have you got up your sleeve?'

Laura didn't realize Patrick was speaking literally until Declan shook out the arms of his sweater and several cards fell onto the floor. That made them all laugh.

Laura was still giggling as she drove back home, but at the same time something was niggling her. She was worried about intruding on Declan's and Patrick's lives – they'd been so supportive and the last thing she wanted to do was become a burden. But she enjoyed their company and for the minute she desperately needed them. She was doing her best to stand on her own two feet, though. She felt as if she was making progress in her sessions with Robert and finding ways of moving forwards, ways of healing.

That reminded Laura of her membership request to the terrorist attack support portal. As soon as she got home, she checked her phone. And there it was. She'd received an email, informing her that her application had been approved. She just had to click on a link to confirm her email address.

She decided to post a message on the forum right away. That was the reason she'd become a member, after all. She changed into her pyjamas, made herself a mug of herbal tea, sat cross-legged on her bed with her laptop on her knees – she would be able to type more quickly on that than on her phone – and logged in to the website.

She needed to choose between two of the categories: "Survivors of *La Voie Lactée* terrorist attacks" or "Those who lost loved ones and friends". She typed a few lines in French about herself in the "survivors" category.

My name is Laura. I'm 30 years old. I'm from Northern Ireland. I came on holiday to Lyon with some friends to see *The Naturals* in August. Two of my friends were killed and another one was seriously injured during the terrorist attack on *La Voie Lactée* concert hall. I was one of the eleven hostages. I was released unharmed.

She reread her message. It occurred to her that the last sentence was far from true, so she added one word that for her said it all: physically. I was released physically unharmed. Then she clicked on *envoyer* – send.

Chapter 23

4 MONTHS AFTER

Sandrine

They hadn't seen Maxime for four days. This wasn't unusual and Sandrine wished he would spend more time at home, but she didn't want him to come back in the evenings after school because he was forced to, but because he wanted to. Clearly, that wasn't the case. He slept over at his friends' houses, on their sofas – more than he slept in his own bed – and she couldn't blame him. She imagined he wanted to get as far away from home as possible. This house had an atmosphere of shame and sorrow, guilt and grief.

Even though there were no longer any photos of Antoine on the walls and none of his stuff lying around, everything here served as a reminder of him and there was no getting away from what Antoine had done, no getting away from Antoine himself. So, as much as Sandrine wanted Maxime to be around more, she tried not to put any pressure on him. All any mother could wish for her child was that he was happy, and if Maxime was happier somewhere else, Sandrine had to accept that. She could certainly understand it.

When she sent text messages to Maxime, he replied. Maybe not immediately, but she always got an answer. When she asked where he was, he told her – he was usually at his friend Benoît's house. At least that way she didn't worry about him. She did worry, though, that she might be doing something wrong. Was she neglecting him because she was so caught up in her grief over Antoine?

'Do you think we give Maxime enough attention?' she'd asked Sam one day.

'It would be far easier to give him attention if he came home more often,' Sam had growled. Then, no doubt seeing her expression, he'd softened. 'He's seventeen. We have to give him some responsibility and freedom. We can't keep him cooped up so that we can keep an eye on him. He would think we didn't trust him. He knows we're here if he needs us.'

She would have to get used to Maxime leaving home altogether soon enough. He'd talked about moving to Marseille at one point, although Sandrine didn't know if that was still his intention. Even if he stayed in Lyon to study after his *baccalauréat* exams, it would be no more than a few years before he left home for good.

Sandrine was overjoyed when he strolled through the front door that Friday evening. She'd hoped he would. He came home on average every other weekend, if only so he could dump his dirty clothes in the laundry basket and pick up some clean ones.

When he did come home, she did her best to make everything comfortable and pleasant for him. She didn't badger him about anything; she tiptoed around the house until midday at the weekends so he could sleep in. She tried to get the balance right, showing an interest in his life but not asking so many questions that he would feel as if he were being interrogated.

Now he was home, Sandrine was determined to make this weekend as enjoyable for him as possible. She hoped Maxime would want to do something with Sam and her, go out together as a family. They could go into Lyon. She was dreading their first Christmas without Antoine, but perhaps they could go to the Christmas market anyway. There were always lovely arts and crafts things there, and there would be stalls selling hot red wine to warm them up. Or maybe there was a film they could all watch together on television or at the cinema.

She cooked his favourite meal for dinner – *boeuf bourguignon* – and as he tucked in, she put her suggestions to him. His answer came as a bit of a blow.

'I'm going to *Mamie* and *Papy* Hamadi's tomorrow,' he said, his mouth full of food.

'For *Papy*'s birthday?' Sam asked.

Sandrine threw her husband a look of surprise. He hadn't seen his parents for several years and yet he was clearly thinking about his father's birthday.

'That's right. Abdel's taking me. He'll pick me up just before lunchtime. They'll all be there.'

That meant Sam's parents, his brother Abdel with his wife, Yasmine, and their four children, Max's cousins. There would be couscous on the menu, Sandrine knew. From what Abdel and Maxime had told her, Sam's mother still made the North African dish in the traditional way, rolling the semolina by hand and using a copper couscoussier.

Sandrine felt torn. She'd always been pleased that her sons had been able to see Sam's family thanks to Abdel, even though she resented Sam's parents for their lack of toleration when it came to Sam and her. But they'd offered Sam no support whatsoever when Antoine had died. Her own parents had been amazing, but Sam's parents hadn't so much as sent a message or a card.

'Surely they must know what it's like to lose a son,' she'd said to Sam at the time.

'They didn't lose me,' he'd retorted. 'They discarded me. There's no comparison.'

She realized her logic was flawed, although she wondered

160

whether her parents-in-law had now disowned their eldest grandson in their minds too. But she didn't bring it up again.

As far as she knew, this was the first time Maxime would see them since the events of the summer. She supposed she should be grateful they still invited him. Perhaps without admitting it to herself, she had apportioned some of the blame for Antoine's actions to Sam's parents. After all, they'd represented his only contact with the Islamic faith during his childhood.

But her resentment was infused with guilt that she could think that way at all. Antoine had made his own choices. What he had done was no more the fault of Sam's parents than it was Sandrine and Sam's fault. And there was a world of difference between being a practising Muslim, like Sam's parents were, and becoming an extremist or a terrorist as Antoine had.

Sam didn't talk about his parents a lot, but when he did, he always spoke highly of them, even though they hadn't welcomed Sandrine into the family. Sam had had a happy childhood, like Sandrine. They'd been brought up differently, but they'd been indoctrinated in similar values. Sam's parents had taught him right from wrong, just as Sandrine and Sam had brought up their own children according to those principles.

'Shall we go into Lyon and buy *Papy* a present?' Sandrine asked Maxime.

'Already sorted, *Maman*. Don't fuss,' Maxime said.

'I'm sure you'll have a lovely time,' she said brightly. She hoped her tone of voice concealed what she felt. She still didn't want Maxime to go, although she couldn't tell if it was because she didn't want him to see Sam's parents or because she would have preferred him to spend the day with her and Sam.

Chapter 24

Laura

There wasn't a lot of food left in the fridge and cupboards. Laura would have to go out and buy some groceries. She couldn't remember the last time she'd had any appetite. She hated going to the supermarket at the moment. She wasn't inspired and bought very little.

Laura knocked on Mrs Doherty's door to see if she needed her to run any errands. The elderly woman handed Laura two envelopes.

'Would you pop these into a letterbox for me?' she asked Laura. 'They're for my granddaughters. Both at university now, at Trinity, so they are.'

'Of course, Mrs Doherty.'

'I took evening classes, you know,' Mrs Doherty said, peering at Laura over her glasses, 'but I couldn't get my old head around this Internet yoke. So I'll stick to snail mail – that's what they call it, isn't it?'

Her neighbour's talk of the Internet reminded Laura of the

forum. She was keen to see if anyone had posted a response to the message she'd written. As soon as she got back from the supermarket, she booted up her laptop and logged into the support portal.

She'd received four replies. The first was from another concert-goer who had had a seat near the back of the arena. She and her boyfriend had both escaped and were safely outside minutes after the first round of gunshots had burst out.

The second was from a man who had played dead in the pits and managed to leave the venue once the terrorists had taken the hostages – including Laura – to the corridor on the floor above. As she read his words, Laura's mind flashed back to her own ordeal and the moment when she had lain immobile on the floor, willing herself not to move, so that the gunmen would assume she was dead.

The memory made her shudder. She tried to shut out the images projecting themselves in her head, but they kept coming, one after the other. She remembered thinking that they would see her shaking and that would give the game away. In the end, one of the terrorists had kicked her in the side, catching her out, but instead of shooting her, he'd hauled her to her feet.

Her mouth felt dry and her hands were clammy. She was shaking now, feeling cold all over, just as she had that night. She fetched herself a glass of water, then sat back at the computer. She should stop. This was too much for her. Perhaps she shouldn't read the other messages at all.

She reached out to close the lid of her laptop, but her hand hovered over the computer. *You wanted to hear from people who had similar experiences*, she told herself. *These people have been through the same thing.* She felt she owed it to them to at least have a look at what they had to say. Plus, it might help her, as she'd hoped. She took a few sips of water and looked at the screen again.

The next one was written by a father who had taken his son

and his son's friend to the concert. His son had died of his injuries a week after the terrorist attack. The father and the son's friend hadn't been hurt. His account was succinct and factual. He described neither his emotions nor his reactions, but it still made for a heart-wrenching read. Laura wondered if he'd seen his son gunned down in front of him, just as she'd witnessed Zak shooting Claire. That memory exploded before her eyes like a bright orange firework. Tears rolled down her cheeks.

Once again she wondered if she should stop there. Was this doing her more harm than good? *There's only one message left*, she thought. *You can do it.* She wiped her eyes with her sleeve and blinked to bring the final message into focus. It was from a man who had carried his injured fiancée along a corridor and outside to safety through a fire escape. He went on to say that his fiancée's injuries hadn't turned out to be serious and that she was now dealing with psychological rather than physical damage. The man told Laura that they'd been fortunate. It could have been worse, for both him and his girlfriend.

Laura could identify with this. She felt fortunate, too. She'd been spared. She didn't know why, but she had survived the attack. She hadn't been wounded and had only psychological scars. Ava and Claire hadn't been so lucky. Neither had Sarah. She'd been badly injured. She was bound to be struggling with both physical and psychological trauma. Laura wished she knew how her friend was doing.

All of the messages, even the one from the father who had lost his son, began by saying how sorry they were for Laura's loss before describing their own experiences. Each account had been condensed into no more than three or four sentences, summarizing an event that would cause them a lifetime of pain. Laura realized that there was so much more behind each story, so much that was left unsaid.

These people – these strangers – had had similar experiences to her, but despite being in the same place at the same time, everyone had a slightly different story to tell. But everyone involved had been damaged in some way. None of them would ever be the same again. There was a before and an after the night of the terrorist attack.

Laura wanted to reply to each message, but what could she say? How could anyone express their sorrow or sympathy? But surely it was better to say something than nothing at all. So Laura replied to all of the comments on the thread she'd created, each in turn, offering her condolences, too, even though it seemed shallow to her, as if she were spouting trite platitudes.

She sighed as she typed more or less the same thing four times. She'd been hoping to make contact with someone who was encountering the same difficulties as her. She'd done that, but it hadn't had the effect she'd expected. She'd thought she might find some inspiration that would help her with her own healing that she could then pass forwards to someone else. But this was so anonymous; it was all too detached. She couldn't put faces to these people. Like her, most of them hadn't added a profile picture and they were going by their usernames, not their real names, and although she could relate to what had happened to them, the connection stopped there.

As she posted her last message, another reply to her post appeared. The username was *Famille Morvan*. It started in a similar way to the others, but this one stood out. It had been written in English instead of French. Laura read it. Then she reread it more slowly.

Hello Laura,

I was very moved to read your message and can only imagine what you've been going through. I'm so sorry about your friends.

My son died that night, too. It has been a difficult time for my family and me. We'll never get over it, but we're doing our best to get through it.

165

I am French and I live on the outskirts of Lyon, but many years ago, I spent a year in the UK, where I worked as a language assistant, and I know that when I was worried or agitated or upset, I found it hard to express myself in English. In difficult situations, I always felt the need to revert to my mother tongue. My English is a little rusty, but if you'd prefer to exchange with someone in your own language, or even a mixture of French and English, please don't hesitate to contact me. I would love to hear from you. famille.morvan@tellcommnet.fr

Laura couldn't tell if the message had been posted by a man or a woman – a father or a mother. It occurred to her that had it been written in French, she would have known this because of the gender agreements. The email address and username didn't give any clues. Presumably, Morvan was a surname, but there was no first name. It appeared to be an account for the whole family. She thought of the man who had posted earlier, the one who had lost his son at the concert. This person had also lost a son.

Laura found it ironic that even though she didn't know the gender or first name of the person who had written to her, the message seemed more personal than the others. It had somehow struck a chord within Laura.

Without giving it any more thought, she brought up her emails on her laptop and clicked to start a new one. This time the words came easily. It wasn't simply because she was writing in English, but also because this person had reached out to Laura and she felt a connection. And a glimmer of hope.

Chapter 25

4 MONTHS AFTER

Sandrine

Sandrine still felt a little uneasy when the doorbell rang the next day. She walked with Max to the end of the drive and Abdel leapt out of the car to give her a warm hug.

'We'll have Maxime back by early evening,' he promised as though reading her mind. 'He says he still has some homework to do.'

'Thank you.'

Abdel let go of Sandrine. She leaned in through the open driver's door to greet Yasmine, who was sitting in the passenger seat of Abdel's Renault Grand Scenic.

'Hello,' Yasmine said in a quiet voice.

Abdel's wife was shy. She was ten years younger than Abdel and eight years younger than Sam and Sandrine. She didn't say much to anyone, although she smiled a lot. Sandrine was surprised to notice she was wearing a headscarf. It covered her hair, but not her pretty, round face. Perhaps it was for the benefit of Abdel's parents, although Sam's mother hadn't been wearing any head covering the one time she'd seen her. She'd never seen Yasmine in a headscarf before, but then she'd only ever seen her indoors – either at Abdel and Yasmine's home or at her own. Secretly, Sandrine thought it was a shame. She had such lovely long, shiny hair.

Sandrine said hello to the four children. The smallest two kids were in the seats in the boot and Maxime was now sitting between Abdel and Yasmine's two eldest in the back seat.

'Hi, Aunt Sandrine,' they chorused.

'Wow! Haven't you all grown?'

'We must get together some time soon,' Abdel said.

'That would be good,' Sam replied. Sandrine hadn't realized he was behind her.

They hadn't had a meal together for a while. They used to have barbecues in the summer and dinner parties in the winter. They would take it in turns to host. Sandrine knew how much Sam loved these family gatherings. Had that stopped because of Antoine? Perhaps, like all Sam and Sandrine's friends, Abdel and Yasmine didn't want to associate with them anymore. Or maybe they didn't know what to say around them or to them. But Sandrine rejected those notions. Abdel had been very supportive after it happened and he still called at least once a week to ask how Sam was. He'd spoken to both her and Maxime on the phone, too.

'That would be lovely, Abdel,' she said.

Sam put his arm around her as Abdel drove away. It felt nice. After Antoine had died, he hadn't touched her for ages, but he gave her an occasional hug now and then for no particular reason and he held her hand in bed again, like he used to, until they fell asleep.

They waved them off, watching the car disappear around the bend in the road, and Sandrine felt more relaxed about Maxime going. He would enjoy himself with his uncle and aunt, cousins and grandparents and it would do him good.

With Max gone for the afternoon, Sandrine knew what she wanted to do. She'd been itching to boot up her computer for a few days, ever since she'd received that email. She'd been wondering how to phrase her reply, turning sentences around in her head. Even though she couldn't tell the whole truth, she wanted to be as truthful as possible.

As if she'd spoken her thoughts out loud, Sam asked, 'So, how's the website coming along? Anything new?'

When Sandrine had first told Sam about her idea, he hadn't been very enthusiastic. She'd hoped that he would help her with it – after all, web design was his job – and show her what she needed to do as moderator. He did both those things without questioning Sandrine's motives. He seemed to understand she wanted to do this as a way of trying to help – even in a small way – everyone who had suffered at the hands of their son. But Sandrine sensed his heart wasn't in it.

Sam's main concern about the website, Sandrine suspected, was that their identity had to remain a secret. No one could ever know that the support portal had been set up by the parents of one of the terrorists. Sandrine had qualms about this, too, but she told herself – and Sam – that this was the only way they could reach out to people affected by the shooting at *La Voie Lactée*.

Sam worked diligently on the website and spent every spare minute on it. But he remained aloof. Once it was up and running, however, he showed more interest. They were inundated with messages from people who had been injured during the attack or had witnessed it; people who had lost loved ones; first responders on the night in question and volunteers, especially health care professionals, who wanted to offer help and advice.

To Sandrine's delight, Sam decided he wanted to be involved every step of the way. They continued to work tirelessly on the website nearly every evening. It had given them something to do and something to talk about. It brought them closer together and helped to bridge the gap that had formed after the night it had all happened.

As they walked back up the path to the house, Sam kept his arm around Sandrine's shoulders. She didn't answer him immediately. She hadn't intended to say anything to Sam about the email, but now that he'd asked, she wanted to tell him.

'Yes. There is something new.'

Sam stopped in the hallway and looked at Sandrine attentively.

'There's this woman, from Northern Ireland. Her username is Belfast Girl. She's from the same city as the band that played in *La Voie Lactée* that night. I approved her membership request and she posted a message on the forum.' Sandrine paused, worried that Sam would think her silly, or worse, obsessed. 'I replied on her thread, then she wrote me an email.'

'OK. What did she say?'

'That she was there, that night.'

'A lot of people who have posted on the forum were at the concert.'

'True.' Sandrine was about to drop the subject. She shouldn't have mentioned it.

'So, what makes her so special?'

Sandrine shook her head. How could she explain to Sam that she wanted to know everything about Antoine's words and actions that night? She knew her son and he would have shown some humanity at the end. Would her husband understand her need to prove that, if only to herself?

'Come on,' he coaxed. 'There must be something about her if you gave her your email address so she could write to you. Tell me.'

Sandrine took a deep breath. 'Her name is Laura. She was one of the eleven hostages,' she said. 'She must have been one of the last people to see Antoine alive.'

From: Laura Davison
To: famille.morvan@tellcommnet.fr
Mon, 17 Dec at 14:47
Subject: forum for survivors & families of victims

Hello,

Thank you for your reply to my message on the forum. I was so excited about finding this website. I felt the need to see how other people in my situation were coping. It's such a good idea. I think it must be recent because not all the pages seem to be active yet. I expect it's even more useful for people who live in France. Perhaps I should contact the moderator and offer to translate the website into English.

You are right about it being easier for me to communicate in English! It was a struggle while I was in France to understand everything that was going on and to talk in French. It was even more difficult, of course, on the night of the terrorist attack because everyone was speaking so fast and because I had to concentrate even though I was panicking. Afterwards, the doctors and police officers mainly spoke to me in English.

I think your English is excellent! I studied French at university and loved it, but unfortunately I fell ill and I didn't complete my course. I've kept up my comprehension skills over the years by reading French novels and listening to the French news. You can forget a foreign language so quickly! I hadn't spoken much French since I left uni, but it came back quickly in the few days I spent in Lyon.

I'd never been to France before last August. My friends and I were on holiday there. I didn't want to go to tell you the truth – I'm not very outgoing and I'm terrified of flying! But we all loved the band and couldn't get tickets to see them here in Belfast. I thought the city was beautiful, especially the basilica and the old quarter.

I'm afraid I don't know your name. Is Morvan your surname? I wasn't sure if I should start my email with 'Dear Mr Morvan' or 'Dear Mrs Morvan'!

I'm so sorry about your son. You must miss him terribly. What was his name?

I hope to hear from you soon,
Laura

De : Famille Morvan
À : laura.davison@ezmail.co.uk
Dim 23 Dec à 11:30
Sujet : Rép : forum for survivors & families of victims

Dear Laura,

Thank you for your email. I'm sorry it has taken me so long to answer. Let me introduce myself. My name is Sandrine but when I was living in England, my friends there called me Sandy, so you can call me Sandy if you prefer! You've guessed correctly about Morvan being my surname. It's my maiden name. It's a Breton name as my family are from Brittany. I grew up there and I enjoyed living near the sea. I would like to move back there, but my husband works in Lyon. Maybe one day ...

I have a confession to make after reading your email. I am the moderator for this website! I set it up because I wanted to help people, like myself, who have lost loved ones and friends or who didn't know where to turn. If you have time, I think your idea of translating the website into English is a great one! As the band was from the UK, there must have been lots of English-speaking people at the concert. We could do it together, if you like. Perhaps this would be a good way for me to brush up on my English and for you to keep up your French!

Thank you for asking about my son. His name was Antoine. He worked at *La Voie Lactée* as a barman and he was there that night. He was nineteen. We all miss him very much: me, my husband Sam, and Antoine's younger brother Maxime. Antoine was in higher education and wanted to work in the hotel industry. My sons got on well together. It was a terrible shock for all of us to lose Antoine in such a sudden and unexpected way. I'm sure you miss your friends, too. You said in your post on the forum that two of your friends died and one of them was injured. What were your friends like? I'm sure they were generous and helpful like you. How about your friend who was wounded? How badly injured was she (or he)?

More importantly, how are you? It must have been terrifying for you to be taken hostage. If you think it might help to talk about it, I'm not a doctor or anything, but I am a good listener!

It was lovely to hear from you and I hope you will keep in touch.

All the best,
Sandy

Chapter 26

Laura

Despite driving at a careful pace, Laura arrived in Bangor nearly twenty minutes early. On the way, she'd thought about the email from Sandy who had asked how badly injured her friend was. Laura hadn't replied to the email yet because she didn't know the answer. But she was about to find out.

Once she'd parked, she paced up and down the seafront, past Bangor Marina and back to the harbour. She pulled the collar of her coat up against the blustery weather and thrust her hands into her pockets. She told herself she was stretching her legs, but deep down she knew she was anxious about seeing Sarah. She hadn't seen her since the night of the terrorist attack. What should she say? What if she said something wrong?

The B&B that Sarah's parents ran in Seacliff Road was a beautiful, cream-coloured three-storey traditional townhouse. Laura had never been to the house before, but she knew that Sarah had grown up here. A ramp ran adjacent to the steps up to the front door. It must have been added because of Sarah's injury when she'd moved back in with her parents.

Laura rang the doorbell and smoothed down her red hair, which she thought must be more dishevelled than usual because of her windy walk along the promenade.

The door was opened by Mrs Lynch. A round-faced woman, she looked like Sarah, right down to the bright blue eyes and the fair hair scraped back into a ponytail.

'Hi, Laura. How lovely to see you again. Come in quick, pet. It's freezing out there.'

'Thank you, Mrs Lynch.'

As Laura stepped into the narrow entrance hall, she heard piano music. It wasn't until Mrs Lynch showed Laura into the large room at the front of the house that Laura realized it wasn't a CD or the radio. Sarah was sitting in her wheelchair playing a keyboard piano. Laura stood in the doorway, listening to the music and scanning what must once have been the family's private living room but was now clearly Sarah's room – her bedroom and her living area. Books and Get Well cards were crammed onto the shelves, there were leg braces and a walker in one corner and a television in another, a bed along one wall, the piano along the opposite wall, and a large window at the far end of the room with a view of Belfast Lough.

'Hello there,' Sarah said brightly, stopping mid-phrase. She used her joystick to turn the wheelchair round so that she was facing Laura.

'Hi. I didn't know you played. You're very good.'

'Well, I've had a lot of time to practise lately. Anyway, thank you for coming to see me!' She motioned for Laura to sit on the bed and came towards her.

'It's lovely to see you, Sarah,' Laura said. 'I'm so sorry I didn't come before.'

'Not at all,' Sarah said. 'You tried. I'm the one who didn't return your calls and texts. I pushed everyone away, including my boyfriend. He was doing his best to be supportive. I wasn't having it. I'm so glad you kept sending messages and didn't give up on me.'

'Still I should have—'

'I was in hospital for nearly two months anyway,' Sarah continued, 'and then until recently I had to go in nearly every day for physiotherapy once they let me out.' She spoke without a scrap of self-pity.

'I'm afraid I don't know much about your injury. I don't suppose you want to talk about that, though. I'm—'

'No, I don't mind. The bullet grazed my spine before continuing its trajectory through my stomach. It hit my pancreas and lodged in my abdomen.'

Trajectory. It occurred to Laura that the trajectories of all their lives had been thrown off course that night.

'I had three operations in France before I was repatriated,' Sarah continued.

'Are you still having treatment?'

'Oh yes. Four times a week. Three times at the Royal Victoria, although one of those sessions is with a psychologist rather than a physiotherapist, and once here. Then I have exercises to do at home. I try to do them every day.'

'I noticed you had leg braces and a walker in the corner …' Laura broke off, unsure if she was being nosy or offensive. But Sarah seemed fine with it.

'I can walk short distances with the help of those. I can get dressed and take a shower now. Mum and Dad had a shower added to the downstairs cloakroom.'

'Is there any chance you'll—?'

'Make a full recovery? I'll probably never be the same as before. But there's still a lot of room for improvement, apparently. I was lucky. If the bullet had been a few millimetres to the right, I'd have been paralysed.'

Tears welled in Laura's eyes and threatened to spill over, but she couldn't allow herself to cry when Sarah was putting on such a brave face. How could Sarah describe herself as lucky? This wasn't luck. She'd had months of hospitalization and treatment and had a long road of rehabilitation ahead of her.

Laura couldn't think of anything to say, but just then Sarah's mother entered the room carrying a tray with two mugs of tea and some caramel slices.

When she'd gone, Sarah picked up from where they'd left off. 'I'm well looked after here, as you can see. Anyway, enough about me. How are you?'

'I'm seeing a psychologist, too. It's helping.' Laura noticed the raw, angry skin around her thumb where she'd been picking at it. 'I've been having nightmares and flashbacks, that sort of thing.'

'Yeah, me too.'

'I think I'm making progress, but I can't bring myself to go back to work yet.'

'No, well, I can understand that. I wouldn't want to go back to the library, either, without Claire and Ava.' Laura nodded. 'Perhaps you could do something else. You're so bright.'

'Like what?'

'Well, your French is excellent. What about teaching?'

'I'd be useless. I couldn't control a class of children! Anyway, I didn't finish my degree. I dropped out of Queen's before the year abroad.'

'Well, there are Open University courses. And maybe there are grants. You should look into it. I want to do one. I thought maybe I could do an English course and then work partly from home. Freelance journalist or copywriter or something like that. I've not thought it through, but I need to do something. I get a bit bored.'

'That's a great idea! Good for you!' But Laura didn't think a change of career was what she needed. She longed to have a familiar routine again, and that would mean going back to work at the library one day, even though her friends would be all the more present in her mind for their absence.

Sarah broke into Laura's thoughts with a thought of her own. 'Do you ever ask yourself why we escaped while Claire and Ava didn't?' she asked.

Why me? These words often went through Laura's mind. Why had Zak given her the choice between her and Claire? Why had he chosen to release her? Why had she survived unscathed when Sarah was so badly injured and Ava and Claire had been killed?

'All the time,' she said.

'Aye. Me too. Did you go to their funerals?'

'No.' Laura felt a stab of guilt. She hadn't known about the funerals and she hadn't tried to find out. She hadn't thought about it until it was too late. She'd been a complete mess when she first got back from France.

'No, I don't blame you. I wouldn't have gone even if I'd been able to. Must have been absolutely awful.'

Sarah changed the subject then and Laura stayed for a couple of hours. The conversation flowed easily and they found they had plenty to talk about – current affairs, TV, music, Sarah's parents, Laura's mum. Sarah was as garrulous as Laura remembered. She'd changed – they both had – but in essence both of them were still the same as they were before the attack.

As she was getting ready to leave, Laura asked if she could pop in again.

'That would be great,' Sarah said. 'But, Laura?'

'Yes?'

'I have … well, let's put it this way. Some days are better than others. Some weeks, actually. This is a good day.'

Laura understood. 'That's fine. We'll fix a day and then I'll check with you by text before I come round. If it doesn't suit, we can postpone.'

Sarah smiled. 'I knew you'd get it. Thank you.'

As she drove along the A2 towards Belfast, Laura reprimanded herself again for not going to see Sarah sooner. At the least, she could have sent a card or an email or chocolates or something.

She felt terrible about not attending Claire's and Ava's funerals, too. She felt guilty pretty much all the time at the moment. About everything. Was this part of her survivor's guilt, too? *No, Laura,* she thought, a wry smile on her lips, *this is your Catholic side.*

She made three stops before going home, one at a florist's and the other two at cemeteries. When Laura had told Sarah she would like to lay flowers on their graves, Sarah had called in her mum, who had all the information she needed. Claire had been cremated at Roselawn Cemetery. Ava had been buried at Milltown Cemetery, the very place she'd been taken to on one of the disastrous dates she'd told them about all those months ago in Muriel's Bar.

Laura was tearful as she finally headed home. It felt loud and crowded in her head, as if her thoughts were jostling for attention. She could still hear a few bars of the music Sarah had been playing earlier on the piano. It somehow sounded even more melancholy now. Sarah's voice spoke over the music, repeating her question over and over. *Do you ever ask yourself why we escaped while Claire and Ava didn't?* Five months after the attack, Laura was still trying to work out the answer to that question.

Chapter 27

5 MONTHS AFTER

Sandrine

Sam traced his finger along the wrinkles above the bridge of her nose and Sandrine realized she was frowning. Touched at this intimate gesture, she forced a smile as he handed her the little espresso cup with his other hand. But as she breathed in the smell of the coffee, her mind was still on the email she'd written to Laura a few days ago.

She told herself she hadn't lied but a voice in her head kept saying, *Now you're lying to yourself.* There might not have been any barefaced lies in what she wrote, but her reply was full of half-truths and lies of omission. She'd intentionally led Laura to believe that her son was a victim. How ironic when Laura and her friends were her son's victims! She'd insinuated that he'd died while on a shift at work that night. Instead, he'd gone to his place of work on one of his nights off and shot dead as many innocent people as possible.

As it was, Laura didn't even know Sandrine's real name. Sandrine had created a new email account, deliberately using her maiden name. The irony of that wasn't lost on her. The words the police officer had said to her on the night of the terrorist attack as she was arrested echoed in her head: *Your older son, Madame Hamadi, you called him Antoine, but he called himself Zak*. And now she was going by her maiden name, Morvan, instead of her married name, Hamadi.

She'd taken a risk telling Laura that her son's name was Antoine. But even if Laura had followed the news, there was little chance she would put two and two together. Antoine had been referred to as Zakaria in the media – nationally and internationally.

On top of that, Sandrine was pushing Laura into opening up to her about her ordeal. Here again Sandrine had been devious. She'd pretended she wanted to help Laura. This was partly true – she'd set up the website in the first place in order to help her son's victims. But of course she had an ulterior motive. What she really wanted was to glean as much information as she could from Laura about her son's last moments alive. Had he had second thoughts? Maybe he'd shown signs of regret? These were the questions she was desperate to have answered.

All of this felt surreptitious and deceitful. She'd wanted to be as truthful as possible in her correspondence with Laura, but there was no way Laura would write to her if she knew the whole truth. Sandrine had resolved not to mention anything that could give away her real identity but glossing over details or keeping silent about them altogether was not much better than blatantly lying.

Sam slurped his coffee. 'So, did you write back to that Irish girl?' he asked, as if reading her thoughts.

'Yes,' Sandrine said, turning away to avoid Sam's disapproving eyes.

'What did you say?'

'Oh, nothing much,' Sandrine said. 'She offered to translate the website into English and I thought that would be a good idea.'

'Oh! That *is* a good idea,' Sam said. 'There must be several

English speakers among the people needing help seeing as the band was from the UK.'

'That's exactly what I said.'

Sandrine wasn't only deceiving Laura; she was also being dishonest with Sam. For both of them, the truth was hiding in what Sandrine hadn't said. She resolved to answer him honestly if he pressed her, but to her relief, he said no more on the subject.

'The weather's glorious,' he said instead. 'Shall we go for a walk?'

'I was going to go to the graveyard,' she said. There was an awkward pause. Then Sandrine said, 'I can do that another day, when you're at work. Let's go for—'

'We can walk to the cemetery together if you like.'

'Are you sure?' Sandrine didn't think Sam had been there since the day they'd buried Antoine.

'Yes.'

In unspoken agreement, they avoided the town centre and took a long route round so that they wouldn't bump into anyone. But they needn't have worried. Apart from a couple of runners and a dog walker, there was no one about.

As they walked, hand in hand, Sandrine remembered the day of Antoine's funeral. It was pouring with rain. She, Sam, Maxime and her parents were the only people there. Sandrine had wanted to ask Abdel and his family to come, but Sam had been categorical. They were not to be informed about the funeral.

'Abdel said that our father is insisting that the Imam of their mosque conduct the ceremony,' Sam had informed Sandrine. 'It will only get back to them if Abdel and Yasmine come. Best not to say anything at all. Anyway, even my brother would disapprove of a cremation.'

Sandrine had tried hard not to imagine what was left of Antoine's body. He'd blown himself up. They had the remains of his remains cremated. It had seemed like the best option.

The mayor of their town had initially refused to allow Antoine's ashes to be buried in the local cemetery, but she came to their home one evening unannounced to say that while she was against the idea, by law they had the right to bury their son in the municipality in which he'd resided. She asked them to hold a low-key funeral. She'd allocated a plot for them to bury the urn in a far corner of the cemetery and stipulated that there was to be no headstone or nameplate – not even a tree – as she was anxious to avoid the burial site becoming a place of pilgrimage. Sandrine and Sam readily agreed to the mayor's conditions, although Sandrine thought it more likely Antoine's grave would be desecrated by vandals than visited by pilgrims.

The mayor organized for a non-religious celebrant to conduct a discreet ceremony. Thinking about that now, as they climbed the steep hill to the cemetery, Sandrine wondered if that would make Antoine turn in his unmarked grave. Did he expect a Muslim funeral? Or had he not thought about that at all?

As they rounded the corner, a few stone crosses appeared, peeping out over the top of the high stone wall. The graveyard was a good kilometre away from the church, where the short ceremony for Antoine's funeral had been held.

Sam held the iron gate open for Sandrine. As they approached the grave, Sandrine felt his hand squeeze hers. Then he stopped in his tracks. She glanced at him and then followed his gaze. Her body stiffened and she let go of Sam's hand, her own hand flying to cover her mouth.

'Oh no.'

She could see red. Red on the little mound of earth under which the urn containing Antoine's ashes was buried. They'd vandalized her home, painting insults on the front door, time and time again. And now they'd found the grave.

She walked towards the grave, almost in a daze. It wasn't what she'd thought. She'd assumed the red was paint that had been tipped over the grass. But it wasn't paint. A pot of red flowers had been placed on the grave and a handful of rose petals had been scattered around it.

What was this? Idolization? Hero worship? Was veneration worse than vandalism?

'Is this some kind of religious ritual?' she whispered.

Sam was silent for a moment, pensive. Then he said, 'I don't think so. Not a Muslim custom, anyway. The Prophet is said to have put leaves from a date tree or a palm tree on the graves of two sinners to lessen their torture so they could rest in peace. I think you can do something similar with petals. But I doubt that's what this is. It just looks like an expression of sympathy to me.'

'But who could have done this?'

'I don't know. But we should get rid of it. It could draw attention.'

Sam knelt, careful not to kneel on the grave itself, and started to pick up the rose petals, putting them on the ground by the plant pot. Suddenly, he stopped. He looked over his shoulder at Sandrine, his eyes wide. Sandrine bent over to see what the matter was. Sam had uncovered a small, wooden mount with a rectangular plaque stuck on it. It had been concealed under the petals. She straightened up, staring in disbelief at the gold nameplate. It was the sort of nameplate you would expect not on a grave, but on a letterbox. On it were two words in black letters. But it wasn't her son's name. It didn't say *Antoine Hamadi*. It didn't even say *Zakaria Hamadi*. Instead, Sandrine saw a familiar phrase in Arabic.

'*Allahu Akbar*,' Sam read aloud.

'What does it mean?' Sandrine asked, but she thought she knew.

'Literally, God is greater,' Sam said.

Sandrine could feel herself frowning and Sam's gesture earlier, when he'd brushed the lines on her forehead with his hand, came to her mind.

184

Greater than what? she thought.

'Those were his last words,' Sam said.

'What?' An icy hand gripped Sandrine's heart. 'Whose last words?'

He didn't answer. Even now, standing next to her by their son's unmarked grave, he couldn't say his name. It was as if her son no longer had a name. They hadn't been allowed to have his name on his grave and her husband couldn't say it. It made Antoine a nobody.

'How do you know what his last words were?' she breathed.

'The police told me when they questioned me. On the night of the terr … on the night he died.'

Allahu Akbar. God is greater. Sandrine knew the meaning of this phrase had been distorted. It had been co-opted as a battle cry by extremists for some time now. Sandrine had been desperate to know about his final minutes on this earth, certain that he'd died having second thoughts. She'd been hoping to squeeze the facts out of Laura.

Allahu Akbar. Had he died believing in a cause? She dismissed that thought from her mind as quickly as it had entered, stubbornly holding on to the faith she had in her son. She was determined not to allow Sam's revelation to shatter it. Antoine had to have shown a trace of empathy towards his victims at the end.

It struck Sandrine that Sam had known more about Antoine's last moments alive than she had. Just as Laura knew more than she did. Sandrine had to find out. She had to know for sure if Antoine had done something to redeem himself at the very end.

'The police didn't say anything about that to me,' she said. She sank to her knees, not to help Sam scoop up the petals, but because her legs gave way.

'I shouldn't have told you,' Sam said.

From: Laura Davison
To: famille.morvan@tellcommnet.fr
Sun, 13 Jan at 20:29
Subject: translation for website

Hi Sandy,

I'm enclosing a few pages that I've translated for the website. I've started with the home page and the pages giving advice on how to support victims and survivors as I thought these would be the most useful.

From what you've said, your son Antoine sounds lovely and that makes what happened to him all the more tragic.

You asked me what my friends were like. My friends Claire and Ava were wonderful people. Claire was kind. Everyone liked her. She was the one who organized our trip and she was so excited about it. They were both younger than me, but Claire made sure I always felt included in their plans. She was considerate like that. Ava was a hoot. She had beautiful skin, but her hair was a bit wild, like her. She insisted on wearing ridiculously high heels everywhere! She even wore them walking up the hill to the basilica when we were in Lyon and she was wearing heeled sandals at the concert the night she died.

I visited their graves for the first time the other day. I'm ashamed to say that I didn't go before. I didn't even go to their funerals, although looking back now on those first few weeks after I came home, I'm not sure that I would have been up to it.

It's nice of you to ask after my friend who was injured. Her name is Sarah and I went to see her not long ago. She was shot in the back by one of the terrorists as she tried to escape and initially her doctors didn't know if she would walk again, but she's determined and she can

186

now walk a little with the help of leg braces. She has had to move back in with her parents, who take her to the hospital several times a week for treatment. She plays the piano beautifully and she reads a lot. When I saw her she was cheerful, but some days are harder than others for her.

You also asked me if it was difficult for me to discuss what happened that night. I struggled to put everything into words to begin with and every time I tried, I got distressed, but I've been seeing a psychologist – Robert – and he has helped me immensely. He's easy to talk to. He said that it was important to verbalize my feelings and also to describe my experience in detail. When I find it hard to talk about my memories, he encourages me to think positive thoughts. That way I can control my fears.

You're right. It was terrifying to be taken hostage. I didn't think I would get out of that concert hall alive and I still have nightmares, but I was one of the lucky ones.

I hope you and your husband are well and Maxime, too. I'd love to hear more about Antoine.

Take care,

Laura

De : Famille Morvan
À : laura.davison@ezmail.co.uk
Lun 14 jan à 15:37
Sujet : Rép : translation for website

Hi Laura,

Thank you so much for your email and for the pages you've translated. If you go on the website, you'll see that they're now live! I'm enclosing another of the advice pages, which I've had a go at translating. I was hoping you would take a look at it and correct any mistakes. It's only fair that I should help you out!

I felt saddened when I read about your friends. I'm sure their parents are utterly heartbroken. I know exactly how they feel. Sarah does indeed sound like a determined young lady. I do hope she'll continue to make progress. Perhaps one day she'll walk without the leg braces.

I think you were right not to go to their funerals. Perhaps it was better both for you and your friends' parents that way. They must have been horribly sad occasions. Last week my husband came to our son's grave with me for the first time since the funeral. I wish he'd come before, but people deal with grief differently, don't they? I don't think there's a right or a wrong way.

Antoine was lovely. Thank you for saying so. He was tall and had brown hair and hazel-green eyes. I think he was a handsome young man, although I'm obviously biased! He was passionate about the things he was interested in. For example, he went on marches to raise awareness about the environment and he was the one who took out the recycling bin for collection at our house. He didn't do much else to help around the house, though! He was a typical teenage boy in many ways! That said, he kept his things tidy, especially his bedroom.

He loved reading and he was good at foreign languages. He was doing a two-year course with a view to working in the hospitality industry afterwards. He would jump on every occasion to practise his English. He was good at Spanish, too, and he often said he'd like to go to Spain. You can drive to Spain from Lyon. It's less than 500 kilometres to the border. We always said we'd go one day, but it's something we never got round to doing and it's too late now.

We didn't have a pet, although he wanted one. He loved cats and dogs and he couldn't stand cruelty to animals. He was in love with a girl he was dating. He wanted to marry her and would have done anything for her. Unfortunately she ended their relationship and it broke Antoine's heart. I hate to think that he might have been sad before he died, but I think he knew how much his family loved him.

I'm glad to hear you have a good psychologist. You said you didn't think you would get out of *La Voie Lactée* alive? Did the terrorists threaten you? Or did they treat you with some humanity? Were you there until the end when the police made their assault? I hope you don't mind me asking. I'm so glad that talking about your traumatic memories to Robert has helped you. Do you confide in anyone else? Are your parents supportive?

All the best,

Sandy

Chapter 28

6 MONTHS AFTER

Laura

'Ta-dah!' Laura said shyly as she let Declan and Patrick into her new flat. It had taken her most of the afternoon to put together the shelving unit that now separated the dining area from the living area, but she was ridiculously proud of herself, as if she'd chopped down the tree, designed the piece of furniture and made it from scratch herself.

'Ooh, has the man from Sky been?' Pat exclaimed, walking round her carefully assembled unit, grabbing the remote control and flopping onto the three-seater sofa that they'd picked up from IKEA the previous day.

Declan rolled his eyes at Laura. 'Ignore him,' he said, making a show of admiring her handiwork. 'That looks grand.'

'You got it easy, girl,' Pat said, his eyes on the television screen as he flicked through the channels. 'When I moved in with your cousin, ooh, fifteen years ago now, there was no IKEA in Ireland. There were organized trips to Scotland on the ferry and everyone brought back their bedrooms and kitchens flat-packed in the hold of the bus.'

Declan and Patrick had recently persuaded her to move into their block of flats off the Antrim Road, not that Laura had needed much persuading. Their elderly neighbour had gone into sheltered housing and their landlord, who owned several of the flats in the building, was looking for a quiet tenant to replace him.

'You need the support of your family after what you've been through, and your mam's been feckin' useless so far, so you're lumped with our Pat and me,' Declan had said. 'It will be easier if you're right across the hall.'

Laura scanned the room. Her last flat had been furnished, so she'd had to buy everything for this one. Yesterday's round trip to IKEA would hopefully be their last. Not only did the place look homely now, it also felt like home. Bright and modern, small, but cosy rather than cramped, it was a far cry from the grotty flat she'd just moved out of. Plus it was closer to the centre of Belfast, a short ten-minute walk from the library, when she felt up to going back to work. Taking the flat was a good move, in more ways than one. The only thing she would miss about her old flat was her neighbour, but Laura had promised Mrs Doherty to drop in from time to time.

'What's this?' Declan asked, picking up a newspaper clipping from where Laura had left it on a shelf of the new unit.

Laura didn't answer. She observed her cousin while he studied the article. He took his time reading it, although he must have known more or less what had happened that day.

The third of December, 1994. Her dad was supposed to take Laura and her mother to pick out the Christmas tree that day. They'd planned to go together – all three of them – to the garden centre off the Lisburn Road. But in the end her dad had to go into work to cover for one of his colleagues, who had gone down with a stomach bug. Laura's mother had taken Laura to get the tree. They would have it up and turn the lights on for Laura's daddy coming home. They were in the middle of decorating it, Laura and Noreen, when the telephone rang with news that would change their lives forever.

Laura didn't remember much – if anything – about that day. She wasn't even sure that the memory of decorating the Christmas tree was real. Perhaps she just remembered her mother telling her about it and the images she could see in her head had originally sprung from that. The third of December 1994. A Saturday. The day her father was killed. Laura was six years old.

She'd found the newspaper clipping one day in a drawer in the sideboard at her mother's house and kept it. It was yellow with age now. It had fallen out of a folder earlier when Laura was unpacking boxes and she'd read it, as Declan was doing now, although she'd read it so many times over the years that she knew it by heart.

Her father, a Royal Ulster Constabulary officer, was severely injured in an IRA mortar bomb attack on Stewartstown RUC station. The 200-pound so-called "barracks-buster" bomb narrowly missed the main buildings and landed in the car park, where her father was getting into his car, having finished his shift. He died in the ambulance as he was being taken to the Royal Victoria Hospital. The three bombers escaped in a Honda Civic, which had been hijacked in town three hours before the attack by men wearing balaclavas.

There were two illustrations. One was a photo of her father in his RUC uniform, looking into the camera with a stern expression on his face. The other photo showed the extensive damage the homemade explosive device had caused to the RUC base.

There was no mention in the article of the man who should have died instead of Laura's daddy. Billy Hamilton. Did he still think about her father? Was he plagued with survivor's guilt because he'd lived while his colleague was killed? How had he lived his life afterwards to make up for that? If Billy hadn't been off sick that day, Laura's father wouldn't have been killed.

The more Laura thought about Billy, the more convinced she became that he had the answers to the questions that were tormenting her. She was struggling to get her head round the fact that Claire and Ava had been shot dead when she hadn't. Billy must have felt the same way when Laura's father was killed. If anyone could provide her with some sort of answer or insight, surely he could.

Declan put the newspaper article back on the shelf.

'I was thinking of going to see him,' Laura said tentatively.

'The peeler?'

'Yes. I've not seen him for years and he'll not recognize me, but he won't have forgotten me.'

She knew where the Hamiltons lived, unless they'd moved – on Montgomery Road, near the Lisnasharragh Leisure Centre, or the Robinson Centre as it was known back then. She'd gone there as a child as Billy Hamilton and his wife used to be close friends of her parents.

'Sure, what good will it do you to drag up the past?' When she shrugged, he said, 'Aye, I get it. It has to do with what you're going through now. Is that the way of it?'

'Something like that.'

'Will I take you to see him then?'

'Oh, no, Declan, there's no need. I know where he lives, or where he used to live anyway. Hopefully he's still there. I can drive or take the bus.'

'No, you can't. I'll run you over, so I will. Let's go.'

'What now?'

'No time like the present.'

That sounded like something Sarah would say, which made Laura wince.

Patrick was so engrossed in the programme he was watching, he didn't even look up as Declan told him they were going out.

While Declan drove, singing along to a song on the radio, Laura looked out of the window. What would she say to Billy Hamilton? She hadn't had time to think this through. As the road accompanied the River Lagan for a stretch, she stared at Samson and Goliath, Harland and Wolff's gantry cranes. The shipyard, famous for having built *RMS Titanic*, had almost collapsed in recent years, but the twin yellow cranes were still standing tall, dominating the Belfast skyline from Queen's Island.

Laura found the Hamiltons' terraced house fairly easily. Declan parked in the street. The vertical slats of the blinds in the front living room and the frosted glass of the front door made it impossible to see if anyone was home, but there was a car in the driveway, half-hidden from view by a sprawling monkey puzzle tree.

'Ready?' Declan asked.

'No.'

'Well, that's OK, we'll sit here for a while longer, so we will.'

She shouldn't have come. Perhaps she would bring back bad memories to Billy Hamilton. She didn't want to do that. And maybe talking about her dad wouldn't do her any good, either.

A familiar song came on the radio. Declan quickly turned it off. Laura continued to sing it in her head, trying to identify it.

'Come on,' Declan said, undoing his seatbelt.

Laura followed him up the drive to the front door and rang the bell. No one answered. She tried again. Then they turned to go. It was only as they were walking back down the drive that it came to her. For a moment, strobe lights flashed before her eyes, blinding her. She tripped and instinctively held her arms out to break her fall, but Declan grabbed her and pulled her upright, holding her against him.

'Are you OK?' he asked.

'The song … I've just realized what it was.'

'I know,' Declan said. '*The Naturals.*'

But he didn't know. Not all of it. "Don't let this be the end."

They'd been playing that song at the concert when the first shots were fired. The irony of the title hadn't struck her until now.

They stood for a few seconds in the driveway until Laura felt steady on her feet again. Then she became aware that Declan was staring at something over her shoulder. She turned her head to see what had caught his attention.

She noticed a face peering through the blinds in the front room move. Someone was at home.

Seconds later, a man opened the front door. He was a stranger to Laura.

'Damn! They must have moved,' she muttered to Declan.

But then she recognized him. She didn't think he could possibly recognize her, but he held out his hand to shake hers.

Chapter 29

6 MONTHS AFTER

Sandrine

Madame Roux, the new headmistress of Max's school had a firm handshake and a sympathetic face. She was tall and exuded confidence. Sandrine warmed to her immediately, although she felt intimidated by her at the same time. Sam had met her – once – at a parent-teacher evening at the beginning of that school year. He'd insisted on attending it despite the recent events. Sandrine had known he would be eyeballed by other parents all evening long and she hadn't offered to go with him.

'Thank you for coming in today,' Madame Roux said, releasing Sandrine's hand and motioning for her to sit down. 'It's nice to finally meet you.'

There wasn't a sliver of a reproach in her kind tone. Seeing the pity reflected in the older woman's dark brown eyes as they looked into hers, an inexplicable spark of anger flared in Sandrine. But it failed to ignite, doused in the wave of sadness that quickly replaced it. She lowered her gaze.

'Firstly, Madame Hamadi, let me say how sorry I am for every-

196

thing you must be going through. Many members of my staff taught Antoine when he was a pupil here and I know that they were fond of him and that they were all extremely shocked by what happened last summer.'

'Thank you.'

'I've asked you in today, Madame Hamadi, because Maxime's teachers are concerned about the adverse effect his brother's death is having on him. It seems to be affecting him more now than it did at first, in fact.'

Sandrine's head jerked up. The headmistress had phrased that diplomatically, but Sandrine had grasped the subtext. Maxime must have done something wrong. Was he acting up? Misbehaving? 'Why? What's …?'

'Don't alarm yourself, Madame. I'm sure together we can find a way to help him. As you know, he has been absent from school a lot.'

'Absent? No, I didn't know. How would I have known?'

'When one of our pupils is absent, we send an email to the family.' Madame Roux shuffled some papers on her desk. 'According to my records, Madame Hamadi, you justified those absences to begin with by return of email.'

'No. No, I didn't. I never received any notifications of his absences.'

'Well, this is the email address I have. This was the form we sent home with your son to check through back in September.' The headmistress, turned a page of A4 paper the other way up and slid it across the desk for Sandrine to see.

Sandrine looked at it. The form contained contact details and information about her and Sam, their jobs, et cetera. It also had a section where the pupil's brothers and sisters were supposed to be listed with their ages and classes. It said on the form that any corrections had to be made in red ink. Dutifully, a line had been scored through Antoine's name with a red pen. That brought tears to Sandrine's eyes. Her email address had also been crossed out. A new address – one she didn't recognize but that contained her name – had been written next to it.

'I'm afraid I'm not the one who made these amendments,' Sandrine said. 'The email address that has been scored through is still valid, but I don't recognize this one at all.' She tapped on the paper with her index finger.

Madame Roux was silent for a few seconds. She was holding Sandrine's gaze again. 'Ah,' she said at the same time as Sandrine said, 'Oh dear.' Sandrine looked at the fake email address. It was unmistakably Max's writing.

'So you weren't aware of your son's irregular attendance at school?'

'No, I wasn't.'

'OK. Up until three or four weeks ago, we received emails from this address in response to our own emails to provide reasons for Maxime's absences from school. Usually the excuse given was "family problems". His attendance was irregular, but not alarmingly so. We decided to show a little leniency in dealing with this situation as we realized things must be extremely difficult for him, so of course there were no punishments, although his form teacher has talked to him about this on a few occasions.'

'I see.'

'Recently, his absences have become so frequent that we can no longer turn a blind eye to them, which is why I asked you in today. For a few weeks now we've received no explanation for his lack of attendance at school. We have encouraged Maxime to see the school psychologist and the school doctor on a regular basis, but I think we need to work together with you and your husband now, as his parents, in order to better help your son.'

'He used to like school,' Sandrine said, thinking aloud. 'Is he in school today?'

'No. I was about to ask you if you knew that he hadn't come in today, Madame Hamadi.'

Again there was no underlying current of disapproval in the

head's voice and Sandrine had to choke back tears. She would find it easier to hold herself together if the older woman criticized her or implied that she was unfit as a parent. Clearly she was an incompetent mother. She'd been so wrapped up in her own grief for her elder son that she'd neglected her younger son, who was grieving, too.

'No. I didn't … I haven't been … He doesn't always sleep at home.'

'I don't think you should blame yourself, Madame Hamadi,' the headmistress said, reaching across her desk and placing her hand briefly on Sandrine's.

'He has his *baccalauréat* exams this year.' It came out in a half-sob, half-wail.

'Yes, he does. And I won't lie. This term his grades have dropped significantly. However, he did have a reasonably good start to the school year. It's only been over the past few weeks that we've had cause for concern, so Maxime could still turn this around.'

Sandrine felt unnerved by the headmistress's stare, which was both benevolent and insistent, and she scanned the room as Madame Roux talked to avoid making eye contact. A Klimt print hung on the wall of her office and there was a large round table in the corner with piles of papers and folders on it. Two photo frames sat on the desk angled towards the headmistress so that Sandrine couldn't see the pictures in them. Her children, she supposed. A blind was lowered halfway down the large window behind the headmistress, perhaps to keep the glare of daylight off the computer screen. Sandrine wondered if pupils were scared of coming into this office. Perhaps the headmistress had a fearsome side that she reserved for troublemakers.

Sandrine only realized she'd tuned out when the headmistress stood up.

'Let's keep in touch, Madame Hamadi. If it's all right with you, I'll phone you in a week or so, but feel free to call me before then if I can be of any assistance.'

199

Sandrine drove the short distance home in bewilderment. Sam, who was working from home that day, had offered to go with her to see the headmistress, but Sandrine had declined. After all, he'd braved the parent-teacher meeting alone at the beginning of the year. She found him in his study. She told him about her meeting with Madame Roux and he gave her the impression that he was listening to every word. But when she'd finished, he said nothing.

Sandrine felt a stab of disappointment. In the weeks after the attack, she and Sam had barely talked to each another, but their communication had been better over the last couple of months, since Sandrine had come up with the idea of setting up a website and Sam had ended up not just helping her out, but playing an active role in it.

Sam waved his mobile, signalling that he had to make a phone call and Sandrine left the room, feeling let down. She sent a text message to Maxime to ask where he was and if he was OK. She hadn't seen him for the last two days.

Chapter 30

6 MONTHS AFTER

Laura

She'd not seen Billy Hamilton for about twenty years, but in that time her father's colleague appeared to have aged by over half a century. He had two or three strands of grey hair stuck to his otherwise bald head, his face was criss-crossed with a network of deep wrinkles and he was hunched over, bent almost double at the hips.

As Laura shook his hand, staring at him open-mouthed, his wife appeared behind him. She was wearing a low-cut pink top and a pleated floral skirt that reminded Laura of her mother's tablecloth. Mrs Hamilton had aged, too, but Laura would have recognized her. She looked like a woman her age should, which highlighted her husband's transformation. She bundled her husband back into the house, throwing a mistrustful glance in Laura and Declan's direction.

'Hello, Mrs Hamilton,' Declan said.

'Do I know yous?'

Declan nudged Laura.

'It's Laura Davison, Mrs Hamilton. I'm Martin and Noreen's daughter? This is my cousin, Declan.'

Minutes later, Laura was sitting on a worn leather sofa, sandwiched between Mr and Mrs Hamilton, with Declan sitting opposite them, perched on the end of a matching armchair. Mrs Hamilton fussed around Laura, talking incessantly.

'Haven't you grown!' she exclaimed, and, 'You've a look of your daddy. You're the spit of him, so you are.'

Mrs Hamilton left them for a few minutes to make some tea. While she was gone, Mr Hamilton didn't utter a single word. Laura glanced at him, trying to work out if he was shy or just used to leaving the talking to his wife. When she caught his eye, he smiled, then looked away. Laura was trying to come up with something to make polite small talk when Mrs Hamilton returned with a tray in her hands. She sat down and poured tea from a pot into chipped china cups before leaping to her feet again. 'I'm forgetting myself,' she said, her hands covering her mouth. 'You'll be wanting a wee cake with that.'

'No, Mrs Hamilton. Don't bother yourself,' Laura said. 'We just wanted to call in. Well, *I* did.'

Mrs Hamilton sat down again. She'd finally stopped talking, but Laura still didn't know what to say.

Declan broke the ensuing silence. 'I don't know if you remember the terrorist attack at a concert in France this summer, Mrs Hamilton,' he began.

'Yes. The band were from around these parts, weren't they?'

'Aye, that's right.'

'I was there,' Laura said. 'I lost two of my closest friends. Claire and Ava. I saw one of them ... she was gunned down in front of me.' In a voice so quiet it must have been inaudible, she added, 'Instead of me.' Laura noticed Mrs Hamilton wring her hands, her head lowered. 'Another of my friends, Sarah, was seriously injured,' she continued. 'She's in a wheelchair. The doctors don't know if she'll recover completely.'

She paused, hoping Mrs Hamilton would help her out. But the woman remained silent.

'I ... um ... I've been thinking a lot about my daddy recently, I suppose because he died in a terrorist attack, too, you know, with the IRA mortar bomb, and well ... I wondered how Mr Hamilton had coped with losing his colleague the way he did.'

'Coped?' Mrs Hamilton scoffed. 'He hit the whiskey bottle, so he did. Became a drunk. Lost his job, lost us all our friends. We almost lost the house. I'm not sure you'd call that coping.'

Laura looked at Billy Hamilton, but he didn't react. She wasn't sure if he registered what was going on around him.

'He couldn't get it out of his head that it should have been him, not your da. Then he had a stroke a few years ago. It knocked that notion clean out of his head. At least it stopped the drinking. But it stopped him thinking straight, too.'

'I'm sorry,' Laura said. 'I had no idea.'

'Is that why he doesn't say anything?' Declan asked. 'Did the stroke affect his speech?'

'No. He's barely strung two sentences together since Laura's daddy was killed.' Mrs Hamilton turned to Laura. 'I'm truly sorry about your friends, pet, and I understand that must have brought back all the memories of losing your da, but you won't find any inspiration here.' She nodded her head towards her husband. 'Yer man's a dead loss.' Mrs Hamilton stood up and smoothed down her pleated skirt.

'We'll be on our way, so,' said Declan, taking his cue.

'Goodbye, Mrs Hamilton. Goodbye, Mr Hamilton,' Laura muttered, following her cousin out of the house.

As Declan turned right onto the Cregagh Road, Laura said, 'That was a waste of time. Sorry, Declan. I'm sure you've far better things to do.'

'Not at all,' he said.

Her mind was elsewhere. She wondered how the other survivors from the terrorist attack were getting on. Did some of them talk about it together? Did that help? The only other person she knew who had been through it and survived was Connor.

'How's Connor? Do you know?'

The other two musicians had travelled back with the road crew the day after the attack, cancelling the rest of their tour, but Connor had stayed for a couple of days to sort things out and he'd ended up on the same flight as them back from Lyon. The last time she'd seen him, he was waiting for his luggage at Dublin airport. He'd looked much how she felt. Exhausted, shocked, broken. A shadow of the man he'd been when she talked to him on the café *terrasse* the evening before the concert. Declan had held him in his arms, a gesture that spoke louder than any words.

'I've not seen himself, but I saw his ma when I went to mass with Mammy last Sunday. She said he wasn't doing too well. I'll tell her you were asking after him next time I see her.'

Was Connor was going through the same thing she was? She'd seen her friend Claire shot before her eyes; Connor's best friend, the band's frontman, Niall O'Donnell, had died on stage in his arms.

As Laura rested her head against the cool window of the car, she could see Connor's clear blue eyes and hear his soft voice in her head. She remembered him telling her how apprehensive he was that day – more than the usual stage fright. Laura had felt something similar on the plane to Lyon. An irrational sensation that she was hurtling towards some inevitable disaster. Just the memory of that emotion caused her to feel anxious now. In retrospect, her fears didn't seem so unfounded.

Chapter 31

6 MONTHS AFTER

Sandrine

Sandrine spent the rest of the day feeling anxious, even though Maxime had replied to her text message, insisting he was fine. But she knew he couldn't be. He was having trouble coping with things – his brother's death, his own life, she didn't know what exactly. They needed to help him urgently.

He was at Benoît's house as usual. She should ask him – *tell* him – to come home so that they could talk to him, but Sam seemed to have left her alone in this and she was afraid to tackle it without his input. She was disappointed that her husband hadn't shown more concern or come up with a plan. She decided to bring that up with him first so they could present a united front when dealing with Max.

It wasn't until that evening, when Maxime sauntered through the front door, that Sandrine realized she'd misjudged her husband.

'So, what's the biggie?' Maxime asked over dinner.

'I wanted you to come home this evening because your mother and I need to talk to you—'

'Oh?'

'—about school. More precisely, about your poor attendance and grades,' Sam continued.

'Oh.'

'What's going on, Max?'

'I … it's just …'

'Is this because of Antoine?' Sandrine asked gently.

'Sort of,' Maxime replied. 'It made me realize that there are more important things in life, that's all.'

'More important than school?' Sam's tone of voice was firm.

'Well …'

'Young man. From now on, unless you want your allowance to be cut off, I suggest you get your arse into that *lycée*. You need to think about your future. And you could spare a thought for your mother, too. She's had more than enough on her plate without you playing up. The last thing she needed was to be summoned to school by your headmistress because you've been playing truant.'

Max looked from his father to his mother. Sandrine tried to read his expression, but it was inscrutable.

'And why did the school have a fake email address?'

Sandrine winced as she thought of the email address she'd created for the sole purpose of communicating with Laura. *Like mother, like son.*

'I set one up so Mum wouldn't be bothered, you know, on top of everything.' He reeled off his explanation and Sandrine couldn't tell whether it was rehearsed or the truth. 'I'm old enough to take care of stuff like that myself.'

'That's what you'd think, wouldn't you, at the age of seventeen. But clearly you're not mature enough. I don't believe you. I think you deliberately changed that address so you could intercept the messages about your lack of attendance and bad marks.'

Maxime didn't deny it. He merely lowered his gaze.

'According to your headmistress,' Sam continued, 'you've been skiving off school since September, but it's got worse recently.'

'Are you being bullied at school?' Sandrine asked.

'No.'

'Don't you like school?'

'Not particularly, but there's nothing wrong, *Maman*. No one's picking on me. Mostly everyone stays well away from me. You didn't need to worry about me.'

'Of course your mother has been worried about you. We've both been worried sick. And there must be some sort of problem when you don't show up for class. Are you taking drugs?'

'No!'

'What do you do when you're not at school? Where do you go?'

'I just walk around. Think. You know.'

'Walk where?' Sandrine asked. 'It's been bitterly cold outside.'

'The shopping centre at *La Part-Dieu*. The one at *Confluence*, too.'

'On your own?'

'Usually. Not always. I hang out with friends sometimes. We even go to the gym a bit.'

At least Maxime wasn't moping around by himself. 'Friends from school?'

'Yes. I expect Roux called their parents, too.'

'*Madame* Roux,' Sam corrected.

'We haven't been absent from school that much, *Maman*. The last few weeks, mainly. Roux – Madame Roux – likes to think she's efficient. There's nothing wrong. Nothing for you to fret about. I ... miss Antoine, that's all. It got to me with the New Year and all.'

'That was weeks ago!' Sam said. 'And what's that got to do with your friends?'

'Nothing. They were just being supportive.'

Sandrine felt a pang of guilt. Clearly she and Sam hadn't been supportive enough.

'Well, from now on, during the week, you will sleep here, in this house. Not on your friends' sofas.'

'*Papa!*' he wailed, sounding like a young boy.

'And unless you have badminton, you will eat here, at this table. Breakfast and dinner. With us.'

Sandrine didn't say anything, but she knew that Max's sports bag – with his racket and shuttlecocks inside – hadn't moved from where he'd flung it into the corner of his bedroom several weeks ago. And she hadn't washed his kit since then. Max wasn't going to school. He wasn't going to badminton practice. He no longer showed an interest in the things he used to love. Was he depressed? Or was he shunned by his friends like Sandrine was herself?

'And you will go to school. Every day. Without fail. From now on, I'll drop you at school on my way to the office.'

Maxime's mouth opened in protest. And closed again as Sam added, 'You can drive.'

Maxime had passed the multiple-choice theory test, albeit on his second attempt, and he'd done the required twenty hours' driving with an instructor, so he was now allowed behind the wheel as an accompanied learner driver. He'd driven a bit with Sandrine before the events of the previous August, as Antoine had when he'd been a learner driver, but Sandrine couldn't relax in the passenger seat while her sons drove and Sam was much more patient. She was grateful to Sam for this idea. It was a good way of making sure Max got at least as far as the school gates.

Getting up to clear the dishes away, Sam said, 'And Maxime, you should be ashamed of yourself, causing your mother concern and embarrassment after all she's been through.'

Maxime lowered his head. 'Sorry, *Maman*,' he muttered once Sam was in the kitchen out of earshot. 'I only ever wanted to make you proud.'

Sandrine's heart swelled. She *was* proud of Max, but he got up to help his father tidy up before she could tell him. She was also overwhelmed by Sam's support. He'd always been happy to play bad cop to her good cop and neither of them had ever criticized the other's methods. They'd always completed each other, acting as a team in their parenting. Their parenting skills had failed in Antoine's case, but it wasn't too late to help Maxime fulfil his potential and thrive. They would do their best. Together.

That evening, instead of shutting himself up in his bedroom with his mobile, computer or console, Maxime stayed with Sandrine and Sam, watching some spy film that Sandrine was having difficulty following. Her mind was elsewhere, as was so often the case these days, but although she didn't feel happy exactly, she felt something approaching contentedness. It was nice to have Max home. It occurred to her that the last time Max had watched the television with her, it must have been the news on the night of the terrorist attack. And the last time Maxime and Sam had watched a film together, it was with Antoine as well.

Sandrine spent most evenings now working on the website, often with Sam. She was itching to boot up her computer to check for any new developments – above all, she wanted to see if Laura had written – but she didn't dare to move, afraid she would break the spell. So she stayed put, her gaze alternating between the TV screen and the rapt faces of her husband and son as they watched the film.

'Thank you for sorting that out,' Sandrine said as she and Sam were getting ready for bed.

'No problem. I'm not sure that it's sorted out as such. Maxime is obviously not dealing with his brother's death very well.'

'Antoine's death and the whole stigma attached to it.' Seven months on and she still couldn't say the words "terrorist attack" out loud, just as Sam could never refer to their elder son by name.

'You took him to see a psychologist, didn't you? Is he still going?'

'No. He said he was seeing one through school. I'll make another appointment, though.'

'Yes. Do that,' Sam agreed. 'We need to keep an eye on him.'

Chapter 32

6 MONTHS AFTER

Laura

Their session began in the usual way with Robert asking about her anxiety and how she was feeling. Laura had been sleeping better and had fewer panic attacks. She still woke up in the middle of most nights and had difficulty getting back to sleep, but on the whole she felt less tired.

'I feel like I'm moving forwards,' she said.

'It certainly sounds like it.' Dr McBride rolled up the sleeves of his navy blue Aran jumper. Although he was dressed more casually than usual, he must be uncomfortable under all that wool, Laura thought. It was unseasonably warm outside and stuffy in his office. 'One of the things I wanted to discuss with you was your social relationships. Do you feel up to talking about that today?'

'Yes.'

The book he used to take notes was open on his lap, but he hardly glanced at it during their sessions. He barely even looked down when he scribbled in it. Either he remembered everything

Laura told him or he revised quickly before she came in each time.

'You told me before that you haven't been out a lot since the incident and other than with members of your family you haven't socialized much.'

He was being polite. She'd told him she hadn't been out at all.

'I went to see Sarah,' she said, feeling pleased with herself.

'This is your friend who was injured that night?'

'Yes. I'd been putting off going for a while.'

'Why do you think that is?'

'Good question.'

'Thank you.'

Laura smiled. He was joking with her. That helped her to talk about the serious stuff. 'I think I'd been avoiding her because she came out of this so much worse off than me. I mean, I wasn't hurt at all whereas Sarah's injuries were so severe that the doctors didn't know if she'd walk again at first. She's made terrific progress, but she mightn't ever recover fully. She's walking a wee bit with leg braces.'

'So, you felt guilty because she was physically injured and you weren't?'

'Yes. That's right. I also wondered what we'd say to each other. She still spends a lot of time at the hospital and I didn't know if she'd want to go into that. And I could hardly tell her about my nightmares and flashbacks and all with her in the condition she's in.'

'I see. And what did you talk about when you met up with Sarah?'

Laura chuckled. 'Well, we talked about her treatment at the hospital and my nightmares and flashbacks.'

Now it was Dr McBride's turn to smile. 'But it went well?'

'Yes, it did.'

'Will you be going to see her again?'

'Yes. I hope to see a lot more of her.'

'OK. That's all very positive. Have you seen anyone else? Apart from your cousin Declan and his boyfriend Patrick – I know you see them regularly.'

'My mum,' Laura said weakly.

Robert gave her a look that said that didn't count.

'I've been for a few swims, but I went alone.'

'That's great, Laura. It's important to do an activity, as we've discussed before. Walking, swimming, cycling. It can be gentle, but it gets you out and it's beneficial for the body and the mind. You need those endorphins. Are you planning to go again?'

'Yes.' She remembered the flyer she'd picked up at the pool. 'I thought I might put my name down for Zumba classes, too.'

'Good idea.'

'Thank you.'

Robert smiled again. 'My wife does Zumba.' It was the first time he'd told her anything personal. 'She loves it. Exercise, music and a girlie natter. Only two men in the class, apparently. It sounds to me like that could be a way for you to combine a physical activity with a bit of socializing.'

'That's what I thought.'

'OK. Now, last time you mentioned you were dreading going back to work, but you had to at some point for financial reasons. Have you given that any more thought?'

'Hmm. This is also something that came up when I was at Sarah's. I've been thinking about it ever since. I'm not sure I'll be able to work at the library anymore. I don't think I could go back there without Claire and Ava. And of course Sarah.'

'That's understandable.'

'But I do need an income and I'm not qualified to do anything else. I did like my job. I also feel the need for a familiar routine. I can't see myself working elsewhere.'

'So it's your place of work rather than your job itself that's the problem?'

213

'Yes.'

'Why don't you try going back to the library for a visit? You must like books if you're a librarian? You could maybe get a book out?'

'I haven't been able to concentrate on the plot of any novels since I got back from France.'

'It's normal after a traumatic experience to have difficulty concentrating. It's not easy to pay attention or listen attentively. That will come back, gradually. Why don't you go to the library with someone? Maybe your cousin would accompany you? Does he read? You could help him choose a book?'

'Yes, he reads. Non-fiction, mainly. Not my area, but I could go with him.'

But when the session was over and Declan was driving Laura home, she didn't bring up Robert's suggestion. This was something she had to do by herself. It had been a while since she'd last tried to read a novel. Perhaps her concentration would be better now. She could try something light-hearted or funny. Failing that, she could take out some magazines. But that wasn't the point. It wasn't about what she borrowed from the library; it was about going there.

Once Declan had dropped her off, Laura made herself a cup of tea and sat on the sofa. Harry immediately jumped onto her lap and made himself comfortable. Laura sent a text message to Sarah, telling her she was thinking of going to the library for a visit. Her phone pinged immediately with Sarah's reply.

Good for you! When?
(No time like the present.)

Sarah really did have a saying for every situation, just as Claire had once remarked. That thought made Laura wistful. Sarah was right, though. Laura could go to the library right

214

now. She had nothing better to do. She was meeting her mum for coffee later, but the café was as near to the library as it was to her flat. She'd planned to continue working on the translations for the support portal. She wanted to check the web pages Sandrine had translated before replying to her email, but she could get on with that later.

She drained her tea and gently lifted Harry off her lap, putting him on the sofa. Annoyed, the cat leapt off the sofa and slinked off in the direction of the kitchen, no doubt for some comfort eating.

The library was within walking distance – supposedly one of the benefits of her new flat, although that was turning out to be inconsequential. The sun warmed her face as she walked. One foot in front of the other. One step at a time. It wasn't hard. She felt ashamed of herself for waiting so long before going to see her boss, Nina, who had been extremely considerate, telling Laura to take her time, assuring her the job was being kept open for her and showing genuine concern about her well-being. At the same time, Laura was proud of herself. Like going to see Sarah, this was something she'd been putting off and now she was doing it. She was convinced that it would work out easier than she'd anticipated.

She was standing right in front of the main entrance when it hit her. Perhaps it was the grandeur of the imposing, red sandstone building that set her off. It all became too much, too big. Even the revolving doors suddenly became an insurmountable obstacle.

Oh no! she thought. She hadn't seen it coming at all. A forceful wave of panic washed over her and she felt as if she were drowning. She couldn't catch her breath. Her heart was pounding hard and fast, in her chest and ears. She leant against the wall of the building as her legs refused to hold her up. Concentrating on her breathing, she tried to inhale deeply and count to four. That's what Robert had told her to do. Her breaths were still coming in short gasps. She could only count up to two. That alarmed her even more.

She tried to focus on something – anything – and stared at her shoes as they skidded into focus and then blurred again.

'Are you all right?' Laura looked up into the face of a small, dark-haired woman. 'Can I do anything for you? Would you like to sit down?' The woman was younger than Laura. She had a Southern Irish accent.

Laura looked around for a bench, but there was nothing. She shook her head. The woman put her arm on Laura's shoulder. She kept talking. Her words were muffled, as if Laura were under-water and the woman above the surface. Although Laura couldn't make out what she was saying, her touch and voice were comforting.

It must have been over in minutes, even though it felt like hours.

'Panic attack,' Laura mumbled. 'I'm fine now.'

'If you're sure,' the woman said.

'Honestly, I'm better now,' Laura said. 'Thank you.'

A few passers-by were staring Laura's way, out of concern rather than curiosity judging from the expressions on their faces. When Laura returned their gaze, they walked away.

She walked off, aimlessly, in the opposite direction. She couldn't go into the library today. Some other time. Maybe. For now she wanted to get as far away from here as possible.

But as she waited to cross the road, she experienced an over-whelming sinking feeling. It wasn't at all like a few minutes earlier when she'd had the impression she was drowning. It took her a few seconds to identify what it was. A sense of failure. She'd set out to achieve something and she hadn't managed it.

She didn't notice the green man at the pelican crossing. Nor did she register the beeping signal. A few pedestrians brushed past her to cross the road as she stood still. She didn't deliberately change her mind. She wasn't conscious of giving it any reflection.

She retraced her steps, her movements mechanical and automatic, as if she were in a trance.

She paused in front of the library entrance and took a deep breath. Then, with renewed determination, she walked through the revolving doors.

Hello Sandy,

I've had a look at the pages you translated for the website and I've suggested some tweaks, but there weren't many mistakes. Your English is brilliant! It's not rusty at all, contrary to what you said!

I'll try to answer your questions. You asked if my parents were supportive. My daddy died when I was six. He was an RUC (Royal Ulster Constabulary) officer – that was the police in Northern Ireland during the Troubles and before it was replaced by the PSNI (Police Service of Northern Ireland). He was killed by an IRA bomb on his police station. He shouldn't have been working that day. He'd gone in to replace a colleague who was off sick. I went to see that colleague recently as I thought maybe he'd experienced some sort of Survivor's Guilt, as I do, but he has had a stroke and couldn't talk. I wish I had more memories of my father. I was very much a daddy's girl. He used to read me stories and he had this infectious laugh. People who knew him always speak highly of him.

My mother hasn't been the same since my daddy died. I think the way he died makes it difficult for her to help me with what I've been going through. I was scared of telling her I'd been held hostage in a terrorist attack and I rang my cousin from France instead! I see a lot of my mother but we don't get on as well as I'd like.

I do have support, though. My cousin, Declan, and his boyfriend, Patrick, live across the hall from me. I see them every day. Declan insists on driving me to all the appointments with my psychologist. I don't have any brothers or sisters, but I think of Declan as a big brother.

You asked if the terrorists threatened me and if I was there until the end. There were eleven hostages altogether and two of the terrorists – their names were Zak and Ali – held us at gunpoint in a corridor on the first floor of the arena. They pointed their automatic weapons at us and made us give them our mobiles. They humiliated a few of the hostages by making them do embarrassing things such as barking like a dog, stripping off their clothes or singing a nursery rhyme. I don't think Ali had any good in him. He shot a passer-by, or possibly a police officer, out of the window for fun.

As for Zak, I'd seen him earlier, before the main act came on, in the ladies' toilets. He scared me because he and I were in there alone and I thought it was strange that he hadn't gone to the men's. I remember seeing his maniacal gaze in the mirror. I think he'd hidden his weapon in one of the toilet cubicles, although obviously I didn't realize that until afterwards.

Later, he spoke to me in English. He behaved in a way that was absolutely barbaric. I saw him play Eeny Meeny Miny Moe with some of his victims. And then he made me choose who got to live between my friend Claire and me. I'm not sure why I'm telling you this. I haven't been able to tell my psychologist Robert or even my cousin Declan. Perhaps it's easier writing it down than saying it out loud. Anyway, Zak shot my friend dead in front of me. I'm crying writing this. There are no words to describe how awful that was. It was just a game to him, though.

But when we were in the corridor and the police negotiated for one of their officers to take the place of a female hostage, Zak let me go. There were five women, but he chose me. I think it was because he recognized me from earlier, in the toilets. So to answer your question, no, I wasn't there until the end. I was released before the police assault. And no, the terrorists didn't treat me, or anyone else, with any humanity. I often ask myself whether they were born that way or if they were brought up like that. You have to wonder what their parents were like, don't you? Either way, both Ali and Zak were pure evil.

I've reread this, Sandy, and it's all rather depressing and doesn't make for easy reading! But you're right. It does help to talk (or write) about it. Robert suggested I should keep a journal and express my thoughts. It has been cathartic getting down those words! I ought to follow his advice.

On a brighter note, I've finally been back to my place of work! Before the trip to France, I worked in the main library, here in Belfast. I'd been putting off going as I couldn't face the thought of being there without Claire, Ava and also Sarah. I nearly bottled out, but I did it! I'm insanely proud of myself and also ashamed that I didn't do it before. I had a good chat with my boss, Nina, and she has been very understanding. I've agreed to go back. Nina has suggested that I start off with half days here and there and gradually build up.

I hope you're well, and Sam and Maxime, too.

Take care,

Laura

Chapter 33

7 MONTHS AFTER

Sandrine

It was nearly twenty to eight. Maxime would be late for school if he and Sam didn't stop squabbling and leave soon. Sandrine was staying out of it, but listened in as she sipped her black tea.

Antoine had always been the one to pick fights with Sam, who, because of his naturally placid disposition, would often take himself off rather than take the bait. Max was normally calm, like his father. He'd always been more docile than Antoine, too. Since Sandrine and Sam had tackled the problem of his truancy, Maxime had eaten and slept at home every evening, following Sam's rules to the letter, but sometimes three became a crowd and lately Max had been more argumentative than usual.

This morning the row was about the photos of Antoine. Or more accurately, the lack of them. Max demanded to know why his father had taken them all down.

'I get that you think he was misguided, even evil, but he was still my brother! You can't pretend he never existed!' Maxime thumped the table with his fist, but it made a dull thud on the wood and Sandrine doubted this was the desired effect.

'If you want to have pictures of your brother in your bedroom, that's fine by me, but I don't want to be reminded of him. And this is my house.' Sam hadn't raised his voice, but Sandrine could tell from the twitch around his mouth that he was irritated.

'Sam, *chéri*, Maxime's first lesson begins at eight,' Sandrine said gently, hoping her intervention would defuse the situation. 'Max, you need to do your teeth and grab your bag.'

Maxime looked at her and she thought he was going to turn on her, although she didn't know what for. Treating him like a child or not standing up for him, perhaps. But if that had been his intention, he thought the better of it and obediently headed for the bathroom.

When Sam and Max left a couple of minutes later, she saw her husband smile tentatively at their son. Maxime hesitated, then returned the smile, all trace of confrontation dissipating. Sam threw him the car keys.

It was quiet once they'd gone. Almost too quiet for Sandrine's liking. She decided to check her messages and see if Laura had written back to the email she'd sent her the other day. Sandrine was growing attached to Laura and still felt terrible about concealing her real identity. But what choice did she have? She desperately wanted to know more about what Antoine had said and done that night. She was convinced he'd shown some consideration in his final moments and that Laura could provide the proof of that.

She cleared away the breakfast things, sat at the kitchen table and booted up her computer. She logged in to the email account she had created just for Laura and was excited to see she had an email in her inbox.

But as she read Laura's email, a feeling of utter disbelief quashed her excitement. She read it again, slowly, grappling with Laura's account of how her son had behaved. Not only had he not shown any mercy towards the hostages, he'd humiliated them, forcing them to carry out degrading acts such as singing, stripping or barking.

She didn't specifically say if it was Ali or Antoine who had come up with these demeaning ideas, but what she did say about Zak was condemning. He didn't shoot indiscriminately. He'd targeted specific people. He made Laura choose between her and her friend. He'd invented a sadistic game and forced people to play it at gunpoint. The losers lost their lives. The winners got to live with that for the rest of theirs. Sandrine could not take that in.

She didn't want to believe Laura. She wanted to cling to the belief that her son had been brainwashed into doing what he did, that he'd acted reluctantly. Laura must have made a mistake. Maybe she'd got them muddled up. Perhaps she'd meant Ali when she said Zak.

Zak made the effort to speak to Laura in English. He released her. Surely that showed a tiny shred of kindness? Or was her mind twisting everything, finding excuses where there were none? She had no idea why her son had talked to Laura when he refused to talk to his colleagues. It might have been nothing more than an opportunity to show off his language skills. And he chose to let Laura go, but the police had negotiated the release of one of the female hostages. In her email, Laura said there were five of them. Laura had a one in five chance of being released.

Sandrine remembered the letter she'd found in the garage. When she'd read it with Sam, there were whole paragraphs she hadn't taken in. No, she hadn't *wanted* to take them in. But it was coming back to her. Antoine had said something about letting someone choose. What were his exact words?

She got up and walked into the living area on shaky legs. The letter was in the drawer of the coffee table. She took the pages out of the envelope. It was on the last page. She skimmed it until she found the passage she was looking for.

She could hear her Antoine's voice, as if he were reading out the sentences aloud, validating Laura's accusation. *I get to play God. I'm the one who will decide who lives and who dies. But it might be more fun to let someone else choose ... your husband or your father? Your girlfriend or your sister? Your daughter or your son? You ... or your friend?*

Sandrine let out a howl of anguish, a cry that was both visceral and animal-like. It was all there in black and white, like a written confession. Sandrine had chosen not to see it, preferring to believe in her son. She'd wanted to prove he'd done something good at the end, but he'd planned his atrocious acts and carried them out to the letter. The letter. She continued to bellow as she tore it up, dropping the tiny pieces to the floor. Then she sank to her knees and cried.

She didn't know how long she stayed like that, but when the crying had subsided, her pain was replaced by a seething resentment. It wasn't rational, Sandrine could see that, but in that moment she hated Laura for forcing her to face up to the truth about Antoine. She didn't want to write to or hear from her ever again.

But the feeling was transient, eclipsed by a different emotion that it took Sandrine a moment to identify. A strong maternal instinct, a feeling of protectiveness, directed not at Antoine, but at Laura.

This girl had reached out to Sandrine. She had opened up to her. Laura had a therapist and a cousin for support, but she had no father and by the sound of it, her mother wasn't very sympathetic. Besides, she'd told Sandrine something that she hadn't been able to confide in anyone else. Sandrine had a responsibility towards Laura now as well as a duty to at least try to redress her son's wrongs.

She picked up the pieces of paper and pushed them into the envelope. She stood up and took the envelope into the kitchen, where she threw it into the bin. Then, even though her thoughts were clashing and her emotions were colliding in her head, she forced herself to sit back down at the kitchen table and type a reply to Laura. Sandrine owed her that much. She couldn't ignore her, not when she'd been the one to contact her in the first place, and especially not after what Laura had been through at the hands of Sandrine's own son.

De : Famille Morvan
À : laura.davison@ezmail.co.uk
Mar 02 avril à 15:15
Sujet : Rép : Your questions

Hi Laura,

Thank you for the pages you've checked through.

We're well, thank you, although my husband and I have been worried about our son Maxime. He doesn't seem to be coping with Antoine's death very well and has been skipping school. I fear we have neglected him but we'll keep a better eye on him from now on.

I'm so sorry to hear about what happened to your dad. How tragic. I'm glad your cousin and his partner are supportive. Declan does indeed sound like a protective big brother.

You can't imagine how horrified I was to read your account of being held hostage. I am so sorry for everything you have gone through. You have experienced something that is utterly traumatic and you were wounded in your own way, too. I hope that you will heal in time, even if you will always carry the scars.

I can see why you didn't think you would get out of the concert hall alive. You wondered if Zak and Ali were raised that way or if they were born like that. The nature or nurture question is an interesting one. I remember reading somewhere that one of the terrorists was born to a Muslim father and a Catholic mother, but neither of his parents practised their respective religions. Furthermore, the father's family had disowned him for marrying a Catholic girl. I think that might explain a lot. Their son almost certainly felt torn between two cultures. Granted, his parents weren't religious, but maybe that made it worse. Perhaps their son needed something to affirm his identity or needed to feel that he belonged in one world or the other rather than in limbo between the two.

I'm so pleased it helped you to write about your experience. If you feel like writing any more, I'm here for you!

I look forward to hearing from you,

Sandy

P.S. Well done! You were very brave indeed to go back to the library. You're right to feel proud of yourself and you definitely shouldn't feel ashamed that it took some time for you to pluck up the courage to go there! I think that's only to be expected in the circumstances. I'm glad your boss is being understanding. When are you going back to work?

Chapter 34

8 MONTHS AFTER

Laura

Laura thought she'd feel nervous on her first day back at work. Not that she'd be doing a lot. And it could hardly be called her first "day" back. Her boss, Nina, had asked her to do Rhythm and Rhyme, which Laura had always enjoyed. She wouldn't be on her own – one of her colleagues, Orla, had organized it and all Laura had to do was assist her. After Rhythm and Rhyme, Laura was to send out emails for overdue books and finally put the returns back on the shelves. She would only be working in the morning. Nina couldn't have made things any easier for her. Despite all that, when Nina had put the idea to her, it had seemed daunting. Laura was secretly convinced she'd get cold feet at the last minute.

But here she was, striding towards the library, feeling, not nervous, but annoyed. Her mind wasn't on work at all; it was on the email she'd read this morning before setting out. She'd grown fond of Sandrine and she felt let down. Laura had confided in her, telling her about being forced to choose between herself and Claire. She hadn't been able to disclose that to anyone – not even

228

Declan or Dr McBride. True, she hadn't told Sandrine everything. She'd left out the part she couldn't admit to herself. But if Sandrine had asked how Laura had responded, she would have told her. Probably.

She'd hoped that instead of asking more about it, Sandrine would reassure her, tell her the same things Laura tried to tell herself. *It wasn't your fault. It was Zak's choice to kill Claire, not yours.* Maybe she would believe that if someone else said it to her. But Sandrine hadn't even referred to the incident in her reply.

What Sandrine had written in her email had also infuriated Laura. Was it her imagination or was Sandrine finding excuses for one of the terrorists? Reading between the lines, Laura got the impression Sandrine was defending him, blaming his abominable deeds on the fact he'd been confused growing up in an interfaith family.

Laura was the product of a mixed marriage, too. Her mother was a devout Catholic and her father had been brought up a Protestant. She shuddered, disturbed by the thought that she could have anything in common with one of the gunmen. According to Sandrine, the terrorist's father had been disowned by his own father for marrying a Catholic. That was the case for Laura's father, too. None of that had made Laura into a violent person.

But maybe she'd read too much into it. You got no sense of tone from an email. Plus Sandrine wasn't writing in her mother tongue but in a foreign language. Sandrine wasn't minimizing his actions. She was simply telling Laura about something she'd read. And Laura supposed that everyone looked for answers when something awful like this happened. She shouldn't feel angry. Sandrine had been nothing but supportive. Laura had told her something personal. Maybe Sandrine didn't want to probe and assumed Laura would tell her the rest of it when she was ready.

By the time she'd arrived at the library, Laura's irritation with Sandrine had simmered down a little and her mind turned to the panic attack she'd had last time she came. She stood outside the entrance for a few seconds, half-expecting it to happen again. But other than an uneasy flutter in her tummy, she felt all right. It seemed to take several seconds to get through the revolving doors and the fluttering became stronger, but as soon as she stepped into the entrance hall, Orla called out to her, waving from the foot of the library's impressive sweeping staircase.

'Laura! You're here! Great.'

Laura walked towards her young colleague. The feeling in her stomach was normal, the way she used to feel when she'd had a test at school or a driving lesson. She was actually looking forward to this.

'Do you want to grab a cup of tea or would you prefer to have a look at what I've got planned for Rhythm and Rhyme today?' Orla asked.

A memory crouched at the back of Laura's mind, threatening to jump out at her. Claire making tea for everyone in the staffroom, Ava flashing her wide white smile and Sarah looking on with a serious expression on her face. Laura couldn't place the moment. It might have been an amalgam of different memories. She didn't try to retrieve any of them. Instead she pushed the image firmly away.

'Hi, Orla. Why don't you show me what you've got and what you want me to do?'

Orla nodded, making her long, spiral earrings jiggle. That was clearly the right answer. She was pretty, although her cropped black haircut was rather severe. Her hair had been longer last time Laura had seen her, but the short hairstyle made her striking blue eyes stand out all the more. Laura realized with a pang that she looked a little like a younger version of Claire.

Laura and Orla walked together up the stairs to the first floor. Once inside the Reading Room where the Rhythm and Rhyme was to be held, Orla turned to Laura and said, 'I just wanted to say how sorry I am. It's awful what happened to you and your friends. The atmosphere at the library was unbearable for weeks.' Orla's face coloured. She looked down. 'Sorry, I shouldn't have said that.'

'No, that's all right. Thank you,' Laura said sincerely.

Today's session was built around Michael Rosen and Helen Oxenbury's *We're Going on a Bear Hunt*. Laura had read this book once before herself in Rhythm and Rhyme. While Orla read it, Laura got the kids doing actions with their arms to show "over", "under" and "through". The group of under-fives, sitting on the floor or on their accompanying adults' laps, made squelching and splashing noises. For the younger children, concentration waned a little towards the end of the story, but most of them sat mesmerized, hanging on Orla's every word.

When she'd finished reading the story, Orla got up and fetched a guitar from the corner of the room. Some of the kids squealed with excitement and one of them crawled towards her, his hand outstretched to try and touch the guitar strings. His mother pulled him back and managed to keep him locked in her arms even though he struggled and whimpered to get free.

Orla then sang a counting song about some grizzly bears, strumming the chords on her guitar. There was an easy chorus and Laura encouraged the children to join in, first counting on their fingers, then singing. Not that they needed any encouragement. Laura didn't recognize the song and wondered if Orla had made it up.

Finally, Orla and Laura got the children to do the actions to the song, walking up and down the imaginary mountain and wading across the invisible river in the Reading Room.

The half hour flew by and Laura enjoyed herself. She had a chat with Nina and Orla afterwards and agreed to organize the story-time event that Saturday for the four- to eight-year-olds. Orla would come to help her out. The rest of the morning, despite the mundane tasks Nina had set Laura, also went by quickly.

A smile stretched across her face as she left the library, and as she walked down Royal Avenue, she did a discreet air punch. She'd promised to ring Declan when she'd finished work, so she took her mobile out of her handbag.

'I did it!' she said when he answered the call.

'Och, well done. I'm proud of you. Did it go all right?'

'Yes. It's stupid. I'd been dreading it for so long and in the end it was fine.'

'Aye, well, I knew you'd smash it, but it's not stupid. That was a big step you took today, so it was.'

'Thank you. I'm going back on Saturday to do Story Time Extra and then we'll discuss my phased return to work in more detail, Nina said.'

'Busy day on Saturday, then.'

'Yes, yes it will be.'

Laura had offered to help Declan and Patrick get everything ready for Declan's birthday party. But she was only working in the morning and the party was in the evening. She'd be free all afternoon to give them a hand. And knowing Dec and Pat, they wouldn't even be out of bed by the time she got home from the library.

'Are you looking forward to it?' she asked.

'Oh, yes. Well, the turning forty part not so much, but sure everyone enjoys a hooley, don't they? And I looove presents!'

Laura chuckled. That was her mission now. She was heading for the CastleCourt shopping centre to hunt for a decent gift.

'Are *you* looking forward to it?' Declan asked.

Laura wasn't. Parties and lots of people were even less her thing now than before, but after her morning at the library, she felt capable of anything. A lot of their family members would be there so it wasn't as if she'd have no one to talk to apart from her cousin and his partner.

'Aye, of course,' she said.

'Your favourite guitarist was asking after you.'

Laura could tell by Declan's tone that he was teasing her, but she had no idea what he was talking about. She realized the bear song from earlier had become an earworm – she'd have it stuck in her head on an annoying loop all day now. She could even hear Orla strumming along.

'What guitarist?'

'Connor. Who else? He's coming to my party. I think he has a wee notion of you.'

'Ah. OK. You'll not be getting a present from me in that case,' she said, playing along with her cousin's joke.

'Oh. That's not on. Why not?'

'Because I was on my way to buy you one, but I'm going to have to get my nails and hair done instead.'

Declan roared with laughter. Laura held the phone away from her ear until he stopped.

'Haha. I'll tell him that one,' Declan said.

'You will not!'

'See you later, Cuz. It's our Pat's turn to make tea this evening.'

'Oh, God.'

Declan burst into another guffaw.

Laura ended the call. Arriving at the shopping centre, she realized the fluttering feeling in her stomach was back. What was she worried about? Finding the perfect present for Declan? That was ridiculous. He wasn't difficult, not like her mother. It took her a few seconds to admit to herself that she was nervous about seeing Connor again.

Chapter 35

8 MONTHS AFTER

Sandrine

Sandrine had just sent the email to Laura when her mobile rang. Her heart recoiled in her chest when she saw the caller ID. It was Maxime's school.

Leaning back in her chair, Sandrine swiped at the screen to take the call. *'Allô?'*

'Madame Hamadi?'

Sandrine recognized the headmistress's voice before she identified herself. Why was she calling? She'd rung every week since Sandrine had gone to see her. Maxime hadn't missed a day of school since then. Madame Roux had assured Sandrine that his teachers were doing their best to get him back on track and that he stood a good chance of passing his *baccalauréat* exams later that year. So what was the problem?

'Hello, Madame Roux. My son can't be absent. He must be in school today. Was he late this morning? I'm terribly sorry.' Sandrine was gabbling, but she couldn't stop herself. 'My husband was a bit late leaving the house, but he definitely took Maxime to school.'

'Maxime is in school this morning, Madame Hamadi.' The words should have been reassuring, but her tone wasn't. 'That's not why I'm calling.'

'Oh.'

'It has come to our attention that there has been a case of bullying at the school, cyberbullying to be more precise and—'

'Maxime's bullying someone?'

'No, Madame Hamadi. Maxime has been bullied. Online.'

'Oh,' Sandrine repeated, thinking, *I knew it!* 'I asked him if he was being bullied and he said no.'

'Some of Maxime's classmates have circulated messages about him over Snapchat and WhatsApp.'

Sandrine didn't have any social media accounts and although Sam had a Facebook account, he seldom went on it. She only had a vague idea of how these platforms worked. 'What sort of messages?'

'Hateful messages. Rumours. Lies.'

Sandrine wondered if that was why Maxime had been confrontational at times lately.

'The pupils seem to have invented some sort of game to see who can post the most horrific thing about your son,' the headmistress continued. 'Many of the remarks are racist. There are accusations that …'

Madame Roux broke off. Perhaps she thought that she'd said too much. It was a lot for Sandrine to digest, but she felt the need to hear the end of the headmistress's sentence.

'Accusations?'

'One or two of his classmates have branded him an extremist.'

'Oh, God.'

All this was because of what Antoine had done. They would pay for his actions forever. His death would always prevent them

235

from getting on with their lives. If only Maxime had said something. Why hadn't he told her?

'How did you find out about this?' Sandrine asked.

'One of the more sensible pupils in Maxime's class came with
the class representative to my office. They showed me screenshots.
They left the WhatsApp group. A few others followed suit.'

'Does Maxime belong to this group? Did he see the messages?'

'No. The whole point was to exclude him. He wasn't added to
the groups.'

'But he knows that he was the object of this ... vitriol?'

'According to the two girls who came to see me, yes. Apparently
most of the bullying occurred online, but it had spilled over into
the classroom, too. The other pupils whispered about him, kicked
his chair, stole his pens, that sort of thing. It's childish and
cowardly, but bullying can have a devastating effect on the victim.'

'That explains why he didn't want to go to school.' On hearing
her voice break, Sandrine realized she'd spoken her thoughts
aloud. Her hands were shaking and she tightened her grip on her
mobile phone for fear of dropping it.

What could be done about this? What could she do to help
Maxime? She didn't voice these thoughts, afraid she might break
down and cry, but it was as if Madame Roux had read her mind.

'I have suspended the pupils involved. They will come to see
me in my office with their parents and will be expected to write
letters of apology and delete the applications from their phones
before I will allow them back in school.'

'OK,' Sandrine breathed. It was all she could manage.

'The head teachers have talked to all the pupils in the class
and their parents will be alerted today.'

'I see.'

'If you wish to do so, after our meeting you can report the
abuse both on Snapchat and WhatsApp. You can also go to the
police if you want to.'

She paused, but Sandrine was so upset by now that she couldn't even respond in monosyllables. Unbidden, an image popped into her head. Her vandalized house with the red paint on the front door. She could hear Sam's voice in her head. *We never report it.* She knew Maxime wouldn't agree to report it to the police. He was like her in that he didn't want any fuss. And if he hadn't admitted it to his own mother when she'd asked him, he certainly wouldn't tell the police he'd been bullied.

'I've also arranged for a specialist in Cybercrime who works for Interpol here in Lyon to come to the school to talk to all the pupils about the dangers of the Internet in general,' the headmistress continued.

'Thank you.' It came out as a whisper.

'Madame Hamadi, I'll let you talk this over with your husband. I will keep you up to speed with everything from this end. You're more than welcome to call me back about this matter or come in and see me. I will continue to ring you, anyway, every week.'

Sandrine made an effort to compose herself. 'Thank you, Madame Roux.'

Sandrine was still sitting at the kitchen table, her computer in front of her. She stared at the screen, stunned. The wallpaper image was a photo she'd taken one summer's day on a small, secluded beach near her parents' house in Brittany. A beautiful cove with turquoise water, there were never many people even at the height of the tourist season for it was a little-known beach and accessible only by steep steps. Sandrine and Sam used to take the boys there when they were little, to play in the sea and hunt for crabs in the rock pools.

After looking at the photo for several minutes, trying to lose herself in memories of the past and forget the reality of her present, she realized she was still clutching her mobile. She snapped the lid of her laptop shut and phoned Sam.

Chapter 36

9 MONTHS AFTER

Laura

If Declan was to be believed, he'd been a bit of a party animal in his younger years, by which Laura supposed he meant when he was at university. He'd gone to Trinity rather than Queen's in a deliberate attempt to get away from home and sow some wild oats. That was how he told it, anyway.

Whatever he'd got up to at uni, he threw a party every year, either on his birthday or Pat's. He liked to consider them lavish, but they were just an excuse for Declan to get his whole family and as many of his friends as possible under the same roof for a few hours.

In the end, there wasn't a lot of preparation for Laura to help Dec and Pat with. They only had to pick up the cake. The previous year, they'd celebrated Patrick's birthday in a community hall somewhere near Enniskillen, where Pat was from, and there had been a lot to organize, not least because it was eighty miles away and many of the guests, including Laura, needed accommodation. Laura and her mother had made a lot of the food. Thankfully, this year that hadn't been necessary.

Declan's fortieth birthday party was being held five miles away from the centre of Belfast in a golf club that could be booked for private functions. Guests bought their own drinks at the bar and the club provided the catering, which made everything easier. The head chef was a local celebrity that Pat had been raving about but Laura had never heard of.

'The chicken fajitas are to die for, apparently,' Pat informed them from the passenger seat as they headed to the golf club in Declan's car. 'Slow down, Dec. The cake's in the boot.'

'I can make chicken fajitas!' Declan exclaimed. 'Why would you need some top chef for that?'

'I doubt he buys the tortillas and the seasoning mix in a packet from the supermarket, though,' Pat pointed out.

'Aye, fair enough.'

'That's it! On the right. Turn right! You've missed it, you bollix! I told you to slow down.' Patrick said all of that without taking a breath or raising his voice. Laura was amazed at how they were able to bicker and banter and yet it never turned into an argument.

'I'll pull a U-ey.'

'You can't. There's a roundabout further along the road. OK, well *you* can, clearly. Right, so. Well, it's on your left now.'

The twenty-seven-hole golf course was spread out across woodland and a huge lake. The views, even from the car park, were pretty good, but from the huge dining room upstairs, they were absolutely stunning. Patrick set the birthday cake on a table in the corner, angled so that everyone would see it. The tables were beautifully laid out with candles, Irish linen tablecloths and serviettes and place cards with the guests' names written in calligraphy. Balloons were tied to the backs of the chairs. Laura took some photos of the lake and of the room before they went downstairs to the bar to wait for the guests.

Laura's mother had already arrived and was standing at the bar with two of her older brothers, including Declan's dad. Declan's mother was there, too. It was early evening, and some of the club members were still at the bar, enjoying a beer after playing a round of golf, but Laura's uncles looked to be on the whiskey already.

'Hello, dar-ling,' Noreen trilled loudly. Laura thought that the greeting must be more for the benefit of the people at the bar than for her since her mother had never called her "darling" in her life. She preferred to call her "dear", which she knew Laura hated. Noreen gave her an air kiss somewhere near one of her cheeks.

'Mustn't smudge my lipstick,' she whispered in Laura's ear.

'Hi, Mum. You look nice.' Noreen was wearing a fuchsia summer dress with matching hat, handbag and lipstick. She looked overdressed for a birthday party at a golf club where the only dress code was no jeans or trainers.

'Noreen.' Declan nodded at his aunt. 'I'll get the first round,' he said to Laura. 'You having a beer?'

All of Laura and Declan's uncles and aunts and most of their cousins had arrived with their families before Connor arrived, carrying a huge present that partly concealed his face. He was dressed in smart navy trousers and a light blue shirt that accentuated his blue eyes. Last time Laura had seen him, he'd been wearing shorts and a T-shirt. She smiled to herself. Connor scrubbed up well.

Connor obviously knew some of Declan's friends and he chatted with them before coming over to greet Laura, who was talking to one of her cousins. He kissed her cheek and she inhaled his lemony smell, which she remembered from the evening they'd spent on the *terrasse* in *Le Vieux Lyon*. Her cheeks were burning and she knew that her face now matched her fiery hair.

When everyone trooped upstairs to the dining room, drinks in hand, she found herself seated next to him, which she knew had to be Declan's doing. They talked about all sorts of things as the waiters and waitresses served the starters and they tucked in. Connor told Laura that he was a full forward in his local hurling team and then he gave her a rundown on the rules because she'd never been to see the Irish field game. Laura said she was going to her first Zumba class the following Wednesday. It sounded a bit lame to Laura given that Connor played his sport at inter-county level, but he listened attentively and said all the right things.

Laura told him about her phased return to work and about her idea of starting a monthly book club. After discussing it at length that morning with Orla after Story Time Extra, her plans were now beginning to take shape. Laura had always wanted to belong to a book club.

'I like reading,' Connor said. 'Will it be a particular genre?'

'Well, hopefully if we get a few members with different reading tastes and we take it in turns to suggest books for everyone else to read, there won't be just the one genre. Part of the fun is reading books you wouldn't normally have chosen.'

'Will there be booze?' Connor asked. 'Is it a female-only group or are men allowed?'

'There are only two rules: members must read the book each month and drinking wine at each meeting is compulsory. At the minute, there are only two members: my colleague Orla and myself. You'd be welcome to come.'

'Well then, make that three members.'

'Great! Orla plays the guitar, by the way. Do you still play?'

'Aye, I do, but just for myself, like. At home. I've not been on stage since … you know.'

'Are you not working in the music industry anymore then?' Laura asked. 'Sorry. Am I being nosy?'

'Not at all. I'm still earning money from mechanical royalties, but not from public performances, obviously, so I've been doing a bit of work for a friend on a building site. The manual labour has done me a lot of good,' he added. 'Plus it's giving me pecs.' He made a joke of pushing up his shirt sleeves and flexing his arms to show off his muscles.

'I think those are your biceps.' Laura laughed.

'I was about to say, *and biceps*, young lady. I know my way around my own body, so I do.'

The main course came. Laura had taken Pat's advice and gone for the fajitas whereas Connor had ordered sausages and champ, the Northern Irish spin on bangers and mash with scallions mixed in with the creamy potatoes. Laura hadn't felt this hungry for months and thought that she could devour both meals given the chance. Her face felt like it might split from smiling so much. She remembered how easy the conversation had been with Connor the evening before the concert. She was just thinking that she hadn't enjoyed herself this much in ages when Connor asked a question that floored her.

'So, are you planning to go back to Lyon this August?' he asked.

Laura choked on her beer. Why had he asked that? Why on earth would she want to go back to Lyon? 'Wh-what?'

'You know, for the one-year anniversary commemorations.'

'I didn't know anything about it,' Laura said. 'I suppose there would be some sort of ceremony.'

'Yes. For the families and friends of the victims. For the survivors, too. It's a big deal, I think.'

There was a pause while Laura let this sink in. Then she asked, 'Are you going?'

'I don't want to, but I've been asked to play in this gig they're doing for charity. A couple of big bands. *Foo Fighters* and *Coldplay*. They want Tom, Rich and me to play a song to kick it all off.'

'How do you feel about that?' She sounded like Robert. Her psychiatrist often asked her that question.

'Scared. Nervous. Reluctant. The concert is going to be held at *La Voie Lactée*. They're refurbishing the concert hall and they want to open it with this event.'

Laura shuddered. 'Really?' She couldn't think of anything else to say, but she understood Connor's reluctance to participate. It was an awful lot to ask of him. She couldn't imagine ever going to another concert, let alone one in the venue where the terrorist attack had taken place.

'It would be weird the three of us playing without Niall,' Connor continued, 'and it would be taking stage fright to a whole new level.'

'What do Tom and Rich think?'

'They're keen to do it. They want to do an acoustic version of "Don't let this be the end". It's the song we were playing when—'

'I know. I remember.'

'I don't want to go. At the same time, I don't want to let Tom and Rich down. And you know what they say about when you fall off a horse.'

'I don't think this is anything like falling off a horse.'

'No, you're right. Bad analogy. Anyway, I can't think of a better way to honour Niall's memory. He was my best mate. I just don't know if I'm up to it. I was wondering ... would you consider going with ... No, forget that. I've no right to ask.'

'What? What were you going to ask?'

'I was going to ask would you like another beer to go with your dessert?'

'Oh.' Laura's half-pint was sitting in front of her, nearly full. She looked at it, and then at Connor. 'Yes, please,' she said.

She watched him through the glass panels in the heavy wooden doors as he headed for the stairs to the bar.

Was he about to ask her if she would go to Lyon with him? But the more she thought about it, the more improbable that idea seemed. He'd have Tom and Rich for support. He'd hardly need her. And anyway, how could she possibly set foot in any concert hall ever again, let alone *La Voie Lactée*? It had taken her months to go to the library, and nothing bad had happened to her inside that building. Even when she had plucked up the

243

courage to go there, she'd had a panic attack outside and almost bottled out. The library was only a few minutes' walk down the road whereas to get to Lyon, she'd have to get on a plane. There was no way she could go.

Connor's words echoed in her head. *I can't think of a better way to honour Niall's memory.* She should be thinking of her friends. She should go to Lyon to honour Claire's and Ava's memories. And to support Connor.

Noreen barged in on Laura's thoughts as she sat down in Connor's empty seat. 'I'm on my way to the loo, dear. Then I'm going to nip downstairs and buy some more drinks. Do you want something?' She placed her hand on Laura's arm. 'A drop of alcohol might loosen you up a bit. You've got a long face like you're at a funeral, not your cousin's party.'

Laura almost retorted that her mother looked like she'd dressed for a wedding, not her nephew's party, but she bit her tongue in time. It didn't do to argue with Noreen. Laura knew from lifelong experience that she couldn't win.

'No, thank you,' she said pleasantly. 'Connor has gone to fetch some beers.'

'Ah, Connor, is that his name? Lovely-looking man. Easy on the eye. Don't go getting your hopes up, will you? You'll end up getting hurt. He's too old for you and way out of your league.'

And in a cloud of potent perfume, she was gone. Laura saw Connor hold the door open for her as he came back with their drinks.

The mood wasn't the same after that. Conversation with Connor dried up. Laura painted a smile on her face as Declan cut the cake and opened his presents. She'd bought her cousin a beer-making kit as he'd often said he'd like to have a go at brewing his own. Connor's enormous present turned out to be a state-of-the-art coffee machine, which Laura thought must have been expensive.

'I think I'll call for a taxi,' Laura said to Connor as the other guests filed out of the dining room to the dance floor downstairs.

'Would you like to share one?' Connor asked. Laura hesitated. 'It's OK. My intentions are honourable,' he said.

On the way home, Laura barely spoke. She berated herself for allowing her mother's snide remark to ruin her and Connor's evening. She wondered again if Connor had wanted to ask her to go with him to Lyon. That made her think of the support portal. She'd become a member and posted on the forum in order to find people who could relate to her experience. She'd found Sandrine, who had been very supportive.

Perhaps Connor felt that she could relate to what he'd been through. Tom and Rich had fled from the stage and managed to escape as soon as the first shots burst out, so they might not be as traumatized as Connor. That would explain why they both wanted to play at the anniversary concert whereas Connor wasn't as enthusiastic. He'd held his best friend until he'd bled out and died. Claire was shot dead in front of Laura's eyes. She and Connor had the same wounds, the same scars.

As the taxi pulled up in front of Laura's place, she turned to Connor. She didn't know why, but she badly wanted to tell him something – the secret she'd been keeping all this time. All of it, not just the truncated version she'd told Sandrine.

'The terrorist made me choose,' she said. 'He made me decide who got to live: Claire or me.' She heard Connor's sharp intake of breath.

'What did you say to him? I mean, what were your actual words?'

Laura lowered her head to avoid Connor's blue gaze. When she spoke, it was no more than a whisper. 'I said, *please don't shoot me.*'

Please don't shoot me! The plea echoed in Laura's head. Had she known when she said that what would happen? Had she deliberately implied that Zak should shoot Claire? Or had the words slipped out before she'd had time to think? Was she simply begging for her own life? After pushing it out of her mind for so long, Laura no longer knew for sure what was going through it at the time.

'He gave you no choice at all,' Connor said. 'If he'd made you choose between Claire and Ava, that would have been a horrific decision to have to make. But nobody in your situation would have sacrificed themselves. That bastard was playing a cruel, sick power game. You couldn't win, no matter what you said.'

Tears pricked Laura's eyes and as she went to wipe them, she realized Connor was holding her hand. She squeezed his hand to thank him.

'And actually, you didn't choose for your friend to die,' Connor continued. 'You implored the terrorist to let you live. I expect when you cried out, it was simply out of fear, Laura. It was instinctive.'

Laura was on the verge of breaking down, but did her best to hold it together. 'I keep asking myself if there was something I could have done that might have saved both of us, you know?' she said. 'If I'd reacted differently when Zak ordered me to choose, maybe the outcome would have been different. Perhaps Claire would still be alive.' A quiet sob slipped out before she could add, 'I'll never know if my words sentenced her to death. Maybe I should have stayed silent, refused to respond.'

'If you'd said nothing at all, he might have shot both of you. Did you ever think of that?'

Laura shook her head. When she could speak again around the tightness in her throat, she looked at Connor again and said, 'Can I give you my mobile number?' Her mother would have called that brazen, but Laura no longer cared what Noreen thought of her.

Connor slid forward on the seat and took his mobile out of his trouser pocket. Laura gave him her number and Connor punched it in.

'That way if you decide to go to Lyon, you can let me know.

I wouldn't blame you if you chose not to. But if you do go, I'll go, too.'

And with that, she got out of the cab and shut the car door without giving Connor a chance to respond. She felt her cheeks flaming for the second time that evening as she walked away, towards the entrance door to her building, willing herself not to look back.

Chapter 37

10 MONTHS AFTER

Sandrine

Sam burst through the front door. His cheeks were red and he was out of breath. He'd said he would come home for lunch that day, so Sandrine had been expecting him, but the bemused, angry look on his face took her by surprise.

'What on earth is the matter?'

'I've just seen Maxime,' he said, kicking off his shoes.

'Where? Isn't he at school?'

'He was in front of the school. I saw him when I drove past. He didn't see me.'

'He must be on his lunch break.' Sandrine went into the kitchen and Sam followed her. She looked at Max's timetable, pinned to the fridge with magnets. 'Look! He has two hours off. From midday until two. What's the problem?'

'He wasn't alone.'

'That's a good thing, isn't it? If he was with friends perhaps the bullying has stopped.'

'Not friends.'

'Then who?'

Without answering, Sam strode out of the kitchen and along the hallway to Max's bedroom. It was Sandrine's turn to follow him. Sam threw open the bedroom door and looked over his shoulder at Sandrine.

'We need to find out what's going on,' he said. 'We need to check his room.'

For a moment they stood in the doorway, about to cross a line by stepping over the threshold. They'd never pried into Maxime's personal life; never gone through his things. They'd always trusted him. They'd never had any reason not to. This bedroom was his space. His secrets should be safe here.

Sandrine's eyes swept the bedroom. Lying on the floor next to his unmade bed was a pile of clothes that hadn't yet made it as far as the laundry basket. On a shelf under his desk, she could see his game console. But her attention was drawn to a photo taped to the top-right-hand corner of his computer. She'd never seen the picture before. He must have stuck it there recently, after his argument with Sam about there no longer being any photos of Antoine in the house.

She walked over to the desk, peeled the snapshot off the computer and examined it. Maxime was standing next to Antoine with his arm around his brother's shoulders. Max was beaming while Antoine was making faces at the camera and rabbit ears behind his brother's head. Sandrine didn't know when that photo had been taken – four or five years ago at a guess – or where, or who the photographer was. They were outdoors, but nothing in the background gave a clue to the location.

She turned round. Sam was on his knees looking under the bed.

'Who was he with? What was he doing? What are we looking for?' The questions tumbled out of her mouth one after the other.

'Anything. We're just checking.'

Sandrine didn't like the idea of looking through Max's stuff.

It was an invasion of his privacy and that made her uncomfortable. But more than that, she realized she was afraid of what they might find.

A memory came to her then. She'd brought a pile of clean laundry in here one evening, a week or so ago. She always put the clothes on the bed for Max to tidy away. She didn't know he was in his bedroom and she came in without knocking. He was sitting at his desk and hastily minimized the browser window on his computer screen before turning to face her. The first thing that entered her head was that he had a girlfriend. She remembered smiling to herself. Antoine had been secretive about Océane at first. She knew the signs.

'Was it a girl he was with?'

Standing up, Sam said nothing, but gave her a look that spoke volumes. She suddenly understood exactly what he was thinking. It felt as if her husband had reached inside her and squeezed her heart hard. Now she knew what she was looking for. She really did know the signs.

'Oh, no. No! That's impossible.' But even as she said it, she knew she'd also been thinking that something wasn't right. Something had been wrong for a while, in fact. 'Who was he with?' she asked again.

'I recognized the car. The Renault Grand Scenic. It was parked in the car park in front of the school. I slowed down and got a good look. Maxime was sitting in the passenger seat. Next to—'

'Abdel. But what makes you think …?'

She scanned the room again, the photo still in her hand. Until this moment, she would have described it as the bedroom of a typical teenage boy. But now Sam had planted that poisonous thought in her head, nothing appeared innocent anymore. The PS4 wasn't plugged in, but the games were piled on the desk. Stand Off, Agony, Call of Duty, Fortnite. Weren't those violent video games? Then again, he also had FIFA 20. That couldn't be particularly brutal. There were two posters of bands on the wall

250

above his bed. Like the photo, the posters hadn't been there last time Sandrine had come into his room. She knew one of the groups. *The Naturals*. The Northern Irish group that had been playing at *La Voie Lactée* that night. The other band's name was familiar, but she couldn't think why. *Eagles of Death Metal*. Did they sing aggressive songs? She didn't know. *The Naturals* didn't. They sang love ballads. Rock songs.

'The police asked me a lot of questions about my family, but especially Abdel, the night we were arrested. They obviously suspected him of something.'

'But you didn't?'

'He's my brother,' Sam replied, as if that answered the question.

'Have you changed your mind?'

'Yes. No. I don't know. Maxime seems to be spending more and more time with him.'

'Abdel's his uncle. Perhaps he confided in him about the bullying. They may have been eating lunch together in the car today.'

Sam shook his head.

'What? What is it? There's something you're not telling me.'

'I saw Ant … Abdel was with him on the day of the concert.'

'You saw Abdel with Antoine on the day of the attack on *La Voie Lactée* – is that what you're saying?'

'Yes. Not the day. In the evening, actually. Abdel picked him up. I was on my way home. I saw him get into Abdel's car. Just around the corner. It would have been about two hours before the start of the concert.'

'And from that you deduce that Abdel is responsible for … what? *Grooming* our sons?'

'There have been other things,' Sam said. 'Things with Maxime. He seems to spend a lot of time holed up in his bedroom. On the Internet mostly, I think. When he's not in his room, he's always looking at stuff on his phone. These are warning signs. I've read up about it.'

She'd pored over similar articles online. Signs of radicalization. How to tell if your son is an extremist. But she'd blamed herself because these were the red flags she should have spotted with Antoine. She hadn't read the articles thinking that this was what she should be looking out for with Maxime.

'Lots of teens do spend way too much time online, Sam. I thought Max might have a girlfriend.' But as she heard her own words, she wondered if that's what she'd told herself rather than what she'd believed. Had she been deliberately turning a blind eye? *Again?*

'He's been quite aggressive recently,' Sam continued. 'He won't listen to anyone else's point of view. He firmly believes he's right when he's spouting rubbish.'

'He doesn't go to badminton anymore,' Sandrine said quietly. 'That's not a good sign.'

'I didn't know he'd stopped.'

'None of this proves anything, though.'

There was such torment in Sam's eyes that Sandrine had to look away. Her gaze fell upon the posters on Max's wall again. And that's when it came to her. *Eagles of Death Metal* had been playing at *Le Bataclan* in Paris on the night of the terrorist attack there a few years ago.

She stuck the photo back on the computer and started to search. She rifled through the chest of drawers; rummaged through his wardrobe. After that, she leafed through all the books – school textbooks, mainly – for something he might have hidden among the pages.

On a shelf under his desk was a pile of rough paper. One side of each sheet had writing on it or something printed on it. The other side was blank. Sandrine sat cross-legged on the floor and skimmed the used side of each page in turn.

Out of the corner of her eye, she saw Sam check under the mattress. He pulled out some magazines and hastily put them back where he'd discovered them. Sandrine felt a sliver of optimism. If the worst thing they found in here was a couple of porn mags, then perhaps their younger son was just a normal teenager.

'Do you know how to get into that?' she asked as Sam sat down at Maxime's computer.

Sam spun the office chair round to face her. He shrugged. 'I gave it to him. It's an old Mac we didn't need anymore at work when we updated. I know a lot about computers, but I'm no hack. He might not have changed the password, though.'

Sam booted up the computer and typed in his old password. It worked. After a few minutes, he said to Sandrine, 'OK. He hasn't cleared his browsing history for at least two weeks and he's used password autofill for all the sites he visits regularly. If there's anything on here, I should find it easily enough.'

While Sam searched through Max's computer, Sandrine poked around the things on his desk. She looked under textbooks and inside his pencil case. Then she ferreted around in the desk drawers. There was nothing much in the top one. Glue, Post-its, Sellotape, that sort of thing. But the bottom one wouldn't open. It had a small keyhole. She hadn't seen a key anywhere.

'I might have found something,' Sam said, tapping the computer screen. 'His phone is synced to the computer. You can see his text messages. He sent one today at eleven fifty to Abdel.' He tapped the screen and read the message aloud. 'Can't go through with it. Sorry.'

'Go through with what? Did Abdel reply?'

'No.' Sam clicked on a green and white icon showing a phone. 'But Abdel called him. Just after the text was sent. Look! This is Maxime's call history.'

A text and a phone call? That wasn't enough to go on. 'Max could have been referring to anything. Maybe he meant he couldn't go through with his lessons this afternoon. Keep looking.'

'OK. But I think we need to hurry.' Apprehension was etched all over Sam's face.

Sandrine took a metal ruler from the pen pot on Max's desk.

With some difficulty, she prised open the drawer, breaking the tiny lock and splintering the wood around it in the process. She peered inside. She had no idea what she was expecting to find, but it wasn't that. Apart from a packet of chewing gum, a paper-clip and a receipt, the drawer was empty.

'What do we do now?' Sandrine asked.

'I don't know. Shall we phone the police? I've got the card of one of the officers who questioned me that night. Maybe we should ring him?'

Sandrine remained silent. *I've lost one son and one daughter*, she thought. *I can't lose Maxime. He's the last one.* She was torn. They had to do the right thing here. But what was the right thing? Should they assume that their younger son had also been radical-ized? Was he up to something? What proof did they have? That he was closer to his uncle than before? That he came over as narrow-minded at the moment? That he was argumentative? That he was spending more and more time on his own and on the Internet?

Maybe they should they trust their son? Was he capable of plotting anything or harming anyone? If it hadn't been for Antoine would they have suspected him of ... of what? What exactly did they suspect him of?

Sam was staring at Maxime's computer screen. Sandrine reread the short text message that Maxime had sent Abdel. *Can't go through with it. Sorry.* What the hell did that mean?

She bent down and took the receipt out of the drawer. It was crumpled and she smoothed it out. She read the amount – fifteen Euros. It was from the *cordonnier* in the town next to theirs. Sandrine knew exactly where it was, a few metres away from Maxime's school. The cobbler himself was a friendly chap. He did a lot more than repair shoes. She'd had holes punched into her belt recently as she'd lost weight and he'd refused to take a centime for it. He also did engravings. That's what this receipt was for. *Plaque boîte aux lettres 10€. Gravure 5€.* He'd bought a name plaque for a letterbox and paid for it to be engraved. Except he hadn't used it for a letterbox.

Oh, God. She closed her eyes, but even with them squeezed tight shut, she could see Antoine's grave. The red petals and the plaque. She knew the inscription. *Allahu Akbar.* God is greater. Antoine's last words. The words Maxime had had engraved on a metal plaque. He'd obviously stuck the plaque not on a letterbox, but on a wooden mount for his brother's grave.

Wordlessly, she handed it to Sam. It took him several seconds to grasp what the receipt was for. Then he looked up, his eyes locking on to hers.

Just then they heard a text notification sound. Sandrine looked around for her phone but she didn't have it on her. It was Sam's. He pulled his mobile out of his back pocket and looked at it.

'Fetch yours!'

His voice and face were both so serious that Sandrine didn't question him. She ran out of the room and along the hallway, hearing Sam behind her. She found her mobile in the kitchen. She'd received a text, too. From Maxime. Words that under other circumstances might have warmed her heart, but instead made her feel as if her entire body had been plunged into ice-cold water. Sam caught her as her legs buckled beneath her.

Je t'aime, Maman.

Sandrine couldn't remember the last time her son had told her he loved her, much less written it.

'What does yours say?' Her voice came out croaky. She reached out and angled the phone in Sam's hand so she could see the screen. *Pardonne-moi, Papa,* she read. Forgive me.

There was no longer any doubt in her mind. 'Do you think he's still at the school?'

'We'll go there and find out. But first we need to call the police.'

Chapter 38

10 MONTHS AFTER

Laura

Laura took the number 81 bus into the city centre. As usual, Declan had driven Laura to the hospital for her appointment, but he hadn't waited for her as she was meeting her mother in town.

She was feeling calm and confident after her session. She'd finally told Dr McBride about the choice Zak had forced her to make between herself and Claire. The whole story. She'd been holding on to her secret – *with*holding it – all this time – and after confiding in Connor, she'd come to realize that it wasn't her fault after all. Laura wasn't the one who had chosen to kill Claire. Zak had made that decision. Once she'd told Connor the truth, it was easier to tell Dr McBride what had really happened that night. It came as no surprise to her when the psychologist said much the same thing as Connor had.

But when she'd told Robert she was going to Lyon for the one-year commemorations, for once he'd been at a loss for words. Looking out of the window of the bus, she smiled to herself, remembering their conversation.

'This isn't what you meant when you advised me to confront my fears through reminders of the event, is it?' Laura had said half-jokingly.

'I think my exact words were *gradually* confronting your fears through *safe* reminders of the event,' Robert had replied, his tone also jocular. 'I meant watching the news and through exposure to the trauma narrative, that sort of thing. Another key phrase I used was *in a controlled way*.'

But Robert had understood that going to Lyon was something she needed to do. They would work again on all the problem-solving skills and relaxation techniques he'd shown her in case something triggered a traumatic memory once she was in Lyon.

She hadn't shared her plans with Noreen yet. Would her mother be as encouraging as Dr McBride had been? Laura doubted it. Noreen wouldn't approve of Laura going back to the scene of the attack, even if Connor, Rich and Tom were with her.

She got off the bus in Queen Street and spotted the coffee house she'd found on the Internet a few feet from the bus stop. Upon entering, she scanned the room but Noreen hadn't arrived yet. Laura chose a table with some high stools by the window. She sat down and got her book out of her handbag. She'd borrowed a psychological thriller from the library about a stalker. She'd scared herself silly reading it in bed the other night, but at the same time, paradoxically, it had made her feel safe.

She quickly lost herself in the pages of the novel. It was the first time she'd been so engrossed in a book since the attack. Her reading mojo was back.

'A-hem.'

Laura looked up. 'Oh, sorry, Mum. Didn't see you there.' She stood up and gave Noreen a quick hug.

'So I noticed,' her mother said huffily, taking off her cardigan and hoisting herself onto the stool opposite Laura. 'Had trouble finding this place. Bit shabby, isn't it?'

Laura would have to tread carefully. Her mother was clearly

in a provocative mood. Whether it was because Laura hadn't chosen a suitable coffee shop or because she hadn't been watching for her mother to arrive was anyone's guess. Thank God they were only having coffee, not lunch.

'So, how was your session with the psychiatrist?' Noreen always asked this and Laura never knew how to answer. When it came to Laura's therapy, her mother was sceptical, to say the least.

'He's a psychologist, actually.' Laura instantly regretted contradicting her mother and hoped Noreen wouldn't pick up on it. 'It went well, thank you.'

'What's the difference?'

'I don't know, Mum, to be honest. I think both psychiatrists and psychologists can treat you for trauma and PTSD.'

'Would you not be better off with a psychiatrist?'

Laura tried to catch the waitress's attention. When she failed to do so, she turned back to Noreen whose pose – elbows on the table, chin resting on steepled hands – indicated that she expected an answer.

'I think you're right, Mum.' Laura hoped that would pacify her. 'There's not much difference.'

Noreen smiled, as if she'd scored a point. She enquired about Laura's phased return to work and they chatted less awkwardly for a few minutes.

'The service is slow in here, isn't it?' Noreen remarked after a few minutes.

'I can order at the counter if you like. Do you know what you want?'

'No, not yet. Sure, we're not in any hurry. We'll sit tight until the waitress comes over.'

Laura felt the tension leave her shoulders. Whatever had got Noreen's back up, or rather, whatever Laura had done to get her back up, it seemed to be over and Noreen was being nice. Now might be a good time to tell her mother about the trip to Lyon. She hadn't been putting off telling Noreen; it just hadn't come up.

'So, Mum, I've been meaning to tell you something. The first anniversary of the terrorist attack is coming up and I've decided to go to Lyon for the commemorations.'

Noreen's over-plucked eyebrows shot up. 'Do you think that's wise?'

'It's something I feel I have to do.'

'I'm not sure that's such a good idea. Perhaps you should reconsider.'

'I'm going, Mum. I've already bought the plane tickets.' Laura realized she was picking at the skin around her thumb and made a conscious effort to stop.

'Oh. So you decided this some time ago then? Who are you going with? Your friends are ... I can't understand why you would want to go back there. Won't it be too stressful for you?'

Your friends are what? Surely she wasn't about to say "dead"?
'It's bound to be traumatic, but I want to go. I want to honour Claire and Ava, and I also want to support Connor.'

'Ava, she was the one with the teeth, wasn't she?' Laura ignored her. 'And Connor, is he your man from our Declan's birthday party? Do you think you're up to supporting someone else?'

Trust her mother to ask all the questions Laura had been asking herself. Laura was determined not to let her mother fuel her self-doubts.

'You're still messed up yourself, so you are,' Noreen added.

Biting her lip, Laura turned her head and pretended to study the large chalkboard on the wall behind the counter. She wouldn't let her mother rile her. 'I fancy a vanilla latte,' she said in an attempt to change the subject. She half-expected her mother to advise her to go for something less sugary. She could almost hear Noreen thinking, *You don't want to put on all the weight you lost.*

But instead, Noreen said, 'Mmm. That sounds good. I'll have the same.' Before Laura could steer the conversation onto a safer subject, she added, 'Do you think there will be people you know at the commemorations?'

Laura had considered this. 'I might recognize some of the other hostages if they go,' she said. 'And I've been writing to a woman whose son was killed that night. I'm going to email her to ask if we can meet up.'

'You didn't mention you had a penfriend.' Noreen sounded piqued, although Laura couldn't imagine why.

The waitress came to take their order. When she'd finished, Noreen asked, 'Do you think that woman will be there?'

'Who? Sandrine?'

'No. Who's Sandrine? Your penfriend? I meant Romane. Wasn't that what you called her? You know, the one whose boyfriend died instead of you?'

Laura stared open-mouthed at her mother. She always found clever retorts to her mother's thinly veiled barbs, but only in retrospect, when she replayed the words in her head.

'Mum, can we talk about something—?'

But Noreen would not be silenced. 'Don't take this the wrong way, dear,' she said. 'I'm just curious.' Laura resisted the urge to put her hands over her ears and braced herself for a disparaging remark. 'Do you ever think, I don't know, that you should do something with your life?'

At her mother's words, anger caught inside Laura like a match. 'What do you mean?' She didn't want to know, but the words tumbled out of her mouth before her brain had time to filter them.

'Well, you said he had a girlfriend, a promising career. He was obviously a brave young man with his whole life ahead of him.' She lowered her voice so that it sounded almost conspiratorial. 'Of all the people in the room – what was it, eleven of you? Of all the hostages, he rescued *you*.'

Laura was burning with rage now. 'The task force asked for a female hostage to be released. There were five of us,' she hissed, trying to keep the quaver out of her voice. 'And the police officer didn't choose me. The terrorist did.'

'Even so. Does it not make you think that you should do something for someone else? To prove yourself worthy because he died for you?'

Laura narrowed her eyes. She'd been over this before, both in her own head and with Robert. She'd come to realize that if Zak had released a different hostage – Henri's wife, Elodie, for example – Pierre Moreau would still have lost his life. In the end, all the hostages had been released uninjured. Only Pierre had died.

'He didn't die for me.' Laura was shaking uncontrollably now. 'He took my place, but he died saving all of us. All eleven of us.'

The waitress arrived with their coffees and spilt some of Noreen's when she plonked the mugs on the table.

'Don't worry about it,' Noreen said to the apologetic waitress. 'No harm done.' She waved the waitress away and grabbed a wad of paper napkins to mop up the mess.

Without a word or a backwards glance, Laura got up and walked out of the café.

From: Laura Davison
To: famille.morvan@tellcommnet.fr
Tues, 11 Jun at 17:24
Subject: anniversary commemorations

Hello Sandy,

Just a quick message to ask if you're going to the one-year anniversary commemorations in August. I don't know much about it all except that there will be a ceremony and a concert to pay tribute to the victims. I'm coming with a friend of my cousin's, Connor. Well, I suppose he's a friend of mine, too. He was a member of *The Naturals*, the band that was playing on the night of the terrorist attack. Connor's best friend, the lead singer of the group, was killed in the attack and Connor and the other two musicians are playing the opening number at the concert.

It's important for me to be there. I want to support Connor and also honour the memory of my friends Claire and Ava. Obviously, I'm nervous about coming. Actually, that's an understatement. I'm dreading it. I think it will be extremely difficult to go to the place where it all happened and I'm sure it will bring back a lot of traumatic memories from that night.

I thought you'd probably be there as it's local for you and I'm sure you want to honour your son's memory, too. I thought it would be a good opportunity for us to meet in person. That would give me something to look forward to!

Let me know what you think.

I hope you and your husband are well and that Maxime is happier at school.

Best wishes,

Laura x

Chapter 39

10 MONTHS AFTER

Sandrine

As Sam drove at a reckless speed in the direction of Maxime's school, Sandrine tried again and again to get through to Maxime on his mobile. He wasn't answering. She'd already left two voice messages. In her head she could hear him say the words he'd written in his text message. *Je t'aime, Maman.* His voice was an octave too high, as if he was a young boy again, or else terrified. She typed a message back to him, hoping that if he wouldn't – or couldn't – answer his phone, he might at least read her text.

Je t'aime aussi.

Then she sent another one, begging him not to go through with whatever he was about to do:

Ne fais pas ça, je t'en prie.

She held her mobile, staring at it, willing it to ring or beep with a message from Max.

'Try the school,' Sam said.

Sandrine did, but she got the engaged tone.

They couldn't get anywhere near the school – there were people everywhere and the traffic had ground to a halt. They parked at the supermarket at the bottom of the road, leapt out of the car and ran from there. Pupils – some of them with their parents – were running down the hill, in the opposite direction, away from the school.

As they got nearer, they could see more parents jostling or shouting from behind police cordons. Some were holding phones to their ears or typing frantically on them. There were fire engines and all sorts of police vehicles in the school car park and even on the pavement. It appeared that everyone had got there before them and yet they lived less than five kilometres away.

'Someone else must have called this in before us.' Sam's voice was strained. He was clearly thinking along the same lines as Sandrine was and he sounded as panicked as she felt. Her heart was thumping and she could hear blood rushing through her ears.

They were at the back of several rows of people and Sandrine had to stand on tiptoe to see over their heads through the school gates. She spotted *gendarmes* in their blue uniforms at the front of the crowd, and armed police in the school grounds. She only realized she'd gasped when a woman in front of her turned round. The woman had her fingers in her mouth and was biting down hard on her nails.

'My daughter's still in there,' she said, her eyes wild and her face pale. 'It's been ages since I got her text message. Her class hasn't been evacuated yet. It's the last one.' She resumed chewing on her nails.

'What's going on?' Sandrine asked as the woman turned away. She felt Sam nudge her sharply in the side.

The man on her other side answered. 'There's been shooting inside the school. A school shooting.' He paused as if the words sounded foreign to him. As if this couldn't happen in France. 'No idea how they got in now they have all that security.' He pointed towards the turnstiles that had been installed the previous year to keep out intruders.

'They?' Sandrine whispered to Sam.

'The last few classes have come out through the main entrance,' the man continued.

The gate next to the revolving portals was open. Helmeted, armed officers in black uniforms and bulletproof vests stood sentinel at either side.

Neither the man nor the woman had recognized Sandrine. She was surprised. But why should they? It was several months since there had been a few grainy pictures of her in the papers and some footage of her on the television coming out of the police station, head down and face hidden by a curtain of hair. To them, she was another worried parent, waiting to find out if her child was all right. That much was true. But that was all they had in common. They had no idea that her son was behind all this whereas there wasn't a shred of doubt in Sandrine's mind. Her son was nothing like their children.

Holding Sandrine's elbow, Sam steered Sandrine away from the crowd, to the side of the school. There were fewer people here, waiting behind police tape. They appeared calmer than the crowd at the main entrance, more disciplined somehow, and Sandrine couldn't tell if these were parents, silenced by their anguish, or passers-by who were curious to find out details of what was happening.

They stopped, behind the cordons, next to two journalists with long-lensed cameras who were snapping photos enthusiastically. Sandrine looked to where they were aiming their cameras and watched in shock as a stretcher was lifted onto a fire engine several metres away.

'Oh God,' she whispered. 'There are victims.' She glanced at Sam. He looked horrified and she realized that the expression on his face must mirror her own.

A police officer asked the reporters to move back as the siren started up, making Sandrine jump.

'What can you tell me about the condition of the injured pupil?' one of the journalists asked, tapping the police officer's arm as the fire engine drove away.

'Nothing.'

Undeterred, the journalist persisted, 'Is he seriously injured?'

'*She* had a panic attack or fainted or something, apparently,' the officer relented. 'There aren't any injured pupils that I'm aware of.'

Sandrine felt a twinge of something she couldn't identify. A mixture of hope and relief, perhaps. But it was short-lived.

'Maybe they haven't brought out the wounded yet,' the journalist said.

'How many shooters are there?' his colleague asked.

The police officer sighed. 'As far as I know, just the one.'

'Former pupil with a grudge?'

A voice from the other side of the journalists piped up. 'I've heard it's the brother of one of the terrorists who attacked *La Voie Lactée*. He was a pupil here, you know. They both were.'

His words stopped Sandrine's heart. It skipped two or three beats before reluctantly starting up again, too fast, shooting pain down her left arm. And yet this merely confirmed what Sandrine and Sam had suspected. Sandrine didn't dare look at the man. Clinging to Sam, she shivered as her face flamed.

Someone shouted as the doors of the nearest building opened. Another shout. 'They're coming out through the canteen!'

A stream of pupils rushed out. Thirty or forty in total, Sandrine guessed. This must be the last class to evacuate. Some of the people around them, ignoring the police officer's protests, slipped under the tape and ran towards the teenagers. There were squeals and tears as fathers and mothers were reunited with their sons and daughters.

Behind and beside Sandrine and Sam, more parents appeared. They had obviously heard the commotion and rushed round from where they were waiting by the main entrance. The crowd surged under the tape and up the slope to meet the pupils running down it.

The woman who had spoken to Sandrine earlier materialized at her side. She was out of breath and Sandrine heard her before she saw her. She appeared to be gnawing on her whole hand now rather than just her nails. Then her arm lifted in a wave and her face lit up.

'Marine! Marine!' she called.

The police officer had given up trying to keep people back and he held the cordon up for the woman to dive under. She sprinted towards her daughter who threw herself into her mother's arms, almost bowling her over. Sandrine heard the woman ask her daughter if she was all right and strained to hear the girl's answer, anxious to glean any information at all about the situation, but Marine's face was buried into her mother's shoulder and if she spoke, it was drowned out by everyone else's excited shouts and chatter.

Minutes later, there was hardly anyone else around except for the two reporters and the police officer. As if by unspoken agreement, Sandrine and Sam waited until the journalists moved away, heading towards the main entrance, no doubt to see if there was any more action around the corner.

Then they approached the police officer.

'Our son is still in there,' Sandrine began.

'There's nothing I can do,' the police officer said. 'I don't know what's going on inside for the moment.' He seemed to appraise them and Sandrine wondered what he was thinking. 'You can't go in,' he said, his eyes flitting from Sam to Sandrine and back again.

Sandrine heard Sam clear his throat.

'Our son ... we think he's involved in this,' Sam said.

'Involved in what way, *Monsieur*?'

'We think ... we have reason to believe that ...' Sam's voice cracked.

Sandrine squeezed Sam's hand and finished his sentence. 'Our son is the shooter,' she said.

Chapter 40

1 YEAR AFTER

Laura

Not for the first time, Laura wondered why Sandrine hadn't replied to her emails. She'd already written two emails to say that she was coming to Lyon. It wasn't like Sandrine not to write back within a few days. It had been several weeks now since she'd heard from her. Laura had been hoping to meet her friend in person and she couldn't understand Sandrine's radio silence.

She wrote one last email from her mobile at Dublin Airport, aiming for short and sweet, in case her first two messages had landed in Sandrine's spam. Three times was more than enough, though. Laura didn't want to pester her. Then she turned on the airplane mode on her phone. She would check her emails again when she landed if she had 4G, and if not, she'd use the Wi-Fi at the hotel.

To Laura's relief, the flight was smooth and stepping off the plane, she realized it was a lot cooler than it had been the last time she'd come to Lyon. It was also a relief to discover that their hotel was a safe distance from the self-catering apartment where she'd stayed with Claire, Ava and Sarah. It was situated right in the city centre in the second *arrondissement*. Connor had chosen it because it was a stone's throw from *La Place Bellecour*, the square where the first part of the commemorations would take place the following day, and the concert hall was easy to get to on the underground.

When the four of them checked in, they were informed by the young receptionist, who seemed keen to practise his English, that the street behind their hotel, *Rue Mercière*, was famous for its restaurants. Tom suggested they get cleaned up and book a restaurant for later that evening, after their rehearsal at *La Voie Lactée*.

The bedrooms were on the same floor and they rode the small lift up together, although it was a bit of a squeeze with everyone's suitcases and the two guitars. The receptionist had told Laura that her room had a view over the River Saône. She opened the door with the key card, lifted her case onto the luggage rack and went over to the window.

She pulled open the curtains and gasped. Her pulse quickened. The view that greeted her was not what she'd expected. At the top of the hill behind the river towered the majestic basilica of *Notre-Dame de Fourvière*. Memories of the day before the concert came flooding back to her – walking up the steep hill in the stifling heat with her friends, her knee throbbing with pain, the welcoming cool temperature as they stepped inside the basilica, Ava crossing herself, Sarah reading aloud from the online guide-book on her phone.

Laura sat on the bed and breathed in deeply through her nose and out through her mouth a few times, her hand on her stomach. Then she got up and drew the curtains. She would leave them closed while she was here.

She showered and pulled on a sundress. A few minutes later, they were on their way to *La Voie Lactée*.

'You don't have to come in,' Connor said to Laura, as they got on the tube.

Laura, who had insisted on accompanying them, didn't want to set foot inside *La Voie Lactée*, but she did want to be there for Connor. 'I'll see how it goes,' she said. 'I'd like to come in for a bit, maybe watch you play, then I'll wait outside.'

'We won't be long anyway,' Connor said. 'We've got a full rehearsal tomorrow. This evening's just a recce. We need to check out the equipment and so on, and Tom wants to try out the drum kit.'

Since *The Naturals* had been on tour the previous summer, they'd had their road crew and a bus full of equipment with them. This time, as Connor had explained to Laura, they were singing only one song and were travelling light with just two acoustic guitars. The two main acts had offered to lend them any instruments they required and *La Voie Lactée* had its own technicians.

For a moment, Laura thought that she would have a panic attack right outside the concert hall, as she had outside the library the first time she'd gone back there. But the tightness in her throat eased and a couple of deep breaths were enough to slow her heart. It helped that they went into the building through the performers' door instead of the main entrance.

'Are you all right?' Connor asked.

'Yes. Are you?'

Connor nodded, but Laura could tell the smile was for her benefit.

Inside, the concert hall had been completely refurbished, just as Connor had said. It smelt of paint, wood and chemicals rather than gunpowder and blood. Although Laura was fairly sure the layout was the same as before, it looked like a different place with no audience, noise or dimmed lighting.

Laura stayed for a while, until she'd listened to their song once, then she left to get some fresh air and stretch her legs after the plane ride. Connor signalled to her from the stage that he'd ring her once they'd finished.

Outside, to the front of the building, was a large forecourt, behind the main entrance. Laura knew that part of tomorrow's commemorations would be held here. This was where the president of France himself would unveil the plaque with the names of all the victims. She wanted to take a closer look, but she was ushered out through a side gate by a security guard. She walked round to the front entrance and peered in through the railings of the fence but other than a lot of people getting things ready for the following day, there was nothing to see. She stood there and watched anyway.

After a while, Laura became aware of someone standing beside her. It was her baby who caught Laura's eye. It was in a baby carrier and also appeared to be looking through the railings. Laura looked from the baby to the woman carrying it strapped to her chest. The baby's mother was small-framed and attractive, around the same age as Laura, with long, dark shiny hair.

'Your baby is very cute,' Laura said to her in French.

'It's a girl,' the woman replied.

Her voice was vaguely familiar. Laura looked at her more closely and with a jolt, she recognized her. Laura was aware she was staring, but couldn't seem to stop herself.

'Do I know you?' the woman asked.

Laura wasn't sure what to say. A long pause stretched the short distance between them as they scrutinized each other. 'We haven't met,' Laura said eventually, 'but I've seen you before.'

A strange look had come over the woman's face. She had placed Laura, too.

Chapter 41

Sandrine

In the days following Maxime's arrest, Sandrine and Sam were cautiously optimistic. Sandrine had contacted Maître Guillet, the lawyer assigned when she herself was arrested, and he'd agreed to represent Maxime. Since the plot was foiled and there were no victims – indeed, no rounds were even fired from Maxime's automatic rifle – Maître Guillet was confident that Maxime would benefit from a juvenile diversion programme.

'The idea of this,' he'd explained, 'is to keep first-time low-risk offenders like Maxime out of the criminal justice system while still holding them accountable for their actions.'

'What does that mean?' Sandrine asked.

'It means that your son would be given community service to do and he'd have to attend deradicalization counselling sessions.'

That didn't sound too bad. Max would avoid a prison sentence, even if in the meantime, while the investigation was ongoing, he would continue to be held in a juvenile detention facility in Lyon.

According to Maître Guillet, Max had been questioned at length about the role of his uncle, Abdel Hamadi, in coordinating the attack on *La Voie Lactée* as well as in planning the school shooting. From what Sandrine could gather, Abdel had been on the radar of the intelligence services for some time. The fact that Max was being cooperative and providing the police with vital information would work in his favour. Sandrine and Sam were also interviewed by the police, but it was clear they weren't suspected of being involved in any terrorist activities.

But their optimism was brief. Although as a minor Maxime couldn't be named in the media, the law ensuring his anonymity didn't extend to social media, where the rallying cry was for public naming and shaming rather than privacy or protection.

The news reports on television, on the radio and in the local and national papers were also far from impartial. After five days, it was still the main news story in France. Amid such mounting public pressure and tension, Sandrine was worried that Maxime would be made into a scapegoat.

Her fears seemed confirmed when Maître Guillet called her on her mobile one afternoon while Sam was at work to tell her that he had some bad news.

'I'm afraid the SDAT – the counter-terrorism division of the judicial police – have swooped in and taken over the investigation. Maxime will be moved to their headquarters in Levallois-Perret in Paris.'

Sandrine and Sam hadn't been allowed to visit Max since his arrest anyway and she didn't immediately grasp how this changed anything.

'Unfortunately, legal proceedings are almost inevitable now,' the lawyer continued.

'You mean Maxime will be prosecuted?'

'Yes, that's the most likely worst-case scenario.' Sandrine remembered that expression of Maître Guillet's from before. She hadn't found it reassuring then, either. 'The SDAT will be looking to have Maxime brought to trial within the criminal justice system for a terrorism-related offence.'

'But I thought you said … He's still a child! Can they do this?'

'There are international laws protecting minors allegedly involved in terrorist activities, especially those who have been recruited by adults, but at seventeen Maxime is well over the minimum age of criminal responsibility and this creates a grey area.'

'But this isn't terrorism! He didn't go through with it!

'I know, Madame Hamadi. There's still a chance Maxime won't have to stand trial, but we should prepare ourselves for—'

'How long will it take?' Sandrine asked.

'We're looking at several months – I'd say nine or ten – before this goes to court,' Maître Guillet said. He added hastily, '*If* it goes to court.' Sandrine swallowed hard but it didn't stop a sob escaping from her throat. 'But even if it doesn't, Maxime will be held in detention for much longer than we first hoped.'

Sandrine spent most of the next three days in bed. She barely had the energy to get up for the easiest of tasks such as going to the toilet or fetching a glass of water. At the end of the third day, Sam told her that he was putting the house on the market.

'You were right,' he said. 'Let's move away from all of this. We'll sell up and start over somewhere near your parents' place, near the sea. If Maxime is in Paris, Brittany will be just as handy.'

'What about your business?' she asked.

'I can set that up in Brittany. I can always come back to Lyon every now and again to see clients. I'll have to work out whether to keep my employees on here or let them go. But most of what I do can be done over the Internet from anywhere. You and I can pack up and go. We'll rent for a while until we find a buyer for the house.'

The move gave Sandrine a vague sense of purpose if only because she needed to make a start on the packing. So she got up, showered and got dressed. But while boxing up their stuff kept Sandrine busy, it didn't occupy her mind. Her thoughts taunted and tormented her with loud, incessant voices inside her head. She asked herself the same questions as she had when Antoine had died. How did it come to this? Could she have prevented this? She blamed herself for bringing up not one extremist son, but two. To Sandrine, this was proof that she was to blame. Perhaps all those years ago when she'd lost Léa, it had been a warning sign, telling her that she wasn't fit to be a mother.

In spite of the situation she found herself in, Sandrine couldn't help thinking about Laura, who had written a few times now to say she was coming to Lyon for the one-year anniversary commemorations. The ceremony and concert would take place in three weeks' time. Sandrine knew the date well. It was the date on which Antoine had died.

In her last email to Sandrine, Laura had asked to meet her. There was no way Sandrine could go to the memorial ceremony. Even if Maxime hadn't been arrested, she couldn't possibly have gone. For a start, someone might recognize her. This didn't scare Sandrine for herself, but she definitely didn't want to upset anyone. These commemorations were being held in honour of her son's victims. No one would want her there. She wouldn't be welcome. She had no right to be there.

Perhaps she could meet Laura somewhere else, on the day before or the day after the tribute. Sandrine had often thought how much she would like to meet her. She'd often wondered what she looked like. She imagined her as being a bit older than Antoine, but really she had no idea how old she was. But she quickly dismissed this idea. It was one thing pretending in her emails that she was the mother of a victim rather than a terrorist. Lying to Laura's face would be far worse. Unthinkable.

But she should at least have the courtesy to answer Laura's emails. Sandrine taped up a box full of bubble-wrapped plates and went into the living area, where she sat on the sofa and booted up her laptop. She started typing, but after her first sentence, she stopped. How could she explain why she hadn't replied? What excuse could she give for not attending the commemorations? She couldn't just say she wasn't coming and leave it at that. She snapped the lid of her laptop shut and drummed her fingers on it while she thought about what she could write.

There was no way around this. She was going to have to lie. Again. She didn't like that idea. She hated the fact that her online friendship with Laura was founded on lies. There was no way Sandrine could ever meet Laura in person for that reason. She didn't want to lie to Laura anymore. But she couldn't tell her the truth. If Laura knew the truth, she wouldn't want anything to do with her. Sandrine resolved to stick as closely to the truth as possible, as she always had.

It took her more than an hour to draft the email even though it was relatively short. She wasn't at all satisfied with it. The story she'd come up with would ward off any further questions on Laura's part, but it was another blatant lie. The irony was, although Sam was being so supportive and Sandrine felt closer to him than she had for several months, she longed to be able to confide in a friend about everything that had happened.

With a sigh, Sandrine read through the email one last time and sent it.

De : Famille Morvan
À : laura.davison@ezmail.co.uk
Jeu 01 août à 11:33
Sujet : Rép : anniversary commemorations

Dear Laura,

I'm terribly sorry I didn't reply to your last email sooner. I know it's been weeks since you first wrote about coming to Lyon and you must be wondering why it has taken me so long to get back to you. I'm afraid we've had a family emergency and I've been preoccupied by that. Our son, Max, has been unwell and is currently being treated in an institution in Paris.

We're also moving house at the beginning of September. I think I told you in one of my previous emails that I'm originally from Brittany. Many years ago, before my children were born, I got my first teaching post near Lyon, where I met my husband, Sam, so I ended up staying here. I've wanted to move back to Brittany for some time now, but after Antoine died, we stayed in Lyon for the sake of Max. Anyway, my husband and I have decided that now would be a good time to go and live near my parents, so we've put the house on the market and I'm busy packing boxes. We hope that Max will be able to join us in Brittany soon.

Because we're moving house and because Max is so ill, I'm afraid I won't be attending the anniversary commemorations in Lyon. I would have loved to meet you and I'm so sorry that I won't get to do this. I think you're very brave to go and pay tribute to your friends and it's kind of you to want to be there for your friend Connor. I hope that he will give you some support, too.

All the best,
Sandy

Chapter 42

1 YEAR AFTER

Laura

'You're Laura, aren't you?' the woman said in French, holding out her hand for Laura to shake. 'Laura Davison, is that right?'

'Yes,' Laura said, surprised that she knew her name. It all felt surreal.

'I'm Romane.'

Laura nodded. 'I know.' She remembered Romane clearly from the police station. She was the girlfriend of Pierre Moreau, the police officer who had lost his life that night. Romane had seen Laura in Commander Roche's office. She'd known who Laura was.

Romane stroked the top of her baby's head. 'And this is Mila,' she said.

Laura looked from Romane to Mila. This must be Pierre's baby.

'I'm so sorry for your loss,' Laura said. She felt a little intimidated by Romane and her voice came out hoarse.

'Thank you.'

There was an awkward pause. Laura couldn't think of anything to say.

'I used to think it was my fault, what happened to my boyfriend,' Romane said eventually. 'I think I was rude when I saw you that day in the police headquarters. At that point I wanted to believe it was your fault.'

'I didn't find you rude,' Laura said. 'Anyway, I didn't understand much of what you were saying to your colleague – Commander Roche, wasn't it?'

'I doubt that's true,' Romane said. 'Your French is excellent.'

'At the time I remember thinking you and I probably had the same thoughts going through our heads,' Laura said.

'Oh? What was that?'

'I kept thinking it should have been me.'

'In that case, you were absolutely right. I'd told Pierre that morning that I was pregnant. When the terrorists demanded a female member of the task force in exchange for a female hostage, there was no way Pierre would have let me go in. I was the only woman on the team. Pierre said there were none and he took my place.'

Then he took mine, Laura thought. 'Do you think even if you hadn't been carrying Pierre's child, he would have let you go in?'

'You sound a lot like my therapist,' Romane said.

'I sound like mine sometimes, too.'

Romane's lips turned ever so slightly upwards at that.

'I didn't see you that night,' Laura said. 'I was debriefed – the police tactical unit had set up their command centre in a restaurant. There were loads of officers there. But I didn't see you.'

'There were lots of us. Lots of teams working together. Outside, inside the concert hall. My team – Pierre's team – was already inside the arena.' Romane looked down at Mila, then turned to Laura again. 'Can I ask you something?'

'Of course. Anything.'

'Can you tell me what Pierre's last words were?'

'Oh, God, no, I'm sorry. I can't. I—'

'I mean, I know he stayed in there after you'd been released, but before that, what did he say?'

'The thing is, he didn't say anything when he came through the door into the corridor,' Laura said. Romane looked crestfallen. 'I remember him slipping a mobile phone behind his back. And I remember being amazed at how unbelievably brave he was. The terrorists were holding Kalashnikovs and wearing suicide vests and Pierre was so calm and confident.'

That seemed to satisfy Romane. 'Thank you,' she said. 'That's good to hear.'

Mila whimpered a little, but then she became distracted by Romane's finger, which she gripped in her tiny hand. A slight breeze made the leaves rustle in the plane trees that lined the avenue, but the sound was barely audible above the noise of the traffic. Laura tried not to think about taking it in turns to sit in the shade of those trees while they queued for the doors to the arena to open that night.

For a few seconds, Romane and Laura stood side by side, the silence between them comfortable now. Then Romane spoke. 'You know, I'm surprised you recognized me,' she said. 'You only caught a glimpse of me that day.'

'I'm good at remembering names and faces,' Laura said with a shrug. 'I've got a good memory in general, although I often wish my mind had blanked out some of that night and the following days. I'm surprised *you* recognized *me!*'

'Well, you have a distinctive look with all your beautiful red locks,' Romane said. 'Strangest thing, though.' She paused and Laura didn't think she would continue. Mila was getting agitated again. 'She's hungry. I'll have to go soon.'

Just then Laura's mobile phone rang out. She fished it out of her handbag. It was Connor. She answered the call and told him she was outside the main entrance.

Then she turned back to Romane. 'What was strange?' she asked.

'In the days and weeks after the terrorist attack, my colleagues had to take statements from a lot of people – witnesses and survivors like yourself, but also members of the terrorists' families and their friends and colleagues, that sort of thing.'

'Go on.'

'Well, one of the people they interviewed was the ex-girlfriend of one of the terrorists. Her name was Océane Renard. I was supposed to be off work, but I went in from time to time and I sat in on her interview.'

Mila was crying now and Romane tried to calm her for a little longer by putting a dummy in her mouth and rocking her own body from side to side. Laura waited patiently for her to continue.

'She was – well, she was younger than you, but she looked just like you. It stuck with me because hardly anyone in France has naturally red hair, you know. For all I know she dyed it, but it looked natural to me. And her surname – Renard, like the animal, the fox – I suppose it was sort of fitting. When I first saw her, I thought she was you.'

Laura mulled this over for a few seconds. She felt as if Romane had given her a vital piece of information, like a piece of a puzzle, but Laura couldn't see where it fit into her own story. 'Which terrorist?' she asked.

Mila had spat out her dummy and was wailing loudly now. Laura picked the dummy off the ground and handed it to Romane.

'I'm sorry?' Romane said.

'You said she was the ex-girlfriend of one of the terrorists. Which one?'

'Zakaria Hamadi.' Romane gave a little wave of her hand. 'Listen, I do have to go. I'll look out for you tomorrow.' And with that, she walked off.

Laura saw Connor approaching from the other direction, flanked by Tom and Rich, and made her way slowly towards them.

Thoughts were chasing each other through her mind. *I look like Zak's ex-girlfriend. Did I remind him of her? Is that why he stared at me in the mirror of the ladies' toilets?* It came to her then and stopped her in her tracks. *Is that why he didn't kill me? That's it! That's why he didn't kill me.*

Laura had asked herself countless times why Zak had picked her out, why he'd made her choose between herself and Claire and why he'd let her live. She'd been terrified it was because he'd recognized something of himself in her. She'd spent months worrying that she and Zak were similar in some way when all along he'd toyed with her and then spared her simply because she resembled his ex-girlfriend.

She shuddered, struck by the realization that he could so easily have had a completely different reaction.

From: Laura Davison
To: famille.morvan@tellcommnet.fr
Thu, 01 Aug at 22:21
Subject: Re: re: anniversary commemorations

Hello Sandy,

I'm so disappointed you're not planning to come to the commemorations! I'll be in Lyon for a few days, though, so if you change your mind about meeting up or find that you have time to grab a coffee somewhere, just send me a text message. Here's my mobile number: 0044 7700 900901. I'm staying in the city centre, near *La Place Bellecour*.

I'm so sorry to hear Max has been ill and I hope he gets better soon.

I moved into a new flat a few months ago, so I can sympathize with you packing boxes!

Take care and please keep in touch. I hope I will get to meet you one day!

Laura x

Chapter 43

Sandrine

Sandrine had always hoped that she would get to meet them properly one day and that Sam would see them again. She knew it would mean a lot to him. But she didn't believe it would happen.

No one ever rang the doorbell now – except for the occasional Jehovah's witnesses or door-to-door salespeople, so it came as a complete shock to open the front door and see them there. She didn't recognize them at first. It had been so long and she'd only ever met them once, although she'd seen photos of them with Sam and Abdel as children and more recently with Antoine and Maxime.

She opened her mouth to greet them politely, but no words came. Instead, she turned her head slightly, her eyes remaining riveted to the faces of her parents-in-law as she shouted over her shoulder for Sam.

Her mother-in-law looked smaller than she remembered her, diminished somehow, although it might have appeared that way because she was lower than Sandrine, standing at the bottom of the steps. Her face was desiccated with age or anguish, or a combination of both. Like Sandrine, she didn't seem to know what to say. But she smiled – hesitantly, apologetically – and the expression on her face spoke more eloquently than any words.

Sandrine had imagined this moment, had envisaged it as a tearful and joyful reunion between Sam and his parents. The repentant return of the prodigal parents. They would hold their long-lost son and beg for his forgiveness and accept their daughter-in-law into their family. But it was by no means a happy occasion. Sam's mother wailed when Sam held her in his arms. Her words spewed out in an incomprehensible rush into Sam's shoulder.

Sam shepherded them inside and made mint tea, and for once Sandrine welcomed its sickly sweetness. They sat around the coffee table. Sam's mother was calmer now and for a while, no one spoke.

'Would you like to be alone with your parents for a while?' Sandrine whispered.

When Sam didn't reply, she got up to leave the room, but her mother-in-law reached over from the armchair and placed a warm, bony hand on Sandrine's arm, a silent request for her daughter-in-law to stay. Once divided because of religious differences, the older Madame Hamadi now had something in common with her daughter-in-law. They were bound by a strong, tacit understanding. They had both tried in their own ways to be good mothers to their sons and they'd both failed.

'We're so glad you came,' Sam said. He was too choked up to say anything more.

His father took over. 'This visit is long overdue,' he said. The lines sounded prepared, but that was of no importance. 'We should have come months ago.'

'*Years* ago,' Madame Hamadi corrected. Sandrine caught Sam's mother throwing a reproachful look at her husband.

'We wish it could have been in other circumstances,' Sam's father said.

They asked for news of Maxime. Sam squeezed Sandrine's hand and she answered for him. She tried to sound positive, even though Maxime's future was cloaked in uncertainty for the moment. Briefly, she told them that Maxime was being held in a facility in Paris. He would undergo a process of deradicalization. He might not get a prison sentence.

'He can come back from this,' Sam managed. He didn't add what Sandrine was sure he was thinking. *Unlike Antoine.*

'That's good. He's a good person,' Sam's mother said. 'It wasn't his idea. It wasn't his fault.'

'Yes, he is. No, it wasn't,' Sandrine agreed robotically. It was comforting to hear her mother-in-law say that.

'Have you seen him?'

'No,' Sandrine said. 'We're not allowed to visit him yet.'

For a few seconds no one spoke. Sam's mother sipped her tea. Sandrine could hear Sam breathing, rapidly and heavily, next to her on the sofa.

Sam's father broke the silence. 'We want to assure you that we knew nothing about this,' he said. 'We didn't suspect for a moment that Abdel could be involved in anything like this ...' Sandrine knew that feeling. She hadn't foreseen it with Antoine, either. 'And we thought Abdel had a positive influence over Antoine and Maxime.'

'That's not how Abdel was brought up,' Sam's mother added. 'There's nothing in the Koran about ...' It was too much for her. She broke down and sobbed.

'We don't know where we went wrong,' Sam's father said.

Sandrine tuned out. She was lost in her thoughts. Sam and Abdel had had the same upbringing and the same education, but they had gone down different paths. Perhaps some of it was due to nature and it wasn't all about nurture after all. Maybe some people just had it in them. Not the desire to kill, exactly, but the ability. And this ability could be exploited by the wrong sort of person.

'It's OK … Dad,' Sam was saying. 'We don't blame you. In fact, we blame ourselves, in the same way as you're blaming yourselves. Don't we, Sandrine?'

She nodded.

'We didn't see the signs,' Sam's mother said. 'It's almost as if our son is two separate people. What I mean is … oh, I don't know.'

But Sandrine knew exactly what she meant. The Antoine she'd known and loved was nothing like the monster – Zak – who had carried out the terrorist attack and she would never reconcile the two of them. For months she'd clung resolutely to the belief that her son had shown some compassion even though he'd committed the most atrocious crimes, but there was nothing remotely redeemable in his actions. She would never understand it, never forgive him. The only way she could deal with it was to continue to love the son she'd known before he'd become Zak and walked into *La Voie Lactée*, armed to the teeth, that night. Sandrine knew her parents-in-law were coping with what Abdel had done in the same way.

They talked a little more and cried a lot more. Sam's mother asked if they could see each other again. Sam's father asked about the boxes stacked around the room.

'It's difficult for us to be in Lyon after everything that has happened,' Sam said, 'so we're moving to Brittany, to live near Sandrine's parents.'

Sandrine's mother-in-law looked heartbroken. She'd just been reunited with her son and he was about to move to the opposite end of the country. 'That's so far away,' she said.

'Maybe when we've settled in, you might consider visiting us,' Sandrine said.

'Or we could meet up somewhere in the middle,' Sam said.

Sandrine's mother-in-law brightened at their suggestions. It occurred to Sandrine that although they'd soon be living further away from Sam's parents, in time the distance between them might not seem so vast.

Chapter 44

1 YEAR AFTER

Laura

Eighty-two people killed. At *La Place Bellecour*, a huge open red-gravelled public square in the centre of Lyon, the mayor had finished his speech, but these words still echoed in Laura's head as a choir sang and a military orchestra played the French national anthem. After the final notes of "La Marseillaise", there was a minute's silence before the loudspeakers around the perimeter of the square crackled into life and two voices – a man and a woman – took it in turns to read out the names and ages of all the people who had lost their lives that night at *La Voie Lactée*. All eighty-two of them.

Laura had learnt in the news how many people had lost their lives, but it was only now, as this long list of names was read out, that she grasped the scale of the destruction. She was also struck by how young most of the victims had been – in their twenties or thirties. She and Connor, who was standing rigid beside her, listened out for Claire's, Ava's and Niall's names. Ava's was the first of the three names alphabetically – her surname was Duffy.

Laura heard Pierre Moreau's name. Then came O'Donnell – Niall, and finally Claire Quinn. Connor put his arm around Laura's shoulder when Ava's name was pronounced and kept it there until the end.

It took more than ten minutes for the names to be read out. A sort of roll call for the victims who would never again answer to their names. Laura supposed the death toll was eighty-five if you counted the three terrorists who had also died. Their names weren't read out. Nor were those of the more than three hundred injured, people like Sarah, some of whom were present at the ceremony in wheelchairs, accompanied by health professionals in orange and grey uniforms.

A few French singers – no doubt famous artists, although Laura had never heard of them – were scheduled as the next part of the commemorations. After the first song, everyone looked to the sky as multi-coloured balloons – purple, blue, pink, orange and green – were released. Laura had no idea how many balloons there were – hundreds, maybe thousands. It was beautiful and Laura was moved.

Tom and Rich stayed to listen to the rest of the music, but Laura and Connor wanted to get away from the crowds for a while. Connor took out the map of Lyon he'd picked up at the hotel. The city centre was situated on a sort of peninsula, sandwiched between two rivers. To one side of *La Place Bellecour* flowed the Saône with the *Vieux Lyon* at the foot of the basilica on the other side of it. It was an area they'd both visited the previous summer. They'd even had a beer there together. But the old quarter would be a painful reminder for them of their friends, so they set off in the other direction, towards the Rhône.

They passed a sports shop with the mannequins in the shop window dressed in blue, white and red T-shirts, shorts and caps. From the balcony of what looked to be a private flat above the shop hung the French tricolour flag. From another window, three pairs of boxers – blue, red, white – swayed gently in the breeze as though their wearer had hung out his washing to dry. Laura took photos of all this with her phone and sent them to Sarah.

They crossed a long, wide bridge over the Rhône to the opposite riverbank, where there were fewer people. As they reached the other side, Laura spotted a florist's with red and white petals strewn on the ground outside.

After a relaxing walk along the river, Connor and Laura found a bistro and had lunch on its pavement *terrasse*, then Connor accompanied Laura back to the hotel. He, Tom and Rich had their full rehearsal that afternoon and Laura had decided to ring Declan, then take a nap. She was exhausted.

'I'll join you later at *La Voie Lactée*,' she promised. 'I'll be there in time for the unveiling of the plaque.'

'Are you sure?'

'Yes. And I'm definitely coming to the concert, so make sure you sort me out for a ticket.'

'Already done.' Connor patted the pocket of his shirt and smiled.

A loud siren woke her up from her nap. She was soaked in sweat and her heart was pounding. Damn! It had been a while since she'd had a nightmare. As usual, she'd dreamt about the terrorist attack, but this time they were inside the refurbished concert hall and Connor had been shot instead of Niall. The strobe lights in the concert hall morphed into the flashing blue lights of the emergency vehicle that sped off for the hospital with Connor inside. Laura reached out to stop the alarm on her mobile phone, silencing the wail of the siren as she did so.

She tried to push away the intense images that lingered in her head – it was only a nightmare – but she was still shaken up as she took a shower. As she got dressed, her hands continued to tremble and she fumbled with the button of her skirt and the straps on her sandals.

She reasoned with herself. She'd known before she came that traumatic memories would resurface. Coming back to Lyon and going back to the scene of the attack was bound to be unsettling. Her nightmare simply reflected that. It didn't mean anything bad was going to happen tonight, not to Connor or anyone else. There would be a lot of security everywhere. A year on, France was still under a national state of emergency.

She took the tube and arrived in good time. She called Connor who came to meet her at the entrance. He'd got hold of passes and this gained them access to the private space on the forecourt of the concert hall, reserved for the families of the victims and away from the media and crowds. As they took up their position, Laura and Connor were handed white roses to lay at the foot of the plaque once it had been unveiled.

'Where are Tom and Rich?' Laura asked Connor.

'We were given just the one pass each, so we were one short,' Connor explained. 'They said they'd stay together and watch from outside the main entrance.'

'That was good of them.' Laura looked towards the place where she'd stood the previous day, next to Romane, watching the preparations through the railings.

To Laura's surprise, the president didn't make a speech, perhaps to avoid making this tribute about politics or popularity. He simply pulled the cord to open the red velvet curtains, revealing the plaque. Then the family members walked past the plaque in single file and laid their roses on the ground around it. When it was Laura's turn, she scanned the plaque for her friends' names, but the line had to keep moving and there wasn't time to find them. She decided to come back after the concert and take a photo for Sarah, too.

It was over. Some people stood around and talked; most started to disperse. Laura saw Romane, but she was too far away for Laura to call out. She realized the concert would soon begin and a few drops of perspiration slid down her face.

As if reading her mind, Connor said, 'You can come in with me through the stage door.' He led the way and she followed. As they stepped inside, he handed her the ticket. 'You're in the first row of seats behind the pits.' He pointed to a seating area opposite the stage that sloped upwards. 'You'll have a great view of the stage.'

'Thank you,' said Laura, relieved to learn she wouldn't be standing in the pits.

'There will be three free seats around you. Don't let anyone sit in them, will you? They're for Tom, Rich and me. We'll join you as soon as we've sung the opening number.'

'Thank you,' Laura said again.

'Declan would be so jealous. He loves Coldplay and Foo Fighters!'

'Are you nervous?'

'Oh, yes. Normal stage fright, though. Well, nearly normal. It's terrifying to be going on stage again after all this time. But, you know, it feels like I'm doing a good thing.'

'Good luck.' Laura stood on tiptoe and kissed him on the cheek, amazed at her own audacity. Then she turned and went to find her seat.

The concert hall was soon full. Laura hadn't expected that as the performance tonight was mainly for the families and friends of the victims and survivors. She felt uneasy. As she waited for the concert to start, her mind drifted back in time, and panic bubbled up from within her as she couldn't find her friends through the sea of people. She jumped as a sound detonated in her memory. She could even smell her fear.

But all of this faded as Connor, Tom and Rich came onto the stage and a cheer rose from the audience. Laura was instantly brought back safely to the present.

Before they opened the concert, Connor had to make a speech. It was only a few sentences, but Laura knew he was more apprehensive about that than performing the song. He spoke slowly in the hope that people would understand him despite his Northern Irish brogue.

'Tonight, we are here to honour the people we loved and lost a year ago in this auditorium,' he began. 'Many of you were present and Tom, Rich and I know that it takes a brave person to come back here this evening. Let's remember our loved ones tonight and celebrate through our music the lives they led and the ways they touched our own lives.'

Then he took a deep breath. Laura knew what was coming next. She was no longer thinking about what had happened in this very place that night. She was focusing on Connor, her stomach somersaulting with nerves for him. This was the bit she'd helped him with. At his request, she'd translated his words and coached him with the pronunciation and accent.

When he started to repeat what he'd just said in French, there were loud cheers and an enthusiastic round of applause from the audience. Laura felt a surge of pride rise inside her as Connor waited for the clapping to stop before he continued.

When he'd finished, he asked for a minute's silence.

Then the stage was lit up. Rich and Connor perched on high stools in the centre of the stage, their guitars on their laps, while Tom took his seat at the drums. Laura felt her chest tighten as she had a sudden vision of the last time she'd seen Connor on stage, covered in Niall's blood as he tried to save him. But she forced the image away.

They played their acoustic version of "Don't let this be the end". Tears streamed down Laura's face the whole way through it.

Shortly after Dave Grohl and his band had taken over the stage, Connor, Rich and Tom slipped into their seats next to Laura.

'You did it,' she said, turning her face, which was still wet with tears, to his. 'That was beautiful.' Rich pushed a packet of tissues into her right hand as Connor squeezed her left hand.

There was no strobe lighting. In fact, the lights were never completely dimmed. Every now and then, memories would squeeze their way through cracks in Laura's mind – pictures of her friends from that night – and she let them in. She was here to honour the memory of her friends. If that meant allowing her own memories to filter through, then so be it. After a while, the flashbacks stopped and when Laura closed her eyes, she could see her friends' faces. They no longer looked terrified, but happy, smiling as they had been the day before the terrorist attack. Laura relaxed and started to enjoy the concert.

Although underscored with solemnity, the mood came close to jubilation as they got a taxi back to the city centre. Tom, Rich and Connor were understandably pleased with themselves and Laura felt proud of herself, too.

The four of them went for a beer and something to eat in the *Rue Mercière*, or the "restaurant street" as Tom called it, before going back to the hotel.

It wasn't until Laura was getting ready for bed that night that she saw she'd received a text message. Opening it, the first thing Laura noticed was the number +33, the country calling code for France. She assumed it was from a mobile phone service provider and was about to toss her phone onto the bed when she spotted the name at the bottom. It was from Sandrine.

Laura read the message. Sandrine wanted to know if it was too late to meet Laura before she left Lyon. Was it too late? She was going home tomorrow. They'd planned to visit the *traboules*, the secret passages in *Le Vieux Lyon* in the morning – not Laura's idea, but something Niall had apparently wanted to do when they were here last year. Then she and Connor had a flight to Dublin in the afternoon. Tom and Rich were taking the train to Paris where they would be joined by their girlfriends.

Laura sent a text message to Declan to say goodnight and then another message to Connor to tell him about Sandrine's message. Declan replied straight away, sending a photo of Harry, curled up on Patrick's lap. Then her phone pinged with Connor's reply. She read it before typing out an answer to Sandrine, wondering what had made her change her mind.

Chapter 45

1 YEAR AFTER

Sandrine

Sandrine washed down a couple of paracetamols with a gulp of apple juice. She attributed her splitting headache to stress and lack of food – she'd lost her appetite again since Maxime's arrest. Sitting at the table, she tried to swallow a few mouthfuls of the toasted *baguette* and jam that Sam had made her for breakfast while he stood behind her and massaged her shoulders.

In the end, it had been Sam who persuaded her. He told Sandrine she'd regret it if she didn't. Sandrine knew he was right.

'At least ask her if it's not too late,' he said.

'But what will I say to her? I've spun a web of lies and I'll get caught in it.'

Sam didn't have an answer for that. Sandrine decided to stick as close to the truth as possible and avoid any questions she couldn't answer honestly.

They arranged to meet at ten, which would give Laura plenty of time to get back to the hotel and have lunch before setting off for the airport. Sandrine offered to come to the city centre or *Le*

Vieux Lyon, but Laura seemed keen to meet elsewhere, so Sandrine suggested *Le Parc de la Tête d'Or*. Laura could take the tube from *Bellecour* to *Masséna* and walk to the entrance on *Boulevard des Belges*. And, with a bit of luck, Sandrine would find a space near there to park her car.

Her headache hadn't eased off much as she parked up and got out of the car, so even though it was overcast, Sandrine put her sunglasses on. Then she walked towards the deer enclosure, where she'd suggested they meet up. She was a little early and expected to arrive before Laura.

At first she thought it was a trick. She hadn't arrived first, but it wasn't Laura sitting on the bench waiting for her. Her initial instinct was childish – she wanted to run back to the car or hide behind a tree. Instead, she stood rooted to the spot and did a double take.

It took her only a second or two to realize that this must be Laura, but she continued to stare at her in disbelief. The resemblance to Océane was uncanny. Laura was absorbed in a book, looking up from time to time to watch the deer. She hadn't noticed Sandrine. Standing a few metres away, Sandrine could see Laura's profile clearly.

She was older. Older than Océane, but also older than Léa would be if she were still alive. For some reason, Sandrine had pictured Laura as a young woman who looked much like she imagined her daughter would look now. Sam's hazel-green eyes, dark hair in ringlets. But Léa would be in her early twenties. Laura was in her late twenties or early thirties. Léa could look nothing like Laura. But in eight to ten years' time, this is how Océane would look.

It came to her then. She'd often wondered why Antoine had spoken to Laura. He had refused to speak to his female colleagues at the supermarket, and yet he'd made the effort to speak to Laura in English. When she'd read Laura's account of that night, particularly the part where she was held hostage, Sandrine got the impression that Antoine had singled her out. Laura was the hostage her son had chosen to release. Laura had assumed it was because he'd recognized her from when he'd bumped into her earlier that evening in the toilets. But studying her now, Sandrine knew exactly why Antoine had fixed on Laura. With her tumble of untamed ginger curls, Laura had reminded him of the love of his life, Océane. The woman he'd wanted to marry.

Laura must have sensed Sandrine watching her for she looked up then and turned her head, then smiled falteringly.

'Hi,' Sandrine said in English, walking towards her as she got to her feet. 'You must be Laura. I'm delighted to meet you.' She kissed Laura on both cheeks, as she would once have greeted her French friends.

'Thank you for making time to see me while I'm in Lyon,' Laura said.

She looked at Sandrine through her striking green eyes and for a split second Sandrine got the impression Laura could see through her and knew she was a fraud.

Sandrine thought conversation might be stilted if they sat on the bench, so she suggested they walk around the lake. But she needn't have worried. Laura was bubbly and chatty. She admired the beauty of the park and Sandrine told her a little bit about its history, that a treasure – a golden head of Christ – was supposedly buried here and that *Le Parc de la Tête d'Or* had opened the same year as Central Park in New York. She also told her there was a zoo and botanical gardens.

Laura told her about the commemorations, the ceremony where the victims' names were read out, which had evidently left a mark on her, the unveiling of the plaque and the concert that Connor had opened with his speech and song.

'I went back after the gig to take some photos of the plaque for my friend Sarah,' Laura said. 'I looked for your son's name, but I couldn't find it. Then I remembered you said that Morvan is your maiden name. Does Antoine have a different name?'

Laura had shot that question alarmingly close to the mark. 'Yes, yes he does,' Sandrine said in a voice that came out sounding hoarse. *His name is Zakaria Hamadi, but it won't be on the plaque.*

Sandrine cleared her throat but when she didn't elaborate, Laura stopped walking and took her mobile out of her handbag. 'You can look at the photos if you like, see if you can find Antoine's name.'

'Could you send them to me? These aren't prescription sunglasses and I can't see up close very well.' The lie rolled off her tongue easily, as if she'd learnt her lines by heart, although a sharp stab of guilt accompanied their delivery. She'd intended to dodge the questions she couldn't answer truthfully, even if that in itself felt dishonest. Yet here she was, adding another coat of lies to the layers of deceit she'd already painted.

She had a sudden urge to blurt out the truth, to tell Laura everything. But before she could think of how to start that conversation, Laura changed the subject.

'Are you looking forward to moving? Have you found a place in Brittany?'

Sandrine relaxed, on safer territory with this topic. 'I can't wait to get away from here, actually. We'll stay with my parents in Brittany and take our time looking for a new home. We've had an offer on our house here, though.' It was a low offer, but they would accept it anyway. They'd been scared no one would be interested.

'How's the packing going?'

'It's coming along. The hardest part is sorting through the boys' stuff,' Sandrine said earnestly. 'I don't know what to keep and what to throw away. There's no point holding on to Antoine's clothes and books, and yet I can't seem to bring myself to throw them away. It's not much fun trying to box up everything, to be honest, and I'm the one doing the bulk of it because my husband is working hard to sort out transferring his business.'

Laura politely asked what Sam did for a living. Easy questions.

Honest answers. Even the one about whether it would be difficult for Sandrine to leave her friends behind in Lyon.

'I don't think so. We don't have many friends here anymore. We had lots of friends when our sons were younger – mainly parents of their classmates. We were close to many of them for years. But then the boys grew up. And since Antoine died, we haven't seen any of our friends. People have avoided us.'

Laura nodded. 'My mother said that happened when my daddy died. Her friends didn't know what to say, so they said nothing at all. And she said her married female friends felt threatened by her. They left her to mourn alone.'

'How is your mum? And your cousin?'

'Declan's fine,' Laura said. 'I'm not sure about my mum. I haven't seen her for a while.'

'Oh?'

'She said something rather mean. Well, something incredibly hurtful, in fact. I haven't been in touch with her since. I suppose you could say I'm not talking to her for the minute.'

'What happened?'

Laura told Sandrine what her mother had said about her being unworthy and needing to do something with her life. She told her story succinctly and without a scintilla of self-pity, but Sandrine's heart went out to the younger woman. Poor Laura. She could do with a supportive mother after what she went through. But Sandrine was in no position to criticize someone else for their lack of maternal skills, so she just tried to say the right things.

'That must have been upsetting,' she said. 'Do you think you'll patch things up with her?'

'At some point,' Laura said. 'But she can make the first move for once. I'll wait for her to apologize, although my mother can be stubborn and it may be a long wait.'

They stopped and watched a family boating on the lake. Swans circled them and the scene was like a postcard. The two children laughed and squealed as their father used his oar to flick water at them. Beside Sandrine, Laura chuckled but Sandrine felt a pang of nostalgia for a time when her boys were still innocent, when they were still a happy family.

After Laura had told her about the incident in the café with her mother, Sandrine again found herself tempted to come clean about all the lies she'd told Laura right from the start. Laura was so candid and spontaneous whereas Sandrine ran every sentence she uttered through her head first, weeding out anything that would arouse suspicion or invite an awkward question.

As they completed their walk around the lake and headed back towards the deer park, Laura said, 'I was very sorry to hear that Maxime was ill. How is he?'

'He's ... I'd rather not talk about it, if that's all right,' Sandrine said. She hadn't meant it to sound so abrupt.

'Sorry,' Laura said quickly. 'I didn't mean to pry.'

Sandrine couldn't bear it any longer. She couldn't keep up the pretence. Without slowing her stride, she said, 'I haven't been honest with you, Laura. I think the time has come for me to tell you the truth.'

'OK,' Laura said, sounding uncertain.

'I'm afraid from the beginning, I've led you to believe that my son was ...' Sandrine stole a glance at Laura, then focused her gaze firmly on the path in front of her.

She would lose Laura if she told her she'd masqueraded as the mother of a victim and was really the mother of a terrorist. That would be the end of this friendship. She couldn't do it. The dense silence between them seemed to magnify the sounds around them – geese honking, children chattering, leaves rustling in the breeze, and from beyond the park boundaries, the noise of traffic.

'It's all right,' said Laura. 'It's none of my business. You don't have to tell me anything.'

'No, I want to.' Sandrine stopped walking and looked Laura in the eye. 'I led you to believe that my son Maxime was ill and implied that he was in some sort of mental institution in Paris.' Sandrine paused again and cleared her throat. Then it spewed out. 'He's actually in police custody in Paris. He ... he plotted a school shooting. In his own school. He didn't go through with it, thankfully, but he was arrested.'

It wasn't what Sandrine had planned to say. She'd been about to tell Laura about Antoine. She'd been so afraid of Laura's reaction, so scared of losing her that she'd changed her mind at the last minute. To keep her friend, she needed to keep silent about her elder son. So she'd told Laura about her younger son instead. It was almost as if this were a test. If Laura passed, maybe one day Sandrine could make a full confession.

'I'm so sorry, Sandy,' Laura said. 'That must be absolutely awful for you. For you and your husband.'

She'd expected Laura to get angry. Her sympathy brought tears to Sandrine's eyes. She'd been holding her breath and now she exhaled. She was glad she'd told her. Relieved, too. It was only part of the truth, the easiest part, but it felt good to confide in Laura about it.

'I can only imagine what you must be feeling,' Laura continued, 'especially after losing your other son in such a tragic way.'

Sandrine's headache was clearing. The clouds, however, were not, and she pushed her sunglasses onto the top of her head. The huge wrought-iron gates were just in front of them, exiting onto *Boulevard des Belges*. Sandrine asked politely about Laura's flight.

Then it was time to say goodbye.

'It was lovely to meet you,' Sandrine said. 'I hope you'll keep in touch.' She kissed Laura on both cheeks again, noticing her freckles this time. As Laura tucked a wavy strand of hair behind her ear, Sandrine couldn't help staring at her. Even her mannerisms were similar.

'What?' Laura smiled and she tipped her head to the side.

'It's just that you look a lot like my older son's ex-girlfriend,' Sandrine said, shaking her head in amazement at the resemblance.

'It's the red hair. She inherited her grandmother's Irish genes.' Sandrine saw Laura's face fall, her eyebrows furrowing, but she wasn't sure how to interpret that. 'She was very pretty, like you.'

Laura's emerald eyes bored into her and again Sandrine got the unsettling feeling that Laura could see through her.

'What was her name?'

Was it Sandrine's imagination or had Laura's tone hardened? 'Océane,' she said. 'Didn't I mention that in my emails? Her name was Océane.'

'No, you didn't. Océane Renard? Like the animal. Red hair like the fox. Was her surname Renard?'

'Yes,' Sandrine said, rubbing her temples. Her headache was back all of a sudden with a vengeance. She couldn't think straight. How did Laura know that? 'Antoine was in love with—'

'Antoine?'

Laura spat out his name and Sandrine realized that somehow her lies had caught up with her.

'My son's full name is Zakaria Antoine Hamadi,' Sandrine said. 'I wanted to tell you. I tried to …'

But Laura had already gone. It took all Sandrine's strength not to crumple to the ground. Tears streamed down her face as she made her way back to the car. She knew she'd lost Laura. The pieces of their fragile friendship had been sewn together with lies and now they had come apart at the seams.

Chapter 46

1 YEAR AFTER

Laura

Laura had to get away. She couldn't listen to any more. She ran all the way to the tube station, looking over her shoulder two or three times, terrified that Sandrine would run after her. When she got there, she couldn't catch her breath – because she'd been running or because of the shock, she didn't know.

It was only when she was sitting in the underground train, speeding towards *Bellecour*, that she gave in to her tears. Thoughts and questions stampeded through her head, ramming into a jumble of emotions. Hurt, confusion, anger. Sandy had deceived her, betrayed her. She'd been lying all along.

Sandrine is Zak's mother. Those words were on repeat in Laura's head, but they wouldn't register. Should Laura have realized who she really was? Was there any clue in Sandrine's emails as to her true identity? Laura racked her brains, but couldn't come up with anything.

Why had Sandy befriended her? Did she need a friend to comfort her because she'd lost a son? But Sandrine had been an immense comfort to her. She'd been caring; she'd given good advice and encouragement. She'd been more supportive than Laura's own mother. Surely it couldn't all have been an act?

With hindsight, she could see that Sandrine had pushed her to describe Antoine's last moments alive, pressing her for details. Perhaps she'd thought one of the other terrorists had carried out the truly horrific acts. Maybe she wanted to find out if her son had shown some remorse or kindness to those who were about to lose their lives or their loved ones. Laura had told her what she wanted to know, although it certainly wasn't what she wanted to hear.

She understood now why she'd got the impression that Sandy was defending him in her emails, suggesting that he might have been struggling with his own identity because he'd grown up feeling divided between two cultures. Sandy hadn't read about the terrorist's upbringing, as she'd pretended – she'd brought him up! But did the fact that she'd raised Zak make his actions her fault?

A dormant memory suddenly stirred and Laura realized that she'd seen Sandrine before that morning, long before their meeting in the park. Two days after the terrorist attack, when Laura had gone to the police station, she'd seen Sandrine coming out of the building and stepping onto the forecourt where she was swamped by raucous reporters. She remembered feeling sorry for this slim, brown-haired woman until someone called out her name. Then Laura's pity had given way to rage as she'd understood that this was the mother of one of the terrorists – the one who had shot dead her friend in front of her.

The teenager guiding Sandrine through the pack of journalists that afternoon must have been Maxime. Sandy's younger son. The one who had plotted to shoot up his school. When Sandrine had told Laura about that not more than a few minutes ago, Laura's heart had gone out to her. And yet she didn't feel even a shard of sympathy when it came to Sandrine's elder son. One son hadn't executed his plan; the other had executed dozens of people, including Laura's friends.

Laura was so preoccupied that she almost missed her stop. She made it through the sliding doors of the train just in time. As she emerged from the underground station onto the *Place Bellecour*, her phone pinged. She had two texts. One was from Sandrine. It simply said she was sorry and would write Laura an email to explain and apologize properly. Laura didn't reply to the message, but she knew she would read Sandrine's email when it arrived in her inbox.

The second message was from her cousin. She typed an answer to him as she walked the short distance to the hotel. Connor was waiting for her in the lobby, even though she was earlier than she'd said she would be.

Connor had encouraged Laura to go and meet Sandrine when he'd replied to her text last night and Laura had talked about her friend at length that morning over breakfast. She'd been so excited about meeting Sandy.

'How did it go?' he asked.

He was clearly in good spirits. Laura remembered allowing her mother's comment at the wedding to spoil their evening and she decided not to tell him what had happened just yet. She didn't want to ruin his mood. She didn't want to discuss it anyway. So she asked him how he'd enjoyed his visit of the secret passages.

'Declan says he's invited you round for dinner,' she said to Connor, when he'd finished.

'Yes, he sent me a message.' Connor grinned. 'Apparently it's Pat's turn, but Declan is cooking.'

'Thank God for that,' Laura said, hoping she sounded light-hearted. 'Pat's no cook.'

'So I hear,' Declan said.

The hotel receptionist called them a taxi to take them to the airport.

As Laura and Connor waited to board the plane, Laura took

out her phone to switch on airplane mode. She noticed there was an email in her inbox, but she didn't check to see if the sender was Sandrine. She couldn't deal with it yet. She remembered checking her mobile to see if Sandrine had sent her an email before taking the flight from Dublin. The irony wasn't lost on her.

It had only been a few hours since Laura walked away from Sandrine in the park. And it had been a few weeks since Laura walked out on her mother in the café. At some stage Laura would have to face both these situations, but she needed some time to work out what to do. For now she had no desire to see her mother and she hadn't assimilated Sandrine's deception yet.

'Are you sure you're all right?' Connor had asked Laura that at least ten times since they'd left the hotel. 'Do you want to talk about it? Did the meeting with your friend not go well?'

Laura sighed. She was trying not to think about it, but she couldn't get it out of her head. It would do her good to talk.

'I considered her a friend,' Laura began. 'She has been so supportive. I couldn't wait to meet her, but it turns out she has lied to me from the start.'

When she'd told Connor what happened in the park, she turned to look at him. He was gaping at her. He'd probably been expecting her to tell him about some misunderstanding or petty argument. Not this. He seemed shocked and speechless.

Their flight was boarding, which saved Connor from having to respond immediately. Once they were sitting on the plane fastening their safety belts, he picked up the conversation from where they'd left off.

'So let me get this straight,' he said. 'You're saying that Sandrine is the mother of that terrorist – Zak. The one who killed your friend Claire before your eyes.'

'Yes.'

'And she's been pretending all along that her son was a victim.'

Laura felt an inexplicable urge to vindicate Sandrine in some way. She knew that she would never have written to Sandrine if she'd known who she really was. 'I'll have to reread all her emails. I'm not sure if she just implied her son was a victim or if she told me outright lies.'

Connor narrowed his eyes at Laura. She understood his meaning.

'No, you're right,' Laura admitted. 'She deliberately misled me. She said so herself. She used her maiden name. She has probably always called her son by his middle name, Antoine, but I wrote to her about Zak. She asked me questions about him.'

'It's unbelievable. And if the police officer's girlfriend – what's her name again ...?'

'Romane.'

'If Romane hadn't mentioned that you looked like Zak's ex-girlfriend Océane, you wouldn't have put two and two together. You still wouldn't know the truth.'

'I think Sandy was going to tell me. She said it was time she told me the truth. But in the end she told me about Maxime instead.' She was finding excuses for Sandrine again. 'She'd lied about him, too,' she added.

'Jaysus. It doesn't bear thinking about, does it? One son turns out to be a terrorist and blows himself up. The other one tries to shoot up a school and gets arrested.' Connor tutted and shook his head. 'What are you going to do?'

Laura didn't have an answer to that. Right now she didn't want to do anything. On some level, she understood. Sandrine hadn't chosen her sons any more than Laura had chosen her mother. What they'd done wasn't her fault. She continued to love her sons unconditionally, no matter what. And she'd shown Laura nothing but kindness. She'd reached out to her and offered support and advice. In fact, the whole idea of setting up the website had been about helping those who had suffered at her son's hands. But that didn't redeem her betrayal. Laura found it all a bit confusing.

'I don't know. It's too hard to digest. I don't want to think about it anymore for now.'

She felt better for having told Connor. Just putting everything into words had helped. And he was so easy to talk to. She still felt let down and shaken, but she knew she would get over it eventually. The last thing she wanted to do now was spoil Connor's mood and ruin their flight home.

'OK. Let's see. What can I do to take your mind off it?' Connor said. 'What do you want to think about?'

'A happy occasion. Dinner this evening with you, Dec and Pat.'

'That should be fun.'

'It will be. Also, I was thinking how brave we've both been, going back to Lyon and how incredible you were on that stage making your speech and singing your song.'

'Laura, I couldn't have done that without you.'

'Nonsense. You had Tom and Rich.'

'I'm serious. I wouldn't even have come to Lyon if you hadn't offered to come with me. You gave me strength. And anyway ...' he elbowed her playfully in the ribs '... Tom and Rich can't speak French. I needed you to translate the speech.'

'Glad I was useful,' she said. She managed a little smile.

As the plane taxied along the runway, Connor took hold of Laura's hand. Laura turned to face him, a question in her eyes.

'I remembered you saying how scared you were when you first took the plane,' he said. 'I couldn't hold your hand on the way here because you were across the aisle.'

'Oh. Well, I'm getting used to flying now,' she said.

'Yeah, I know. It's just an excuse to hold your hand.'

'You don't need an excuse,' Laura said.

He let go of her hand, put his arm around her shoulder and pulled her to him. She barely noticed the armrest digging into her side as she snuggled into him. Closing her eyes, she breathed in the tangy scent of his eau de cologne, now a familiar smell. Then she smiled as he kissed the top of her head.

Epilogue

2 YEARS AFTER THE NIGHT THEY DIED

De : Famille Morvan
À : laura.davison@ezmail.co.uk
Sam 02 août à 10h51
Sujet : 2 year anniversary

Dear Laura,

Thank you for your card. It arrived in the post today and I was very touched. I wanted to let you know that I'm thinking of you today, too, and I'm sure you're thinking of your friends. Two years ago today and in some ways it seems like yesterday. The pain and shock still feel raw. In other ways, though, a lot has changed in that time.

Sam and I have planned to go for a long walk along the coastal path this afternoon. We are going to throw flowers into the sea in memory of the people who died that night. We know that today, on the second anniversary of *La Voie Lactée* terrorist attack, hundreds of people will be mourning loved ones who died at the hands of our son.

Because of this, it doesn't seem right to us, but Sam and

I also want to remember today the good times we had with our son. Sam wouldn't say Antoine's name for a long time, but now we talk more openly about him. It has been as hard for my husband as it has for me to come to terms with the fact that the son we brought up and loved is the same person who committed the most hateful deeds imaginable. Sam's parents have faced similar issues and it has helped Sam immensely to be in touch with them again. It disturbs me terribly to think that we would still not be on speaking terms with Sam's parents if Antoine and Abdel hadn't done what they did.

In your last email, you asked about Maxime, which was kind of you. He is doing well. As you know, he was lucky enough not to get a prison sentence – I think the last time I wrote to you, his release from the detention centre in Paris was imminent. He has now been living with us in Brittany for about a fortnight. He is still following an obligatory deradicalization programme and he has to do several hours of community service. He is genuinely remorseful and blames only himself for what he did. We are all very thankful – no one more than Maxime himself – that he didn't go through with the school shooting. He spends all his free time fishing with his grandfather. He's talking about taking his *baccalauréat* exams next year through a correspondence course.

I hope you're well, Laura. I also hope that you will find something good in today even though it is the two-year anniversary of the terrorist attack. I will be thinking of you, as I said. As I've told you before, I'm so grateful that you were able to forgive me a year ago and I hope one day to meet you properly.

Your friend,
Sandrine

From: Laura Davison
To: famille.morvan@tellcommnet.fr
Sat, 02 Aug at 19:12
Subject: Re: 2 year anniversary

Hi Sandrine,

I was delighted to see I had received an email from you when I came in this evening. You're welcome for the card!

I liked the sound of your idea of a walk with Sam along the coastal path to throw flowers into the sea and I think you were right to remember Antoine as well as his victims.

I, too, wanted to find something nice to do despite the date. I didn't want to be mope around the flat and feel depressed, but I did want to remember my friends.

This morning I had my last appointment with Robert, my therapist. I haven't had any nightmares or panic attacks for many months and since I've gone back to work, I've been more confident and sociable. I'm also doing more exercise and eating better. Robert said I didn't need him anymore! I can contact him by email at any time or make another appointment if I need to, which is reassuring, and otherwise he will ring me every couple of months to check up on me.

I think we had a similar idea to you. This afternoon I also went for a walk along the seafront – with Sarah, in Bangor, where she lives. I hadn't seen her for a few weeks and she has made amazing progress with her recovery. She can walk with a cane now. Claire and Ava were on our minds all day long and a bit like you, we threw wreaths into the sea and shared our memories of the two of them with each other.

I'm so glad that you and Sam are reunited with his parents and that it's going well. I don't think my mother and I will ever be close, but she likes Connor and refrains from making jibes when he's around. Perhaps I should refuse to see her unless he's with me!

Speaking of Connor, we've been together for a year now and he's moving in with me. There are boxes all over the place, much to the delight of my cat, Harry. He loves to hide in them! Declan is also ecstatic about having his best mate live across the hall!

It would be lovely to see you again one day. I'm not that keen on flying, but I could always take the boat instead of the plane to get to Brittany! I'd love to meet Maxime and Sam. Connor and I have been thinking about driving down the west coast of France next summer. Perhaps we'll come and see you if you'll have us.

In the meantime, let's keep in touch.

Your friend,

Laura x

Acknowledgements

A HUGE thank you to …

… Abigail Fenton, my brilliant editor: This book is far better than I could have achieved alone thanks to your hard work and insightful feedback. I'm so glad I got to work with you and hope I'm lucky enough to work on my next book with you, too!

… the whole team at HQ.

… Sam Copeland, my multi-talented agent, at Rogers, Coleridge & White.

… my beta readers: my mum, Caroline Maud, my cousin, Anne Nietzel-Schneider and my writing buddies, Louise Mangos, author of *Strangers on a Bridge* and *Her Husband's Secret* and Amanda Brittany, author of *Traces of Her* and *I Lie in Wait*. Your suggestions, reassurance and ideas during the writing process were invaluable.

… Annabel Kantaria, author of *I Know You* and *The One That Got Away*: Thank you so much for reading the synopsis and the opening chapters. Your feedback was amazing and changed this story completely.

… Michael Moran: my most valuable contact! Thank you for your help with all my questions concerning counter-terrorism procedures in France. Any mistakes and exaggerations are all mine.

… all the bloggers and Bookstagrammers who have read and reviewed or posted about my books. Special thanks to Mark Fearn for sharing your story with me and for sharing my stories with readers!

… the Savvies for your advice and for making me feel normal!

… and, above all, my family: my husband, Florent, and our children Benjamin, Amélie and Elise, for encouraging me with my writing. An extra special mention for Amélie, who makes innumerable mugs of perfect tea to fuel me. Thanks also to my dad for believing in me, my uncle Barry for being my number one fan, and my cousin Lucy for shouting out about my books on social media. Special thanks to my black Lab, Cookie, for taking me on plot walks and for keeping me company while I write.

And finally, many, many thanks to all my readers, whoever and wherever you are, for taking the time to read my books. I hope you enjoy reading my novels as much as I enjoy writing them.

I am very grateful to all of you.

Diane
xxx

XCLUSIVE ADDITIONAL CONTENT

Dear Readers,

The Silent Friend is a psychological thriller that will stay with you long after you've turned the final page. This well-crafted suspense novel took me on a rollercoaster ride of emotions with each heartbreaking twist and tense reveal – and I was gripped throughout!

When a holiday in France takes a catastrophic turn, Laura is left devastated by the worst night of her life. Then she connects with Sandrine on an online support group, and Sandrine seems to understand exactly what Laura's going through. The pair quickly grow close, confiding in each other, but one of them is lying about who she really is… and there's no going back once the truth is out.

From its dangerously uneasy beginnings, you'll feel totally invested in the precarious relationship between these two intriguing characters. Trust me, this is an absolutely addictive read!

Karin

READING GROUP QUESTIONS

(Warning: contains spoilers)

1. Whose story were you more invested in, Laura's or Sandrine's?

2. How did your feelings for the two main characters change over the course of the novel?

3. Laura and Sandrine are very different and yet they are drawn to each other. How do you explain their friendship? Under other circumstances, how might Laura and Sandrine's relationship have been different?

4. The main twist in this novel occurs not at the end, as we would expect with many psychological thrillers, but in the first third of the book, when we learn Sandrine's true identity. What effect did this revelation have on you as a reader?

5. Laura discovers the truth much later than the reader and when she does, she feels betrayed. Was Laura right to forgive Sandrine in the end?

6. In an email to Sandrine, Laura writes, 'You have to wonder what their parents were like, don't you?' Sandrine also asks herself in Chapter 43 if Antoine turned bad because of nature or nurture. What do you think?

7. Whose point of view is given in the prologue? At what point in the story do we realize whose voice this is?

8. Did you find the ending of the novel satisfying?

A Q&A WITH DIANE JEFFREY

What gave you the idea for *The Silent Friend*?

The idea came to me after the November 2015 attacks on the Bataclan concert hall in Paris. I live in Lyon and I was glued to the news on the television in horror. Two years later, there was also a barbaric terrorist attack on the Manchester Arena. Faced with atrocious acts, many people behave in a selfless way and carry out courageous and heroic deeds. I wanted to portray that in my novel. I also wanted to examine how surviving a tragedy might affect different people in different ways.

Laura and Sandrine are both such intriguing characters, who show plenty of grit in their own ways. Did you identify with either or both of them in any way?

It has intrigued me to read reviews in which some readers have identified with Laura and others with Sandrine. I identify with both of my main characters to a certain extent.

Like Sandrine, I live in Lyon. She is a similar age to me. She's a mother who strives to bring up her children as well as she can. She's originally from Brittany and she misses the ocean. I come from North Devon and I miss the ocean terribly! Lyon is a lovely city, but it's nowhere near the sea!

That said, although Laura is younger, I also relate to her. As my mum is from Belfast, I spent a lot of time there while I was growing up in the 70s and 80s during the Troubles. Belfast is now a very different city, and Laura reflects on this in my novel.

Although I have imputed some of my own personality to both characters, unlike Laura, I'm not shy or particularly lacking in confidence and I don't think I could be as deceitful as Sandrine. But, on the whole, I identify more with Sandrine than with Laura.

Where do you find inspiration for the plots in your novels?

That depends on the book. My novels are either inspired by real life events or by places I visit. For *He Will Find You*, I was running around Derwentwater with my dog while on holiday in the Lake District when I came across this incredibly ugly house that seemed incongruous with its stunning surroundings. My main character, Kaitlyn, moves into the Old Vicarage in Grasmere, far from her family and friends, to make a new life for herself with Alex, the father of her baby. Alex, however, is not all he seems and Kaitlyn soon ends up trapped in her new home!

For the plot of my fifth book, which I've recently handed in to my editor, it was also the setting that came to me before the story. This one is set on Rathlin Island, off the Northern Irish coast, a beautiful place when the sun is shining, but a rather scary place to be stuck during a storm if there's a killer on the island!

Do you know what the twists will be in your books before you start writing, or do you plot them as you go along?

I can't start writing unless I know what the main reveal is. Usually, other twists come to me while I'm writing. For example, there's a final twist in the epilogue of *The Guilty Mother*, which I know left many of my readers reeling with shock at the end. That particular twist came to me in the middle of the night when I was about halfway through writing the book. I had to get up and write it down before I forgot. I often get an idea during the night but usually, in the cold light of day, it doesn't seem like the brainwave it did when my brain was befuddled with sleep! In this instance, however, the twist made it into the book – it occurs in the last two pages!

What is your favourite thing about writing psychological thrillers?

When I'm asked what I like about writing, I usually joke and say the champagne! There's so much to celebrate: completing a first draft, finishing the last round of edits, seeing the cover for the first time, the publication day itself, unboxing my author copies when they arrive, the first positive reviews... The truth is, as I live in France, writing has been a great way for me to stay in touch with my roots and my mother tongue. It has also provided the perfect excuse to drop everything and take off for a few days to a crime festival or to meet up with my editor or agent or writing friends, especially in London. I have made a lot of very good friends through writing.

What I like most about writing psychological thrillers is that it allows me to get in touch with my dark side! I'm fascinated by what makes people tick, why we're different and how the human mind works. I try to create strong female characters who are flawed and damaged, good people who sometimes make bad choices, but who the reader will root for and sympathise with even so. I try to put ordinary people in extraordinary circumstances. I like to ask myself what would she do if…? I also love reading psychological thrillers, so, although I've dabbled in other genres, it had to be this one!

What is your writing routine?

I don't really have a routine. I work full-time as an English teacher in a lycée in Lyon (although I'm hoping I can soon go part-time) and the past two or three years, due to both Covid and an education reform, it's been difficult to find time to write. So, I don't write every day. I just write when I can, often during the school holidays and the weekends, sometimes in the evenings if I can concentrate and even in the car (not when I'm driving, obvs!). When I'm not writing, though, the characters and story are present in my head and, when I can't get to my laptop, I record voice memos or send emails to myself on my phone or jot down ideas or sentences that come to me.

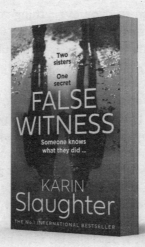

Leigh doesn't like to talk about her sister.

About the night that tore them apart.

About what they did.

But someone else is about to.

How far will Leigh go to protect her family?

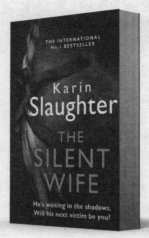

She runs

A woman runs alone in the woods.
She convinces herself she's safe.

He watches

But a predator is watching from the shadows.
Waiting for the perfect moment to attack.

He waits

They thought they caught him.
But another victim has just been found.

The hunt has only just begun.
And the killer is ready to strike again...

Dear Reader,

We hope you enjoyed reading this book. If you did, we'd be so appreciative if you left a review. It really helps us and the author to bring more books like this to you.

Here at HQ Digital we are dedicated to publishing fiction that will keep you turning the pages into the early hours. Don't want to miss a thing? To find out more about our books, promotions, discover exclusive content and enter competitions you can keep in touch in the following ways:

JOIN OUR COMMUNITY:
Sign up to our new email newsletter: hyperurl.co/hqnewsletter
Read our new blog www.hqstories.co.uk
🐦 : https://twitter.com/HQStories
📘 : www.facebook.com/HQStories

BUDDING WRITER?
We're also looking for authors to join the HQ Digital family!
Find out more here:
https://www.hqstories.co.uk/want-to-write-for-us/
Thanks for reading, from the HQ Digital team

ONE PLACE. MANY STORIES